DANCING WITH THE ANGEL

Terri Prone is the head of the successful PR firm Carr Communications. The author of the bestselling novels *Swinging on a Star, Running Before Daybreak* and *Racing the Moon*, she has also written seven non-fiction books and the short story collection, *Blood Brothers, Soul Sisters*. She has a husband and son.

TERRI PRONE

Dancing With the Angel

FLAME
Hodder & Stoughton

First published in Great Britain in 2002
by Hodder and Stoughton
This edition published in paperback in 2002 by Hodder and Stoughton
A division of Hodder Headline

A Flame paperback

2 4 6 8 10 9 7 5 3 1

A CIP catalogue record for this title
is available from the British Library

ISBN 0 340 73327 6

Printed and bound in Great Britain by
Mackays of Chatham plc, Chatham, Kent

Hodder and Stoughton
A division of Hodder Headline
338 Euston Road
London NW1 3BH

In Loving Memory of Brona Coary

Contents

————◆·◆·◆————

I

Standing on an Occasional Table

———◆◆◆———

I have been standing on the table for two and a half hours when I hear my mother's church-going cough.

This particular cough she developed for use during Mass. It could speak volumes. Mostly, it said Behave yourself, Madam, or I'll deal with you later. (I was always Madam when my mother was cross with me.)

The cough – now – comes from the car park, one flight down. I am afraid to turn round, but I am still sure, without ever seeing her, that it is my mother's cough. Her cross cough. Its very don't-make-me-come-over-there authority brings tears to my eyes. At the promise of rescue and punishment it carries. Has always carried.

I blink back the tears and feel my eyelashes clumped and cold with the wetness. Any sensation, other than the marble chill of my feet, is welcome. I concentrate on breathing evenly. A sob would madden him. My left foot cramps, the pain grinding around the bones. I bite into my tongue to create a distracting pain and start to count the flowers in the trellised wallpaper, getting to 3,421. The cramp dies down.

If I had poetry learned off by heart, the way my father has, this would be a lot easier. I could run through poem after poem in my head, visualising every image as I think out the words. But the only poems I ever recall are ones learned in nursery school, like Eentsy Weentsy Spider – and it makes my hand twitch with the dangerous instinct to mimic the spider movements.

Luke shifts, at the table. Easily. Probably, I think, to make himself more comfortable in his misery. In the background, I hear people on the stairs. They will continue up to the next floor of the four floor block. They always do. Nothing to stop them. Nothing to indicate to them that someone in here, in Apartment 3c, needs help. This time, though, the footsteps seem to stop at our landing, then come the short distance to the apartment door.

'Luke, let me in.'

The voice is deep and strong, but muffled.

'Luke, this is your father. Let me in.'

Mr Buckley's muffled loudness is like someone talking a sleepwalker back to bed, not wanting them to wake but wanting them to take action, all the same.

'Luke, let me in.'

Luke never moves. Not a blink. Not that he could blink, with closed eyes. I stay, still and silent. A statue on a stool-sized table, I am. The statue of non-liberty.

'Luke, I know you're in there. Come on. This is your dad.'

There is a long silence. Sometimes, when I'm on the table, Luke listens to music through headphones, but today, he's just there. Slumped. Please don't go away, I pray to his father. Please.

A key turns, the door opens and Luke's father comes lumbering towards his son, as if he expected him to fight, to draw a gun. Luke never moves. How strange, I think. If I'd as much as shivered during the last three hours, he'd have given me hell, but now his father can get right into the room with my mother behind him and he's still frozen.

His father is rendered helpless by his son's inaction. You'd

2

know how to bring Luke down if he fought, I think, looking down at them. You were born to be a barman, Mr Buckley. Or a bouncer. A big quiet man, you always are, without the words to argue. You'd overcome him in a minute, just look at how frail he is.

'Now we have to be going,' Mr Buckley says, softly. 'We're away, Luke. We're away. Off we go.'

He half-hugs my boyfriend upright, the repetitious encouragements becoming more confident now. He must have talked to Luke that way when Luke was three or four, and he knows it's right now, again. Luke crumples into a sad soft acquiescent stumbling. His father turns him towards the door. My mother flattens herself against the wall to let them past, unnoticed by Luke, Mr Buckley murmuring away to him, all the time.

'We'll get you minded, now. We'll get you minded.'

My mother closes the door on the sound and is across the room in a second, two arms up as I come falling, disassembling, almost, off the table. As if I were still a little girl, not a big woman who outweighs her by two stone. She was stronger then and she is stronger now, so I am a child again, being held upright for a minute, then pulled down onto the floor, strong hands rubbing life and pain back into my ankles.

'Jesus, Flannery,' she keeps saying. Reproachfully.

It was always thus, I think, catching one of the big capable hands and holding it to my face. Always the vexed reminders and the physical comfort. Together. 'I *told* you,' sharp, sharp. 'Didn't I warn you? Didn't I? But no, you insisted.'

The captured hand pushes my mousy hair back from my face and palms the tears away.

'Were you in the car park half an hour ago?' I ask, trying out my voice.

'Of course I was,' my mother says, as if it was an argument.

'I heard you cough.'

'I knew bloody well ye were both in here and had been for a while. I tried your phone and then I tried *his* phone and then I just came around and I knew bloody well the two of you were in here. And not asleep, either.'

I smile at her. My mother could not possibly have known Luke and I were awake, but I believe her. Even when I was very small, my mother showed an extra, weird cop-on that was unnerving. Like she could see through walls.

'I walked back, back, back as far as I could in the car park and then I could see your head. Perfectly obvious you were standing on something. Your eyes open and standing still? *You?* Flannery Fidget? I knew he must be making you do it, so I just went and got his father.'

' "Leaps of Logic",' I murmur. I am quoting. It was the title of a poem my father had written. About my mother.

'But first you gave your official cough so I'd know you were there.'

Mam nods, somehow more upset by this than by anything else.

'The idea,' she says, blowing her nose vigorously. 'The *idea.*'

As if getting angry would make it less sad. Getting angry about coughing in a car park, knowing your child will identify both the owner of the cough and the cough's promise of rescue.

'He's very sick, I know,' she says, putting the hanky away. 'It's not his fault. His father says there's a history. A family history. That sort of thing does surface in the late teens, early twenties. I always thought he was a bit strange. Lovely manners. But artificial, somehow, as if he'd learned them on a course and was doing an exam every day.'

4

I am testing out the sore muscles of my legs with probing fingers, letting Mam's words wash over me, listening to the unspoken ends of the sentences. It's not his fault, but it *is* your fault, a bit, for going along with it.

'Ma, it was very gradual.'

'Oh, he started you on stools and worked up?'

The two of us scramble off the floor, me laughing at the acid returning to my mother's voice. I fill the kettle and plug it in, knowing I will never tell my mother how it seemed so flattering, in the beginning, Luke's attention, his sharp-faceted focus on me, me, nobody but me. I have spent so long being Daughter Of that to have a boyfriend who never registered me as anything but me was cool. It was even flattering when something I did wrong put him in a rage. Flattering to have the power to transform him from ordinary humour into a black hole of reverse emotional power, black and darkening and sucking everything into itself. Early on, I could laugh him out of it, apologise, make it better. Then there had come a time when nothing would make it better, a time when the rituals began. Rituals to make me prove I loved him, to prove I meant what I said, to prove, eventually, the unprovable. I have no idea what precise day it started, or what specific incident started it, but over time, he had been training me to an exquisite responsiveness.

'Was he violent to you?'

'Not really.'

'What do you mean, "not really"? Violent is violent.'

'No. He wasn't.'

My mother is sorting items in the kitchen into neat piles, and without ever being told, I know I am being moved.

'Lock, stock and barrel,' I say aloud.

'Entire kit and caboodle,' she responds, but dully.

I rescue two mugs from my mother's evacuation system and make tea. Mam drinks it while she works. Always has. Task, task, task, sip from mug. Task, task, task, sip. I start to help. Or, if I'm to be honest, I make a deliberately ineffectual offer to help and am gestured into sitting down.

But he *was* violent, too, I think. Not the violence of smashing blows and blood-rousing smacks. He is too intense for that release. Instead, his hands had clutched, controlled me by the arms, sometimes the wrists, so my hands felt they would swell and burst, sometimes by the upper arms, his grip like steel so that for days afterwards, I had to wear sweatshirts rather than T-shirts to conceal the navy bruise-imprints of his fingers.

'He brainwashed me,' I think aloud. 'Sort of.'

'Why didn't you go to the college counsellors?'

'They're too busy with suicides.'

'And you don't think someone forced to stand for days on end on an occasional table is a likely suicide?'

An occasional table. That's what it's called, I think. It sounds so casual, so unplanned. He occasionally made me stand on an occasional table.

'I thought *he* might commit suicide,' I tell her. 'Him. Not me. I thought I could keep him from suicide if I just went along with what he wanted. It calmed him down for a while, you know? And then he would be tired and go to sleep for maybe ten or twelve hours.'

The answering sniff says wordlessly that Luke was too inadequate to commit suicide and I too inadequate to know how inadequate he was.

'Take these down to the car,' she orders, nudging two black plastic rubbish sacks, already filled with sheets, towels and pillows. I finish off the tea (see how independent and confident I am with my mother? I can make her wait for at least forty seconds. Maybe fifty.) Then I bump the fat soft bags with their odd protuberances down the stairs. You could lift them, you know, you're not that shook, I tell myself. I know, I answer. I know. But feckit.

I stand at the front door of the little block of apartments, smiling for the first time in a long while. It is so familiar, this internal argument. The mad internal dialogue of the only child, I once described it. To my father, I so described it, and he put the phrase in a poem. It had deteriorated, the dialogue, in the past few months, to a wordless shriek of misery. Oh, please let him be all right tonight. Please let me not have left anything that will upset him. The smile fades.

Craven shite, one voice in my head says.

Anyway, it's over, the other voice responds.

No thanks to you, the first voice says.

'Took you long enough,' my mother says when I meet her back on the landing, surrounded by black plastic sacks, locking up the flat. She sounds like the first voice. Maybe that's what the first voice is, I think. Maternal implant. She heads down the stairs ahead of me.

Always did, one voice says.

Stop you falling downstairs, knocking yourself unconscious, says the other.

Just as well your mother's ahead of you, one voice says. Otherwise she might see you grinning to yourself like an eejit.

'Do your thoughts sound like characters in your head?' I ask Mam, now failing to get the boot closed over all the plastic sacks. Ignoring me, she takes a nail file out of her handbag and stabs several of the bags. I understand I'm to help expel the air from them. Mother and daughter lean, elbows pointed, into the bags which sigh as they collapse. The boot closes easily.

'What?'

'Nothing.'

Bloody right, one thought says. Your boyfriend's just been barrelled off to the loony bin because of voices in *his* head. It's an act you don't want to join, the head-voices advise.

The car noses out onto the main road and gains speed. I unstick a leg from the black plastic sack beside me.

'At least I had enough rubbish bags,' I joke.

'You didn't,' my mother says flatly. 'I brought some.'

'Did you bring a straitjacket, too?'

'For you?'

'No, for Luke.'

'Luke's his father's problem,' she says, crisply. 'You're mine.'

I should be insulted, I suppose. Being regarded as a problem to be brought home in rubbish bags. My mother brakes suddenly and one of the bags on the back seat advances on the back of the head. *Don't make me come down there . . .*

'Sorry,' Mam says, backhanding it into submission. Know your place, bag.

'Did you bring the rubbish bags on spec? Or did you just have them in the boot?'

'I *always* have black plastic bags in the boot,' she says. 'And I wouldn't tell your father much, either.'

Mightn't sound, those two statements, as if they belong together. But they do. You never know when my father will break or spill or retrieve something that needs black plastic bags. And if you tell him anything, it'll end up in a poem. Or a radio reflection.

'Are you on skim milk or what?' Mam asks, slowing down as we come near the big supermarket close to my parents' home.

'Cream, actually. High fat, high protein, no carbs.'

The car swings into a slot in the supermarket car park.

'Your insides must be in a state of complete confusion,' my mother observes, getting out of the car. 'A few months ago it was no fat, no protein.'

A big truck with 'Re-use, Re-cycle' on its side is negotiating with difficulty away from the green, brown and white bottle bins, the driver looking down reproachfully at me. We probably shouldn't have parked here. Then I find myself favouring the truck driver with the radiant smile of a happy discoverer and sliding out of the car, dragging black sacks from behind me and hauling them to the big Cerebral Palsy bin. It has a complicated mouth on it. You pull down the handle and it presents a scoop-shaped metal lip for you to put your discards on.

I horse one of the bags onto the scoop and pull the handle up. The bin swallows and I hear the plastic bag landing deep inside. Scoop, load, plop. Four goes and I'm back to the boot of the car, retrieving deflated saggy bags, checking the contents of each through the holes made by my mother's nail file. Everything but clothes and books goes into the yellow metal bin. Bedclothes – gone. Table mats – gone. Crockery – gone. The crockery protests a bit, but there's no sound of major breakage. Cutlery – gone. The last bag is angular and the scoop can't cope with it. Bloody occasional table. Am I going to lovingly retain my plinth? For future elevation? You bet your ass I'm not. I carry it around behind the bin.

Behind the bin, of course, there is this big enamelled tin sign: a notice warning against abandonment of anything that won't fit into the bin. In spite of its officious tone, I abandon the angular bag. There's no way I can even conceal it very effectively, so I just blow the notice a kiss. There are exceptions, I tell it.

2

Laissez Les Bon Temps Rouler

———◆◆◆———

Decanting clothes into drawers in my old bedroom, I discover a rolled-up, discarded T-shirt, ditched when I moved out two years earlier. Unwound, it reads *Laissez les bon temps rouler*.

'I figured it was a good omen,' I say, wearing it into the kitchen the following morning.

'Omen,' my father reflects. 'A portent of what is to come. A bird of ill omen. Augury or foreboding.'

'Oh, for fuck's sake,' I say.

Normally, my mother would reprove me for using four letter words, but maybe definitions from Da, first thing in the morning, make her want to swear, too. So she mutters about the T-shirt that it may be a good omen, but it's not a great fit. Which is the sort of comment that makes me wish I had bulimia or anorexia. One of them you can blame on parents. 'They precipitated it by making comments about me being too fat for my T-shirt.' But just being a fat serial failure on every diet ever invented is your own fault.

'Now I know why I moved out of here,' I say. But not very sourly, because I am still glad not to be in the flat. My father smiles and touches my arm as I pass.

'We're glad you're back,' he says softly. I do not believe this. I think Mam's glad I'm back, but I've always felt my father regards me as a temporary extra drain on my mother's available attention which should be all going to him.

'Speak for yourself,' my mother says. 'She's eating nothing but cream and eggs and ham.'

'It's the Atkins Diet,' I explain to Dad.

'Could be expensive,' he says mildly.

'You're just sucking up to Ma,' I say. 'And it never works.'

'You're right, she knows me too well.' He's lifting his old suede jacket off the back of his chair and standing for a moment, jacket hanging down his back from a hooked forefinger. Da's movements amount to a series of still photographs. I often wonder is it because he has to pose so often for photographs that he's got into an obliging habit of always being photographable. It is one of the things that make him so likeable, this instinct to be whatever you need him to be.

Whenever we go overseas, he ends up talking like the natives. To Brits, he gets all clipped, to the Welsh he sing-songs, and at the University of Texas, I swear I once heard him y'all-ing. My mother, on the other hand, would never y'all. In the United States, she insists – article-of-faith time – on using Irish terms like 'boot' and 'ten to three' when 'trunk' and 'ten of' would make it easier for the natives to understand her.

'You coming?'

She's wrapping a shawl thing around her. Discount Pashmina. My mother dresses my father in cashmere and silk, herself in whatever is handy and cheap. He is a work of art in process of ongoing composition, but she is just a completed handicraft project.

I shake my head. College? Lectures? Friends asking me about Luke? Me updating them on our shared happy life as a couple – 'Well, I was on this occasional table for a couple of hours and then his father took him to the funny farm'? I don't think so.

My mother stands in the doorway, looking irresolute. This

is new. My father does irresolute constantly. Sometimes he does irresolute and bashful. Right now, he's doing irresolute-but-put-upon. As in 'You're keeping me late for my students, but I'm sure you must have some key priority more important than mine.'

She rubs her eye with the humped back of her wrist.

'I have a scratchy eye,' she says, and goes out of the door.

My father's collusive shrug at me implies, in the nuanced way my father's shrugs always do, that we two are filled with boundless goodwill but must dam it up until something amenable to generalised goodwill comes up, and a scratchy eye isn't it.

Thus did those poor hollowed-out cowering dusted dead react to an equally tiny enormity. Vesuvius? That puff of smoke? Does it all the time.

What my mother did all the time was mind other people's scratchy eyes. Scratchy everythings. A diagnosis waiting to happen, my mother. Somewhere along the line, the Medical-isation of Emily happened and my ma became a medical groupie. She would come home from a college 'do' muttering that she didn't like the cast of Dr So-and-So's skin and a week later you'd hear he was getting chemo. She would know what kind of chemo, too, and if it was worth a toss. Never had any faith in Interferon. Mainly, though, she minded sick people. If it was Victorian times, when the remedy for everything was calves' foot jelly, no calf would have been safe from her. She'd have had them all footless in the interests of some ailing neighbour.

Which was handy, really, because my father had the most fantastic potential as a patient, because he was so distractable. He would get hellbent on where he was going, forget they'd put speed bumps down and hit the first of them like

Schumacher. He punched a Saab into a stationary car that was parked, wreathed in smoke, in the middle of the road, because he thought the smoke was fog and was admiring the way it was roiling.

'I was just thinking,' he explained to my mother as they loaded him into the ambulance, 'I was just thinking that fog doesn't often roil.'

'It wasn't fog, it was smoke and that's why it roiled,' she told him tersely, and you could see the ambulance men thinking this poor artistic man with the seventies rock star hair must have an awful time with such a literal-minded wife.

I'm still sitting in the kitchen, considering another cup of coffee, when I hear the key going into the front door. Jesus, I think, the coffee I've just drunk turning into cold green bile in my innards. That's not the way my mother puts a key in a door. (This was quiet, as opposed to my mother's take-no-shit-from-any-keyhole attack.) That's not the way my father puts a key in a door. (It didn't involve metallic fumblings and droppings of key rings and preliminary cuts at the keyhole, the way someone nerving themselves to slash their wrists has a couple of exploratory goes first.)

Who else has a key? Luke. Luke took my key off my key ring three weeks ago as part of a rant about me going home to my parents too often. I get out of the chair very quietly, backing up against the sink unit, wondering if I can hide. I'm five feet ten and until Atkins kicks in, I'm eleven and a half stone, and I'm going to *hide*? Oh, Christ, I think, looking down at the skimpy T-shirt. He's going to come in here and take one look at the slogan and I'm going to be in shit because he'll take letting the good times roll after I've left him as a personal insult and who wouldn't?

He'll go upstairs first, I think. He'll think I'm still in bed, because he'll think I need the extra sleep after the strain of yesterday, *like* he has the insight to even think being knee-locked on an occasional table was a strain for anybody but him who was looking. The kitchen door opens and he comes in, looking for a place to dump his bag. That done, he turns and yells at me.

'Oh, motherajasus,' is what he yells.

I shake all over. Peeing on the floor is a real possibility.

'I'm sorry,' he says, beginning to laugh. 'I wasn't expecting someone to be in here.'

'You're not Luke,' I tell him, and he agrees.

'I'm Doug,' he says and extends a hand.

'Doug?' I say, like an idiot, giving him a handshake like a withered carrot because I lose faith in whether I should or not.

'Doug Rogan,' he says. 'Who're you?'

'Flannery.'

'I figured you must be something to the Prof. He'd have to call his kids funny names.'

'Doug's a funny name.'

'Nickname. Dougal is my real name.'

'Like the screw?'

'*What?*'

'Wasn't Dougal the screw in *Magic Roundabout* that said it was time to go to bed?'

'That was Zebedee. And he wasn't a screw.'

You sound, I thought, like you're Zebedee's adoptive father getting huffy over me insulting him.

'What was he, then?'

'A yoke on a spring. But at least you're not doing a Father Ted imitation Who was Luke?'

Another yoke on a spring, I think. Another screw. Loose.

'What do you mean, "was"?' I ask.

'Is, was, maybe, Luke? Who you were glad I wasn't?'

'An ex-boyfriend.'

I quite like the way that comes out. It's as if I have them stacked above us, circling to land, all my ex-boyfriends. The reality is that before Luke, there wasn't anything you could call a boyfriend. Cricket club young lads (my mother's phrase) or callow youths (my father's take on the same thing).

'Oh,' he says, losing interest, and goes to retrieve his bag. He has a pony tail. How late nineties, I think.

'Why are you here?' I ask, and he looks surprised all over again as if everybody always knew why he was anywhere. As if everybody was just *waiting* for him to be wherever they were to improve their lives. Not a sufferer from low self-esteem, this one.

'I'm here to put software on your father's computer,' he says. 'I know where it is.'

He's halfway out of the door again when I ask him why, if he knew where the PC's kept, he came first into the kitchen.

'I was going to make a cuppa,' he says.

'My mother says all workmen take the first ten minutes for a cuppa,' I say.

'I wouldn't dream of suggesting your mother's fulla shite,' he says. 'But if she says that kind of stuff, she is.'

He's gone, and I can hear him padding around my father's study. He probably wears those high tops with embroidery-pattern soles that serial killers wear and that get them caught, I think. I follow him into the study. He's wearing moccasins, hand-hewn a lifetime ago by the resident alcoholic on an Indian reservation. They're all tufty hair bunching out of prolapsed seams and he's flattened down the backs so they're like slippers.

'Yes?' he says, and I realise I'm standing gaping at his feet like nobody ever had any before now.

'D'you know that cannibals don't go much for feet because they have so little meat on them?'

Now it's him that's scared, either because he's not used to my scattered mindset or because he thinks I might grill and eat his tootsies.

'Cuppa what?' I ask.

Tea, he says. Weak. I go back to the kitchen and boil up a mug in the microwave. When I feck the teabag in, it seems to enrage the liquid, which boils over in a big burbling spurt, leaving the teabag stranded in an inch of water. It makes me want to cry, for some daft reason, but I start again and this time get it right. I even do him toast. Why do I do him toast? Because I used to do Luke toast. Shit, I'd have done toasted possum for Luke if it had kept him happy.

'You happy?' I ask the pony tail when I bring in the tea and toast. (Triangulated and with crusts amputated. The toast, I mean.)

He's shoving CDs into the server and making right-handed with the mouse. The server does that revving noise computers do to make you think they're going to play with you, and he takes the tea. Looks at the toast with suspicion, then takes one triangle and puts it butter side down on the other, so he has a kind of air sandwich.

'Mmmf,' he says through his nose, chewing.

Amazing, what one non-syllable can convey. It says ' 'Course I'm happy, what a stupid frigging girly question to ask, everybody's happy except planks that don't deserve to be happy and anyway nobody should waste time on crap like that.'

I nod and start to retreat out of the door with his now redundant plate. I'm halfway down the hall when he asks me do I have an e-mail address. Oh, puh-lease, I think, could we be a little less previous?

'Or do people use your father's to get to you?'

'My father doesn't have an e-mail address.' As I say it, I realise I'm wrong. I remember telling Luke about it a few weeks back. My wonderful father. Scholar. Poet – and able to use the Internet, too.

I put the crumby plate in the kitchen and go back.

'Why d'you ask?'

He gestures at the screen and there's a line-up maybe twenty deep of unread messages, all sent over the past three hours. He opens one of them. The two of us read it.

'Who'd'you say this Luke was?'

I stand there, sickening, my hand spidering for the door. He clicks to another of the messages.

'He's some fucked-up weirdo, that's for sure.'

It's at this point that my father's rug comes into play. It was given to him by Colonel Gaddafi or somebody else – one of those guys who lives in a tent – and he's never got that tape put underneath to prevent it slipping, so it suddenly slides from under me, bunching up in corrugations of colour at the foot of the chair the computer guy is in, and I come down on my arse with a whack you could hear in Sligo. The pain is fantastic and I let on this is why I'm crying until I realise this *is* why I'm crying. He gets out of the chair and the corrugations of rug push it neatly under the desk. This gives him enough room to kneel down in front of me. Holy, holy, holy, I think, and this makes me cry even more, which makes no sense, but then, not a lot of my life does make sense.

'D'you want to sue him or block him?'

I ram the tears out of my eye-sockets with the same gesture my mother used rubbing her scratchy eye and find him looking at me, absolutely devoid of sympathy.

'Sue him?'

He does a flail out of the back of him with his hand. I figure it's meant to take in the computer.

'It's illegal, what he's done there. You can put him in clink. Although, you want my opinion, the fucker should be in a mental hospital.'

'I thought that's where they were taking him.'

'When?'

'Last night.'

'What did he do last night?'

'You don't want to know.'

He stands up and yanks me, two-handed, to my feet. My arse does this fantastic echo-pain, like it was saying 'Just to remind you not to do that whack thing again.' I clutch it. He impatiently gestures me to one side so he can straighten out the Colonel's rug.

'Colonel Gaddafi gave that to my father,' I say.

'Bit loud,' he says after a minute, and since this is what I've always felt, I get raging and start to defend it. He indicates that I'm to go to the kitchen, and when we arrive there sits me down and plugs in the kettle.

'Microwave,' I say, as he pulls out two mugs.

'Nobody should ever microwave water,' he says severely. 'Could blind you.'

'You sound like my mother,' I say, smiling.

'Jesus,' he says, with total contempt, lashing hot water into the mugs and beating the hell out of one of the teabags with the back of a spoon.

'My mother is very good to me,' I say and start crying all over again.

So of course I end up drinking tea as strong as undiluted tar, with the detritus of a destroyed teabag in it, while telling him

the whole Luke saga. The only thing that seems to bother him
is my plinth.

'An occasional table?' he asks. 'What's that?'

'You know, those little tables that sort of go into each other,
the little one, then the middle one, then the bigger one and you
pull them out when you're having parties? Nesting, I think
they call it.'

He shakes his head like a novice anthropologist coming to
terms with a tribe that celebrates good years by eating alarm
clocks.

'Occasional tables,' he says. 'Nesting. Right. These'd be
small tables, would they?'

So I'm doing the flat hand, palm down, two feet off the floor
mime and he considers the dimensions indicated.

'Would you not be a bit hefty for that?'

'I don't suppose Luke gave the relative strength of the table,
vis-à-vis my weight, much consideration,' I say stiffly.

'Nah. He wouldn't,' he says.

'How do you know what he wouldn't?' I ask, shifting in the
chair. The movement puts bendy lines and starbursts behind
my eyes.

'The bag of wire hangers who generated the crap that's on
your da's machine wouldn't have enough sane moments to
work out stuff like that,' he says and then asks me why I'm still
crying. As in: I battered you up a cup of tea, I listened to your
story of being victimised by a looper you outweigh by two
stone, what the hell else do you want?

'It's my arse, actually,' I say. I would say it with as much
dignity as I can muster, except that I'm not able to muster any.

'What is?'

'Oh, Jesus, what's making me cry! My arse is.'

There's this long silence and he pulls the end of his pony tail around and chews on it. I shift again and my bottom really, *really* hurts.

'Do you often cry about aspects of your appearance?' he asks. Carefully. And I realise he thinks I'm crying because my arse is too big and pear-shaped, which it is, but I'm long past crying about it. Big pear-shaped arses set in early in life. You get over having one in time. I have.

'I'm not crying over how it looks,' I say, standing up with difficulty. 'I'm crying over how it feels. It hurts. I mean, it's amazing how much it hurts.'

OK, he says, in a this-I-can-handle tone, relieved to be rid of all that other emotional stuff. He'll back the tank up to the front door. Tank? He then leaves, and I can hear a car engine coming closer. Through the open front door I can read what it says on the tyre stuck onto the back. Land Rover Discovery. I walk with some difficulty to the front door and he sort of nods at the open passenger door. I balk.

'Where we going?'

'Beaumont Accident and Emergency.'

'I'm not going there.'

'Why not?'

'They'll take eight hours to find there's nothing wrong with me.'

'Not at ten o'clock on a Tuesday morning. Maybe at ten o'clock on a Saturday night. Or ten o'clock on a Monday morning. Tuesday's fine.'

I'm climbing halfway up in the sky as he talks, thinking this is *not* the kind of car to take a sore arse up into, but next thing I'm strapped in and it's like being on the top deck of a bus. I can see everything. I wonder aloud why Monday morning would be bad in A & E but not Tuesday and he says people save their illnesses and bone-breakages over the weekend thinking they'll get better but when they don't, they take them to A & E first thing the following week to get the best value out of the sick cert.

In Beaumont they triage me and eventually X-ray me and say a consultant will see me presently. I crouch my way back to where I left Doug and find him fast asleep, his beat-up moccasins sticking up at the end of legs that run for miles and cross at the ankle, his chin dug into his chest. I leave him to sleep until the consultant tells me what's wrong with me and says I can go home. Then I wake him up. He comes up from under sleep as if he was a spy, trying to work out where he is but reveal to nobody that he doesn't *know* where he is.

'Beaumont Hospital,' I say. 'Accident and Emergency.'

'That's right,' he says as if I've won a table-quiz. 'Your arse.'

'They say I can go home,' I say and lead the way to his upstairs downstairs car.

'Do we need to go to a chemist?' he asks as we drive.

'No.'

'Was anything broken?'

'Yes.'

'Jesus,' he says, impressed. 'What?'

'My coccyx.'

'Your what?'

'COCCYX,' I yell, and he roars laughing at me. He tries to get serious again, but it doesn't really work. I spell it. He repeats it.

''m I allowed to ask where that is?'

'My arse.'

'Where in your arse?'

'It's the rudimentary redundant tail-bone.'

'Oh,' he says, light dawning. 'Your *arse* arse.'

I, the daughter of Ireland's most popular poet, couldn't have put it better.

'Yeah,' he says. 'Be difficult to plaster that, all right.'

He thinks *that's* an effing riot, too. I feel ridiculous, because it's still bloody painful, but nobody in A & E proffered morphine. Instead, they sort of sniggered and said take paracetamol. By the time we get back to the house, he's completely lost interest in my arse or my gratitude. It was grand, he says, allowed him to catch up on his sleep. He can, he tells me, sleep anywhere at any time.

I'm not sure this is something I need or want to know, but it's difficult to tell a man to shut up and chew silently on his pony tail when he's taken you to ER and back. He tells me he's going to block anything incoming from Luke and asks do I want to read the messages that have already come through. I quell that possibility with a look and tell him not just to delete them but to delete them out of the recycle bin and everywhere else so my father won't ever come across them. At which point my mother comes home. Do I remember to ask her how her scratchy eye is? Of course I don't.

3

Meeting in Gangland

———◆—◆———

The main reason I don't ask about my mother's scratchy eye is that my mobile starts to go. I had turned it to mute, because Luke, months ago, put one of his compositions on it to serve as a ringer, and I didn't need a phone reminding me all day of Luke and of the fact that I hadn't telephoned his father to find out how he is doing. Which I am going to have to do, sooner or later. Now, though, the phone is vibrating itself into an infuriated circle on the table. I pick it up and give it the most cautious 'Hello' you've ever heard.

'It's all *right*,' Lyn says, sounding, as she always does, as if she's spoiling for a fight. 'It's only *me*. Well?'

'Well yourself,' I say. To find out how much she knows. Which is mostly everything, because Lyn is the queen of the networkers. She is the most connected woman alive. Her phone never stops. Half the time, when she's working on her PC, she has the tiny phone to her ear, hidden by the long straight black mane.

'The two of you in hospital on the same day,' she says with a downward inflection that makes quite ordinary comments sound disapproving.

'Yeah, but they let me out,' I say.

'Luke will be in for at least ten days while they do tests,' she says, her voice going into monotone to indicate that this is the party line. 'Of course, they'll stabilise him and he'll promise to take the medication and they'll let him out, but probably not for a few weeks. Hang on.'

I can hear her telling someone across the room how to shift something from one directory to another. Lyn has 'incompetent bimbo' written all over her. As tall as me – taller in the heels she always wears – she's so slender you want to call her 'skinny' but it doesn't apply. She is as improbably perfect as a Barbie doll, only dark. When we were both eleven, I was built like a postbox and she was so fragile, every passing adult wanted to adopt her. Even as a kid, she had these huge, knowing eyes and that slightly wistful beauty.

'I haven't telephoned Luke's father,' I say, when she comes back.

'I'm sure he's so busy, he's grateful to you for leaving him alone. Anyway, you've a broken bone.'

She should be in PR, Lyn. Instinctively comes up with a favourable rationale to agreeably cover whatever you need covered up. A few years ago, my father decided to do some electrical work in the house. Lyn dropped in when he'd finished, and was talking to us when I leaned against the wall and got electrocuted. The shock was so strong it catapulted me right across the hall, which fortunately broke the connection between me and the ESB.

'That wall's alive,' I shrieked.

'Oh, Flannery,' my father murmured in gentle reproof, and put his palm to it. He went rigid all over. Forget languid. His very teeth asserted themselves as his mouth went into an horrific rictus. Lyn lashed out with her backpack and swept him away from the wall, which I thought was clever, although not so clever as suggesting to my father (as she then did) that an electrified wall might be very useful to some department in the college for study purposes. My mother was having none of this. For her, the electrified wall was a cock-up too far. From that point on, whenever anything went wrong in the house, her policy was to Get a Man. My father appeared on a talk show not long afterwards and had everybody in stitches at him electrifying the wall and as a result being demoted, domestically. People kept telling me how funny the electrified wall must have been. With slight envy, they kept telling me this. Yet more evidence of my privileged background. I even got to play with live walls.

Today, though, Lyn is in the accommodation business. My space in her apartment is going to be vacant again very soon, because Meriel the Marriageable is getting hitched within months. I'm welcome to move back whenever I'm up to it. But apart from that, some of the girls are meeting this very evening in Gangland in Temple Bar to hear about Merry's wedding plans, so will I come?

'Lyn, none of them know about Luke?'

'Being in hospital? Of course they do,' she says, as if it had been on all the news bulletins. 'It won't be a *problem*, Flannery. Really it won't. It'll be good. You will come along, won't you?'

I end up agreeing, even though I figure this entire thing is a set-up: that none of them were planning to meet tonight, but will now be dragooned into doing it by Lyn. How the hell she manages to be as efficient as she is, I have never worked out, because either she's tic-tacking with people on e-mail, fending off invitations from celebs or she's on three different phones, two pals in distress on two of the phones and a celeb on the third.

The only disadvantage to sharing an apartment with Lyn is the message-taking and damp-shouldering you have to do, to comfort famous and nearly famous people who have fallen for her and who are getting nowhere with her. She goes out with them and they feel great because she looks better than any other woman at the event. She gives them her e-mail address and says she checks her mail every hour without fail and answers everything. They don't believe her, but she's telling the truth. What they quickly realise though, is that there is nothing to beat instant access for knocking hell out of aspirations of intimacy. They're hardly done pressing 'send' when a response comes winging its way into their inbox, filled with delight, stuffed with some useful information or a contact name, ending with affection, but somehow failing to advance the relationship. The fella wants to do a forty-fathom dive and Lyn is dog-paddling along on the surface. Come up here, the shallows are lovely. You don't want to get the bends, do you?

It's at that point they end up talking to whoever's sharing the apartment with her, which for a lot of our lives has been me. Bit of type-casting, there. Big lump of a plain girl is best friends with beautiful brilliant girl. Whenever I'm going through a downswing, I wonder if Lyn didn't pick me for that purpose. Compare and contrast. On the left we have Neanderthal woman, on the right we have the end result of evolution and healthy living. Except that she doesn't even do healthy living. I've been her food courier. I've brought back those sandwiches haemorrhaging mayonnaise at every bite, filled, as they are, with ham, turkey, tomato, lettuce, mozzarella cheese, basil with a side-order of chips and a cappuccino with two extra shots of espresso. Any one of Lyn's cups of coffee would curl anybody else's hair. But she looks as if she lives on apples and camomile tea, and when she arrives, that evening, into Gangland, every conversation in the place goes hushed for maybe thirty seconds. Then every speaker resumes, pretending they weren't distracted for a minute by this girl with the mermaid fall of wet-shined navy-black hair and the indecent slip dress.

'Lyn looks as if it would show if she ate a Smartie,' Andrea says from the corner where the early arrivers have congregated. Andrea is drinking gin as if she is proving something. I know better than to ask her what it is. Andrea is at war with life, and life is winning. Now, life never asked to go to war with Andrea, but she's always picking on opposition bigger than she is, which isn't hard, because she's 4'11" if the carpet is thick. She has the look of a six-footer who accidentally stood under a car-crusher for a couple of minutes. It squashed her broad. The very lobes of her ears are so stubby, her stud earrings always look like they're going down for the last time.

Lyn takes one look at the group and says we'll order straight away and could we have a menu and she hopes we're not all going to make her look greedy by not having starters because she's going to eat everything. The waiter comes over beside me (to get a better view of her, I decide, bitterly) and chuckles when she says this, obviously thinking she'll eat a leaf of radiccio and then cast down her napkin, unable to swallow another morsel. Stick around, lad, I think, and watch the Eating Machine in action.

Meriel is all ready to launch on her pre-marital problems when Andrea sets the agenda.

'Here's to Flannery,' she says, raising her glass. 'Free Flannery.'

'Free Flannery with every order,' Lyn says.

I ponder the notion of myself as imprisoned, and, like a bad skin graft, it fails to take. You have to be small to be a victim.

'Hope *you'll* learn a lesson from her,' Andrea says to Meriel, who is fishing for fruit in her glass. Waste not, want not. Make a great wife, you will, Merry. Lyn, of course, is drinking pints. Another way to focus the minds of the peasants, I think, noting the number of men glancing at her admiringly. It's the sexy contradiction. Would you look at that black-haired one with the Emma Peel shape and her lowering pints, fair dues to her all the same . . .

'Hardly saw Flannery, once she took up with that Luke,' Andrea comments. 'Oh, no, she was too busy to see old friends, once she had a man.'

I'm sitting on a tall stool at the bar, immobilised by imperatives. One of the voices in my head is telling me to get the hell off the stool, because on it I must be the image of Miss Piggy. Another is repeating the phrase 'took up with that Luke' and wondering what Andrea's mother is like, because this sounds to me like a Mother Phrase. A third is telling me to smack Andrea in the chops with my handbag for the suggestion that I don't have millions of men.

'Flannery's goldfishing,' Lyn giggles. 'We ban goldfishing in our news reports.'

Lyn works for a TV production house. Goldfishing must be opening and shutting one's mouth unproductively. I shut mine. The waiter takes us to our table and Lyn starts to eat like there's no tomorrow. I suddenly wish there would *be* no tomorrow and this surprises me. Without Luke to take care of, to placate, to dread, my life feels like a phantom limb. Of no practical use, but filled with referred pain.

'What about your thesis?' Andrea says to me.

She manages to jerk her head reprovingly at the waiter – enough, already – just before he was going to stop pouring wine in to her glass anyway. He heavy-breathes to keep his temper under control.

'What about my thesis?'

'Have you finished it?'

'No, and I'm not going to, either.'

This surprises the hell out of the lot of us.

'Why not?'

'Because it bores me stupid. I'm going to get a job.'

'You can't just abandon your degree because of Luke.'

'Luke has very little to do with it. I can finish the thesis some other time. I just want to do something that makes money and requires no brain power or effort.'

'If I find a job like that, you'll be the second to know,' Raimonde says.

Lyn spends her life getting past the 'Jesus, you are so beautiful, you must be brain-dead/a bitch/a slapper' grace-before-relationships stage. Raimonde has to get past a version of the same introductory hassle, as people discover that her parents gave all their six children unisex names so (in those pre-scan days) whatever gender the baby turned out to be, it would have had the boost of hearing itself referred to by name while still in the womb. The family goes Raimonde, Hillary, Connie, Raphael and Willi. I baby-sat Willi when she was a toddler, and even then you could tell the damage the name was doing to her. Other toddlers have a pet blanket. She had a pet front doormat. I was always afraid, when I was baby-sitting her, she'd get sick enough to be taken to A & E and I'd get arrested as a child-abuser because of her being worn raw down one side from the mat. Sometimes she even had 'Welcome' embossed in mirror-writing down a leg. I felt she couldn't turn out to be an integrated adult, and I wanted to get offside before she started into the torturing of lower animals phase.

'I'll find you a job,' Lyn says, cleaning her starter plate. Literally. She was a joy to live with, that way. You never had to scrape her plates before you put them into the dishwasher. My plates always had leftovers. Partly because I was always pretending not to really eat anything, and partly because my mother maintained it was not good manners to scarf everything 'as if you never saw a bit'. Leaving stuff on your plate was kind of family PR: no starvation at Stapletons. Plenty of food around here. Can't speak for the neighbours and there may be rationing down at the crossroads, but our fridge runneth over.

Les Girls, warming to the task, begin to ask me in detail how bad it got, with Luke. I stay vague and general. Obsessive behaviour. Controlling. Very depressed. Because Luke did his bachelor's degree in Manchester, they didn't know him prior to me, so they take my side without question. Which is awkward for them, because Andrea is egging to say that this explains why such an attractive guy would have ended up with me (he was barking mad but kept the volume of the bark down temporarily) and Raimonde is dead curious about the specifics, particularly the sex specifics, but doesn't know how to ask. (Raimonde has tapes of every episode of *Sex and the City* and watches them so frequently she talks the same way. The word 'relationship' comes into every third sentence.)

'Meriel, you don't look as happy as I expect a bride to look,' I say, changing the direction of the conversation with the clanging subtlety of a train opting to become a helicopter. Fortunately, Meriel isn't one to hang around waiting for a subtlety. Centre stage was made for her. Our Merry's always braced for the cry 'Strip, you're on!'

'Hotels are just impossible,' she says, with the air of stating what we all know. Andrea nods, rolling her eyes. Don't *talk* to me about hotels. Andrea's earlobes are now not just fat, but red, too. The stud earring reminds me of buttons punched into the middle of leather chair-backs with the chair swelling out all around them.

'No hotel available?' Raimonde asks

'Nowhere.'

'Not even the new ones?' Lyn asks.

Now, you might think it was obvious that if someone has said nowhere is available, that means old and new hotels are ruled out, but what Lyn is doing is not information-gathering. Lyn is doing accompaniment. Twiddle, twiddle, on the minor keys until the next theme picks up. I can see a man at the next table, his back to Lyn's back, listening and half-nodding at how sweet she is being and I get a huge desire to hit her and him with the marble slab the butter comes on. Most of the butter is gone, because Lyn has eaten bread with sundried tomatoes in it, two of the pesto rolls and a brioche I suspect contains soap shavings, because I tried its brother and left half of it. I always hope, when I leave half a roll or brioche, that someone at the table will remark on my self-restraint. Two chances.

'Eighteen months. You have to give them eighteen months' notice,' Meriel says.

'Go to Rome,' Andrea says. Very mannish, Andrea is. Thinks solving the problem is what conversation is about. I must tell her, sometime. For women, *enjoying* the problem is what conversation is about.

'If you went to Rome and just took the two sets of parents, that would get your mother off your case,' Andrea adds.

Meriel's mother (who actually named her daughter Martha, after that fart in the Bible who was always washing and tidying and being on time – it was never going to stick, and at thirteen Martha became Meriel) was a leading figure in the seventies and eighties, fighting for the Liberal Agenda. Contraception, abortion on demand, divorce, gay rights. Except that Mrs Tyler (sorry, she probably calls herself Ms) wanted all that good stuff for the general populace, not including her own children. Like a Victorian do-gooder bringing gifts to the deserving poor, she expected her own to have higher standards.

To prove to herself that she didn't mind when Meriel started living with Adrian, she started to refer to the relationship in heavily perverted commas, talking about them 'living in what used to be called sin' and once, memorably, referring to Meriel as Adrian's concubine. Adrian laughed so much his dinner went the wrong way and for a few minutes his survival was touch and go. He told me afterwards he thought concubines only applied in China and was imagining Meriel with slitty eyes. I think, myself, that it wouldn't require much imagination, because Meriel *has* fairly slitty eyes, particularly in the morning, but you don't say that to a concubine's boyfriend.

Andrea's suggestion of a Rome wedding seems to me and Lyn to have something going for it. Undoubtedly, a five-day immersion in Catholicism in Vatican City would set Meriel's mother up for a while by giving her eternal verities a transfusion, but Meriel isn't having any.

'This is *my* day,' she says to Andrea, so squashingly I get fearful Andrea might move even lower to the ground. 'It's a once in a lifetime thing.'

'Not for Adrian,' comes the unwise response.

Adrian has (Mother Phrase coming up) Cut a Swathe. Had his way with maidens to the left, maidens to the right. And a lot of unmaidenly females, too. First year in college, he married a girl named Nina whose surname none of us could ever remember. Nina worshipped my father and followed me around, all first year, I think in the hope that some of Da might rub off me on to her. I was a terrible disappointment to her. Not only did I not have the draped, freeze-frame by freeze-frame elegance my father has, but I didn't want anybody in college to give me special treatment because of him, so I never mentioned him. You'd think I was an orphan, I referred so rarely to my father. No, in fact, you'd think I was a patricide, because of the guilty start I'd do whenever anybody *else* referred to him.

Nina had a kind of *National Enquirer* approach to her adoration of my father. Any bit of information would do. She'd have gone through our wheelie bin for his discards, if she knew where we lived, I feel sure. Just to see if he wrote anything deathless on paper napkins before balling them up and throwing them out. The day I told her that my father wrote only on hand-bound acid-free paper bound in leather in Italy, she walked around all afternoon with a softened post-orgasmic smile and I wondered how soon that little nugget would surface in some profile about Professor Stapleton. It took nearly a year for her to believe me that my father never noticed women other than my mother. (I didn't think he noticed *her* half enough, either. He always had the air of being about to get around to noticing her.) He was terribly courteous and charming to other women. Did hand-kissing and all that stuff. But it was done in the same slightly absent-minded way new mothers talk about other people's babies: they have the real thing, so they can be kind about the imitations. Nina got very down about the whole thing. An unattainable man is bad enough. But a courteous, charming man who is unattainable because he doesn't notice you enough to find you sexy is devastating to someone like her. A rite-of-passage experience with an older, famous man was integral to her concept of third-level education.

If it were possible to be on the unrequited rebound, I suspect that was what Nina was on when she married Adrian. She couldn't wangle herself into any of my father's tutorials (mainly because he was getting out of doing them, TV being much more lucrative) and I was no good as a substitute, so she turned all her dammed-up passion for him onto Adrian.

Three months after they got hitched, he got one of those travelling scholarships to the States for a year, *and took it*. Nina could make those words into a scream of agony or a whisper of disbelief. *He took it. HE TOOK IT!* I'd be sitting in a lecture theatre, and she'd be beside me, playing mad variations on a theme in a me-directed whisper. *HE* (as opposed to any of the unwed millions who could have won it) *took it*, she would say, forcing me to nod in apparently shared dismay. *He TOOK it* was an alternative. Meaning he could've postponed it but didn't. Then there was *He took IT*, which I took to mean that given a choice between Nina and the scholarship, he took the scholarship.

By the end of second year, I was praying more for Adrian's return to Nina than I was praying for good results for myself, although good results were a high priority for me. If I did badly in college, it would draw attention to the link with my father. Some gossip columnist would talk of him being 'saddened' by me cocking up.

Thinking about Nina has completely distracted me from the conversation (although not from the meal, which is good, or the grinding pain in my coccyx, which is bad) and so I'm surprised to find myself in crossfire between Andrea, who has suggested that Adrian has a lot of marital frequent-flier miles under his belt, and Meriel.

'What a rotten thing to say,' Meriel is now saying to Andrea, who isn't listening because she's trying to locate a waiter. Gangland, at ten thirty, is so crowded that getting a waiter is like catching a salmon in the Liffey: possible, but it surprises the hell out of both sides. Andrea's lack of attention to her is working Meriel into a frenzy.

'I mean, what a *rotten* thing to say. I mean, *shit*. Really, though.'

Meriel did Communications in DCU. You can tell.

'You know the truth,' Meriel suddenly announces, nodding to me.

Me? The truth? Whose? What? Andrea fixes me with a determinedly non-judgemental look. I'm here to listen, says the look. Convince me.

'Flannery got them nullified. Adrian and Nina,' Lyn says helpfully.

'Did you?' Raimonde asks, admiringly. 'I didn't know that.'

'You're not supposed to know,' I say, and that sounds pompous. 'I'm not supposed to tell,' I add.

'Why not?'

Now that I think of it, do I know why not? My grasp of religion is somewhere between Rupert Bear and knock three times on the ceiling if you want me. Half-remembered snippets of heavyweight threats and promises entwined with the seal of the confessional and the Hippocratic Oath. Omerta crossed with Omigod. I tell them my ass is hurting (you have to take the 'r' out of arse in a posh restaurant) and go for a brief walk. I've already done this so many times the other diners are beginning to nod wisely to each other. Twenty-something keeps leaving the dinner table, face scrunched up in misery, disappears for five minutes, comes back, face unscrunched – it's obvious. This time, I sit down, facially unscrunched, to find that the conversation has double-parked waiting for me to get back.

'How did you get Nina and Adrian nullified?' Raimonde wants to know.

'I didn't get them nullified. It was just – if they wanted an annulment, they had to jointly nominate two witnesses to testify at Archbishop's Palace.'

'Jointly?'

'Witnesses to what?'

That surprised me at the time, I remember. Nina got very virtuous with me and told me that as far as she was concerned, I was free to tell the archbishop anything. This blanket permission turns me off more than anything else she could say. I've never felt an urge to tell an archbishop a single thing, and now she wants me to confess at random? No, she says, just she and Adrian are both happy for me to go in and tell it the way I saw it and they won't even ask me afterwards. Who's your other witness? I ask, and she says Luke Buckley, who I've met but don't really know. He's a former flatmate of Adrian's.

'I had to go to Archbishop's Palace in Drumcondra,' I tell them, trying unsuccessfully to distract Andrea from wine-waiter pursuit. 'And there was this old nun with a jotter and she asked me to tell her about Nina and Adrian and how mature I thought they were and whether they should have been married to each other.'

I don't announce that I told the old nun neither of them should ever be married to anybody, but that at least having them wed to each other reduced their potential to do damage on a wider front. It doesn't seem to be the kind of thing to say to the prospective bride of one of them. Anyway, Adrian may have improved over time. Some people do.

'Was that how you met Luke?' Raimonde asks this with piety, as if the relationship that ended yesterday on an occasional table was so precious she's thinking of organising a month's mind for it. What the hell, I think, shrugging (yes, but that's not important), is a month's mind and why is my brain full of my mother's phrases and why didn't I remember to ask her about her scratchy eye, what kind of a self-absorbed shite am I?

'They get it?' Andrea demands.

The brevity of the question is a classic giveaway. When Andrea has had enough drink she starts conversation-texting.

'Get what?'

'Ananunilment.'

'Say that again,' Lyn instructs, catching the eye of a waiter at first go and indicating a coffee requirement for the lot of us.

'Won't.' More text from Andrea.

'They did get the annulment, actually,' I say, cutting to what I think is the chase. 'I asked Nina a few months later and she looked a bit furtive. Eventually she admitted that there was an annulment sitting up in Archbishop's Palace waiting for her. All she had to do was come up with five hundred quid. But she said she was leaving it there because, although she had the five hundred, she was blowing it on a skiing holiday instead.'

'Dead right,' Andrea says, pouring the rest of the wine for herself, presumably on the assumption that nobody but her would want the dregs. 'It wouldn't go away.'

True. You don't often hear reports of unclaimed annulments escaping from Archbishop's Palace and menacing the married in the streets of Drumcondra.

'If hotels are difficult and you don't like the idea of Rome,' Lyn says, 'would you think of an open-air wedding? On a beach, in the sunshine, with a marquee just in case it sprinkled.'

Saying 'just in case it sprinkled' about the Irish weather is like saying 'just in case Tuesday followed Monday'. But Meriel buys the conditionality of the 'sprinkle' without a qualm. The gullible must have a greatly enhanced shot at happiness, I think.

The man who has the back of his chair almost touching Lyn's turns round at her last comment and hands her his business card. She looks at it solemnly under those foot-long eyelashes and says 'Wow!' I've seen her do it so often. Just that one *Beano/Dandy* exclamation. Wide-eyed. Gleeful. Solution to all our problems. Boat on the horizon. Marines arriving. I've never said 'Wow!' in my life. The day I was born, I was too old for 'Wow!'

But the guy glows like a shagging lamp (Andrea's are not the only tumescent lobes in this restaurant tonight) and all us goils lean forward like trained seals waiting for a lashing of mackerel out of Lyn's bucket.

'Robert, here, does marquees,' Lyn announces. 'Now, what are the chances of that?'

I swear I can see the diners at Robert's table, every last one of them, moving gently forward towards Lyn. If the magnetism was any more powerful, they'd end up going smack against her and have to be beaten away the way she beat my father off the electrified wall. One of them hesitantly talks of a private beach in Wexford he has an interest in. I didn't think you could have an interest in a beach. I thought beaches were kind of like air. That the Minister for the Environment owned them and the rest of us got lender's cards. This guy describes a sweeping semi-circle with his left hand, decanting a balloon of brandy into the lap of the man beside him in the process. The man beside him folds a napkin geometrically and leans heavily on the wet bit on his thigh. This is a man who's often on the receiving end of spilt drink.

Overlooking the beach is a Martello Tower. None of us work out what Meriel is going to do with the Martello Tower, but we end up with date, location and even a band. Sorted. The man with the brandy seeping through his trousers owns a bit of Beesleys, a brother-and-sister band he tells me is the sunny south-east's answer to the Corrs. I've been out of circulation standing on tables for Luke too long, I think, realising I've been mishearing radio DJs talking about this band and assumed they were calling it the Bees Knees.

As the bill comes and Les Girls start hitting the table with their chins as they reach underneath for handbags and mobile phones, I begin to work out how much weight I must lose per week between now and when Adrian and Meriel tie the knot. Diets always look dead easy at the end of a good meal. The guy with the beach is exchanging business cards with Lyn. Forget it, fella, I think. Lyn would never go for a man who keeps a matchbox-sized yoke in his pocket for delivering business cards singly.

'Nice man,' she says, joining us outside the front door. Kiss of death phrase, that one.

'Anal retentive,' I say.

'Oh, now,' Lyn says, disallowing the cruelty.

'Ten condom man,' Andrea announces.

'*What?*'

'To be sure, to be sure, to be sure, to be –' Andrea is saying when the guy comes out behind Lyn and hands her another card.

'I've just added the e-mail address I use at weekends,' he says, and Lyn nods, wide-eyed and speechless with the effort not to laugh.

When I get into the house, my mother is already in bed, leaving a message for me from Luke's father. Luke's psychiatrist thinks it might be helpful if I attended one of Luke's group therapy sessions. Love, Mam.

I could leave a note on the hall table saying 'Hey, how's your scratchy eye?' but it never strikes me. I mean, there's a natural order to everybody's priorities. How could a scratchy eye compare with the threat of having to attend group therapy for my former boyfriend?

4

Visiting the Eye and Ear

———◆◆◆———

Just beyond the end of Grafton Street, there's a point where a garda stands, ready to catch ordinary drivers who have turned left at the end of Dawson Street. Ordinary drivers don't realise until too late that this is now illegal. You can see them doing a 'Feckit, too late to go the other way now' shrug as they muscle into the bus/taxi lane and get beeped at by a double-decker. Or – if you go a bit further up – you can see the driver of the double-decker, or of a cab, gloating as the poor hoor gets hauled to one side by the garda and ticketed.

I'm standing near the garda, watching this at the end of a long day negotiating the postponement of my thesis, when my mobile rings.

'Flannery?'

My mother's voice, before I get to say hello.

'Hi, Ma,' I trill, beginning to walk up towards Wicklow Street, thinking that there's no city in the world as beautiful as Dublin when there's a bit of sunshine in the mix.

'Flannery.'

Oh, bloody 'ell, I think. A full stop. My name, in my mother's mouth, can mean any number of things. When I was around ten, I particularly dreaded the version that ended on an upswinging inflection: FlannereeEE! It meant she was standing over something I had hidden/broken/half-eaten and I better get myself lined up for the court martial. A full stop

41

turned my name into a negative statement and that's what I'm now getting. What the frig have I done wrong now? The potentially wrong bits of my life pass in front of my eyes, but none of them justifies the gravity of her tone, I feel.

'Yes, Mam,' I say, huddling back into one of those decorative niches you find along Suffolk Street.

'Flannery.'

Another full stop. Jesus, Ma, we have the dramatis personae sorted. I'm me, you're you. Known you for years. Not going to be fooled by any substitute.

'Flannery, I'm in the Ioneer.'

'OK,' I say, as if this means something to me.

The Ioneer? Could it be the Ironer? Something to do with my father's silk shirts? No. Must be a restaurant.

'Remember I told you I had a scratchy eye?'

'Oh, I know, Ma, I'm a cow for not asking you about it.'

'I decided to go to the Ioneer.'

Long silence.

'And you did,' I say helpfully, mystified.

Slap upside the brain. Eye and Ear. Hospital.

'Oh, you *did*?'

'And they told me to come back for tests.'

'Right,' I say, delighted to be on top of this issue. Finally.

They're keeping me in.'

'They're keeping you in what?

'Overnight. Well, really, for the rest of the week.'

'What's wrong?'

'I have the fastest-growing cancer in my eye.'

'Oh, Jesus.'

'Mmmm.'

The garda is still stopping unfortunate drivers. The activity suddenly seems idiotic.

'What's the treatment, Mam? What do they do for it?'

'Remove it.'

My heart skips a beat.

'Remove what?'

'My eye.'

I will forever feel guilty over the twenty seconds of absolute silence that follow. I know they are making her feel worse. I know they're emphasising the gross horror of what is in store for her. I know there is some response I should make that would be supportive or helpful, but what I want to do is close my eyes in the middle of this busy street and make it all go away. Scream and shout and drown out everything she has said. Open my eyes – Oh, God, both my eyes – and be somewhere else coming out of a dream, sweaty and panicky and grateful.

'Mam, darling. Where's the Eye and Ear?'

She tells me.

'I'll be there soon as I can get a taxi. OK?'

'OK.'

She isn't and won't be and nothing will ever be again, but I can hardly say 'Don't let them take out your eye before I get there' because it would sound as if I want to witness it. I step practically into the path of a taxi and get into its back seat as if I were in London or New York where they have a taxi system that works. Tell the guy to take me to the Eye and Ear. Think about second opinions. That's it. That's where I have to start. You just smile at the surgeon and say 'I'd like to have a second opinion because this is such a serious matter' and the second opinion suggests some dead easy alternative approach. There's always other options. I can go on the Internet. Half the time, backwoodsmen in medicine in Ireland don't even know the kind of state-of-the-art stuff discussed on the Internet.

The taximan is telling me about the Spike. The sculpture that's going to go up where Nelson's Pillar used to be. Before my time, Nelson. But *there's* a guy who did OK with only one eye. Even used to stick his telescope to that empty socket when he wanted to pretend he didn't see something the Admiralty would have wanted him to see. Stole that fat bird Emma Hamilton away from her husband and stayed pals with the husband. Lot of things you can do with only one eye, I think, desperately. It can even look good, if you wear a swashbuckling patch. The thought of my mother dressed up as Long John Silver with an eye-patch strap slanting across her beautiful face reduces me to a silence so profound that the taximan's flow of opinion gets dammed up at source.

At the old Victorian redbrick hospital, I fling banknotes at him as if I was in a movie and don't even tell him to keep the change. My mother is in a room on her own, reading *Hello!* magazine. She despises *Hello!* magazine. She puts it aside unhurriedly and smiles at me. I have decided to be strong and calm, so I burst into tears and clutch her like she's a swimming ring.

'Now,' she says. 'Here's what we need to do.'

She has a little spiral bound notebook with the headings already listed. I am to collect my father by taxi (because neither of us can drive the family car – she's Head of Family Transportation) and explain to him what is happening. He is not to be frightened or upset. Right, I think. Dead easy, that'll be. Hey, Dad, Ma's getting her left eye out, but no problem, you get two of them, the other's fine and they do wonders with plastics these days, don't they?

'Will you be able to drive afterwards?'

She takes a second spiral bound notebook out of her

handbag and makes a note of the question. Hasn't thought to ask that, yet. I feel promoted to the front row.

'Have you thought of going for a second opinion?'

The specialist himself called for a second opinion, she tells me. Because this is a rare cancer, he wanted to be sure. So he got some woman to fly in from Bristol. And (she reaches behind her and finds a sheaf of pages) here are some Internet printouts he gave her so she could be completely informed about the options. I take the sheaf and stick it under the notebook allocated to me.

'And what, exactly, *are* the options?' I ask, in the tone of voice you use to ask someone are they for coffee or tea.

'There aren't any,' she says, pointing to where she has put an outsize X beside text in the printouts. To give myself time, I read the paragraphs. It gives me no time. It tells me the minute this unpronounceable cancer is discovered, the eye must come out faster than fast because the thing migrates into the brain if left. It gives me a handful of references just in case I think there is a way around its argument. They sit, those references, on the page, as disengaged in their venom as a shark. Nothing personal, they say. Nothing but the facts, ma'am. For further links to eye cancers that can kill you, click here.

'I'll still be able to see,' she says. 'Although depth perception may be skewed for a while.'

'Shit, what's a little screwed depth perception between friends?' I ask and feel like I'm feeding her pebbles. She smiles. What nice, clean, *round* pebbles. Oh, Ma, your beautiful eyes. Eyes that—

'The hardest thing will be the poems,' she says. 'So many of them mention my eyes.'

That's true, too. Some critic once commented that Da must be subconsciously competing with Van Morrisson because so many of the poems mention his girl's brown eyes. Never brown, though, give my father that. Honey-hued. Amber-deep. (She told me when she was typing up that one for him she was preoccupied and he was very hurt to find she'd rendered her own eyes 'ankle-deep'.) Tea-dark, streamclear umber. You name it, my father found a synonym for brown when writing about my mother's eyes.

The surgeon, when he arrives, covered in students the way surgeons always move, seems mercifully unaware of my father's existence. This is obvious because he calls him 'Mr Stapleton'. People who know him as a poet tend to call him 'Professor Stapleton'. It's a title to which my father is not technically entitled, and he never lets it pass, gently indicating that he's a lowly lecturer. This, of course, endears him even further. Nothing like modesty, carefully flaunted, for binding the fans to you.

My mother asks if she'll be able to drive.

'I see no reason why you shouldn't continue to drive,' the surgeon tells my mother. 'You'll need to be careful until you get used to the deficit. Well, you'll always need to be careful, and you may have to adjust your driver's licence, I don't know. But lots of people drive with only one eye. The brain compensates.'

He goes off into a 'bet you didn't know' excursion about experiments where people had to live on the ceiling and eat off the floor or maybe it was the walls, and when they took their distorting glasses off after the experiment, they all fell over for a while but eventually went back to eating off wherever they normally ate off. My mother sits through this with her hands folded in her lap and a slight smile on her closed mouth. It is a stance she takes with drunks and other people's naughty children and allows her to check through her mental agenda without paying attention to what's in front of her. When the surgeon finishes she asks him if it's possible to have a false eye inserted tomorrow directly after the surgery. I'm going to throw up, I think. Right here. Right now. On the floor. It's not even my eye, but the thought of popping a plastic marble with iris and all painted on into a socket filled with bloodied bone turns me puky. I put my head down on my knees and the surgeon, who had got launched quite confidently on his response, takes this amiss.

'Go on.' I can hear Mam instructing him to disregard me. 'Go on. She'll be fine.'

Her big cool hand palms the cold sweat off the back of my neck and rubs my shoulders gently. Ma, you're the patient. *I'm* supposed to take care of *you*. And I will, too, the minute I stop yearning to barf over this man's oxblood loafers. The phrase 'oxblood' dances in front of my brain and I do some committed throwing up. Fortunately, a nurse has arrived with a brown plastic kidney bowl and gets it in place at the crease in my chin just as I let go. The timing makes me want to laugh, but I'm too busy trying to get standing to go clean up. Someone steers me into a bathroom and I de-grot, then sit on the edge of the bath wondering if going back too quickly will make me do it again.

Old trick for the nauseous: think of the most sickening things you've ever seen/heard/read about. That feature in the *Grauniad* where the autistic boy ate the cat sick because it was in the place where his food was routinely presented to him. That wedding where confused clamour three cubicles down from me in the hotel toilets sorted itself inescapably into a man having sex with a woman who was simultaneously throwing up. Neither image makes me throw up again, so I must be OK. I stagger to my feet and go back into the ward where my mother says she's got the answer to her question and she'll be wearing a protective patch for a few weeks. There is much talk of prostheses. Meaning false eyes. I try to keep my gaze above oxblood shoes and huge charts of bulbous eyes on the walls and find myself being instructed by a blink from a nurse to go to the door. She follows me.

'You OK?'

'Was it you had the kidney dish?'

'Yeah.'

'Thank you.'

'Don't let your mother be too brave. That's all.'

She goes off somewhere else and I go back to where the surgeon is trying to leave, but failing because he's obviously taken by how stoic and graceful my mother is being about the whole thing. He rolls his cupped hand around her shoulder. She does her aristocratic tolerance pose. She hates being touched. Glaumed, she calls it.

'Look at the time,' she says and I think how all the time we say look at this, look at that, did you *see* such-and-such, didn't like the look of your man.

'And not a child in the house washed,' I say. A mother's phrase. They slide you back into the groove of the normal, those phrases. Not to worry. Win some, lose some. Time heals all wounds.

Not only does she then give me instructions, she gives me a timeline on each of them. If I go over to the college now, I'll be able to get my father on his own, but then he'll have to do his lecture in the afternoon, which will put him at enough remove from the news to cope. He's to have a meal and only then come in to sit with her for a while.

'You're not to come back,' she says, firmly kind in her cruelty. 'You can be more useful to me in the next few days when your father might be too upset. Just make sure he brings me in the things on the list when he's coming this evening. C'mon, I'll walk you to the lift.'

Whatever I try to say to her gets short-circuited by the trailing wires every observation now seems to carry. *I always liked walking alongside you, because of us being the same height* leads to *But in future I'll always have to walk on your right, because you won't be able to see me out of the corner of your left eye because you won't have a left eye to have a corner of.*

At the lift door, I turn to give her a hug, my arms ready to do double or treble duty, ready to convey my understanding of the extra significance of this last embrace before the surgery, ready to indicate the steely supportive strength she needs but I don't have. She manages to half-turn in my arms so the embrace is shortened into what any mother and daughter who are speaking at the time might give each other and, as the doors whoof in from either side, walks away without looking back.

'Let's have no melodrama, now,' she used to say when I'd come home from school swearing never to speak to some girl who had smartarsed me about how fat I was or shopped me to a teacher. 'No melodrama. No *East Lynne*.'

I stare at the sign telling how many people at what weight are allowed into this lift, and, as always, sub-divide one into another to find if I outweigh the average. I don't. Now, *there's* a little ray of sunshine on a dark day, I think, taking out the instructions list, not to read it, but to be connected with her, even indirectly.

My father, when I tell him, is so sorry for me as first recipient of the bad news that he makes me cry. I'd better not learn CPR or the Heimlich, I think. The way I'm wrecking situations where I'm supposed to be helpful today suggests I'd kill the first cardiac arrest or choker I got my hands on. Dad writes DO NOT DISTURB, PLEASE on the back of a student poster and sticks it on the outside of his door with Sellotape, which surprises me. I thought he'd tell other people, but he just sits down opposite me and thinks. At one point he snaps his fingers, says 'Shit!' and disappears out of the door. When he comes back, he's pulling plastic wrapper off a brick of trade paperbacks. His books are always published in that form, he says, because he's not formidable enough to justify hardback and not popular enough for mass market paperbacks. Mass market are the smaller ones.

He hands one of them to me.

Dancing With the Angel is the title. Poems by Edmund Stapleton. Silver embossed lettering against a black and white photograph. I know the photograph. Taken before I was born. Taken by my father. The two of them, on holiday, visited some cemetery early one morning. Family lore records where and why, but I cannot, looking at the grainy blown-up version of the old snapshot, remember either. He gave her a leg-up onto the plinth occupied by the statue of an angel, lifesize. She snuck under the angel's great white wing and was holding onto its out-thrust arm when my father told her to look where the angel was gesturing. The wind played out the hem of the shirt-waist dress and freed her bright shoulder-length curls, giving the photograph the verve of captured movement.

'She doesn't know,' he says, miserably.

'She wouldn't have let you,' I say.

He turns pages in the book and holds it out to me, open to the title poem. It is about her. About her watchfulness, about the impression she gives of being braced to repel boarders. Eerily, it evokes the discomfort I felt when the surgeon massaged her shoulder, because its imagery suggests she is truly at ease only with the infinite cold stillness of the marble statue. The word 'angel' appears nowhere in the poem. In the title, only. And, of course, in the title of the book. Angels sell books. Statues don't. I shrug myself out of the snidery and concentrate on re-reading the poem.

'It's very good,' I whisper, eventually. 'Not gentle.'

He is often accused of sentimentality. When one of his poems was purchased by Hallmark, it gave magazines like *Phoenix* a great chance to torture him, although the royalties from Hallmark (tax-free, thanks to Charlie Haughey) limited the pain.

In the picture, my mother is a beautiful twenty-year-old, her eyes shadowed by sunshine, face filled with the unwise confidence of the young.

'You're going to have to manage the publicity around this,' I tell him. 'Manage it tightly. That's all.'

He nods gravely and puts the books away.

5

Research and Recovery

———◆◈◆———

The first thing that strikes me when I see her a few hours after surgery is how carefree she is. She's actually quite like the girl on the plinth alongside the big white angel, her face lifted up, filled with bright expectation. *We have seen the future and it isn't so bad.* What has she always been dreading? I wonder, kissing her, surprised to recognise this dread. The shadow of fear seems lifted by the delivery of a reality welcomed in its ghastliness. She is merry with survival. Childish curls bursting out around the big bandage, face slightly swollen.

'All gone,' she says, index finger pointing to the part of the bandage hiding the empty socket.

I tell her I am surprised she's not more hung over after the general anaesthetic, and she explains that the surgery took a relatively short time. I try not to think thoughts like 'Well, popping out an unwanted eye *would* be pretty simple', but trying not to think of scooped-out eyes is like trying not to think of a pink elephant. Images of shiny aluminium ice-cream scoops and melon ballers dance before me and I can feel my thumb moving to press the release lever of a phantom ice-cream scoop.

The surgeon appears and beams at anybody who's in the beam-receiving business. It went great, he says, nodding in agreement with himself. Great. Just great. Couldn't have gone better. Yes, it could, I think. You could have found the diagnosis was all a mistake and my mother's lovely amber eye would still be where it should be.

This thought is another pink elephant, because I begin to wonder what they do with a removed eye after surgery and hear again the distraught account I listened to on a radio programme by a father who found the body of his still-born baby abandoned on a metal drainer in a hospital sluice room.

'As opposed to what?' I ask suddenly, to distract myself.

The surgeon turns his head to me. They must do courses in the Royal College of Surgeons in how to patronise people. That's one method. Stand where you are, but turn your head to the person talking to you. Gives them your attention while your body is still turned to something else. Like a vulture physically turned towards its next meal, but listening to what its partner says. Not only does he turn his head to me, but he does that frown-and-smile thing with one bendy eyebrow that means 'What are you talking about, you dumb patient-relative?'

'When you say the surgery went well,' I elaborated, 'as opposed to what?'

Hey, I think, you're pretty good at providing your own sickie images and pink elephant thoughts, why are you asking this fool to add to your collection?

He nods again. Jesus, you missed your vocation, Mr Surgeon. Any time you want to do a nixer, you can go be a little statuette, sitting in the back window of an Opel Corsa and nod, nod, nodding at the car coming up behind.

'You know,' he says, and cups his chin. 'You know, I believe our timing was just right.'

My father arrives and puts his hand momentarily on the surgeon's lower back. Someone should do a glossary of the significance of men touching each other. There's the 'Man, you were *good*,' shoulder-clutch. The 'You'me, lads together, right?' backhanded blow to the upper arm. And this quiet 'Can't say it, but you know how much I 'preciate palm pressure'.

'Isn't she in great shape?' Da says to the room, and Mam is left, for about three seconds, like someone doing a half sit-up, her head pulled up waiting for his kiss. He puts his cheek alongside the unbandaged side of her face, then kisses the bandage over where her eye used to be. He asks the right questions and the surgeon projects his successful performance onto my mother, like an old hoofer looking for a round of applause for the boys in the band. She's a great patient. She hasn't been nauseated.

The nurse who produced the kidney dish for me is standing behind the surgeon to his right. Our eyes meet. *Don't let your mother be too brave.* Pointless, my friend, that advice. She knows it, too, breathing in the testosterone flowing around the ward. She does a minimal eye-roll – *What can you do?* I do a mouth-tweak – *Mam'll be OK, she's actually not responding to this cheerleader stuff. Just letting it flow past her.*

The registrars or students or whatever the retinue consists of begins to shift, bored. What they want is an endless supply of complicated problems to be solved, issues to be intervened in, indications to be contra'd. Patients are just the vehicles. The containers. A profound misunderstanding is always in process between hospital medics and patients. The patients think they're key players and they're not even caddies.

One of the retinue hasn't even bothered to wear a white coat. He's leaning up against the jamb of the door, legs crossed, one foot cocked, toe down meeting floor tiles. He belongs, yet isn't part of the group. None of the others shares glances with him. Which is, I realise, because he's not one of them, he's the computer guy working for my father. The one who took me to A & E. What's his name? Zebedee? Dougal? Doug. That's it. Rogan. Doug Rogan. A man who has shared the experience of my broken arse with me, and I have to work at remembering him. Oops, the surgeon has obviously said something to me, so I give him a radiant smile that could mean anything, and he sweeps off, his comet-tail of aspirants shambling into order.

Doug unravels himself from the wall and comes to the side where my mother still has an eye. He doesn't say anything. Just gets to where she can see him and does a kind of sideways jerk with his head. The howya jerk. She laughs up at him.

'Well, aren't you so good to find the time,' she says, reaching across herself to give him her right hand.

'Picked the wrong time,' he says. 'Entire family here.'

'Sit down there,' she tells him. 'Doug's been doing all sorts of research for me on the Internet,' she tells us. 'False eyes.'

He does a double-take and laughs.

'I thought you said falsies.'

'They don't exist any more,' she says.

'Yeah, they do,' I say. 'Wonderbras.'

'Hello, boys,' my father says, unexpectedly.

'Waterbras,' I add.

'Traffic hazards,' the pony tail guy says.

'Waterbras?'

'No. Those "Hello, boys" posters for Wonderbras. Cars rear-ending each other because the drivers were distracted.'

'The male drivers,' my mother offers, now lying back with an air of benign chairwoman of the board.

'No, believe it or not. More women reacted to Wonderbra ads than men.'

'What about false eyes?' I ask.

Derailed, they all look at me.

'What were you finding out?'

We're like a backing trio, all lined up on the side of the bed where my mother can see us with her functional eye. She laughs.

'Well, if I was a heavy drinker, I could get a sequence of eyes that get progressively more bloodshot, so the false eye could keep pace with the real eye.'

He mutters stuff about eyes for the short term and eyes for the long term and I can feel myself getting queasy again. At precisely which point he turns to me and enquires after – my arse. In precisely those terms. My father thinks it's a riot.

'It's actually very painful,' I say, to get on top of the situation and of course it puts me six feet below, because the minute I have it said, my mother is half off the pillow with concern. Here's your mother, disfigured, destroyed, one of her eye sockets filled with strangled nerve ends withering back into themselves, lying on a plastic-for-incontinence hospital bed and you're whining on about a crack in a bone that got its P45 handed to it by evolution a couple of millennia ago.

'It would be,' my father says.

Answering our surprised expressions, he tells us he was at a dinner a year or so ago in Dublin Castle for some visiting dignitary and got seated beside a former politician, who was in considerable pain because he'd had a hard landing from a paraglider on his holidays.

'I'm surprised he told you about it,' is Doug's response.

I'm not. People tell my father everything. He asks them questions and reacts to the most obvious and banal replies as if the other person were the Angel Gabriel announcing that Dad had won the Lottery. His expression does Lyn's 'Wow'. The guy beside him at that dinner would never have said to himself

'Look, this guy is famous, popular, a household name as a poet, he couldn't possibly find my cracked arse interesting.' The people Dad talks to never do. But then, we're all convinced we're the most interesting people on the face of the earth. Show people Polaroids at weddings and even if there's six people in the shot and each one of the six is better looking or more famous than the person to whom you've handed the freshly developed picture, they'll still look first at themselves and do the *Oh, look how fat I am/how awful my hair is* rif. Or maybe that's confined to women. I must remember to watch it at Meriel's wedding.

'Not only did he tell me about it,' my father is saying, 'he was very funny about it. Until I met him, I thought he was a rural gobshite. Having spent an evening with him, I'm—'

'*Sure* he's a rural gobshite,' Doug supplied.

'No. It's much more subtle than that.'

'Subtle?' my mother says. The queen of the understatement. The rest of us join the dots – how could a big loud-mouthed thick like that politician ever be spoken of in the same breath as the word 'subtle'?

'No, it *is* subtle,' my father says, putting his long-fingered elegant hand gently on hers to take any sting out of the disagreement. 'That man actually does a parody of a rural half-eejit all the time. Pronounces "West of Ireland" as "Wesht" . . . It's as if he's testing out whoever he's with, and if they're stupid enough to take the parody as the real thing, then he has their measure. But if you *don't*, if you go between the lines of the parody, he's quite different. An interesting mind.'

He then has to pull his hand away, because Doug the computer guy stands up and makes to go.

'They letting you out tomorrow?' he asks my mother. Doug, not my father.

'I don't know. I should ask, shouldn't I?'

I am startled at the possibility. The gravity of an ailment, to me, is demonstrated by the length of time spent in hospital with it. Very soon, they'll be doing heart transplants on a day-surgery basis. Also, it's much more virtuously inconvenient to be off visiting your mother in the hospital, as opposed to going next door in the house to see how she's doing.

'Pick you up in the Land Rover, no prob,' he offers, and she goes to shake his hand. It proves to be more difficult than she had expected, because so much of the bandaging is stuck to her hair, it somehow restricts her when she tries to extend her arm.

'I've the car parked around the corner,' she explains, and we remember she drove herself to the hospital and was kept in. I resent him offering to drive her. It implies closeness to her. I've grown up with half the world believing it has a unique closeness to my father. Individuals, once they know I'm Daughter Of, tell me, as if it was a unique benison, how they experienced reading a particular poem. They can remember the room they were in. What they wore. Most of all, they can remember how they felt, finding their thoughts, their secrets, exposed on paper. Exposed better than they could ever hope to do it, they would allow, the implication, none the less, being that in some weird way my father is indebted to *them*. He used them as the subject, the source for his poem, even if he had never officially met them before he sat down to write it. Plus, nobody but them quite understands all the shades of meaning in that poem.

When I was a teenager, he once described himself to me as 'the cut-price Salinger'. When I looked blank, he went into his study and came out with one of those very old paperbacks that's like a sideways flag: broad orange stripe across the top and bottom with a white bit in the middle with the title printed on it and a little bird in an egg at the bottom. *Catcher in the Rye*. Of course, I read it and thought it summed up my life and insights. Which it probably did. The most personalised generic in literary history, that book.

'See what I mean?' my father said when I'd finished it. 'People – particularly adolescent girls – reading my poetry believe they share a special relationship with me. They'll try to further that relationship by getting close to you. Don't let them. It becomes febrile and unpleasant.'

I had no idea what febrile meant, but 'unpleasant' from my father was the equivalent of 'hellish, fiendish, ghastly, ghoulish, grotty, disgusting and unspeakable' from anyone else. I gave the widest berth to people who believed my father was speaking to them and only to them. I pitched my act halfway between his and my mother's. I didn't go down the paternal line of asking them questions about themselves, but I flatter myself I managed to avoid the glazed eyes wide shut expression that tended to come over my mother's face in that situation. Mercifully, my father never wrote much about children, so I was spared poems about me at seven or ten or in the early teen years and the identification of readers with the person being portrayed. That was what exposed my mother so much: the fact that people knew she was the subject of some of the love poems. Not only was my father the cut-price Salinger, he was also the discount Chris de Burgh. If de Burgh's wife ever got fed up being the lady in red, she never let on, just as my mother did her chin-raised, mouth-closed smile whenever women said 'Oh, *you're* "the heartbeat of his life".'

It would have been easier if she was a poet, too. The Brownings could write to each other all day and no skin off either's nose. Or maybe it got to Elizabeth. Else, why would she have been drinking laudanum all the time?

I'm thinking all this while looking at their two hands on the coarse hospital sheet. Hers is slightly clenched. No. Not clenched. That would imply tension, and it is all ease. The fingers are just folded under. On top, my father's long, graceful hand.

'I'm outa here,' I say and, turning, collide with Lyn.

She is clutching a small circular table display of flowers.

'Oh, *freesias*,' my mother says to my father. 'Isn't that just typical of Lyn?'

My father shoves one of those awful metal-legged chairs behind Lyn's legs and she sits, telling me over her shoulder that my phone must be clogged with messages from her. My mother's bandaged head comes up off the pillow for my kiss and she pats the side of my face.

'Turn back on your phone,' Lyn says.

That gives me an extra brownie point, free: Look, she's saying to my parents, see how dedicated Flannery was, she cut herself off, telephonically, from all normal living because of her mother's surgery. I stump down the corridor wanting to hate her. Her, with her fray-seamed low-rise jeans sprayed on. Even when she sits down, she doesn't get a roll of flesh over the top rim of the jeans. Jesus. If low-rise, straight-leg, fray-seamed jeans are in style, put your money on me being in fray-hemmed bell-bottoms fastening just under my armpits. And then the freesias. What flowers do you bring someone who's short of an eye? Something to please their nose. Something already sorted and arranged in a clod of oasis, so issues of perceived symmetry do not arise and humiliate the eye-deprived.

'Jesus, are you fucking blind?' a woman says as I blunder into her at the entrance to the hospital.

No, ma'am. But my mother is half-blind. Wonder if she qualifies for welfare? OK, she can see, but one of her eyes is definitely blind. No. One of the places where eyes are normally housed . . . but a socket can't be blind. Only a leg can be lame. Only an eye can be blind. Or is it a person who's blind? I start sorting my political correctness. My mother is now someone with a visual impairment. Visually impaired. I try it out and bloody nearly walk into another hospital visitor. At a glance, you can distinguish a hospital visitor from a worker. There's something put-upon and urgent about visitors. Visually impaired. It sounds like a negative judgement passed on my mother, whereas 'blind in one eye' evokes a sympathy jolt. Technically untrue, though. Half-blind, yes. Missing an eye? Not cocktail-party parlance, that one. Apart from anything else, it suggests the eye is mislaid and that she just can't be arsed to go find it.

I answer the phone and Les Girls are there in force. Meriel, all hushed sympathy for my mother and me and my father. Andrea, her concern as rough and direct as a swift mugging, with an ultimatum-flavoured offer to be of any practical assistance I might want. The way she phrases it suggests that the world is full of shaggers who can be relied on to give impractical assistance, but that she's standing by to take on the real down-and-dirty stuff. Then there's a long one from Raimonde bringing herself to the verge of tears as she warbles through a wandering reflection on mothers, eyes, hospitals and my father's poetry, which she paraphrases so he sounds as if he was mainlining dishwasher detergent when he wrote it.

Finally, there's another long one from Luke's father, saying in a measured way that he understands from my mother that our family do not believe in me turning up for Luke's group therapy and while of course he and his wife regret this, it is my prerogative. I run it back and play it again to make sure I've understood the prerogative bit. Mr Buckley, in his nice way, is saying I'm a shit but he can't unshit me.

In between all these messages, a string between beads, are short offerings from Lyn. She'll be at such a place until two, and after that, reachable at the office. Knows I'm taken up with my mother – how *is* she?

When I contact her, the following day, my mother is in the kitchen, at home, preparing a meal, having driven herself home and shooed me out of any helper role on the plea that the sooner she comes to terms with being one-eyed the better.

I kick off my shoes and lie down on my bed to tell her how matter-of-fact, even funny, my mother is being.

'But we need to talk about *you*,' she says.

'Why?'

'Because now you need to earn a living.'

Lyn asks me to hang on because another call is waiting and she has to deal with it. She must be talking to me on her mobile, because I can hear the other call, which is mostly her talking.

'I suggest you issue a credit note or something,' she says in that vague girly way she uses up until the point where the other person forces her to bring out the big guns. Today, the person on the other end misinterprets Lyn's girly offering. There's a silence.

'You must be joking,' Lyn then says. 'I am not paying for two Vikings. I didn't order two Vikings. I ordered three medieval Knights. No, they are not the same. I never met a medieval knight with horns out the side of his helmet. It was so embarrassing for me, with my client *there* and your guy thinking he was funny calling himself Olaf. However, my embarrassment is not the issue,' she said in a suddenly generous way. 'The issue is an invoice my financial controller wouldn't consider for a moment, so you'll need to do something about that. You really will. Listen, I have to run. Seeya.'

Her voice comes back into proper volume suddenly. Directed at me. Full blast.

'We need a researcher.'

'For what?'

'For programmes. At the radio station.'

I find out, long months later, that they *always* need researchers, because most people who take on the job actually want to be reporters or anchors and so the attrition is fierce. However, at the time, Lyn gives the impression that the need is sudden and that only I will satisfactorily fill the role. I have agreed before I know why.

I go downstairs and tell my mother, who is putting scones in the oven. I find myself walking around the kitchen, closing the doors of overhead cupboards.

'You'll knock your other eye out,' I say, as if I were the mother.

'You're quite right,' she says with unexpected docility.

It doesn't last long, either, that docility, because a few minutes later she catches me consciously moving to the side her working eye is on and she snaps that I'm not to *cater* to her. She gives 'cater' roughly the toxic weight of a phrase like 'Vichy collaborator'. Huffy, I say I'm just trying to be considerate in not scaring the shit out of her by suddenly appearing where she wasn't expecting me to appear. Just letting her get used to her new range of vision.

'The rest of the world doesn't know I've turned into Cyclops,' she says. 'So there's no point in making allowances for me.'

Maddened, she lifts the flour sifter off the table and very

decidedly opens her hand, letting it fall the inch or two to the draining board. Except the draining board isn't where she thinks it is, so the sifter goes straight down and lands on its arse (moment of referred sympathy pain from my own posterior) sending a cloud of white up to nearly waist-level.

'That'll teach you,' I say unsympathetically, and she roars laughing.

I stand where I am, rather than go to pick it up for her.

'And if I were you, I'd leave that flour cloud settle before I picked it up, because otherwise it'll go into your hair and make you look like you have a case of mega-dandruff.'

But don't forget it's there, I think. Because then you'll fall over it and hurt yourself.

'You'll need to get Dougal,' Mam says, scooping the thing off the floor so swiftly no flour has a chance to settle on her. I scrunch up my eyes, trying to make the connection between the computer guy and anything we've been talking about.

'To teach you the accounting package he's installed on the computer to take care of your father's earnings,' she explains, kindly.

She's right, although I don't want for her to be right. You don't want to ask for help from someone who's seen hate-mail from your daft ex-boyfriend. You *definitely* don't want to ask for help from someone who's seen you break your arse. But I could hire him and pay him, I think. That would put him at the right distance.

'I'll ring him for you,' she offers, turning on the timer on top of the cooker.

Because my mother is a better-now-than-later person, two hours later the pony tail owner and I are in my father's study sweeping scone crumbs away from the keyboard, while he talks, then sets me tasks to find out how closely I've paid attention to him. If I hesitate, he just gestures, back-handed, at the screen. Go find. Fetch. He wanders over to the window and sees our neighbour driving off in his convertible.

'Old farts shouldn't be allowed to drive convertibles,' he says. 'And no fat chicks, either.'

This double-whammy of ageism and sexism floors me. I feel a great commonality with every aged convertible driver in the world. For just a moment, I am at one with every fat chick in the world, too. What am I talking about, 'for just a moment'? I *am* that fat chick. Permanently. Arse that goes from here to there. In fact, if there was any justice, the very scale and external buttressing of my backside should have prevented my coccyx from cracking. Losing three pounds in preparation for Meriel's wedding doesn't seem like much, right then.

'You going to be using this machine?' he asks.

'For a while, yes. Until my mother doesn't find the screen so bothersome on the one eye. Why?'

'Your ma won't mind if I put up a few shortcuts to make things easier for you.'

I watch him doing it, very careful not to let this get in the way of my resentment of the fat chicks crack.

'My mother will be delighted with anything that makes my life easier,' I say.

Not only a fat chick, but pompous with it. Without a conversational backward glance, he's setting me a task to check have I understood the shortcuts and the favourites and all that. I go through it at speed, powered by fury at being even briefly in debt to someone who is so – so—

'Concentrate,' he says tersely.

I get on with the task and he tells me I've been very quick on the uptake.

'Oh, a lot of your students are slow, are they?'

That surprises him even more.

'I don't have students,' he says. 'I never taught anybody before you.'

And I never want to repeat the experiment, is the unspoken addendum. He starts groping in the little dirty-weekend bag he carries all the time (even into the hospital) and comes out with a card.

AMAZING TRACE

it reads and gives his name as Managing Director.

'How many people do you employ?'

Motive behind this question: to expose him as a sole trader pretending to be a company.

'Six.'

Well, you're still very small.

'I develop software that traces patterns.'

'Patterns of what?'

'Everything. Keystrokes, sites visited.'

You know something is really boring when – try as you may – you can't think of anything in it to be snide about.

'How's your arse?'

'Fine, thank you.'

I lie. By this time each day, I'm conscious of dull pervasive pain. One of those non-specific yet ever-present miseries like a toothache.

'Seriously, do you think your company has prospects?'

'I don't think. I know.'

May you rot, you over-confident gobshite, I think. May your willie swell and fester. May you get mange, hoose and worms in your pony tail.

'By the time I'm twenty-five, I will be a millionaire. By the time I'm thirty I will retire.'

'What age are you now?'

'Twenty-two.'

Let's go for one last stab at an insult.

'Oh, I thought you were much older.'

'How much older?'

'Maybe twenty-seven. Or more,' I improvise.

'Good.'

'Why?'

'At twenty-two, venture capitalists will give you seed money. At thirty, they consider you a serious investment prospect.'

'You always so dogmatic?'

'On anything I know all about, yes.'

Lyn, when I e-mail her a summary of my new-found computer competence, rings me to say 'Wow!' Also to ask do I want to go to the Point for the concert the day after tomorrow. The concert being given by a muffin-faced folk singer who has suddenly achieved cult status. Tickets are going in the street for twice their face value. Turns out she met the folk singer somewhere and he is really pleasant.

'Now I'm with you,' I say. 'Fancies the knickers off you, trying to buy his way into them with freebies.'

'Oh, *Flannery*,' she says, self-deprecatingly.

Jesus, wouldn't I love to have something to self-deprecate about, I think, going down to eat the fantastic dinner my mother has cooked, single-handed. Or maybe I mean single-eyed. She is beginning to fiddle with the edges of the bandage, like a dog that's had plaster of paris put on a broken limb and who knows instinctively the fracture is healed. Three weeks from now, she tells my father, she'll have an interim prosthesis in, and after that she'll be in great shape.

Then she gets launched doing PR for Doug the Pony Tail, telling my father how helpful he has been to me. My father looks as near as he can to smug. Usually, when he locates a handyman or a gardener or someone to fix something, the end result is screaming sirens and a pissed-off insurance company. Marvellous youngfla, he says. Be a millionaire before he's twenty-five, probably. Get through the rest of it, I think. Be retired by the time he's thirty.

'I'd be willing to bet Doug will be retired by the time he's thirty,' Dad says, sagely.

I don't quite know how I know there's sage in there, but there is.

'And so very pleasant,' my mother says.

Because she's looking at me for agreement, I can't stay silent, and I can't agree either. So I shrug. More silence.

'He's just not my kind of person,' I say truthfully.

'Who *is* your kind of person, Flannery?' my mother asks in that extra quiet voice she uses for 'think on this' questions. In spite of myself, I end up running an identification parade, submitting a line-up of acquaintances and friends to the test. She's still looking at me. One-eyed, bandaged like a cartoon figure.

You are, Ma, I think. You're my kind of person.

But there's limits to the positive things you can bring yourself to say to a parent. So I close my eyes and do a surly give-me-patience sigh. It takes the life out of the conversation. I'm good at that. Not proud of it. But good at it.

6

Working from Home

———◆———

'I think I have a much better deal than you do,' I tell Lyn a few months later. 'I'm at work five minutes after I get up, in my dressing-gown. Research is amazing. I can do it in bed, if I really want to. Nobody knows, if I e-mail them or telephone them. If I sound awake, they think I'm a dynamo, whereas I'm still a secret slob. You, on the other hand, have to turn up in there every day in your little business suits and your little polished high heels and your fingernails like little square shovels.'

'French manicured,' she says, laughing. 'And fight with the traffic, don't forget that.'

'What are you driving at the moment?'

Another of those deadly silences I've come to understand indicate that the answer is one Lyn doesn't want to articulate because it makes her appear too successful/sexy/beautiful.

'Well, it's only a lend,' she says defensively.

'What is it?'

'Mercedes CLK. Ragtop.'

'What the frig—? Oh, convertible. Is it one of those that swallows its own roof?'

'Mmm.'

'Lyn?'

'Yes?'

'Lent by who?'

She names the son of an internationally known captain of industry for whom I've always felt sorry. Son Of, sympathised with by Daughter Of. Dopy Daughter Of, now that I think about it. This particular Son Of is doing well enough, within his father's empire, to not just own a classy convertible, but own several, so he can lend one of them to a girl he wants to bonk.

We're sitting in a corner of Eden, the restaurant looking out on Meeting House Square. Lyn wanted to sit outside. I'd said no bloody way.

'I'm surprised you even agreed to have lunch with me,' she says, flagging down the waiter with the bread basket. 'I thought you might have joined some secret religious cult. Or Reclusives Anonymous. The girls are all asking what you're doing, outside of work.'

'I would have thought what happened with Luke and then my mother and a new job . . .' I peter out and address the walnut bread.

'Luke's living with his sister in England, did you know that?'

I shake my head. Solid little barrel of supportiveness, his sister. She will make him take his pills on time and – if anyone can – get him to go back to college.

'She'll have the time, too,' Lyn says, in that way we've always had of finishing each other's unspoken thoughts.

'Mmm?'

'She's like me.' Lyn goes wide-eyed at me. 'No man. No spouse. No mate. No partner in life. A reject. Spinster.'

I sometimes think Lyn should be paid to eat in restaurants simply for the delectation of men at surrounding tables. One guy close to us, and obviously waiting for another diner, his chair tipped backwards, bloody nearly upends himself trying to get a look at this rejected spinster. Down, Towser, I think. Back in your box. Does she look like a reject?

'What about Head the Ball the folksinger?' I ask.

'Oh, he's really *nice*,' she says. Compliments to die from, I think.

'And Son of Captain of Industry?'

'He's just a friend,' she says, laughingly midway between self-parody and seriousness. There must be a moral here somewhere, I think, addressing a slab of swordfish with some enthusiasm. Confucius he say 'Beautiful, sexy and successful girls may attract men, but not always right man'.

'Question. Is someone who is up to their armpits in un-wanted fellas, like you, any happier than someone living through a complete dearth of fellas, like me?' I ask.

Lyn ignores this and asks me when I'm going to learn to drive.

'I'm in the process of doing driving lessons,' I lie. It isn't that bad a lie, because I did look up the number of the driving school nearest to me. 'As soon as I've got my licence, I'll buy a car. I should have enough saved by then.'

'So we might get to see more of you?' Lyn observes.

Nobody would want to see any more of me, I think, dragging the duster coat around me to conceal the two stone I've gained in the six months post-Luke, in spite of planning to be thin for Meriel's wedding. This, of course, is why I do not want to see the girls. Either they'll comment, in which case I will want to split them, or they won't comment, in which case I will watch every glance between them and split them when I catch them exchanging the look that says 'let herself go, a lot, hasn't she?' Even if they connect it to Luke's departure from my life, I'll split them, I think as I finish the swordfish. Because one of them will say 'comfort eating' and that's not an acceptable response to trauma. Starvation is an acceptable response. Going back on the fags is an acceptable response. Getting hooked on OxyContin is an acceptable response. Even staying in bed and never washing is a more acceptable response than stuffing your face with tiramasu. Or M & Ms. Empty wine bottles on their sides in corners of your bedroom have a more tragic resonance than empty plastic containers once filled with crème caramel. It must be something to do with the size of them. People count. 'Omigod, she ate fifteen crème caramels' is just disgusting, whereas 'She drank two whole bottles of wine' snaps everybody into thoughts of detox. Which is always more glamorous, anyway, than de-food.

'I'm in contact with everybody be e-mail, what's the issue?' I ask, devoting myself to the pudding menu. I don't care about pigging in front of Lyn. Partly because she's known me fat and she's known me thin and it genuinely doesn't seem to make any difference to her, and partly because she eats like a rhino coming off a diet at all times herself anyway.

'Some things you can't deal with by e-mail,' she says severely.

'Like?'

'Like not letting Meriel turn her wedding into a complete fart.'

The man at the next table laughs straight into the face of his arriving guest, who is miffed by it.

'Farce, I mean. Not fart.'

'If Meriel wants a wedding fart, why shouldn't she have it? It's her fart.'

'There's her parents to consider.'

'Why?'

Lyn turns the Bambi big eyes/solemn truth look on me. It always makes me feel like one of those blown-up tigers on top of petrol stations, bloated with banality.

'Weddings are for parents, really,' she says. 'They should reflect your parents' values and needs, not yours. You've got the rest of your life. It's a sort of thank you. Even if you don't believe in anything, you should get married in a church and wear great clothes and have civilised speeches.'

We work out ways to prevent Meriel wearing a white leather corset that pushes her copious boobs up round her ears. There is the threat of a Jamaican steel band, but Lyn says the guy who's lending her the car – ('Son Of' I say helpfully) – is going to work on Meriel's fiancé to sell him on the idea of a string quartet.

'And then there's Raimonde,' Lyn says, leaning across and forking up some of my pudding. My mother always taught me, even if I was ravenous, to leave something on my plate. Lyn's Ma must have missed this aspect of table manners and left her with a search-and-destroy approach to any leftover food. Even if, I think resentfully, it's not long enough untouched to *count* as leftover.

'True,' I say, unwilling to be turned into the Red Cross for Raimonde, and determined not to be forced into asking questions about her mental or physical health. Lyn orders coffees and looks sadly at me.

'What's wrong with Raimonde?' I ask, trained-seal fashion.

'Well, you know how shy she is and how low her self-esteem is.'

I look out at Meeting House Square, where they have an art exhibition of Heath Robinson mad machines. The whole self-esteem thing boils my mind. To me, low self-esteem is a necessary friend. Low self-esteem is the voice inside my head that says 'You are so piggy you're going to make yourself sick, for Chrissake show some decency and leave it at three Mars Bar ice creams.' Or 'For Jasusake, it's twelve noon, you slob-faced slut, move your bulk out of bloody bed and do some work.' Without low self-esteem, I would not be where I am today. Now, where I am today is nothing to write home about, but it beats the hell out of standing on occasional tables.

I sniff at the cinnamon on top of my cappuccino and get foam on my nostrils.

'Far as I can tell, Raimonde's low self-esteem leads her to drink herself into being the life and soul of any party and go home with any available bloke,' I say.

'Exactly,' says Lyn. She has foam on her upper lip. I swear to God it suits her.

'Exactly what?'

'It's happening all the time, what you're talking about.'

'And that's bad?'

Lyn's neat little pointy tongue – she even has a slim tongue – comes out and nips away the foam. Funny thing. I can spot all the things that make her so fanciable at one remove. I wonder if this is what a gay man feels when he's with a woman he really likes but does not fancy?

Lyn says slowly that Son Of has seen Raimonde in action at parties. And, in a conversation this week, when he momentarily disremembered Raimonde's name, referred to her as 'Your friend, the slapper.' Lyn had been horrified.

'I said to him, "You just think she's a slapper because you know she's been sleeping with a lot of different guys each weekend after parties," and he looked at me and said, "That isn't why I think she's a slapper. That's why she *is* a slapper." But Raimonde really *isn't* a slapper.'

May not be, I think, but the guy at the next table would appreciate it if you dropped him her phone number. After you drop him your own. Mine, he can survive without.

'You know her for so long, you know she's not.'

Lyn is practically in tears. But she still manages to order more coffee.

'Lyn,' I say, clueless as to what I will say next. 'The fact that your lover regards Raimonde as a slapper doesn't really affect Raimonde's life in any terribly damaging way.'

Not lover, she mouths. You have to hand it to me. I know how to bait a line.

'The problem is that you do think she's a slapper, but you think she's not a natural slapper. You think her self-esteem or lack of it is driving her to inappropriate slapperdom and you want me to fix that.'

She does this smiling flinch, to indicate amn't I marvellous and it's such an imposition, but it would be such a good thing to do.

'If I try to do anything about it,' I reflect. 'Raimonde will think I'm just so man-starved I want the ones she has.'

I never do casual sex. Mainly because 90 per cent of the time I'm too fat to socialise and anyway I might want to go to a twenty-four-hour shop for food and you can't say to a guy who thinks he's made the earth move that it was grand, but you're desperate for a Club Milk or three. Plus, I'm bad at positive reinforcement. I can't be arsed telling a man he's the biggest, best, slowest, most considerate, most repetitive, has the best abs/attitude/car/suit or aluminium briefcase. Especially when I know he's going to put his bloody nose beside my ear and in three minutes set in to snoring like a frigging foghorn so my brain goes corrugated and just as I get used to the pattern of it, do that snorting thing like a colicky horse.

Lyn is now happy she has the world sorted and can relax.

'I often imagine you when I ring you in the mornings,' she says. 'You sound all businesslike as if you're surrounded by filing cabinets and scanners, when all the time I know you're sitting like a Buddha in bed surrounded by grot.'

I'm not sure I like the Buddha bit, but there's a grain of truth in all of what she says. My workspace is surrounded by cups of tea, yesterday's tights, piles of paperbacks, all of the Sunday papers (I figure that means the destruction of at least one oak a week), half-eaten apples, empty *Go Ahead* packs of reduced-fat biscuits (of which you have to eat twice as many in order to get the same fat-and-sugar charge), diet drink cans (Red Bull I drink secretly the mornings after I've sat up half the night with a great book, but I hide the cans from my mother who has read the stories about its consumers dropping dead in droves), pens (I have this fetish about fountain pens and ballpoints just won't do), computer leads, mobile phones, kitchen paper (great for mopping up food spills), scissors and blades (for cutting things out of the papers), alarm clocks (plural because I don't trust any one of them), radios, CD players and tape-recorders. Plus free weights because my intentions are always good.

'People talk about working from home and teleworking,' I tell Lyn, 'but they're euphemisms. The real kicker is working from bed. There's a great satisfaction to ringing business-people on the dot of nine, when you know they haven't really got settled or got a cup of coffee or a read of their letters, of all the time sniggering to yourself because you're still in the scratcher. You feel sorry for them when they ask for your number and extension. You say you work from home, and the sigh they let out of them – remembering their bus or car journey and the hour it took them. On the other hand, people who go to an office are in on the office gossip.'

'That's not an advantage,' Lyn says. That's just because you're the subject of the office gossip, I think but don't say.

'You don't get the gossip if you work at home, but you're not at the receiving end of casual snideries, either,' I admit. I can see Lyn thinking about office criticisms. I bet she gets them so rarely she can't remember the last one. I, on the other hand, can remember every criticism ever made of me or to me. I'm thrown into deep terror and affliction by any criticism or joke that reflects on my looks, sex appeal, competence or ability to drive a car. If a bunch of gurriers in the street go into an orgy of laughter, even though they're all total strangers, I automatically assume one of them has ridiculed me.

I know that in the looks, sex appeal and competence areas I rate three on a scale of one to ten, and that as a driver I'm a danger to everything except ten-ton trucks (the guy who's teaching me to drive gives me these unsought testimonials about once a week), but I live in hope not everybody has noticed. I wouldn't exactly say I can't take criticism, but there's a long list of things I'd rather take before it, including gripewater, diesel oil and arsenic diluted in hen bile.

That's the great thing about working at home. The casual sniper is eliminated, so there are fewer occasions of misery about. If someone wants to give me a psychological dig in the solar plexus, they've to go to the trouble and expense of ringing me up to do it, and with any luck, my phone will be under so much debris, it'll stop ringing before I reach it.

'I see your dad's *Angel* book in the bestseller lists,' Lyn says, as we dawdle through Meeting House Square in the three o'clock sunshine. 'I can't ever remember a poetry book selling so well.'

'Oh, I don't know,' I say. 'Didn't that murderer, Catherine Nevin, carry *Beowulf* around with her right throughout the trial?'

'Your dad is so nice, though,' she says. 'I believe he's giving a reading for that young spastic writer. He says the lad is very talented, doesn't he?'

My father is a chronic talent-spotter. One of the oddities of growing up so near him is observing how few of the talent-spottees ever come to anything. But at least he gives them their fifteen minutes of fame, their pleasurable jolt of affirmation from a major figure in the world of letters. He gives endless time to individual kids with handicaps and to organisations that help young offenders and children damaged by traumatic early years. My mother is always trying to curtail it. It requires him to be present in person, rather than her writing a cheque and getting him to sign it, and for some reason she'd always rather send the cheque.

That's what she's doing when I arrive home. Writing cheques and piling them neatly, one this way, one across it so she has a plus sign made of cheques. The top one isn't to a charity but to an Italian bookbinder who supplies the hand-bound antique paper journals within which my father does his first drafts. I know my mother has an eye on how those drafts will look when she donates them to some university archive, and the embossed-leather Italian notebooks knock hell out of a computer disc, although my father is spending more and more time, these days, on his computer, not least because I no longer share it with him. I now have a laptop that allows me to stay in bed a lot. I touch Da's computer only when something mild goes wrong with it. The guy with the pony tail very occasionally drops by, as a favour to Da, when Da manages to collapse or freeze up his PC beyond any re-booting I can achieve.

Watching my mother as she works, spears me with evoca-tive memory. She looks, from this angle, as she always did, and I want to call out to her, like a photographer, 'Hold it there, just as you are.' Knowing that when she raises her face, it will be subtly, crucially different. The false eye is not quite right. People who never knew her would have no clue that her left eye is a prosthesis, but to my father and me, it's very obvious. The new eye is heavier than the real thing, and so it seems to sag slightly. Very slightly. In addition, when she looks left or right, the new eye moves fractionally more slowly than the other. She isn't aware of it, but for half a split second, every time it happens, it makes her look slow, stupid.

The specialist says she might look at lazer surgery around the lid to tighten it up, but for the most part, the specialist uses her as the most wonderful example. He asks her to go to meet people who have to have her kind of surgery, although most of them have it for other reasons. The cancer she had is rare. She was reluctant to do this at first.

'I'm not trained in counselling,' she said to my father and me. 'I might say the wrong thing.'

'So, when in doubt, don't say anything,' my father said.

That's what she did, and she clouted him playfully over the head with her wallet that evening over how well it worked.

'I just sat there and the man talked and talked, and I listened and at the end he told me I was a great help to him. I hadn't said hardly anything other than "Good morning, Mr Durcan."'

Since then she's done a lot of that kind of thing. Not just for people losing their eyes, for people with cancer who get terrified and depressed. Her specialist has this big thing about survivors being fighters. I personally believe it's the greatest horseshit and another way of shifting the blame for failure from surgeons to patients: see, if you'da been more optimistic, your malignancies would've known they were beaten and just gone and shrivelled away to nothing. It's like that thing in the

Bible where Jesus is walking on water and Peter thinks hey, that's cool, gets out of the boat and as he's walking along the surface, loses confidence and begins to sink. The lesson you're supposed to get out of that, I figure, is it's his fault for not having courage. Right. First-timer in this water-walking and he's supposed to have bullet-proof confidence in his own ability? That's like saying you could rollerblade down Mount Everest at first try if you weren't a gutless wimp.

'Your dad's book is on the *New York Times* bestseller list,' Mam says, tidying away her stuff.

'Now, aren't you sorry you didn't let the publicity people say you were the girl dancing with the angel?'

She smiles, tranquilly. She doesn't need to say to me that identifying her as the figure in the picture would have opened self-exploitative floodgates about the eye. Because she is older, although not heavier, because clothes are so different today, because her hairstyle has changed so much, and because the picture itself is a grainy black-and-white, there is no chance that book purchasers, even if they knew her, would make the link.

Only two people have, so far. Both of them people from her past. One a guy she worked with in the Civil Service, who rang one night, pissed as a newt, and, because she was out to dinner with my father, favoured me with a slobbering account of his unrewarded passion for her. There used to be a photographer on O'Connell Bridge, this drunk told me, who took photographs of passersby and he snapped the drunk and my mother one time and the drunk still has the picture. Regal, he tells me. Regal. The head up and that wonderful figure and that f-f-fearlessunafraid stride. Because I have the laptop already on when he rings, I type in what he's saying as he's saying it and when he's done, I proof it, bump the typeface up to 16 point to make it easier for her to read, and print it out. I watch her, later, when she reads it.

'Poor Derek,' she says softly. 'Poor Derek.'

I consider pushing her for the story, but I don't consider it long. She is not that kind of mother. I remember when I was at the groping motor mechanic phase of dating ('What's in here, then? Whoo, one of *them* . . .') I was halfway through an account of a party when a slight change in her expression withered the story at the root. I blithered to a halt, and she smiled at me.

'Any time you do something I wouldn't approve of, you don't have to tell me,' she said, effectively writing *finis* to that brief time in late adolescence when your mother is your rescuer and best friend.

Now, she hands me a fax of a page from the *New York Times* Sunday book supplement. There's the title, Dad's name and 'Poems of epiphany and loss of certitude, from an Irish academic'.

'Loss of certitude, yet,' I say. 'I'm still waiting to acquire certitude. On anything.'

'Oh, no,' she says, getting up and putting the back of her hand to the small of her back, 'certainty is the ultimate sin.'

I must look puzzled. I've always thought certainty was the ultimate aim, in relation to everything.

'It's the people who are certain who kill,' she says, still trying to unkink her back. 'People certain of their dogma, their politics, their beliefs are always the ones who condemn. And kill. Stay with the doubtful.'

Logically followed through, this would allow me never to leave the house, because they don't come any more doubtful than me. I'd make a great horse: Doubtful. Daughter of Bestselling Poet. Out of Angel Dancer.

7

Playing With a Beachboy

———————◆———————

When Andrea rings, I tell her I'm too busy to meet her for lunch. I'll have a drink with her after work on Tuesday. The hidden meaning in this is that I'm on a diet mostly consisting of canned high protein milkshakes that coat the roof of my mouth with what feels like candle-wax. It's probably the diet Oprah Winfrey went on the time she dragged a child's trolley filled with suet onto the set of her programme to demonstrate the awfulness of what she had lost. In theoretical suet terms, I would at this point justify only a quarter of a child's trolley, but twelve pounds is enough to move me out of elasticated-waistband country, so I'm not completely knotted up at the prospect of Andrea seeing me.

I'm knotted up enough, though, to work myself into a temper as I walk to the pub she chose. Although my driving instructor is no longer seeing his life pass in front of him during each lesson, I haven't got to the stage of buying a car for myself yet, although, financially, I'm almost there. I walk along lower Baggot Street, looking at myself sideways in the shop windows, pulling my stomach in until oxygen deprivation forces me to let go and swell back to normal. I must have lost the twelve pounds off my bones, or something, I think, but why do I care, I further think, Andrea is built like a fire plug anyway, who's she to cast aspersions? This, despite the fact that I have never encountered a fire plug and wouldn't

recognise one if I did, and Andrea has never, to my recollection, commented on my weight, never mind got into
aspersion-casting mode.

'Flannery!' she bellows from a dark nook. Just so everybody
in the pub knows who this great advancing tub of lard is. Until
I saw myself in the windows, I had thought that twelve pounds
and black jersey would make me curvy but contained. Amazing how one deceives oneself.

'You're in black, too,' I say, having ordered sparkling water.

'Monday,' she says.

'Monday?'

'Half the women in my company wear black on Monday to
make themselves look thinner after pigging out at the weekend.
It's like we're all on our way to a funeral.'

'Do you pig out at the weekend?'

She gives me the kind of look that disqualifies a question at
source. I shrug, humbly.

'That's one of the reasons I wanted to talk to you,' she says.

I'm now completely lost, because nobody has ever made an
appointment with me, up to now, to discuss weekend pigging.
Sisterhood only goes so far.

'My career path,' she says.

Oh, I think, you have one of them? I must at some stage
pave one for myself. There's something shallow about a year
whose stages are marked by the traumas and achievements of
one's parents and the loss of twelve pounds in preparation for
a friend's wedding.

'I'm one from the top in HR,' Andrea says and I try to figure
out what company is represented by the two initials. It takes
me quite a while to remember that she's in the Irish branch of a
massive multinational and that HR stands for Human Resources. By which time she has established that there are two

things wrong with where she is. One is that it's a pink collar ghetto filled with women. The other is that they apply systems from the parent company to Ireland as if Ireland were a county in Minneapolis. She bangs down her empty glass and I realise her input is finished and I must now do something.

'Pink collar ghetto,' I prompt, thinking I must write this down, because it would make a good item for one of Lyn's radio programmes.

'Nobody ever tells you in college that you should *never* go into PR and *never* go into HR,' Andrea barks. 'Dead ends for women. You never get out of them. People from Accounting end up as CEOs. People from HR never do.'

I'm looking at this little stubby twenty-four-year-old who is drinking gin with the fierce tired concentration of a defeated fifty-something. She's got a title and a direct line and money to burn, but (a) thinks I have a better life, she should see the dressing-gown I live in, any decent derelict would be ashamed of it, and (b) thinks I can give her advice. She'd be better to get (b) from a decent derelict. Andrea's now talking about maybe going back to get a master's degree. The company she's with will pay for her to do it and give her the time off, but she'd have to stay with them for three years after graduating, and they might still not move her out of HR.

'Why's it so bad, there?' I wonder aloud. 'I'd've thought working with people and setting up training and promoting and recruiting would be varied and interesting.'

'It might be if they didn't install these rigid fucking systems where every wanker has to fill in questionnaires about every other wanker and then you sit down with each wanker and "explore" with them the "issues" raised by the "objective feedback".'

The inverted commas around the practices for which she

has contempt are as obvious as an initial daubed in blue on the side of a sheep. I murmur that I thought she said there were a lot of women in this area, and women are supposed to be flexible and creative rather than rigid, so why are they not challenging these systems? I get another disqualifying glare, accompanied, this time, by a sigh controlled to prove patience.

'As soon as you promote women into management, they get fat and fucked,' she announces.

'Sounds good to me,' I say and regret it. Andrea is freighted with rage and I could attract every bit of it if I'm not careful.

'I'm looking around me every day at four women who, when we all joined the company, were going to the gym or just – just *thin*. And now they're all wearing cover-ups and talking about their bloody children and they never talk up at meetings, just gossip on corridors and backbite and have no ambition. I can feel it beginning to infect me, and I have to get out.'

'Feel what beginning to infect you?'

'The internal politics, the bitching, the eating and the way they *talk* about eating.'

This is getting awful close to home, I think, but simply do a Lyn wide-eyed tell-me-more look.

'They talk about "treats",' Andrea hisses, her face twisted with hatred. ' "Treats!" As if they were exceptional. As if they didn't eat junk all day every day. Or they make out that it's because their baby is sick or their husband is being difficult or their mother is dying or something. Oh, I'm sorry.'

I glance around me to see who she's apologising to before I realise she thinks she's insulted my mother by association with the dying. I laugh and flap a hand at her to stop her worrying. I also feel my face getting red, because I may not have said it to other people, but I was kind of hoping anybody who noticed me getting huge would make allowances. Sure

God love her, the pressure she's been under, her mother losing an eye and all. Andrea's now made me feel retrospectively guilty towards my mother. Not that me taking theoretical free-food passes related to her illness could complicate her recovery, but still.

Andrea talks like a ketchup bottle lets go of its contents. Big globs and then complete silence. At the end of one of the big globs, she says bitterly that the only woman in HR she thought was worth *that* (snap of fingers which a barman thinks is directed at him and is insulted by) turned out to be a headbanger who was taking backhanders.

'Meaning?' I ask, convulsed by the realisation that the offended barman has sent us to Coventry and is refusing to serve us. Since we didn't actually want to be served (I don't want any more fizzy water and I don't want Andrea to have any more gin because she's difficult to follow when she's texting, verbally) this suits very well. Sometimes even a bad turn will work.

'She persuaded them, last year, to change provider—' Andrea reverses out of the jargon bog. 'She got them to shift from one pensions company to a different one. Which is quite an achievement, in there. Achieving *any* change in there is a major achievement. Hell of a coup for the pensions company, the business is worth millions to them over the term of the contract. But then it came to light that the new pensions company had given her backhanders – bribes, really.'

'How did it come to light?'

'How would I know?'

'You didn't ask?'

'Why would I care?'

She signals the barman, who by now has forgiven her, and with an air of great generosity comes over to us. We're now into coffee, black for me and a sandwich for her. I'm glad of the distraction, because I'm beginning to realise that wherever Andrea's career path is going won't be helped by her terminal lack of curiosity.

'So is she in jail?'

'No, she got parole or probation or one of those things. First offender, and she had a psychiatrist who said things about her family background. But she was fired without a reference.'

'Never work in this town again?' I ask, trying to sound sophisticated. The question irritates Andrea, probably because it has damn all to do with her career path.

''Course she will. Ninety per cent of employers fail to check with previous employers.'

There's another great item, I think. Then I feel like Simon Legree. I'm beginning, I think, to exploit every poor hoor who crosses my path. They're nothing but a source of ideas for me. I deserve to be fat.

'So how's your love-life?' Andrea barks.

'Oh, I'm still getting over the Luke episode,' I lie. A kind of merciful amnesia has descended on me about Luke. It feels like that was another country, and besides, the wench is dead. 'And yours?'

Why do I allow myself to be intimidated by these looks indicating I'm stupid or impertinent to ask a question she's already asked me? Andrea's a year younger than I am.

'Anyway,' she says, with the sudden decisiveness that comes when what you thought was an open career path turns into a brick wall. 'Have you got your invite to Meriel's wedding yet?'

'No. When is it?'

'June. Tenth, I think. At least she didn't ask me to be a bridesmaid.'

'Me, either.'

87

'Her two sisters are doing it. One of them's making a speech, too.'

As long as Meriel doesn't make a speech, I think. Meriel, when she gets launched, does a stream of half-consciousness that is interesting only as proof that someone can talk without breathing in or saying anything for as long as ten minutes. The inflections and gestures and emphases are all in the right places, so the first few times she fools people, but long-term friends are always ready to fling themselves in her path or rugby tackle her. For her own good.

'I'm going to bring Bruce Green,' Andrea mutters, side-waysing it to give me the option of reacting or not reacting. Bruce Green has a glass-edged voice that jangles my teeth. He's the most nakedly negative human being I have ever met. He will tell you if you've sat on something that left a stain and he will make sure to tell you at a point when you can do nothing about it. He'll tell you right at the end of an evening that you've had spinach on your teeth since the starter. He also has this mannerism of pulling up the front of his trousers and holding it for a few minutes. It got him dubbed 'Numb Nuts'. I forget who did the dubbing.

I flail around for one of those ameliorative comments any woman dating a dud will welcome. Except I can't even say he's good-looking. Bruce Green isn't bad looking, but he's the peel image of the Yorkshire Ripper and also has the biggest arse I've ever seen on a man. It's elliptical, like a swingboat.

How desperate can you be, I mentally ask Andrea, knowing I'm not really positioned to put the question to her out loud. When you've spent three months sporadically immured on the top of an occasional table at the behest of a man everybody but you knew was loopy and not even good-looking, it's not a great idea to start sneering at the escort choices of other women.

'Oh, at least I'll know *Bruce*,' I eventually work up to saying. It seems to serve.

'Have you bought what you're going to wear?' she asks.

I spend my life walking into rules I never knew were there, like a guy riding a motorbike into the path of a low-hanging clothesline. It must be a rule that you can't wear to a friend's wedding anything you already have and like and are comfortable in. It must be new. I tell Andrea that I'm going shopping the following day and I do, mainly because the prospect of me getting, as she puts it, 'at least one decent thing to wear' puts my mother in such good form. She tells me to go to Brown Thomas and buy something classic with a good cut and finish. Like I'd know a good cut and finish from a haddock and chips.

So, to show independence, I go instead to a much more trendy place and find a dress I quite like. Dressing rooms? I ask and the girl points to a spiral staircase in the corner. Up I go. Horrors. At the top is a communal dressing room in which nobody is fatter than Victoria Beckham. Some of them even have Madonna arms with real live tendons in them. I have the kind of arms you get on blow-up armchairs. I consider pretending that I climbed the spiral by accident and do the 'just looking' performance, but an obliging skeleton moves to one side to give me room so that option evaporates. I mess around a long time with my bag, working out how to avoid standing in the middle of these anorectics looking like the post-treatment example that's supposed to encourage them to eat up now. I know, I think: I'll just hold the dress up in front of myself and decide I hate it without even having to try it on. I do this, sigh ostentatiously, gather my stuff and fall down the stairs, not having convinced anyone. Because it's a spiral staircase and there's opposition coming the other way, I can't fall far, but because it's a *metal* spiral staircase, I can fall noisily, and I do and by the time I get out the front door, my face is so red it looks like I've fallen asleep under a sunlamp.

I come home and say I saw nothing I liked in Brown Thomas. Which is unassailably true, because I never went near the place.

'I was thinking you might like to try this,' Mam says, putting out the *Indo*, where there's a big feature about shopping spree trips to the United States. I look consideringly at the page, controlling my desire to yell Yess! and fist my hand in the air, knowing that America is full of women who are fatter than me and who must buy clothes somewhere.

My father makes wounded-in-advance noises to suggest that my mother leaving him alone for four days means he will suffer malnutrition and depression, but she pays no attention to him at all. Instead, Mam gets all businesslike, and before I know where I am, I am in Newark, New Jersey. I'm kind of surprised by this, because the airline that flies into Newark – Continental – doesn't believe in normal transatlantic planes with two aisles. There's only one aisle, which means that by the time you get lunch, you've forgotten they ever served you a drink and they barely get time to run up and down with the duty-free trolley before it lands.

At the shopping mall, Mam goes first to Waldenbooks to check if my father's book is properly displayed. Since I was a teenager, I've pretended I'm not with her when she takes copies of his publications out from the back where they were hidden and puts them at the front. This time, I'm genuinely not with her. I'm in Lane Bryant, buying a size fourteen. It's really a size sixteen, but the American sizing is one down on ours, so I'll be able to hang it up anywhere and passersby will be convinced I'm a size fourteen.

'Well, I followed your advice,' I say when I meet her in the

Food Court, which is, according to a poster, sponsored by Radio Shack. Why, I wonder, does a bunch of fast-food outlets need sponsoring?

'That's new,' she says, trying to get comfortable in one of those chairs made out of an overgrown paperclip and two planks.

'Me following your advice? When have you given me advice?'

She smiles me off that one with the air of someone too old and too wise to walk into so obvious a trap. I try to think if she warned me off Luke. Maybe I didn't let her meet him until it had gone too far for her meaningful glances (back then when she had two eyes she could do meaningful glances) could have made a difference.

'You said I was to buy something that fits me now, rather than something I hope to get thin enough to fit into by the wedding.'

'Oh, good,' she says and burrows a bit in my bag. 'Taupe.'

'I thought it was beige,' I say.

'Same thing.'

'Did you know "beige" is the only word that doesn't follow the I before E except after C rule?'

There is an expression mothers have, which is specific to mothers and only mothers. It signifies that the topic under discussion is mind-bendingly, toe-curlingly boring, but because it has been raised by their offspring, must have a deeply concealed merit.

'What about "weird"?' she asks and I want to go kill whoever impressed me about beige except I've forgotten who it was.

She accompanies me as I search for shoes. I have no problem with shared shoe-buying, because whether you're going up or down in weight makes shag all difference at foot level.

'You'll need to get some colour,' she tells me, when we're seated on the plane, swollen in the feet and depleted in the wallet.

'Colour?'

'A tan. You spend so much time indoors, you have a prison pallor and the taupe will show it up.'

I nod in agreement, but I don't actually plan to do anything about it. Over the next few days, though, she starts nagging me, telling me that this is the summer, after all, we're having a heatwave, she's made up a salad in a Tupperware container and here's the keys to the car. I'm not supposed to drive without a qualified adult in the car with me, but we are apparently going to gloss over that requirement because she says she's feeling a bit achy and going to lie down for a while.

So off I go to the beach, feeling ridiculously happy, like I should have a bucket and spade with me instead of the rug and the Tupperware and the bloody big book about how history is full of lies. I am doing the boring bit of getting sun on my back, and have reached the Rape of Nanking, when this kid walks over my back. Weighs a stone, he does, give or take his nappy, but means no harm, so I stay still and let him pad about.

The problem arises when he gets unbalanced by the weight of his nappy and sits down unexpectedly, catching me in mid-lung and winding me. So winded am I that when he rolls off my now deflated back and sets out to engage me in chat, I am not really in good condition for it.

A little bored, he sticks one exploratory finger in my eye. Just to keep his hand in, I suppose. I am convinced that he'll really get his whole hand in my eye if I don't restrain him, so I haul off and restrain him, sitting up for the purpose. Half the beach falls off my front, and he thinks this is the funniest thing that ever happened. He laughs like water escaping from a bathtub, revealing that he's under-supplied in the teeth department, which is just as well, because he decides to chew on my hand when no more sand falls off my front. You have to fill in that empty time, you know?

I'm sitting there thinking that I can now claim to have given oral satisfaction to a beachboy but the thought seems filthy when I look at this toddler and I wonder at what point I developed a need to make the off-colour crack before somebody else does. Maybe it's a function of being the big plain one, the urge to be more overtly sexual, more knowing. I hate it in myself.

'You have a great future with spaghetti,' I tell the toddler gently.

He unplugs my hand from his mouth and says, with no little affection, 'Dadda.' I scoop him up in my arms and get to my feet at the same time. Then I have to climb out of the valley within the sandunes where I've hidden. The toddler thinks my ploughing progress up the side of a sand dune in hot soft sand is nearly as funny as the beach falling off my front, and almost upends the two of us trying to get a good view of what my feet are doing. Reaching the tough long grass holding together the top of the sand dune, I stand, wobbling, to let any real father in the vicinity spot and retrieve his youngster. No luck. I slither the two of us back down into the valley and put the kid sitting on the sand. (I do lift up a corner of the rug so he's sitting on sand that isn't scorching, but there's no way I am putting him on the rug itself. He needs changing.)

I retreat up the sand dune again, doing a visual recce for people who look as if they're grieving for a lost toddler, but any of the families within range look either as if they have all their kids present and accounted for or if they're missing one and are quite happy to go on missing it. Meanwhile, the toddler in question is not happy in the valley and lets me know at high volume. I slither back down to him, which distracts him for a while, but not a long while.

I am going to have to change this baby, I hear my mother tell me. You cannot leave a baby unchanged. It's one of Nature's rules. God will strike you dead or you'll be had up for child endangerment. I take the nappy off him, and wrap it very tightly inside the polythene bag I've brought all my stuff in, using it first to wipe excess expulsions off him. (It *is* a him, this toddler. Nappy removal proves it.) I then pick him up again and carry him to the water's edge. On the way, he attracts some attention, because the nappy must have been overdue for changing and as a result, his small posterior is as red as a stop light or maybe redder.

The child cries all the way to the water's edge. Gets no charge at all, this time, out of me climbing the soft side of the sand dune. Tears slide down his roundy face and into his mouth, which seems to annoy him even more, but there's no explaining to a baby that if he shuts his mouth the tears can't get in. I am not made for motherhood, I decide, as he gets more excited and opens his kisser so wide I fear the opening will meet behind his ears and the top of his head fall off. Not that anybody has offered me a go at motherhood, I think, dumping him tail first into six inches of chilly seawater.

Silence. Silence so absolute that for a mad moment I wonder have I dumped the wrong end of him in. The silence, however, is caused by surprise. The surprise is so total he gives up breathing for what seems about five minutes. Just as I expect him to turn blue, he seems to cop on that the seawater has cooled his poor overheated bottom by several degrees, and smacks the surface approvingly. Doing a great job, sea. I figure he has heated up the water between here and Holyhead at least two degrees.

Eventually, I remove him from the water and carry him back in the direction of my rug, gazing about me the while and asking my beachboy if he sees his Mamma or Dadda. But he does not seem pushed if he never sees his Mamma or Dadda again, and I find myself back in the dune with a small naked kid who now shows all the signs of being hungry. Not being of the Boy Scout mentality, I do not have much with me in the line of baby food. Indeed, all I have left is a hardboiled egg and an apple. I squash the hard-boiled egg against the inside of the Tupperware container with the fork my mother has so sweetly provided, and feed it to the kid. He eats it all and looks for more. I feed him Diet Coke and he lies down and goes to sleep. I do likewise.

Next thing I know someone is trying to take the eye out of my head. (Another Mother phrase: watch those country people, they'd take the eye out of your head.) It is the child, trying to pry me awake. We wrap ourselves around another slug of Coke and talk of this and that. I have now, I find, glancing at my watch, had this child's company for three hours. Just then, a blonde in a bikini with old-fashioned high-cut legs (bikini, not her) appears and is greeted by the child with wild cries of 'Dadda!' She looks at me with such an accusatory expression that I get furious and silently hand her the plastic bag full of dirty (and by now cooked) nappy.

She decides to be grudgingly grateful and asks me do I have children of my own. I shake my head. You are so lucky, she tells me. Once you have children, you can never again relax on a beach. You spend every minute changing and feeding and entertaining them. I try to put an expression of awed respect for the trials of motherhood on my face, wondering at the same time who she has been changing and feeding and entertaining for the last three hours when I had her offspring all to myself. I could have ransomed him, I think.

'Wave day day to the lady,' she instructs him and he looks at me as if he knew I was *that* much away from ransoming him and won't raise a paw in parting.

That night, my mother has to anoint my back and shoulders because I have got twice as burned as I meant to. But that's after I come home and find the Land Rover in the driveway, the pony tail techie in the study, and the house vibrating to the strangest engine noise.

'You doing that?' I say, sticking my head into the studio.

'The noise?'

'Yeah.'

'No. I think it's your mother.'

I go to their bedroom, but she's not there. Process of elimination establishes that she and the noise are in the bathroom and I remember that the bath has a Jacuzzi capability I didn't think any of us ever used because mostly we take showers. Of course, afterwards – long afterwards – I replay the movie of me standing outside the bathroom door yelling at her does she want a cuppa when she comes out. But making no connections. Leaving the vital links unlinked.

I include Doug in the tea and make some sangers. Mam, now in a towelling dressing-gown, arrives in time to share the food and tells him about Meriel's wedding.

'Oh, I know about this wedding,' he says. 'One of the guys in my company is going to it. Escorting a girl named Linda.'

'Lyn?' my mother suggests.

'Lyn,' he says, snapping his fingers in confirmation.

'What does the guy drive?' I ask.

'Beat-up Ferrari. Why?'

I have to explain that Lyn has been seeing, but very casually, mind, Son Of Captain of Industry and he says oh, no, this guy (name Piers) is completely different and who's taking me to the wedding? I'm so flummoxed by this coming at me that I say nobody is, and he says the invite says 'and Guest', which it does, as he can prove, because he's got it in his hands. He then says he'll take me and my mother laughs and I don't know what to do and all I can think of is that I am as red as my little beachboy's bottom.

You can't say to a guy, 'Look, no offence, but I have no problem going to this wedding on my own, indeed I would greatly prefer that as an option to going with a know-all computer nerd wearing a pony tail who is just not my kind of person and who my girlfriends will all look on as a step worse than Luke whose mad effusions you read on my father's PC.'

Or maybe you can say that, but I don't and so end up going to Meriel's wedding with him.

8

Meriel's Wedding

————◆•◆•◆————

On the day of Meriel's wedding, if there's spot prizes, I figure we'll get the one for Most Unsuitable Couple. Dougal does his best, admittedly, arriving in a suit and demanding that my mother agree with him when he says he scrubs up good, but I am dying to poke the pony tail down the inside of his jacket. I can hear the comments the girls will make about it already. Most of them in Andrea's bark. Once we've left the house, it's as if he gets renamed. I try calling him Dougal a couple of times, but people laugh and say 'Oh, Father Ted' as if it were a joke.

On the other hand, Piers and Lyn would be picked out as Best Suited Couple. Most men look less attractive alongside Lyn than they do in circumstances that don't include Lyn. She sort of takes the shine off them. This guy, you could take wire wool to and you couldn't take the shine off him. He knows it, too. He is consciously casual and easygoing and self-deprecating in a way you expect of very famous people slumming. George Clooney going incognito. People turn to look at the two of them and it isn't just that they are so beautiful, it is because there is an assumption that he must be someone off the telly. And accordingly, of more importance than any of us real mortals.

When Doug the Techie introduces us, Piers gives Lyn a shove with the back of his hand.

'Sit down there beside your friend and stop drawing attention to yourself,' he says. 'Else the bride will never speak to you again. The groom's already bursting to come over and chat you up.'

Lyn sits down. Beside me. Just what I need. Up to this point, I was reasonably acceptable, if a couple of notches short of actually being attractive, but when Lyn sits down beside you, bang, bang, you're dead. I am glad I brought the camera. The plain girl always brings the camera. It's an unrecognised law of nature. I get it out of its case and check all its instructions. It still won't work.

'You're the technical genius,' I sour at Doug. 'You make it work.'

'I know shag all about cameras,' he says, handing it on to Piers. Who hands it back to me, two seconds later, smirking and handing me the lens cap. Which, of course, had been covering up the lens and preventing it from working.

'The offspring of famous people never amount to anything,' he says.

I look reproachfully at Lyn who is stung into denying she'd told him about my father.

'He's just one of those people who know everything,' she says. With *admiration*? O, Jesus, Lyn, no. He knows bloody well what I'm thinking and favours me with a smile that shows all his teeth. Like a fender. He has good teeth.

'Two knowalls together,' I mutter, and Doug laughs as if it were a compliment.

I stand up and tell them to move closer together. Piers puts his arm around Lyn's shoulders as if he'd known her for years. Doug puts his arm over Piers's. All comrades together. Guard of Honour instantly formed. I take the shot and sit down again. Piers takes the camera from me and presses the play button.

Up comes the picture in the viewfinder. The two men start to come up with captions.

'The Brightest and Best,' suggests Piers.

'No, only on your side,' Lyn says and I have *such* a desire to break the camera over her head.

'Beauty and the Beasts,' says Doug.

'I wonder if we should check on Meriel?' asks Lyn.

'Check on her for what?'

'She's late.'

'Like brides are ever on time,' Doug says.

I would be, I think. I'd be up at dawn, getting dressed. Not that it will ever arise. The single life suits me. You don't have to dress up for it. At dawn or any other time.

'She's probably getting sewn into her dress,' I say, aiming the camera at the groom and his father. The father, just as I click the shutter, looks at his wristwatch with manifest irritation. It is a great picture, I know without looking at it. Piers points an index finger at Doug and demands to know what famous figure in history had been sewn into her dress. Doug looks blank. And bothered by looking blank. Piers moves the finger so it points at Lyn.

'Marilyn Monroe,' she says. 'To sing Happy Birthday to John F. Kennedy.'

'Give the girl the prize,' he says. 'The Mind Filled with Trivia Prize.'

Lyn laughs. Don't feed this ego, I mentally shout at her. It's already nourished to within an inch of its life. Piers looks at me as if he knows exactly what I'm thinking, but before he can sharpen a put-down for this, bigger, target, there's that re-lieved anticipatory movement within the crowd that estab-lishes the bride has arrived. Meriel's dress looks like it's made from tights, bleached. When she stands with the sun behind her, she could be starkers.

I take a picture, just to see if I am imagining it. I'm not. The playback gives no evidence that she has any underwear on. But she's proud. Man, is she proud. This is not the dumb innocence of the picture of Lady Diana Spencer with the kid on her hip and her thighs showing through a thin skirt. Meriel is being a suburban version of that girl from the Cranberries who got married in her knickers. The groom and his father move forward to the Pavilion where the ceremony is to happen, and I can see the groom's father making the decision that he's going to like the dress. If the choices are like it or lump it, publicly, on your son's wedding day, I imagine you like it.

The priest does that gather-round-folks gesture that always makes me want to ungather. Doug gives me what I could interpret as a shove and I flare a look at him.

'You're one of her closest friends,' he says reprovingly. 'Move forward.'

I try to, but the heels of my shoes have sunk into the earth and I'm stuck. To pre-empt another shove, I hiss the situation at him. He drops on his hunkers and unsticks me. We move forward into the inner circle of close family and friends. For the first time, I notice Raimonde, looking preoccupied but pretty. No doubt preoccupied: working out who she's going to get laid by later, I think, and wonder why a woman's mind is always filled with poisonous observations about those she supposedly loves. It then strikes me that maybe the mind of every other woman in sight is as clear of poison as a well-scrubbed kitchen and it's only me who thinks these bad thoughts.

The priest gives us a specially encouraging don't-be-shy-now nod before making a speech about how wonderful it is, on this glorious summer day, to be together here in the outdoors where we can appreciate the beauty of our surroundings as we witness the coming together of Meriel and Adrian. Meriel and Adrian have been coming together with record-breaking frequency over the last two years, but it doesn't seem the time or the place to mention it, particularly because the priest is working so hard at not calling Meriel Muriel, which most people do. Thank you, Mam and Dad, I briefly think. There's not that many mistakes anyone can make with a name like Flannery.

'And I want particularly to welcome Meriel's friends,' the priest says, and directs his gaze at each of us in turn. 'Lyn. Andrew. Flanagan.'

Andrea looks so mad, it takes the sting out of Flanagan for me. I put my two hands out in front of me and look at them to concentrate on not laughing. A thick passing bee takes this as an invitation, and suddenly I have this great fat fur-coated bumbler walking around the backs of my outstretched hands.

'Stay still,' Doug hisses. 'They only sting when they're annoyed.'

Brilliant, I think. So how do we know my fat fur-coated friend here hasn't had a bad day before he ever landed on me? He sounds mad as hell and determined not to take it any more and I, who haven't done a bloody thing to him, yet, could be picked as the receptacle of his rage. I mean, how sequential is the thought process of the average bumble bee?

'Stand still for how fecking long?' I hiss back.

This bee is so stupid, he's now investigating my rings to see if he can get pollen out of them and everybody my side of the congregation is finding it a whole lot more interesting than what the priest is saying. Which is not surprising, because he's doing a generic, one size fits all, nothing personal kind of wedding liturgy. In spite of the beachside setting, it has a generic flavour to it. The bee keeps wandering my hand, which is now trembling slightly.

'Bees die if they sting you,' Doug says under his breath. 'So they don't do it lightly. A wasp'll sting the shit out of you just for spite.'

A woman in front of us turns round and looks disapproving at this. Must be you can't say shit at a wedding. The bumble bee doesn't think much of it, either, and fecks off. I stretch my hands in relief and a wasp lands on the left one. I'm not taking no air traffic control directions on this. I flap him into kingdom come and he buzzes the face of the disapproving woman, who says 'Shit' in panic and gets a disapproving look from her aged husband, who hasn't seen any of the wildlife visitations.

I keep my eye on the bee lest it come back to me. It does a Garryowen so high in the sky it's a danger to passing planes, and then dive-bombs the priest, landing on his chin. It gets a good purchase there, then stings him. The priest doesn't say 'Shit', which impresses us all, but he goes white as a sheet, puts down the prayer book and swells up. Right there and then, his chin swells as if someone is inflating him from behind.

'D'you have a syringe, Father?' this is from Doug. I haven't noticed him leaving my side.

The priest nods, groping under his robey thing for his trouser pocket. Piers is beside the two of them, grabbing the keys. He gets a description of where the car is and takes off like Maurice Greene. The congregation opens ahead of him like that Biblical Sea. Doug looks up so authoritatively from where he is undoing the priest's neckwear that someone in response starts the 'Move along now' routine to get the gawkers leave the priest to swell up on his own. Meriel's groom grows into his new role and leads her over to Les Girls to get kissed and congratulated.

I'm not sure she's actually been married, but I clutch her as if I do believe it, and tell her she looks amazing. Which is true. She looks pretty amazed, as well, but, given the fact that the officiating priest's face is now unrecognisable and he's having difficulty breathing, amazement is a fair response. We might even have a joint wedding/funeral here, I think. Buy one, get rid of one free. Piers arrives back just as fast as he left and hands something to Doug, who pulls the lid off it, points it up in the air, squints at it and then jams it into the priest's arm. The two of them then wrestle the clergyman, his vestments everywhichway, into a sitting position and look at him. Breathe slowly, Doug says. The priest seems to be having difficulty breathing at any speed, but the swollen face does a breathless nod. Doug appears to give Piers instructions, and Piers comes over to Lyn and me.

'He'll be OK. Adrenalin always works for anaphylactic shock,' he tells Lyn. Not the two of us. Just Lyn.

Hey, I'm sorry, what about me? The big one in the middle? Like I don't care about this poor inflated cleric? Anna what shock? Before I can voice any of this, he's back on the other side of the priest. Someone hands him a plastic bucket of ice with a towel draped over it ready for champagne. He looks puzzled. Doug mutters at him and he clunks ice cubes into the towel, rolls it over and applies it to the priest's neck.

'How do they know stuff like that?' I ask, trying to take back control and wondering if curtailment of the liturgy means we'll get fed faster. I can see, out of the corner of my eye, Bruce Green hoving to, and if there's one hove I want to prevent, it's Bruce Green's. 'I mean, Doug's parents aren't doctors or anything?' We know shag all about Piers's parentage, I think but don't say.

'No, Doug and Piers just watch the Discovery channel a lot,' Lyn says.

She moves forward as she speaks, noticing that the guys are about to hoist the priest onto his feet. Doug flicks his pony tail back over his shoulder out of his way, Piers relinquishes the towel-pad of coldness to Lyn, who holds it in position at the priest's chin as they get him upstanding again. The two guys talk quietly to the priest, whose eyes are swollen shut but who seems to be breathing easier. He does not resist as Piers pulls the top vestment over his head and hands it to Lyn, who stands back to let the two of them half-carry the priest to Doug's car and take off in it.

'They're taking him to the hospital,' Lyn says, folding the vestment as if she did vestment folding for a living.

'Shucks,' I say. 'Thought they might be off lapdancing again.'

Then I realise I am wasting my time with the sarcasm. Sarcasm on steroids is not going to pass the barrier of adoration for Piers which now surrounds Lyn. Once upon a time, I think, I had a bright interesting friend and then she fell for a showy bollix with teeth and you couldn't get a word of sense out of her.

'Is he at least rich?' I say, through gritted teeth because I'm trying to smile for official photographs. History, as defined by photographs, is going to show that I had no fella at Meriel's wedding, whereas the truth is I did have a fella. A poor thing and not mine own, but male and *there*, up to the point where he turned into the Emergency Services.

'Piers?' She caresses every consonant, croons every vowel, in it. Thanks be to Jasus it's a short name or it'd be multiple orgasms every time she had to call him in for his tea.

'No, the priest,' I say.

'No. He will be, though. Doug and he will be. Not that it matters.'

Andrea bricks up beside us with Bruce of the Elliptical Arse in tow. She's so low to the ground, I always try to be sitting down when I'm talking to her, because otherwise I can't hear her that well. Otherwise applies in this case. From the snippets I catch, I get the impression she thinks a wasp was the least the priest deserved for calling her Andrew. I think Andrew quite suits her, and he also called me Flanagan and lost me my escort, and anyway it was a bee, but I say nothing. It is now very hot, very sunshiny, and the duster coat of my outfit is roasting my half-healed sunburn. I slip it off quietly and put it loosely over my shoulders in the hope that this will stop me looking like a pot-bellied stove in overheat mode.

'Doesn't Meriel look so *cool*,' Lyn murmurs reverently.

Yes, and cheap and half-naked with it, I think. Andrew/Andrea thinks the same, to judge by her expression. Bruce appears with a tray of Heineken. I would rather die than drink that stuff, but I smile graciously. The glass is at least cold. I can see the car pulling up and the two guys getting out of it in that very guy way where they almost kick the doors closed behind them, never looking back to check have they latched, the way I always do. But then the previous week, I found myself repeatedly trying to close the door of my new car, using my mobile phone instead of the right remote-control gadget. People were watching me, mesmerised. I pretended I wasn't with me and walked away as casually as I could.

Doug doesn't even bother coming to say hello to us, just goes off and gets drinks. He does get the *right* drinks, though, so when he arrives with his tray, I stick the Heineken glass behind a shrub and Lyn does likewise, falling on her pint with chirrups of delight.

'They're lighting the barbeques,' Doug says to me in the tone you'd use to tell a dehydrated half-dead castaway that there's a sail on the horizon. I raise my eyebrows at him in puzzlement. Interested in food? *Moi?*

'Or trying to,' says Piers, reappearing with a saucer of peanuts. I turn down the peanuts, but civilly. After all, he does seem to have part-saved that priest's life, which is the first sign I've seen that he might serve more than decorative purposes or cheap laughs.

'How d'you mean, trying to?' I ask, never having run a barbeque.

'They're not in a sheltered enough place,' he says. 'Oooh,' he adds, disapprovingly, and, following his gaze, I see a young fella sloshing some liquid out of a can onto the barbeque nearest to us.

'Back!'

The yell comes from Doug beside me as he claws a handful of Lyn's dress between her shoulders and reverses her, forcibly, by about four feet.

Simultanously, another guest who's been in line with Lyn moves to get away and the sudden movement swings out the woman's long hair just as a sheet of white flame comes up out of the barbeque and in that split second, she is alight and screaming. The coat is off my back a second later, and Doug has her downed and doused with it as if he wanted to suffocate her or beat her unconscious, him thumping all sides of her swathed hidden head before he lets her out and she returns her scream to full volume from the muffled level it was at, under the coat. Not that much of her hair has burned, but some of the back of her dress is singed and she is beginning to choke on her own screams. Her husband appears and pastes her to his chest, talking to Doug and Piers over her singed shoulder and then carrying her to Doug's car. Be right back, I think. Yeah, right. See you, lads. We'll hold the fort here until you get back. Weddings are such dull events, aren't they . . . ?

Someone brings me my coat, with an air of including me in any credit that's going for heroism. It is burned on the inside and covered with grass stains and mud on the outside. I'm stuck with wearing just the dress for the rest of the day. The problem is that, having bought the dress knowing I would fit into it, I then abandoned the diet, so now I really *don't* fit into it. Not to mention the fact that my sunburn is peeling. My little beachboy friend should see me now, I think. He'd never like me enough to call me Dadda.

The other barbeques have been lit and heated without problem and food is cooking on all of them. It could, I think, be cooking on the one that went on fire, too, except that in peculiar deference to the woman whose hair went on fire, they've left that one black and smoking sulkily to itself. You'd nearly feel you should visit it and kneel down and pray in front of it. Shrine to the shorn.

'Disasters go in threes,' I say grimly to Andrea and she moves away from me. Superstitiously, I think, but also perhaps because Bruce has discovered my glass of Heineken behind the shrub and is standing in a way that begs for his offendedness to be noticed. Lyn makes her way over to be nice to him. Hell with this, I think, and get a plate. Food is your only man. In fact, at this wedding, food seems to be the nearest to a man I'm going to have.

The two heroes get back just before the speeches, and the hotel manager makes a big thing of having saved food for them. She gives them a platter of lobster salad with tiger prawns, oysters and caviar. It would feed six, so I help them with some of it. Doug is now so dishevelled, he looks exactly like the guy I'm used to seeing around my father's study. The other guy's looks have stood up to the pressure of repeat heroism somewhat better. He's standing, now, raising a glass of champagne to Lyn, across a bunch of fans who are telling him how marvellous he is. And the guy in the pony tail, I think, and, as if they've heard me, some of them say, 'And your brother, too.'

The speeches, when they eventually happen, are a mixture of average to good, with an awful lot of votes of thanks, including one to the hotel, which seems excessive to me since they set fire to one of the guests, which is not usually thought of as part of the service, although they can't really be held responsible for the wasp.

Having caught one of Meriel's sisters snorting a controlled substance off a surface in the Ladies' during an early visit to the loo, I put off a second visit for as long as I can. Rightly, as it turns out, because the woman who disapproved of me saying 'Shit' during the ceremony is heading in there just as I arrive, with a female pal of even more fortyish formidable faith and fortune, both evidenced by a gold crucifix that shrieks it's an antique.

I'm about to enter a cubicle when the crucifix woman asks me if I'm my father's daughter. I figured someone would, after the best man read one of my father's more romantic offerings in the middle of his speech. I nod and am bolting the inside of the door when she calls over the top that my mother did lose an eye, didn't she?

That's true, I say quietly. Because my voice can't be heard over a crowd of women who have come into the loo after us, her friend repeats the question from the cubicle on my left. At the top of *her* voice. You're four vodkas down from the properness you were showing at the bee-sting stage of this wedding, I think, and answer more loudly. All of the women, inside cubicles and outside cubicles, go quiet for a moment.

'And your father still wrote that poem to her,' the woman in the cubicle on my right says.

He did, but it was before she lost the eye. I refrain from bellowing this information to the entire restroom.

'You know, I feel sorriest for *him*,' says the woman in the cubicle on my left. Unbelievably, I hear a murmur of assent from the ones outside and for a mad minute find myself in an internal debate as to whether I'll go over the wall and kill her or go out the door and kill them. Sanity and the need to pee prevents me from doing either, and by the time I go out, the two of them are gone and the others are immured in booths.

I come back to our table so obviously enraged that they all ask me what on earth happened. I tell them. Piers scrooches his mouth in 'So what?' mode. I am speechless.

'Kind of a victimless crime,' he says. 'Your mother's never going to know it was said unless you tell her.'

'And if you *did* tell her, she'd laugh,' Doug adds.

That's true, but makes me feel worse.

'It was a stupid insensitive offensive sexist thing to say,' Lyn says, taking her elbow away from where it was touching Piers's.

This puts paid to conversation around the table for quite a while. I drink wine and concentrate on calming down. I'm not very good at this and so, after about three minutes, another offence burbles up in my memory.

'And you can shag off, too, with your comments about the children of someone famous being crap,' I tell Piers. 'A lot you know about it.'

Doug seems to find this a lot funnier than was intended and I wonder how drunk he is.

'Piers *is* the son of someone famous,' he says. 'His father was Greg Watson.'

Greg Watson was a kind of upmarket successor to Terry Wogan, presenting books programmes on British television and sharpening his jawline in profile shots by sticking a rigid index finger along it. He had done a media death a couple of years before, writing a book about his AIDS or Hep C or something while he died of it. Him being such a creepy self-publicist, even in death, makes me feel sudden, overwhelming sympathy for Piers.

'Wouldn't be hard for you to be less crappy than your father,' I say and then apprehend that this may not be experienced on his side as sympathy. I apologise. Clumsily. How could I do something that dense? God knows I've had enough offensive things said to me by people who (a) think you exist only as an extension of your father, and (b) who think that referred fame means you have no feelings. I apologise again, this time with such fervour he begins to laugh.

'I didn't know my father, really,' he says, being kind to me. 'He left my mum when I was six.'

'You're better looking than he was, too,' I say. 'Why aren't you in TV instead of something as boring as – as Amaze Me—'

'It's good, if you want to insult a company, to get the name right,' Doug says mildly. 'Amazing Trace.'

Piers looks at me as if I'm barking mad and tells me TV couldn't be anything like as exciting as what they're doing. They've got the first product that can do the kind of thing he did when the priest got stung. He did educated guesswork – this software is the most sophisticated tool for that. It takes the guess out of it. It traces patterns, not just of consumption or hits on websites, but gathers and interrelates them across time and distance, so you end up knowing what way your person is likely to think in a given circumstance at a particular time of the day.

'What the hell is the use of that, other than to brainwash people to buy stuff?'

'If you know someone is going to freeze and panic if an airplane comes down hard, you could insist that they get survivor training before letting them fly, because that's the only way they'd survive in a crash. Or if you know someone with a new girlfriend is going to drive like a bat out of hell, then you—'

'What? Put a governor control in their car that doesn't let it go above thirty?'

'Maybe,' he says slowly, not liking where he has got himself to.

Doug intervenes, almost casually, and says that probably the key benefit to society from what they've developed is to catch criminals. He talks about the Menendez brothers, who murdered their parents in the most brutal way and who were caught because material they had deleted from their computer was recovered by computer experts. If their computer had been destroyed, they wouldn't have been caught, couldn't have been convicted. But Amazing Trace would be able to link up the sites they'd visited and the people who they'd sent correspondence to, even if the original source computer had been completely destroyed.

'But isn't it erosive of human privacy, human rights, to be able to do that?'

He takes my hands and turns them palm side up on the table, then touches the tips of my fingers.

'Everywhere you go, you leave evidence,' he says. 'You can't help but leave it. Before someone worked out that fingerprints were particular to each person, the argument you're making against our software could have been made against fingerprinting.'

'Fingerprints aren't amenable to much besides pursuing criminals,' Lyn points out.

'So?'

'So the software you've invented can be used for much more malign purposes,' I say. 'And anything like this is more likely to be used for commercial purposes than for the good of humanity. For bad rather than good.'

'Oh, crap,' says Piers.

'Oh, bullshit,' says Doug.

'Oh, charming,' I say, looking for a high horse to get on.

'For Jasus' sake,' Piers says, trying to control his temper. 'Prove that about any computer application.'

'Punchcards used by the Nazis, bought from IBM,' Lyn says. I've never heard about this and neither have the two guys, but she can't remember the details, so it gets dismissed. But dismissed kindly, because it was her suggestion.

'Give me one single solitary example,' Piers says, 'of Power-Point being used for evil.'

I mutter that PowerPoint is so mindbendingly boring that you could say it was always used for evil, and he goes into a sulk.

'What I'm doing is bringing Locarde's principle of transference into the twenty-first century,' Doug says.

'By Jesus, there's a conversation-stopper,' I respond and he laughs. But he's not going to be deflected, and I begin to like that. He insists on telling us about this French guy in the twenties in France – a detective – who worked out that every human contact leaves a trace. Long before electron microscopes revealed fibres left by a person's body when they were left in a car or a room even for a brief period of time, Locarde had it figured. Human tracing can now identify bodies of men killed in the First World War. Electronic tracing of human patterns must inevitably develop in the same way.

'You can choose not to use a computer if you're really paranoid about leaving those traces,' Piers adds, getting involved again because he can't resist it. 'But that would be like deciding never to write, once you cop on that every time you take pen in hand you leave clues about yourself.'

'It does mean,' Doug says, slowly, 'it does mean people won't be able to disappear. Walk away. Develop a new identity. That's already becoming much more difficult because of CCT cameras everywhere. But why would you want to disappear unless you'd done something criminal?'

'If you were being stalked by someone,' I say. 'That would be a good reason for wanting to disappear.'

'But Amazing Trace would probably be more useful to someone being stalked than to anybody else,' he says. 'Because it would pull together the patterns of the stalker, and as soon as this kind of evidence is familiar in court cases, it would convict him.'

'Or her.' This is Lyn, being fairminded.

'If you were the child of someone you were ashamed of,' I offer recklessly, 'then you might want to escape and be someone else.'

'Naah,' Piers says, raising his voice over the tuning up of the musical instruments. 'What you want to do in that situation is be so successful and famous, you make everybody forget your parents.'

Lyn goes off to talk to Raimonde, who is at a table with three couples and not circulating. Usually, once Raimonde has two and a half glasses of wine in her, she circulates with crudely obvious intent. Intent like a heat-seeking missile. You own a penis, you qualify. She must have tight shoes on, I think. The guys are now talking about needing someone to head up HR for them, now they employ more than twenty-five. This activates something at the side of my mind, but Lyn coming back to the table distracts me from it, so I never recommend Andrea to them.

'Raimonde's not drinking,' Lyn says approvingly.

Lyn mustn't be an alcohol addict the way I'm a food addict, I think. Addicts like me don't take to abstention on a big food and drink occasion, a birthday, Easter. Christmas or Sunday. Monday morning is the day for tightening belts, pulling up socks, turning new pages and going cold turkey on KitKats.

The best thing about the evening is the music. No steel band. No string quartet, either. Someone has got the Guinness Jazz Band, and they're lashing out Dixie long after night has fallen and we're dancing with bug-lanterns all around the edges of the dance floor that's been laid on the beach. Perhaps because so much has gone wrong, I've relaxed and am having a great time. Doug can dance and when he shuts up about business, which doesn't happen except when he's dancing, is good company. He excuses himself at some stage and wanders off down the beach, head on one side, talking into his phone.

'Captain of the Rescue Squad,' Piers mutters. 'Ringing the hospital.'

Not long afterwards, Meriel climbs onto a table, claps for attention and tells the assembled guests (and those who are visibly disassembled) that the priest and the guest have both done really well and have been released from the hospital. We all applaud, and Meriel's mother, who is seriously under the weather, insists on the band playing 'The End of a Perfect Day'. Which, in my view, is overstating it a bit.

9

Testing, Testing

———◆—◆———

Even though, as weddings go, Meriel's was perhaps a little too eventful, Lyn and I end up talking to each other on the phone quite a bit about it. We agree that it was much more enjoyable than we can ever admit, because we have to be grave and take the injured priest very seriously, not to mention the girl who had to get four inches cut off her hair the next day because it was burned lopsided. The only thing that bothers Lyn is that, technically, Meriel may not be completely married.

'Listen,' I say, ready to conclude the phone call because I'm coming up to my own front door, 'Being incompletely married is probably a very good thing for Meriel. That is one union of free spirits that's going to ferment awful fast.'

'You think it's not going to work?'

'Lyn, you and I know it's not going to work. So it would be much better if all she has to get out of is the state contract, not the church one. This way, none of us will have to drag ourselves up to Drumcondra and tell the Archbishop's little old nun stories of how we didn't prevent our demonstrably ill-suited friends from predictably awful marriages. They'll have just been living in sin.'

It takes Lyn four weeks to talk me into it, but eventually I am persuaded to visit the HQ of Amazing Trace. It overlooks a thing that was once a river but now seems to be a dumping ground for old prams. From the other three sides, though, it's

OK. Red cobbly paving surrounds it and it's glass clad from top to bottom. Amazing Trace has the second floor with plans to take over the whole building. Non-representational art everywhere and greenery. The staff look as if they've wandered in off the street and there are cardboard-sleeved coffee shop cups everywhere. The largest size. It's all open plan, so the Head of HR sits next to a lowly programmer. Doug has theories about this. They sound to me like Feng Shui mated with Military History. Something to do with putting people together and watching how leaders emerge.

I am listening to him with the rapt attention that comes of rooting round in your own mind for a missing connection when that connection clangs closed in my brain cells. I excuse myself to make a phone call, hitting the speed dial as I walk away from the group. (Of course there's a group. Lyn is like a snowball. All you have to do is roll her around and people stick to her.)

'Andrea,' her voice snaps: OK. Cut to the chase, I don't have time for crap.

'Flannery, Andrea. Remember you told me the name of the girl who was taking the backhanders? I need you to remind me of it. Tell you why later.'

I wait for her to add two and two together and get three, because she never told me the name. She does now. I thank her and tell her I'll get back to her.

Piers is coming down the blond hardwood floor towards me. No doubt Lyn has told him I might get lost if he doesn't come and steer me back down the absolutely straight corridor.

'C'm'ere to me,' I say, and position the two of us leaning on the steel bar that runs along the windows, giving a spurious cruise-ship feel to the building from the inside.

'Yeah?'

'Nicola Warden.'

'Head of HR.'

'Who hired her?'

'Doug. Why?'

'She permanent?'

'Yes. Why?'

'She's crooked. Got fired from her last job.'

'You sure?'

'Very sure. I knew about her before you hired her.'

'You knew we were looking to hire someone.'

'Oh, so I should respond to any casual conversation by telling you that there is one potential applicant out there who I know for a fact has been ripping off her employer?'

'Leave it with me.'

Twenty minutes later, as I'm getting into the car, Doug says quietly to me that he believes I know Nicola. I tell him truthfully that I don't know her from a hole in the floor, but that, coincidentally, I had learned about her leaving another organisation under a cloud. Even if he didn't know when he hired her, I point out, she can't be more than two or three weeks on staff and therefore, no matter what Piers says, can't be permanent. Anyway, I add, warming to the task of disaster-prevention, if she made false claims to get employed, it nullifies the contract of employment. Probably.

'Leave it with me,' he says. I left it with Piers earlier I think, and where did that get us?

When I get back to the house that evening, I can hear the jacuzzi going the minute I put my key in the front door. Largely because my father is in Los Angeles for three days to discuss an offer from some studio to make an animated film out of a long anecdotal poem he wrote to keep me amused when I was three or four. I am convinced that my mother made up the basic story, because I have a recollection of her telling it to me over a number of weeks at bedtime, but when I said her name should be on any movie based on it, she laughed at me. My father's name was saleable, she said. Marketable. Bankable. Hers was not. So what would be the point?

The silence when the jacuzzi goes off is wonderful. Whenever my father is in the house on his own, he has music playing. Either Tom Waits or classical or Dixie. Now, however, I can hear the birds singing through a partially opened window. Which window may be a mistake in late August, I think. A relative of the wasp that did in Meriel's priest could be out there, just waiting for this chance to have a go at Mam and me.

I have tea made when Mam appears and nods in response to the offer of a mug.

'Doug was on,' she says.

I decide not to tell her about Nicola the Crook and she wonders, aloud, if Doug should be rung back. He might have tickets for something. I think she sees him as good for me, in the same way fresh air would be. She's convinced that me being indoors, working on Lyn's research, will give me gangrene or terminal mildew or something.

'How's Lyn doing with that partner of his?'

I shrug. At one point during Meriel's wedding, Piers made this big speech about how he was never getting married or having children, which, since nobody had invited him to do either, was one large irrelevancy. It may have been a late response to the talk about his father, and it's understandable that he might not have the best precedent in the world to fall back on, but it was a little off in front of Lyn. Not that she hungers to populate the world or have weddings, but it was like an advance warning that he was always going to have two or three girlfriends on a rota. A rostered harem.

'Raimonde also rang.'

I smile at Ma, knowing she's the only mother of all of the girls that Raimonde would talk to. Not only does this take Raimonde off my back, but my mother will have gently tried to steer her away from slapperdom and alcoholism.

'She still off the booze?' I ask.

'Very much so.'

'Very much so?'

'She's pregnant.'

'Oh, bloody 'ell. Since when?'

'A few weeks before Meriel's wedding.'

Better get a move on, Ray, I think.

'She's going to keep the baby.'

Forget the last advice, Ray. Stock up on ginger ale.

'She doesn't know who the father is for sure.'

'Which of many, you mean?'

The minute I have it said, I feel as if I've endangered my mother's purity. Since I entered my teens I've been trying to protect my mother against learning awful things I was doing and my friends were doing. Now, she smiles at me with an infinitely tired kindness.

'Flannery, the world doesn't change that much from generation to generation. Each generation is secretly convinced that it did invent sex and will prevent death. No generation is right on either.'

'No, I think my generation thinks it invented certain *kinds* of sex.'

I think about Egyptian hieroglyphics and other evidence of exciting antiquity and amend this.

'We probably do more varied stuff than—' (– your generation did.)

The look she gives me quells that one. My imagination is

just not up to coping with thoughts of anybody of my mother's age and niceness doing anything other than missionary position sex.

'Oh, come on, Mam, there were virgins in your time,' I say, trying to shift the conversation onto some unembarrassing level.

'Not many, and not for long,' she says, quite seriously. 'But there was passion. And fun. And dancing that spins in your dreams forever. People fall in love and continue to fall in love and all the other rubbish gets swept away.'

She says it with such peaceful fervour, I want to buy in. I hope so, Mam, I really do. Even if not for me, for Lyn. But, Jesus, Raimonde.

'Has she told her parents?'

Raimonde's father is a mid-level civil servant who is tied up in every little local organisation of the Catholic Church. He's one of those guys up at the altar rails along with the priest each week. Cannot see why Raimonde can't live at home. Because she couldn't bring home a different sex partner as soon as she's drunk enough any weekend, Mr Father Figure.

'They seem to be so relieved about her not having an abortion that they're coping better than she expected,' my mother says. 'She's told them at work, too.'

Now I know what Raimonde is at. Telling all the key people and the non-key people like my mother. Because once you've done that, you can't go back. It's the quiet little nun-y ones that get rid of the problem most effectively. They know that three friends can keep a secret if two of them are dead. They tell nobody. They fabricate a trip to termination land and they come back to get-over-it country. Memories contract like hard small scars if unshared. I must get on to Raimonde and see what I can do. Working the way I do, I can make my own hours and, now I have a car, I could be useful to her.

'Anyway,' I say to my mother, always good for a conversational change of gear that grinds like a train crash, 'you haven't half fallen in love with the jacuzzi. You've spent half the last month in it.'

'Lot of back pain,' she says. 'Do me a favour?'

'Mmmf?' Eyebrows raised, mouth full of biscuit, head nodding to show willing.

'Come with me to the specialist tomorrow.'

'Wof speshflst?'

'A guy called Wellfleet.'

'Speshflst 'n what?'

'Oncology,' she says, standing and stretching.

The ancient Chinese had their own kind of lie-detector test. They would feed the accused dry rice and then they would ask questions. The innocent could summon up saliva, swallow and respond. The guilty went lethally dry-mouthed. I do my modern version, biscuit crumbs dry, shards of sweetness, crumbled piles of deadwood, a mouthful of postponement, a heart full of frozen terror.

'Whof time?'

'Half ten,' she says over her shoulder as she heads upstairs to get out of the dressing-gown. 'He'll have the test results.'

Even then, all the bits don't fall into place. I am that self-absorbed. But even the self-absorbed can see the obvious. If the test results are good, they ring you and say 'Nothing to worry about, glad we did them and I do want to see you, but we just need to work on getting your weight/cholesterol/mood/whatever under control . . .' You don't need to be accompanied, when you go to get those results. Where you need company on the day you go to get the results, it is

because you know in advance that the results are an ultimatum, a sentence. When you ask someone to go with you to
hear what the tests reveal, it is because you know you will be
too shrivelled by the overall awfulness to pick up any ameliorative details.

I will be my mother's note-taker, I think, opening the lid of
the sani-can and letting the dry biscuit mass fall from my open
mouth into it. I will be crisp and clear. I will— Oh, who gives a
fuck what you'll be? This is Mam. The girl laughing into the
sunshine under the angel's wing. The woman with the cough
to let you know she's going to rescue you. The friend with the
big beautiful hands and the assumption that no matter what
has gone wrong, you are never to blame, you are the victim,
you are the one to be minded.

Now it is time for you to get out of the encircling arms. To
grow up. To mind. For Chrissake, take the focus off your
bloody soft fat self and for once in your life turn all your
candlepower on someone else.

I do manage to keep her laughing, in the waiting room
before we go in, by telling her about Doug's Greek mytho-
logical approach to management.

'There were these two sisters,' I tell her. 'I forget their
names. But one of them was into prevention.'

'So if you kept fit and ate from the top of the pyramid and
never smoked, you'd be big pals with her?'

I nod.

'And if you were a couch potato, stuffing yourself with
hamburgers and chips and chainsmoking, you'd be big pals
with—'

'Maurice Nelligan,' the only other person in the room, a
heavy middle-aged man, suggests. Nelligan is the big name

heart transplant guy. We both laugh and he looks guilty for invading our conversation. I'm only delighted and include him in the sweep of my Doug interpretation.

'Doug maintains that good management should be based on that model,' I tell the two of them. 'One key top person pushing everybody to perform, and one remedial person catching non-perfor—'

My mother gets called and the pretence of no worries, smalltalk on demand, evaporates. She walks into the specialist's office and I lumber after her, trying to keep mobile phone, pen, pad and car keys together. Introductions: You're very welcome, Ms Stapleton. Please call me Flannery. Do sit down.

He takes out charts and folders and gets launched. She will remember her eye operation. She nods as if this wasn't an idiotic question along the lines of 'Well, Mr Passenger, you will remember your trip on the *Lusitania*?' He has heard of the marvellous work she has done in the interim with Dr Potterton's patients. She nods again. Please, I think. Please get to the effing point before I sink my teeth in the corner of your desk and start chewing my way towards you. I could do without wood splinters in my tongue. The spectacled eyes turn to me. I may be aware, he says, addressing me as if I were a small seminar, that your mother presented some time back with back pain. Now it's me who has to do the nods, like physical punctuation in this man's talk. A number of tests were done, and a scan last week, and they've now examined all of the tests in some detail.

Any introduction this long has a weight swinging behind it like a wrecking ball. If tests have shown shag all, you don't expound on them. You pay for them without complaint because that's the price of a temporary clean sheet. But if you get the chronology of the tests, the tests have found you out. I want to touch her, but she is too far away. Looking at him watchfully but without fear. It was like this when the eye thing happened, I think. All worries gone, all anxiety calmed by the proven presence of disaster.

The specialist, directing himself between the two of us, is emboldened by our silence into going plural. What we now know, he tells us solemnly, is that the eye cancer was a secondary. Wait a second, I think, but do not say, for fear of making things worse. You mean she had cancer someplace else, and it spread to the eye and you people only caught the eye cancer? There is a mad table-tennis match going on in my head. I'm writing down the technical terms but thinking if you don't catch the primary cancer, you're bunched, aren't you? Or maybe that's only if the primary cancer is a stinker. But if there's now a problem, is that a tertiary cancer or is there such a thing?

Melanoma, my notes say. Lovely name for a girl, Melanoma. That's what the first cancer was. Wherever it was. Doesn't matter now. A silence happens and I go croaking into it, getting clarifications on things. I can see him looking at her, wondering if she's going to come apart at the seams. You don't have to worry, I think at him. Blubber in front of a stranger she will never do. It would be against good manners. The danger with my mother is like that she will be too brave. Fat payoff there's been for bravery up to now. He is talking about a survey of therapeutic options and I can't make head nor tail of it. But I know that one more question will bring me into a place out of which I will not be able to reverse. He knows it too, and works hard at maintaining a bland expression. I scrabble through my pages to work up to whatever I'm going to say next. In fact, though, my mother gets in first.

'Dr Wellfleet.'

Oh, you poor man, I think. When she turns your name into a statement, you're in trouble.

'Dr Wellfleet, Flannery will have understood all of the information you have given us, thank you.'

Isn't it strange? For the first time in my life I realise that Mam never refers to me as 'My daughter'. As long as memory goes back, I have been Flannery, a named individual, not an adjunct, to be taken seriously, not just referred to.

'I would just like to know' – oh, Mam, the gentle self-dismissiveness of that 'just' – 'how bad it is.'

'How advanced the—'

'How bad my situation is. My prognosis.'

Her sentence, I think, her ultimatum, her deadline. He looks down for a moment.

'Mrs Stapleton,' he says, with infinite gentle rigor, 'in this situation, they used to advise patients to get their papers in order.'

She smiles at him. Liking the way he has done it. The breath slides out of him and he has to make an effort not to let it be noisy.

'Will I see Christmas?'

He could answer straight away, but takes half a heartbeat's time in kindness.

'This Christmas, probably.'

'Thank you so much,' she says, rising and extending the hand, the gloves ready in the other hand. When she turns to the door, he does a tiny helpless gesture and I don't shake hands with him, but follow her, trying to summon up a smile for the Maurice Nelligan man, admiring the speedy grace of the way she walks, wondering will I now watch and admire and regret every second spent in inattention up to this.

As we go down the steps of the clinic, I fumble with the remote control and accidentally make the car beep.

'That's in case you lose it in a car park,' I say when she jumps.

'I just thought it was getting *very* clever,' she laughs. 'It was smart enough, the way it flashes its lights at you.'

We get into the car and I have to restrain myself from leaning across her and fastening her seatbelt. She gets comfortable and tells me, when we reach the big pillars at the exit, that the road is clear on her side.

'I'll want you to talk to him tomorrow again,' she says. 'We'll need to find out how long I'll be able to manage and we'll need a prescription for very strong painkillers and sleeping pills. Immediately.'

I glance at her and she is looking at me. You know what I mean, that look says. I do, my flinching glance says in return. She leans forward and puts on music. Tomorrow, I will get the prescriptions and count the tablets.

In another six weeks, I will get another prescription, because he will not, even for a cancer patient, be allowed to write ad lib repetitions on the prescription. Meanwhile, she will bear as much of the pain as she can, spacing out the serious painkillers with Solpadeine and glasses of brandy. The percentage of the painkillers and the sleeping pills actually ingested will go up as the months pass – if there are months – but there will be enough for the day she decides is the end of it.

I know, because we talked when the papers were full of a famous cancer patient who died with such quiet dignity. Just came home from hospital when there was nothing more they could do for her, gathered her family around her like in a Victorian painting, and slipped away. And my mother, the weekly Mass-goer, had smiled grimly and said no natural death was ever that beautifully timed and managed. I had been stunned, still looking at the television, shallow-breathing to understand it, waiting for the moral condemnation, hearing instead only a soft-voiced approval, like a prayer, a voicing of the belief that no God would want otherwise, no God would want His to return to him shredded by the cell mutants, swollen by organ failure, skin sloughing away.

The road ahead of me is warbled and corrugated by my tears, but I will not blink and let them fall where she will see them and be saddened by the small splashes of them.

10

Coming up to Christmas

———◆◆◆———

Next day, when the specialist sees me, it's as if my mother has gone to the wrong end of the telescope. She's this little figure, quite distinct, but very small, the subject of our discussions, which mainly concern data. Data, wonderful data. Look on this X-ray and on this. Never mind the victim, feel the information. Up goes the bluey frame with the bleached-out skeleton within it, genericising my mother. His pen touches small flaws in the print that turn out not to be small flaws. Here. And here. And in this organ. And in that lung. There are bigger words for them, but they are cancers. Some of them have joined up with others, all together now, lads, in clusters. Some are small outriders, fearlessly going where no carcinoma has gone before.

He pulls the chest X-rays down and replaces them with that ultimate generic, the skull shot. I wonder if my mother had to take out the false eye before she had these pictures taken. He points to tiny dots, not much bigger than full stops. Brain cancer. The lightbox goes dark and an assistant shuffles the big dark sheets into a portfolio with my mother's name on it. We go to the other side of the room and sit down.

'The eye cancer was a secondary, right?'

I take out my spiral bound notebook and pen and feel the atmosphere go chalky solid around me. If I'm taking notes, the relationship has changed, changed utterly. I'm now not the willing acolyte, not the head-shaved novice, hands steepled, listening to the Master. If I'm taking notes, I'm one of those litigious bastards media coverage of the occasional case has created. Sue over anything, they would. Have sent malpractice insurance so high there are whole *states* in the USA where they don't have a gynaecologist or an obstetrician, because it's just not worth the medics' while to pay the insurance.

'We believe so.'

For a moment, I sit, head down, eyes on notebook. Without raising my head, I look at him. Long and cool and suddenly confident. Yesterday, I was shocked Daughter Of. The big awkward lump of a one dropping keys and pens and handbags everywhere. Today, I am in charge and if you try pulling the vagues with me, Mister, I really will turn into a litigious cow. Watch me.

'It was, yes. A secondary.'

Now, doesn't that feel better? Letting go is so pleasurable. Hold to that thought, that attitude and this will hurt only a little.

'Why were we not told at the time it was a secondary?'

He shifts in the chair.

'You'd have to ask Dr O'Kane that. But the eye would have to have come out, anyway.'

'Why?'

He is affronted by the dumb simplicity of the question.

'*Why?*'

I keep the head still, look up at him again, blinking rapidly, as in *Don't understand why you're making an issue of this.*

'It would have metastasised,' he says.

Big word like marmalade, metastasised.

'Spread, right throughout her body? And brain?'

He nods. With relief. Even a slow student can understand if you just give them time.

'And amputating the eye prevented that, right?'

The corner of his mouth flickers in reaction to 'amputating'. Dear, dear, the terms these lay-people use. Then he realises where I'm going and starts waffling in increasingly technical terms. I listen very politely, very attentively and make no notes whatever.

'Let me get this right,' I say. 'The eye cancer was a secondary. So there was cancer already somewhere else?'

He nods. Don't put words on it. A nod is not going to stand up in court.

'Which wasn't looked for or found,' I say, quite cheerfully. Just establishing the first of the mistakes, lads.

He sits very still, and I am sorry for him. He did well, this man, with my mother, yesterday. He should not have to carry the can for whatever earlier halfwit failed to investigate what was eating holes in my mother. But if he wants to be medically collegial, that means carrying the other wanker's can.

'And, because no further investigation was done,' I continue, keeping the tone light, as if the issue were of no particular significance, 'there may well have been other secondaries already established at that time elsewhere in my mother's—'

For some reason, the word 'body' makes me balk and lumps up my throat as if using it were to categorise her as already dead. He does another nod. Little dots, I think. Little full stops like the ones on the picture of the skull. Already dug in more than a year ago. Rendering the removal of the eye useless. Mutilation to no purpose.

He gets launched on an explanation that veers between indicating that oncology is not an exact science, that individual patients vary in their responses to therapies, but it may be that removing the eye may have slowed the progress and blah and blah. Oh, right, I think. The little full stops sitting on her liver, when they heard about her eye being removed, would have felt threatened. They probably all went and hid in her pancreas for six months until the coast was clear for them to come back and metastasise.

I'm looking at him so blankly that he ends up half-offering me radiation for her. This would shrink some of the tumour mass somewhat, he explains. This is how it goes, I think. Owners of cancers turn up, braced and brave, for the sentence, get unbraced in discussion and both sides end up in a craven dance of death dressed up as 'treatment options', buying bad time with worse suffering, making hope out of deferral, but always contributing to those statistics of survival, puking their bald contribution to some study in the *Lancet* proving life extension of three months on this new combination of tortures. I dismiss the possibility of radium or chemo, one-handed. He looks relieved.

'What happens next?' I ask, and the relief leaves his face. No, I think. I do not mean that I expect you to go in surgically and take out all those full stops. I've been proof-reading my father's work for long enough to know that a full stop is The End. End of progress. End of image. End of thought.

He looks surprised, as if he is not often asked about the predictabilities of the dying. Even when he talks about it and I make notes, there is a slightly distant, academic tone to his listing of the possibilities, as if he knew them just from books, rather than from experienced reality. I write, distracted by this thought, until it becomes obvious to me: this is the point where specialists hand over to nurses, visiting less frequently because my mother will now be a reminder of failure, and, because of not taking the radium or the chemo, unworthy even as a subject of scientific research. There is no unkindness in it, but then there's no unkindness when a cold-eyed shark shears away the pulsing muscle from a swimmer's thigh, either. We do what we have to do and that's what oncologists do.

I try to discern a pattern in the notes in front of me. There is none. She will just die, that's all, but the proximate cause cannot be predicted. It could be a fall or a massive infection. He gets busy writing prescriptions and at some stage mentions hospice care, which – unfairly – makes me want to say 'Oh, yeah, don't want my mother clogging up one of your money-making acute beds, sure you don't?' But that is not what he has meant and not what I should think, so I nod as gratefully as I can, waiting for the final right question to strike me.

'Is there anything else I should be asking you?' I say when the final right question fails to materialise. He leans back and looks at the ceiling. Shakes his head. I stand. He comes forward and out of the chair and we shake hands. Warmly. Firmly. You've done your best. Not gonna sue *you*. Sorry to give you such bad news. S'OK. Telephone if we can be of use. Sure. Absolutely. None of it said, all of it conveyed.

I drive home slowly enough to get beeped at by those drivers filled with freefloating hostility who assume anybody getting in their way is doing it deliberately, with malice aforethought. No, I think. Just sadness and indecision. You kid yourself that once you have the information, you will process it, come out with the right answer and move seamlessly to the implementation phase. Maybe it works that way in business, but real life doesn't do the progress thing so evenly.

'Real life is not orderly, you know that?' I say to my mother when I get in.

'No, and Raimonde needs a lift home from Holles Street,' she says, very speedily, as if her words can prevent me from sitting down. I'm half-crouched, arse halfway to chair, and the arresting of the movement makes us both laugh.

'Jesus, what's wrong with getting a taxi?' I ask.

'You live in a world all your own, Flannery,' my mother says, shaking her head in something close to admiration. 'There's a taxi strike on, today.'

Never knew, I think. Feck, I think. I could've used the bus lane, coming home. If it's not being used by taxis, it probably doesn't legally apply.

'But anyway, it's because she's weakish. Lord love her, she had a miss.'

Miscarriage. My first reaction is irritation. Jesus. Ray, you got us all worked up into a collective support system, you converted your father from being a bigoted old bollix into being a proper paternal non-judgemental Dad and now you've abandoned the whole baby thing. Meanwhile, my mother, who is dying of little dots, is consumed with sympathy for you. It's disproportionate, so it is.

'Did she specifically want me to take her home?'

I am suspicious. My driving is competent, but not so outstanding as to have potential passengers lining up, slavering for a lift. My mother looks furtive.

'Oh, she really wanted *you* to drive her home,' I say.

'I knew you'd want to be the one to do it,' my mother says, and because we both know it's a lie, we laugh again, but a bit guiltily.

One of the Dublin radio stations tells me that the taxi strike is not as big as when they blockaded Kildare Street and the airport. I veer away from the bus lane I was about to enter and get beeped at. Bad. On the other hand, getting to Holles Street will be a lot easier if Kildare Street is driveable.

The minute I see Raimonde, I want to lift and carry her to

the car. Not practical, because although she's a lot lighter than I am, she's still a big girl. A big, pale, raccoon-eyed girl, now, pulling a pretend leather coat around her. She slides into the passenger seat and thanks me quietly. I touch the back of my left hand to her cheek and move out into the traffic, trying to give the impression that my silence is caused by the complicated driving choices I have to make, while I work out what I'm going to say to her.

'How bad?' I eventually blurt.

She goes a grimace that pulls in her lower lip.

'Very sore?'

That seems to confuse her, and I feel stupid for asking her. The overall malaise and coldness are visible and she's still clutching the PVC of the coat as if it was likely to escape if she didn't. Everything that I might say shouldn't be said. Like: You weren't even sure which guy fathered it, did you want to spend its life searching its features for putative paternity? Like: Look, you can go again once you've picked one right guy. Like: You've actually got a let-off on this one, don't be so fecking sad about it. Sorting through all of these unsuitable gambits takes time and I get worried that I should have said something. Anything. So I pat her PVC'd thigh and am astonished when she grabs my hand and holds on to it. I squeeze the clutching hands and figure this may do instead of words. It does mean we stay in third gear all the way to her home, but she doesn't notice the juddering at low speeds, and the damage to the clutch from just one journey can't be that bad.

'Will there be anybody home?'

She nods, dumbly. I walk with her through their paved-over-for-cars front garden. An old Saab is parked near the house. Probably her mother's, I think, and am surprised when it is her father who opens the front door of the house before we even get to knock and folds her down into him like a big old bird, her back shaking with hard racking sobs as he nods in severe acknowledgement to me, closing me out with the door.

When I get home, my mother has sandwiches made and wants to know all about Raimonde and Raimonde's father. Hasn't he been great, all the same, is the theme, and I eat the sandwiches wondering about that. Amazing, the credit a man can get for playing against the expectations his lifelong membership of the Bollix Union have set up. Much more credit than an ordinary decent human being gets for doing exactly the same shagging things the b. is now doing. I knew you when, I want to say to Raimonde's father. I'm not giving you human being status just because you come through on one occasion.

I wonder, out loud, what this will mean to the relationship between Raimonde and her Da. Or if it will mean anything. Or change anything.

'Dear Flannery,' my mother says, pouring more tea into my cup to heat it up. 'You're so like your dad. Always looking for significance.'

Except, unlike my dad, I won't be satisfied with the simple, surface significance, I think, and the viciousness of the comparison takes me aback. Not to mention the arrogance. Nothing like the illusions of those who not only have never achieved anything of lasting import, but never even tried. We promote ourselves beyond the achievers because, although we can't be arsed to engage in this tedious achieving thing, we're secretly convinced that if we ever *did*, the air would be thick with flying Nobel Prizes.

'Your dad telephoned just before he got on his flight,' Mam says comfortably. Give me another tilly, I think, remembering her phrase for that extra jolt of tea my dad calls the hottener. That restores cooling tea to warmth. The tilly. We tidy up together, the agreement between us unstated: we won't talk about *that*. No full stops in our conversation. No secondaries nibbling at my leader's bum. Nor am I empowered to share it with my father. She will. In her own good time. Or maybe it's now her own bad time. It's not my time, anyway. For this relief, much thanks.

Not that we could have got a word in edgeways, anyway, when my father comes home. He is on such a high, it turns him childish. We have to listen to the whole thing right now, everything else could wait. They are paying him $100,000 in an option fee, whether or which. Mam and I go 'whether or which?' obediently, so he gets to tell us that even if the studio never make the animated film based on his poem, he can keep the $100,000. He lifts my mother into the air at one stage and it is like a blow to me to see how easy the gesture is. She is lighter, she has got thinner without my having noticed her losing weight. I want to tell this child-man to put her down, not be so silly, she could break.

He puts her down to go get the videotape he wants to show us. I yell after him that it probably won't play on our machine if it's an American one, but he calls back that they thought of that and it will. Sits us both down in the sitting room and does his usual monumental fumbling with the machinery before he gets pictures and sound.

He puts it on pause to tell us that what we are about to see is what this studio made of something Ted Hughes wrote for his children. After he retrieved them from the upstairs bedroom under which their mother gassed herself because of his infidelities, I think. My mother says she didn't know Ted Hughes ever wrote anything for children. The videotape decides it has been long enough on Pause, and unravels.

The Iron Giant, the title says. The animation is not Disney. Not art-bettering-reality. There are no cutesy-pie squirrels or long-eyelashed birds helping characters make pastry. The only one making anything is the child-hero's lone parent mother, a waitress. When the giant appears, he is just a big metal shape. My heart sinks. They're not going to be able to make anything emotionally involving out of a big metal shape, I decide. Over the next hour, I get proven wrong. My mother and I sit through this child's movie and snigger and cry at all the right places. If the studio involved can do anything as good with my father's poem, it will be fantastic.

After lunch, my father has to give a lecture, and Mam asks him to drop her at Marks & Sparks and pick her up later. I am tempted to e-mail Lyn and tell her all about my mother, but – although I know my mother would not be mad at me if I did – I don't. Lyn is fighting promotion at work. Her boss does not understand that a Lyn operates best just below the top, smoothing over the abrasions the boss makes at meetings, promoting potential the boss can't find the time to spot, but above all, not complicating the instant hatred every woman feels and the instant appreciation/lustful speculation every man feels in response to her looks.

I have a need for something momentous to happen, but instead, everything seems to be sliding back to normal. As if my mother were not dying. In fact, she's not doing or saying anything to register her understanding that she's dying. It's all normal, routine, except she's using the jacuzzi less. Once you know it's not rheumatism that ails you, maybe you lose faith in the efficacy of agitated water.

She never asks me what the specialist said and I never tell her, although I suspect I find not telling her – not telling anyone – much more difficult than she finds not asking. But then, every time I open my mouth, now, I'm second-guessing myself. Don't mention anything due to happen next year. Don't talk about the flowers that bloom in the spring, tra-la. Don't refer to ordering a desk diary in which to keep Da's business straight, because it might upset her to think she won't be around for some of the pages in the coming year. Don't refer to conferences he's going to speak at.

Sometimes I wonder if, absent my mother, my father will be as bereft as I feel he should be. He has always maintained that once I came along, my mother never paid as much attention to him as she did before my birth, and although it is always said with self-deprecatory humour, there is an edgy whingeing undertone to it. He would much prefer it if she took care of his career instead of having an administrator keep track of the anthologies that include his work and make sure they pay up, but she handed that over when I was a toddler. There is no evidence that he would not be competent to get himself to a conference in California, for example, stand up, do his piece, sit down and get himself on the return flight. It's only around the house that he's noticeably deficient in coping skills. Of course, he maintains he'd like her to travel with him to all of his overseas engagements, but the way he says it, I've never believed it to be more than an extension of his politeness, a saying what he thinks he should say. But maybe neither of them feels whole without the other present. Who can judge parental ties?

It would help if I knew Mam's behaviour was what could be expected at this stage of this disease. None of the websites I visit are useful, because they're most detailed about primaries and what happens within mutant cells, not what happens long after secondaries are found all over someone. Certainly not the behaviour of the cell-owner. The cell-owner is irrelevant.

So, I get through Hallowe'en. The trick-or-treaters are accompanied on their rounds by their parents. I don't know if this is to ensure they get enough admiration for their plastic costumes or to prevent people like me secreting razor blades in the apples we give them. If the latter, they shouldn't bother. I couldn't be arsed putting razor blades into apples and anyway I don't buy apples. My mother may have handed out healthy stuff in the past, but, now that I'm in charge, it's straight carbs and calories. Fun-sized Twixes and Mars Bars by the handful. Hallowe'en is a good excuse for buying sacks of them.

I'm still eating the remains of those treats when Lyn rings me one morning to tell me I have a computer virus.

'It's called KAKworm,' she says, cheerily.

Introductions to strange viruses free, gratis and for nothing. This girl will even network with a goddam virus.

'It transferred to me in that note you sent me. But I have the right anti-virus program.'

'You have the right bloody everything,' I say disagreeably, and she laughs. 'How's Piers?'

Oh, wonderful, she says. Hmm, I think, but don't say. Whenever Lyn puts an Oh in front of something, it queries whatever follows.

I wait for elaborations and, instead, get told that Raimonde is doing all right. Staying off the jar. Totally. And not missing it.

'Which means staying off sex, too,' I say.

Raimonde is so shy, no man gets near her when she's sober.

'The three-Smirnoff Slapper,' I add.

There is a small silence. Lyn lets comments she doesn't like die of lack of support. You are quite like my mother, Lyn, I think but don't say. I mean it positively, but don't say it because it's never a compliment to be (a) likened to someone else's mother, (b) told someone else's mother approves of you.

'Is it true they're making a film of one of your father's poems?'

'How do you know?'

'It was on the MSN site.'

Oh, right, I think. 8 great chat-up lines from poetry. 5 Top Poets of Today. 10 Poems you Must Know. 6 Must Have Culture Tips.

'Yes. Have you ever seen a thing called *The Iron Giant*?'

'The one they made of Ted Hughes' story? It's lovely.'
She quotes some of the lines from it.

'Piers rented it one night for us. He'd heard about it. I don't know that he knew about the Ted Hughes connection, though.'

'The question is whether Piers had ever heard of Ted Hughes, never mind his connection with the film,' I snide.

'By the way,' she asks, having done the obligatory but noncommittal chuckle, 'did you see the profile of Doug on Friday in the business bit of the *Irish Times*?'

I didn't. She'll e-mail it to me, she says. I get it up on-screen an hour later. There is a water-colour sketch of Doug, pony tail over his shoulder, and the headline is *Pulling the Celtic Tiger by the Tail*. It's at this point the machine freezes and no matter how many bent paperclips I poke into the little re-booting slot, I can't get it to do anything.

The doorbell ringing should be a welcome distraction, but it feels like an extra imposition, so I lash it open with a '*YESSS?*' expression crimping my mouth closed, and don't for a second recognise the man standing on the doorstep. Then I laugh.

'Anybody ever fill you in on small details like "Hello, Doug, nice to see you, would you care for a cup of tea?"' he asks crossly. I laugh again. He walks past me into the hall.

'You have a key, don't you?' I ask.

He was in a week ago, although I didn't see him, to show my mother the website he's developed to showcase my father's work. He looks reproachful, as if I'd know he wouldn't use a key when the cars parked outside show someone's home. A smile keeps curling up around my face and eventually I ask him why he cut the pony tail off.

'Or rather, now that I come to think of it,' I amend, 'why, if you were going to cut it off, didn't you have it cut off before the paper did that profile of you.'

'Wouldn't get rid of it to make me fit in with the rest of the suits on the business pages,' he growls.

In fact, he admits, he's wanted to get rid of it for some time, but waited for spite until *after* the profile and its accompanying illustration appeared. And a girlfriend of his *really* didn't like it, he adds, going, ahead of me, into my father's study. I follow him, trying to understand why the reference to one of his girlfriends bothers me.

'I believe you have a virus,' he says, sitting down at the desk and dumping his grotty little bag beside him.

'Oh, Lyn's being a support system, is she?'

He gets the thing going and smiles when he sees I was looking at his profile in the paper.

'Lyn told you about my virus, told me about your profile. Great little operator, isn't she?'

I am sitting at the end of the big desk, swinging a leg. He gets rid of the picture of himself on the screen. I watch him. He not only looks better without the bloody pony tail, I think, he looks younger. Lightened of the weight of the thing, his hair has bounced up and even has a strong wave in it. He is good-looking.

'You have committed one of the fundamental branding errors,' I tell him, happily. 'To establish yourself as a pony tail user in the Paper of Record and then cut off the pony tail is a bad marketing move. Like Michael O'Leary changing to solid colour shirts, Armani jackets and a Blade Two haircut.'

'Ryanair *is* Michael O'Leary,' he grunts.

'If Amazing Trace is anybody, it's you,' I say.

'Probably should be Piers,' he says.

'Why? You invented the system. He came in long after.'

'Better bullshitter than me,' he says comfortably, beginning to hum to himself as he tracks where the virus has reached.

'You should be off making another million,' I say. 'Crazy, to have someone like you doing stuff on Dad's computer a first-year student could do.'

'That's true,' he says equably. 'Tellya, you've pissed off a fair number of e-mail recipients, these last few days.'

'Sent this Kake thing to them, have I?'

'Kak. Yes. Who the hell is Elisabeth Cooper-Rosse?'

I try to remember which overseas contact of my father this may be. He corrects himself.

'Kubler. Kubler-Ross.'

I can see he's in Favourites, checking sites I've clicked on recently.

'None of your business,' I say and mean it.

He looks up at me sideways.

'I'm sorry,' he says. 'You're quite right. It *is* none of my business.'

He puts a disc into the server and it begins to grind through files.

'I never actually got to read the feature,' I say, after a punishing silence. 'What did it say about you?'

'That I have a coherent, self-developed managerial style,' he said, taking the disc back out. 'Am self-assured not to say bumptious, unthreatened by the volatility in the marketplace, but more likely to be taken over than to go for flotation.'
I absorb this as best I can.

'Taken over by who?'

'MicroSoft. SunSystems. Any one of the big guys.'

'Not Bill Gates?'

'Why not Bill Gates?'

I mutter half-remembered prejudices about the evil nerd. Spawn of Satan. He gives one of his lectures. About Beauty contests. Steve Jobs, he says, from the start gave the impression of being Mr Alternative, the maverick putting together cute systems in a garage, whereas Gates was the nerd rushing to become part of the establishment. David and Goliath.

'David isn't always the hero,' he says. 'Underdogs can be shites, too. Jobs won the beauty contest, that's all.'

'So you'd say my father is an international bestseller as a poet because he personally looks good,' I say, testing out something I half believe anyway.

'Of course,' he says.

'What about Heaney?' I ask.

'You don't think Heaney's good-looking?' he asks, surprised.

'I actually think he's a hell of a lot better looking than my father,' I say. 'He looks like his poetry.'

To this he makes no response, and after I think about it, I'm not surprised. Response would not have been safe.

'How'd that profile happen, now that I think about it?'

'Of me? Nicola dealt with the PR agency and told me where to pitch up.'

'How's Nicola doing?' I ask, with studied neutrality.

'When she realises how good she really is, she'll be fine,' he says, patting the machine approvingly. I assume it's now deloused. 'She spends a lot of time proving herself to me. And Piers.'

I'll bet she does, I think. If your new bosses know you ripped off your old bosses and stayed out of clink mainly because you were a first offender, there's a lot of proving to be done.

He says Piers, him, Lyn and I should meet some evening. Have a drink. We must, I nod, not meaning it. Foursomes I can do without. Particularly at a time when, no matter where I am or what I'm doing, I keep getting the feeling that I should be at home, taking care of my mother. The fact that she seems to need very little from me at the moment diminishes this anxiety not a bit.

Not only does she need very little from me, but sometimes, when I get home, I have the impression that I'm interrupting her at something important. Except that the something never *is* important. I keep expecting to arrive in and find her writing her will, or going through old photograph albums, but I'm much more likely to find her watching *Coronation Street*. I keep thinking she should be doing something more important. With a limited amount of time left, should she be wasting it watching an old soap?

But then, what is the proper occupation for someone who is dying? What constitutes wasted time or valuable time? Do I seriously believe St Peter's going to meet her at some celestial gate and give her hell for spending time in the Rover's Return? Are there heavenly Brownie points due if you spend your last months reading Marcus Aurelius or learning to do calligraphy?

The thing that phases me most is that my mother does not seem to be dying at all. Maybe she is going to live until she dies. Live, as in be ordinary. Do routine things. Be *more* routine, *more* ordinary than normal. I sneak glances at her, trying to figure out what she is thinking, constantly disappointed when, at the end of a long silence, she says something mundane. I am hoping, maybe, for a moral lesson, some reflection sharpened by the nearness of eternity.

But when I think something like this, I get shivers. Why is she not more fearful? The specialist did say that in his experience the period leading up to dying was worse for patients than the dying itself, but is she not invaded by thoughts of the grave, of nothingness? Of course, babies do not look as if they've come from that nothingness, so maybe there is no consciousness of it, no dread.

What Doug has encountered in my Favourites is some of the research I have been doing in order to stay on top of this. Kubler-Ross says my mother should be going through phases. There should be a phase where she gets enraged and feels she's been picked on by fate.

I see no signs of that phase at all. Not in my mother. I see plenty of it in me. I keep thinking that although she smoked – because there are photographs of her with my father in the early days with a cigarette held, elegantly, in the long fingers of her hand – she didn't smoke for very long, and it seems unjust that people who smoked forty a day for forty years should be doing nicely thank you while my mother is under a death sentence. One part of me is wondering if I'm just trying to turn my mother into a personal project, while another part of me is afraid that if she doesn't go through these Kubler-Ross phases, she'll die in unhappy disarray.

Then the reality of it comes rolling at me and the terror. The sense that there must be something I can do to freeze this period, lock it in amber, but make sure it is filled with some especially rewarding activities. I know. I know. I'm behaving like those charities that take baldy-headed nine-year-old leukaemics to Disney World. Fulfil their dreams before they die. My mother, in her tranquil disengagement, gives no inkling of unfulfilled dreams. Occasionally, when she asks me for a painkiller, I grind up half of the mildest of the prescriptions and dribble the ground powder into a big empty capsule, one of a hundred I bought in a health food shop.

She has never asked me why I do this, but even though she hasn't come near the end of her first prescription yet, I have worked out where she would be if she had been taking three a day, and will soon go back to have another prescription filled out. That will bring us to what the suicide book says is enough.

Will I be able to do it, when we get to that point? I get chilled by the thought that there would be an autopsy, or is it a post-mortem, and that I would be found guilty of murdering her. Every time I fill one of the capsules, I think this is another step to murdering my mother and that it was a mistake to start it. If she was doctoring her own pills, if she wasn't asking me for her painkillers when she needs them, she would probably take charge of swallowing the hoarded cache when she needs to.

'And then,' the voice in my head says, 'you'd only be an accessory. That make you feel better? Because it's all about how you feel, isn't it? Your mother is dying and you're worrying about being an accessory versus being an active criminal.'

You can't be an accessory to a non-crime, and suicide isn't a crime any more. But what will I do, if she is in hospital when the point comes where she indicates to me that she wants me to do it? How will I get a hundred different pills into her when she may already be nauseated? If we do it slowly, she is less likely to throw them up, but if there is a long time before all of them are swallowed, the first ones might overcome her before she has taken all she needs to take. Will the relaxation the first ones cause make her talkative about what she is doing and thereby endanger its completion?

The fact that she has never actually told to me this is what she wants to do confuses me. I thought she might go into some detail after that last visit to the specialist, that we might face into this together, so to speak, but she is pushing me gently away with little pads of ordinariness. Not me, particularly. All exigent exigencies.

Because I am in the house with her all the time, I find myself, in the middle of doing a bit of research, thinking that I should go downstairs and ask her about the men she dated before she met dad. The two who telephoned after the book appeared with her and the angel on the cover. Who were they, those men? Did she love them? Are they still alive? But I stay at the computer, because if I were to start asking those sort of questions, it would be macabre: tell me things I never asked you before because they were never important enough to ask about until your value went up because of impending death. So I sit, immobilised by misery, at the desk in the study, listening to the distant sounds of afternoon TV or – occasionally – the jacuzzi.

The PC makes its 'You have mail' noise and I click on the newly arrived note. Doug@Amazingtrace.com has e-mailed my father many times, but this one is for me. In the Subject box, he has typed NONE OF MY BUSINESS.

You're welcome to tell me to effoff, the message reads, *but Kubler-Ross and lassitude make me jmp to the conclusion that yr mum is bad. If I cn be any use, say.*

I hit Reply.

Right conclusion. Don't talk me about it. You're v. kind.

Within seconds, another message appears.

:-I

I presume it means shut mouth. I must, sometime, learn all these shorthand icons, I think, and my mind loops back to my mother. There's the nub of the difference between us, now. I am a lazy, overweight under-achiever, but I am possessed of a sense of infinite possibility. Tomorrow, I could choose to learn to fly. To ice skate. To deep-sea dive. To learn show-jumping. To do origami or learn Esperanto. I will not do any of these things. But I can, I could, I might. For my mother, now, there can be no such possibilities. What she has now is all she will ever have. I hope a function of the illness is the removal of any desire to develop some new, different, oddball skill. If she ever had such a desire.

Or – it comes as a helpless ache – is she sitting, now, in front of the TV, not hearing or seeing the programming, but imagining herself flying a kite by the sea or riding a horse bareback? Is there an added wistfulness about not having done those things or is that wistfulness only experienced by someone like me, who is not as immediately threatened by ceasing to be?

I sit, hands on keyboard, knowing that – even in this – I lie to myself. I know I will die, because that's the way the cookie crumbles, the odds play out and the statistics dictate. But deep inside me is a conviction of such profound uniqueness as to justify me being an exception to this dying thing. Fantastic. I amount to the sum of shag all, except as Daughter Of, yet am prepared to submit my beloved mother (but not myself) to the logic of death. Maybe this is why I am willing to hoard painkillers and sleeping pills for her: to confirm to me my superhuman status? Jasus, what a crock.

The phone rings. Andrea. I have to come to a party, she belligerents at me.

'Andrea, some of the girls and me are going to club together and send you on an anger management course,' I tell her.

'What are you *on* about?' she asks, furiously.

'That,' I say, beginning to be sorry I started it, but unsure where there's a back door or if there's one.

'That *what*?'

'Forget it,' I say. 'Scrub it. Erase it. Disregard it.'

'You're spending too much time on your own,' she says.

'You may be right,' I say, pacifically.

'I bet you haven't worked out in weeks.'

'More like months, Andrea, actually,' I say. Use the other person's first name, it's a great anger defuser.

'You're over there doing nothing but reading and eating.'

'Bit of work, sometimes, too,' I say, but lightly.

'Well, of course, work,' she says. 'I wasn't suggesting you don't work hard.'

O, Jasus, she's getting worked up that I have suggested she suggested something she believes she didn't suggest. Only Andrea can add the unimportant to the irrelevant, stir it and get cause for a small claims court case out of the end result.

'How is Bruce?' I ask.

Now, *there's* hypocrisy for you. Like I care about Bruce Green. Like I want to hear anything other than that Bruce got swept into a combine harvester and spewed out as silage, or that he went playing chicken on the edge of the Grand Canyon or got on the wrong side of a sex-starved Giant Panda.

'That's really why I'm ringing you,' she says.

Yay Hay. Maybe Bruce has developed terminal psittacosis or eaten bad sushi. As long as he's been discontinued, I don't much care how. Botulism would be good, though.

'We're getting engaged.'

Close that open mouth and make positive words come out, dopey.

'You're not serious.'

Not positive, thicko. Could mean 'Of all the men in all the world available even to a short hostile bulldog of a woman with a heart – according to Lyn – of gold, you pick the ultimate shite?' *Does* mean that.

'On my birthday.'

Andrea was born on the anniversary of the death of JFK senior, so she gets doubly offended if anybody ever forgets her birthday. No excuse. I know it's sometime in November, but I'll work out precisely when after I've got off the phone. The immediate priority is not to say anything that will let her know I haven't a clue when it is. No. That's the second immediate priority, the first being not to vomit forth my truthful view of her elliptical arsed fiancé. Like saying 'Andrea, you'll have to have nappies purpose-built for any offspring of Bruce's.' The effort not to burst forth with any of the comments dammed up behind my front teeth reduces me to inappropriate silence.

'You can't remember when my birthday is,' she accuses.

'Andrea, of all my girlfriends' birthdays, yours is the easiest to remember, thanks to historic connections.'

Whoo. Next trial of strength, please? You want me to eat maggots? No problem. With or without whipped cream on top?

'Have you picked the ring?'

Safe serve. There are a number of them. Have you picked a name? Are you over it yet? Suppose you're a bit down? Was it great?

'There's a tradition in Bruce's family.'

I'll bet there is. Oversized elliptical arses and traditions and terminal boringness.

'Really?'

I inject more zest into this question than it's really worth, so it sounds as if the tradition (whatever it is) in Bruce's family (elliptical arses to the right and left, evenly distributed) will solve all my problems (multifarious though they may be) and maybe some of the problems of the Peace Process in Northern Ireland.

The enthusiasm injection gets her started and she blithers about genuine garnets. Since I don't think garnets, genuine or false, are worth a toss, this is roughly the equivalent of saying 'genuine toilet paper', but I moan appreciatively, and she gets into antique settings and how much it would mean to Bruce to see his wife wearing the ring he remembers his mother wearing as a boy. The notion that Bruce's mother was once a boy throws me, although it might explain some of his pain-in-the-arse factor. Then I realise it was Bruce who was the boy, which is more likely, but not that much. I forget what happened to Bruce's mother, but she's dead a long time. Which makes me wonder if, when my mother dies, there will come a time when she becomes unreal because her death was so long before.

'I can understand that,' I say. 'What will you do about wedding rings, because it won't be that easy to match a new bright gold ring with an antique, will it?'

Give Flannery Stapleton the smalltalk prize, I think. The conviction with which she's spouting this tripe . . .

'You weren't listening,' Andrea snaps. 'His mother never—'

'–wore a wedding ring, right, right,' I say, scrabbling to get back on the high moral ground, to win back the smalltalk hill. Thanks be to Jasus, I think, for the peculiarity of my brain that allows me to playback with complete faithfulness something

I've just heard but neither listened to nor consciously remembered. It was what made me survive school. Every time a smartarse teacher observed me drifting off to sleep and demanded to know from me what the teacher had just said, I was able to reproduce it, every comma and 'em' in place. The accuracy always mollified the teacher, although the fact that I included their 'ems' in the playback often got them riled all over again. God is not mocked and you take your life in your hands trying a perceived mock on a teacher, because teachers, in their own view, are next best thing to God.

'I'm sure the engagement ring will be just beautiful,' I say. 'What'll you do at the wedding ring part of your wedding, though?'

No problem to Bruce, I think. That guy is such a penny-pinching, sewn-pockets money-grubber, he'll probably slip a rubber band on your ring finger at that point in the ceremony. Or pretend he really had one but the best man lost it. Assuming, which might not be a good idea, that Bruce can drum up a best man. I wonder, guiltily, if any of the venom I'm mentally directing towards Bruce Green can do him any harm. Some of the stuff I've been reading about cancer says optimistic people survive longer than pessimistic people. If you send vanquishing thoughts at mutant cells, they get discouraged. I wouldn't like to equate Bruce Green with a cancer cell, but what if my evil thoughts about him make him fail to thrive? And why does every thought I have, evil or otherwise, loop back to my mother and what's happening to her?

'Of course I will,' I hear myself saying to Andrea. What have I agreed to do? Go to a party. *Shit*. But I couldn't get out of an engagement party. That's a cut above an ordinary knees-up.

'It's going to be a dinner party,' Andrea says smugly and my heart sinks.

'Do I get to bring my own partner?' I ask.

'Do you have someone you want to bring?'

Caught between a rock and a hard place.

'I'd need to think about that.'

'If you don't have someone you immediately want to bring, you don't have someone,' Andrea says with the directness that will make her one fearsome fifty-year-old. 'I'll put you beside someone nice.'

'Thanks,' I say sardonically. Waste of sardonic. She is powering onto the next thing, which is Lyn, who might let that Piers move in to her house if I don't get my act together and go back living with Lyn. There is my role in life, defined. Be the human gooseberry who will physically stand (or maybe lie) in front of Piers Rickard to prevent him establishing a domicile with Lyn. Human speedbump, I am. Barricade the door with Flannery and Lyn will have no problems. Flannery is the sandbag you put outside the door to prevent the floods from entering. The chair you hook under the doorhandle to repel muggers and pillagers. She is never going to be in much danger of pillage herself. Only the pillage idiot would fancy her.

In the old, post-Luke days, I could quote the typical Andrea boots-and-all gaffe to my mother and she would be properly scathing on my behalf. She would even say that much as she loved my friend, I was much more classically beautiful than Lyn. Taller, too. I used to go back to the bathroom and check for any signs of emerging classicism and laugh at myself for listening to mother-talk for even a minute, but there was consolation in it, too. Now, even considering mentioning it to her makes me feel trivial. But, oh, I need mothering *more*, in the face of losing it forever. Maybe, I think, maybe my mother might need to mother me, as well, but this, I figure, is just self-serving projection of my needs onto her. I'm beginning to meet myself coming back instead of being really useful to her, as is made plain when I hesitantly mention the possibility – only the possibility, mind – of me going to Andrea's engagement party.

'For heaven's sake, Flannery,' my mother says, with more rattiness than you'd think a sick person could come up with at short notice, 'I'm not deranged. I don't have to be watched for fear I'll start chewing flexes.'

'Of course you're not deranged,' I say, and the awkwardness of the unsaid 'but you are dying' makes the situation worse. She tells me that I'm hanging around the house to no purpose half the time, even when Joyce, our cleaning lady, is in. I am immediately hurt that she must want Joyce to herself, which is understandable, because Joyce is one of the funniest women alive and is always up to date on the local scandals. She's particularly good on how the neighbourhood is coping with the sixty Nigerian refugees currently billeted in a disused convent up the road from us.

The first anybody heard of that was when my dad was on a radio programme, mostly made up of loving phone calls from women whose lives were changed by one or another of his poems. Women who say their lives were changed by a song or a poem are like men who say their business life was changed by some book or training course: nobody else can see any difference at all, but the people involved are convinced they've made a quantum leap in some greatly advantageous direction.

So my father's absorbing all this praise, mostly by asking these women questions about the great challenges of their lives (a boss who fails to appreciate, a teenage daughter who surls) when one caller comes through who wants to know how Dad is coping with all the blacks in his neighbourhood. You can hear my father groping to understand what he seems to think is metaphorical talk, and the presenter of the programme is even more at sea, which isn't hard, because the presenter wouldn't know a metaphor if it bit him in the knee. His open questions provoke the most fantastic rant from the caller. It's made up of equal parts anti-liberalism and racism.

The anti-liberalism portrays the suburb where we live as a coven of feminists and worse, which is probably true. The woman next door, who should now be drawing her pension and re-reading Ethel M. Dell, has got into Reflexology and when my mother got the false eye, tried to do her feet on the basis that everything was helped by particular pressure points. Anybody but my mother would have hauled out the false eye and thrown it at her. Old liberals think they stay young by wearing denim and getting into aromatherapy.

The guy says it's people like the people of Poplar Park (the site of the feminist and worse coven) that destroyed the great religious orders of Ireland. My father makes some weak noise about being a Belvedere boy himself, which inflames the caller worse. And did he send his kids to the Jesuits? he demands of my father, which wrong-foots my father a bit and causes him to hesitate. No, the caller says, he probably sent them to a non-denominational school which is just another word for Prot-estant. (My father can't cope with this at all, because of not wanting to offend Protestants while wanting to point out that since his only offspring was female, he couldn't have sub-mitted her to the Jesuits because they educate boys only.)

If people like my father hadn't emptied the convents, the caller goes on, they wouldn't be empty and getting filled up with niggers and the nerve of that Bertie Ahern anyway wanting us to vote for the Nice Treaty to let in the African countries.

At this point, the presenter self-evidently gets the earpiece equivalent of a cattle-prod from his producer, to the effect that racism, unchallenged by the voice of the station, could get them shagged off the air, so he reproves the caller and drops him into an electronic garbage disposer (you can hear the caller, on fade, calling them worse than niggers) before playing a disc.

The next day, the *Star* has a picture of the convent, a line-up of black refugees and a photograph of my father, all on its quite small front page in colour.

POET WELCOMES REFUGEES

says the headline, which marginally over-states what my father actually said on the programme, which was that he had total faith that the people of Poplar Park would adjust to the marvellous challenges of the twenty-first century, just as they had in the twentieth century.

The people of Poplar Park, according to Joyce the cleaning lady, are not adjusting so's you'd notice. They can't protest about having two busloads of blacks in their back garden, but they can raise questions about the support systems provided for the refugees. That keeps them on the right side of their own conscience while allowing them to fight like hell to get the kids (these refugees are all teenagers) shifted. Mostly, that fight involves the local TD, who is apparently pissed off at my father because the Taoiseach gave out to the TD when the Nice Treaty got rejected by Ireland because one of the TD's most prominent constituents (my father) had talked about African countries joining the EU when there was never any question of them being let in.

My father ended up writing to the Taoiseach explaining that

it wasn't him who'd talked about African countries, it was a phone caller and he thought the phone caller might have misheard the Taoiseach and other politicians when they kept referring to 'applicant countries'. My father got back a generic-type letter from the Taoiseach's office, which annoyed him more than anything. When you have the American President including lines from one of your poems in his inaugural address, you feel you deserve better than yellow-pack letters from your own prime minister, dammit.

A couple of the neighbours have tried to get my mother involved in discussions as to how best to cope with this new challenge, as my father phrased it, but she's got out of it by overwhelming vagueness. Either she thinks this is a problem she is not going to have to cope with or she thinks it's not a problem. She hasn't commented, either way, to Joyce. I keep waiting for Joyce to notice something different about the way Mam is looking, on the basis that, being with her all day every day, I must miss changes in her condition as evidenced by her appearance, but so far Joyce hasn't said a thing.

My mother says she is going to start her Christmas cooking next week. She invests the marzipan-making and plum-pudding boiling with no trailing clouds of mortality, so I don't either.

I I

Party Time

———◆·◆·◆———

Because the party pulls together betrothal, birthday and housewarming, I figure I have to do a fair bit of expenditure on a gift. I go along to Stephen Cullen's studio and pick out one of his more recent paintings. Time was, I knew what his paintings were about. Now, I just let them smack me in the face and the one that gets imprinted on my retina gets taken home. The price rocks me, but, mid-rock, I remember that I haven't bought anything much recently other than food, petrol and books, so (a) everything has got dearer when I wasn't paying attention, and (b) I have money in the bank and can cope with the cost of the painting. I write a cheque, convinced, as I always am when I visit his back-garden studio, that this man is reading my mind and knows every venal little calculation that goes through it.

It's OK to be a mind-reading observer if you never articulate what you observe, or do it in non-representational painting. The master of the unexpressed thought, Stephen Cullen is. Doug Rogan's partner, Piers, on the other hand, is the master of the immediately expressed and acted-out thought, as I find at Andrea's party.

I arrive to find him in the middle of convulsing everybody with a mad exaggerated replay of my father on the phone-in radio programme. Piers does the racist ('Effing niggers taking up our jobs, not that I've ever had an effing job, you think I'm stewpah or wha'?'), the presenter and my father all at once, yet separately. My father he mostly does physically. For several seconds at a time, a languid draping of a leading hand, or a smile that took fifteen seconds to get from the eyes down to full mouth extension brings my father into the middle of the group with as much vividness as a blow. Some mimics pick up the way people talk. Piers picks up the way people move. I'm still shrugging my way out of my coat when he puts his finger over his mouth to shush the laughter, gestures at me, and imitates the way I'm standing. Until he does it, I don't realise the half-committed, I-will-be-ladylike-about-this stance I've taken, and once he *has* done it, I find myself doing it all the time.

Fortunately, Andrea undoes the wrapping around the painting and makes a fuss of it. Doug Rogan appears with a drink for me and – at a glance – identifies it aloud as a Stephen Cullen. A ridiculous feeling of warm commonality comes over me. Dougal, I think, you're one of us. One of the select group who collect Stephen Cullens. He is oblivious to my warm commonality. Frig him.

Having a painting recognisable as being from some named artist impresses the elliptical Y-fronts off Bruce Green, who decides it must be worth finding wall space for. I wonder if Doug has been laid on for me or for Raimonde, who is skittering in response to every casual comment made to her as if she were auditioning for an ad for panic attack medicine. Piers is there with Lyn, although he is at pains not to be solicitous, and when she tries to damp down his imitation of my father, imitates *her* so ruthlessly that I want to be furious but am laughing too much.

Lyn tosses the black mane and goes off to the kitchen and he tosses his crew-cut and does an exaggeration of the mince her Manolo Blahniks give her.

When we get to sit down, I'm between him and Doug, with Lyn opposite and Raimonde also opposite but down the way a bit. Difficult to work out whether this is just Andrea approaching the issue in the spirit of making a brick wall (they're all the same, all you have to get right is making sure none of them stick out) or if she has a Cunning Plan.

Meriel and Adrian are separated physically, but exchanging those sweetly collusive glances of the truly in love that make any decent person want to clock their two heads together. Over the starter, Piers announces he's starting a support group for people like me and him who have fathers they're ashamed of.

'Flannery's not ashamed of her dad,' Lyn says. 'Her dad's a lovely man.'

'Nah,' Piers says. 'She's in it for his money.'

The woman named Cliona and her partner Mike glance at each other for help as to what millionaire my father might be. I quickly say that my father is a poet, not exactly rich. Piers makes a speech about how nobody who can write even the kind of crap poetry my father writes ('Flannery's father doesn't write crap poetry,' Lyn says. 'Her dad writes lovely stuff') pays any tax on it, because of Ireland's daft tax laws with their ridiculous favouring of artists, so he (my father) is now so rich, he wears sable Y-fronts. This causes Doug to choke himself laughing.

'I know her father,' he tells the rest of the diners apologetically. 'I'm just imagining him in sable Y-fronts.'

'Flannery's father doesn't wear sable Y-fronts,' Piers says in a high voice, imitating the way Lyn routinely contradicts him. 'He wears lovely mink boxers.'

'I don't squeak like that,' Lyn squeaks. Everybody laughs. 'Well, not as bad as that,' she amends.

'Lyn doesn't have the problem Flannery and I have,' Piers says, patting her hand across the table. She snatches it back theatrically and he examines his own hand to see if it was unclean enough to deserve rejection. 'Lyn's father's an ordinary, middle-of-the-road, boring kind of father.'

Even though I know I am now being co-opted into his performance, I rise to this.

'Lyn's father is not ordinary or middle of the road,' I say, and the whole table joins with me as I add, Lyn-style, 'He's a lovely man.'

Piers makes like he's conducting us, and in the process manages to smack Bruce's carrying arm, which is making an ostentatious job of transporting three stacked plates. The plates take to the air, then smash on the Italian-tiled floor. Andrea goes down on her hands and knees to pick up the pieces, giving Bruce a blinding glance as she does so. Bruce doesn't know whether to blame Piers out loud (but can you do that to a guest?) or tell her to stuff her blinding glances (but can you do that to your new fiancée and it her birthday, too?) and so stands, irresolute. Piers tells him kindly to move his incredible oversized arse into the kitchen and get a dustpan or else Andrea will cut the hand off herself on the broken crockery and the marriage will be all off because she won't have a finger to stick a ring on. Bruce Green tries to get launched on the genuine garnets saga, but a ground-level glare from Andrea speeds him into the kitchen to seek a dustpan.

Piers is now in full spate with a criticism of my name.

'I mean, *Flannery*. Jasus. Named after a nightgown.'

'That's flannel,' Lyn says, half-deliberately playing straight woman at this point.

'And there's a difference?' Piers makes them all look at me, and I swear I feel like I'm made out of flannel. Face-flannel. Damp.

'Flannery is named after a famous author,' Lyn says. 'She's named after—'

'Whoa!' Piers says, like she's a horse about to bolt. She unbolts. He sweeps the table. 'Bottle of Kristal for the first guest to name the writer after whom the girl in the flannel nightgown is named.'

'Flannery O'Connor,' Doug Rogan says.

The surprise this causes is slightly damaged by the furtive glances traversing the table indicative of the guests' complete pig ignorance of Flannery O'Connor. Piers starts to maintain that Doug is disqualified because I either prompted him or told him previously (neither of which is true) and that he won't win the champagne unless he can name three of Flannery O'Connor's works within sixty seconds. Piers flails out his wrist and ostentatiously pushes the second hand on his watch.

'*Wise Blood*,' Doug says after a moment's thought. I'm amazed but keep my face blank. '*Dark Sassafras*.' There is another, longer silence, during which Piers sneaks a look sideways at Lyn. Doug snaps his fingers. '*Counting the Bougainvillea*,' he almost shouts.

'Fair dues to you, Doug,' I say. 'I never knew you had it in you.'

Piers wants to get back to the point. Which is that people like him and me, with questionable fathers, spend our lives living them down. Because he is working for Ireland's most exciting software entrepreneur (Doug bows) who pays him more than he is worth, and that's really saying something, he, Piers, is showing signs of healing. But Flannery, who really has no job but stays at home pretending to do something called research, carries the scars of her father's ill-gotten fame all over her and needs help.

Andrea and Bruce must have come to a revival of their working partnership, because they now appear, him holding a tray with six plates on it, she placing them in front of each of us.

'Wow,' Lyn says, and the Cliona woman echoes her.

Andrea has done the whole main course so it is a round tower in different colours, with a stiff fan thing sticking out of the top. She must have bought a set of those round handcuffs for food. I lift off the fan with my fingers and crunch it, because until I see which way other people attack the round tower, I'm not going for any bit that might land in Doug's lap or Piers's lap or both laps. There are three coloured layers, so I could do it turn and turn about. Doug's lap gets the red bit on top, then Piers gets the white one, then Doug gets the green one at the bottom. Under cover of all the compliments to the cook, I lean over to Doug, pretending to draw his attention to a subtlety at the bottom of the tower.

'*Wise Blood*, yes,' I say quietly. 'I'll give you *Wise Blood*. But the other two?'

'You got to admit,' he said, leaning towards me and nodding at the dish in front of him. 'They do sound like Flannery O'Connor titles.'

'You want Brownie points for creativity?'

He nods, thoughtfully.

'When you're cheating on a bet?'

He looks startled, and then laughs out loud.

'You don't imagine for one moment Piers was ever planning to deliver me a bottle of champagne?'

'He wasn't?'

'Ask him.'

I turn to Piers, who is on the second service round and whose food has only just arrived in front of him, courtesy of Bruce.

'Marvellous, isn't it?' he asks gravely, and winks at Andrea, who is so busy slapping the tray down by Bruce's side (*it's empty, you dozer, concentrate*) she misses it.

'What's marvellous?' I am forced to ask him when Bruce and Andrea have retreated out of earshot.

'It's marvellous, the lengths pillocks will go in dressing up food so that when it arrives in front of you, it's been mucked around by eight hands and is rubbery and cold,' he mutters.

'Where will you get the champagne for Doug?'

'What champagne?'

'The bet he just won?'

'Oh, that wasn't serious. We run a mutual tab.'

I glance in outrage at Doug, now eating his dinner with a smirk and none of Piers's reservations about its rubbery coldness.

'Anyway,' Piers says, raising his voice to gather his audience again, 'since Flannery is so – so – *challenged* by her status as Daughter Of the Poet Lurrier, I'm giving her counselling. After all, as you all know, I've had my own troubles in that department.'

He breaks into theatrical sobs and lowers his head onto the naked shoulder of the woman on the other side of him, whose name I missed. She goes along with it by patting the back of his head and saying 'There, there.'

'Wonder why we don't comfort kids by saying "here, here"?' Meriel wonders aloud. She must be pregnant, I think. Meriel never, to my recollection, *ever* spoke of children up to now.

'Because they'd start crying all over again,' Lyn says.

'"Hear, hear" means you approve of what they're doing. "There there" means they do it well, but would they stop, please.'

'You're giving Flannery counselling,' the woman he cried on prompts Piers. He kisses her in gratitude.

'Even better, I'm getting her to watch, all on her own, the ultimate therapeutic films.'

'They being?'

'Cartoons. Son of Sylvester.'

'I know who Sylvester is,' Raimonde says, out of the blue. Several people, startled by hearing a voice from the silent end of the table, turn to her with 'Oh, you can do the speech thing?' expressions on them.

Since the sudden attention will either make her go silent for life or grab the nearest full wineglass, I say 'Attagirl, Raimonde. You tell 'em who Sylvester is.'

Piers comes up off my shoulder, smarting as if my raised voice had been positively raucous. I check to see has he dribbled on me and get a small but significant laugh down my end of the table, which annoys the hell out of him because he missed what caused it. He does a 'keep it coming' gesture to Raimonde.

'Sylvester is the cartoon cat. I tawt I taw a puddy tat. That cat.'

Piers gives her a big hand.

'Not many people know this,' he tells the diners, 'but Sylvester had a son. Who looked like a small, cute Sylvester. He thought his da was God and that Tweety was toast as soon as Sylvester decided to eat him. Every episode he was in, the son would get hugely enthusiastic about his father's schemes, writing off every failure as bad luck. By the end of the episode, it would dawn on him that his da was a fuckwit. When that registered, he would put a paper bag with two eye-holes over his head, say "Oh, the shame" in a small voice and exit stage left.'

What's funniest about the reaction to this is that so many of the diners have either been watching Sylvester recently, or have had a major impact made on them in the past by the cat, because they're all nodding and laughing with recognition.

'In order to come to terms with my own father, I have watched Sylvester's cute little son many a time and oft,' Piers says. 'Bruce, you're going to have to take my plate, Andrea's never going to talk to me again after my lack of progress, but when you talk as much as I do, you don't get to eat even the most delicious food. *Which this wasn't,*' he hisses at me before going warmly back to Bruce. 'Not that it matters, that I didn't eat. Flannery here beside me was eating for two.'

This gets a laugh that wavers midway through as diners ponder the implications of the phrase.

'Not pregnant,' I say, waving a napkin. 'Insulted, yes. Caricatured, absolutely. Pregnant, not even a little bit.'

Somebody else wants to draw our attention to another important father/son relationship in the comics: the bulldog and his son who are up against Tom the tomcat. This doesn't ring quite so clanging a bell. Piers gets absorbed in a three-cornered discussion with the naked shouldered woman next to him and Lyn.

'How the hell did you end up pals with this guy?' I ask Doug. 'He's not at all like you.'

'He's nearly as clever as me,' Doug says.

'Cleverer,' Piers says, not missing a beat in the conversation he's in.

'He doesn't work nearly as hard as I do,' Doug goes on, rolling his eyes at me.

'Geniuses don't need to,' Piers says.

'He's more obviously good-looking—'

'by a mile—'

'but doesn't leave the lasting impression I do—'

'on little old ladies and their pekes.'

This throws me, and even with his back to me, Piers seems to know it.

'Pekinese, dear, pekinese,' he says, patting me, backhanded. His hand goes high enough for me to drop my head and nip it with my teeth.

'Imagine,' he huffs to the woman on the other side of him, 'she bites the hand that feels her.'

'And I find him a useful distraction to have around when investors ask questions to which I have not sufficiently thought out the answers. Other than that, he's a complete waste of space and a wojus git.'

'At least I don't drive a poncy naff Land Rover,' Piers says, with an air of finishing off the discussion. '*I* drive a car that pulls birds.'

'I don't need a car to pull birds,' Doug says.

I nudge him to indicate that not enough fuss is being made of Andrea's pudding, and he manages to quell Piers for about three minutes while he elicits encomiastic comments on the pudding from everybody. Andrea, who is sitting down and letting Bruce take care of coffee, allows herself to be flattered out of her patent anxiety that he'll do it wrong.

'Anyway, I'm going off pulling birds,' Doug says suddenly, much more energy in his tone now he has his duty done. 'Birds are a pain in the tits.'

'How true those words are, even today,' Piers agrees.

'Women, you mean?' Raimonde seems to think we may be still back with Tweety.

'Wimmen,' Piers confirms, in a good imitation of the voice of Grumpy from *Snow White and the Seven Dwarfs*.

The naked-shouldered woman next to him favours him with a collusive smile, conveying she knows he's only kidding.

'Women are the inferior sex, by a mile, and it's time they knew it,' Doug says, and I wonder if he and Piers have rehearsed this. No. They are egging each other on. They may have glanced at the theme before, but no more than that.

'No, I think they really do know they're inferior,' Piers says.

'It's probably their unacknowledged inferiority complex that makes them so needlessly obnoxious,' Doug agrees.

Serendipitously arriving on the words 'needlessly obnoxious', Bruce says something brain dead about feeling obliged to stand up for his future wife and her gender. I can see his future wife dying to tell him to shut up and keep his mind on the job, pass out the coffee and not kid himself that his future wife and her gender will tolerate him standing up for them, never mind appreciate him doing it. Piers doesn't even register the host's intervention. He is surfing along on an exposition of his theme.

'Doug and me; now, there's a good example,' he says, gesturing past me at Doug as if he were a specimen in a petri dish or wherever good specimens are kept. 'We can have a knockdown dragout, fuck each other from a height fight.'

'Verbally, the fucking from a height, verbally,' Doug says, but only loud enough for me to hear him.

'Do you two live together? I mean, are you partners?' This is from Cliona.

Piers does an over-the-top shudder at the possibility of partnership with Doug.

'Working partnership only,' Doug tells her.

'You fight a lot at work?' she asks.

'All day, every day,' Doug confirms.

'Whatever the fight is about gets sorted,' Piers says. 'Either in the office or over a pint later. Right?'

The woman next to him, surprised by being poked with an unexpected question mark, nods, obediently.

'And when we sit down to work tomorrow, there's no leftovers. We can move on together, no problem. But, you have a fight with a woman, first of all, she cries, or she runs away from it, or she concedes, but not really and tells all her friends.'

'Oh, that's not true,' Raimonde says, in such a doubtful voice it serves as a confirmation.

'But you know the real sickener about women in a fight?'

This time it's Doug, and he's poking me with the question mark but I'm not playing. Does my failure to co-operate slow him down? Not at all.

'The real sickener about women in a fight is that they never stay with the specific issue in question. It's never this particular cock-up right in front of you both. Oh, yeah, it starts with this specific cock-up, but as soon as the girl starts to fight, it gets extrapolated out and suddenly you're fighting on every cock-up there's ever been in the entire history of your relationship and not just your relationship but every relationship in the history of the world and it becomes a demonstration of the way you think, how badly you clean up the kitchen when she goes away for a weekend, how annoying you are kidding yourself that you're handy around the house when you're really a complete asswipe, what a living bitch your mother is and how all the other girls warned her you were a manipulative dangerous bullying bastard and to steer clear of you, and now look at the way you have her and what you've made her say, nobody else has ever reduced her to this level and you should be ashamed of yourself, but that's the central issue, isn't it, that you have no shame. Sugar, is it?' he finishes, on a tone of domestic good humour, having worked himself up to screaming pitch before asking me why I was tugging at his sleeve.

'Milk, actually,' I say, in a pretend-scared whisper. 'But I wouldn't want you to take it personally.'

' 'S'all right,' he whispers back. 'It's only women take things personally.'

Piers nods vigorously.

'Sometimes you get a Son Of who does, too,' Doug hisses at him from the other side of me.

'You're right,' Piers says, clouting Doug on the back with such comradely force he nearly puts him face down in the cheese.

'See?' he says to Meriel, who hasn't been paying enough attention to the joint developing thesis. 'See how men can take it from each other?'

At this stage, half the table is in stitches at Doug and Piers, and the other half, including Raimonde, want to mount a major assault on them, particularly on Doug, for their views on women. It is noteworthy that the ones prepared to wave the standard for women are all females. Doug points this out, quietly but seriously, and Raimonde gets rattled.

'Raimonde, he's only teasing you,' Lyn says, as fearful as I am that Raimonde will suddenly take to the drink and revert to slapperdom within the hour.

'I'm deadly serious,' Piers says. 'You deadly serious, Doug?'

'I'm *pretty* serious,' Doug says, and I can feel his arm behind me, the hand sending some signal to Piers, who glances sharply at him.

'But we're being boring,' Doug adds.

There's a fraction of a second before Piers drapes his napkin on his head, and, shrinking down into his chair, says, in the small voice of Sylvester's son, 'Oh, the shame.'

Andrea, demonstrating good timing I wouldn't have credited her with, suggests we move into the other room and Bruce gets into a saga of interminable length designed to illustrate the inadequacy of all builders. The unspoken consensus among the guests seems to be that the host pair deserve a bit of a boost at this point, so nobody points out the gaps in his argument to him. I am sitting in an overstuffed chair that has me so low on the ground I must look like a collapsed circus tent, but do I care? Doug sits on the arm of it, and I expect Andrea to tick him off, but she doesn't. Maybe knowing Stephen Cullen's work has advanced him in her eyes. Adrian, who is being an old charmer, moves the conversation seamlessly from Bruce to Mike and Cliona, who work together in one of the big accountancy partnerships and who are doing, between them, 150 billable hours a week. They are constantly exhausted, they say, and Mike tells a funny story about falling asleep at a meeting with one of the partners.

'Be all right if I dropped around to see your mum, one of these days?' Doug says quietly to me. 'Haven't seen her in weeks.'

My brain gets log-jammed wondering if his visit would make her think I had told him she was dying.

'Your father told me,' he says, leaving me in no doubt what my father told him.

I look up at him, wonderingly.

'I didn't know Dad knew,' I say.

He shrugs. I feel a surge of warmth towards him. He may talk a whole load of women-hating theory, but he doesn't apply it to real people like my mother. Bruce is now talking decibels to Adrian about the flat Bose audio system he's had installed. He keeps turning Guns 'n' Roses' *Patience* to full volume and then down to nothing. Andrea tells him to think about the neighbours, it's nearly one in the morning.

'Some things never change,' Doug says to me, finishing his coffee.

My head is spinning with alcohol and undirected urgency.

'I should go home,' I say to him. 'But I probably shouldn't drive.'

'C'm'on,' he says, and pulls me, two-handed, out of the chair.

We are outside the house, telling Andrea what a great meal it was, trying to force them back to the rest of their guests, before I make a decision. Then I'm in the passenger seat of a car that isn't the Land Rover, leaning back, eyes closed.

'How the hell will I retrieve my car?'

'Take you to my place for a coffee. Get it later.'

'Sounds like a plan.'

I thought he had an apartment, but he has a house. When he opens the front door, a big dog comes lolloping at him and I shrink back. Dogs, I don't know.

'He's a Labrador, for Chrissake,' he says impatiently.

'So?'

'Gentlest dogs in the world,' he says, guiding me into a sitting room. As soon as I'm sitting, the dog puts its chin on my knee and looks soulfully at me. I stroke it tentatively and nothing bad happens. Doug clatters in the kitchen and I half-heartedly offer to help. Help refused. I stroke the dog some more.

'What's this thing's name?'

'Punter,' he says, coming in with two mugs hanging from a finger, coffee pot, jug and sugar bowl held in his hands. Getting them onto the table without spilling any one of them is a challenge, but he does it.

'C'm'ere, you,' he says to the dog in much the same tone he

used to order me out of the chair in Andrea's. The dog's tail starts wagging, overtime, and he galumphs out to another room. I hear the door closing. The man comes back without the dog.

'Food,' Doug says. 'Labs love food. Any food. Anything they decide is food. Remember the moccasins I used to have? Punter chewed them, so even I couldn't continue to wear them.'

'Labs,' I say. 'Is Punter a yellow lab, then?'

'Golden. Golden Labrador. Black Labrador.'

'You don't get spotted Labradors?'

'No. Bastarding Dalmations are the ones with spots.'

He pours the coffee, standing, and drinks from his mug. When I put mine back on the table, he sits down beside me on the couch, throwing his arm over my shoulders. His jacket sleeve catches on the big clothes-peg-like clip into which I've dragged my hair. He turns me to examine it and unclips it, running his fingers through the bends it has made in my hair. Laughing when his fingers find the dampness.

'Couldn't be arsed to even dry your hair before you go to a party,' he says.

I go to pick up my coffee again and when he takes it out of my hand and puts it back down on the table I know I didn't want it. And that I did want what he is now doing. Very gently. Very surely.

'As if you knew me for ages,' I say, letting him.

'Shut up,' he says softly.

'Being masterful, are we?' I ask. With difficulty.

'Practical,' he says, and that makes sense to me.

12

Nothing to Fight Sleep For

———◆———

It is a Black, rather than a Golden Labrador that knocks my mother down, although she says it was her own fault, turning suddenly when she was so near the kerb. When she comes in from a short walk, helped by a neighbour, she looks aged and different and is fighting to be the same.

'Quite all right, now,' I hear her saying, down in the hall, reassuringly. Then I hear the over-loud voice of the neighbour hinting through the house: Anybody home?

I'm out of the study in the ratty dressing-gown without shoes, taking the light weight of my mother from the neighbour, getting her into the kitchen. Mistake, I think. Now I'll have to offer this neighbour tea. But the neighbour shakes her head at me over my mother's head – how that would irritate my mother if she could see it – and is gone, closing the front door after her. I go on my knees in front of Mam and she braces herself, hands on my shoulders. Heavily. Fruitlessly. The pain is not eased.

'Oh, Flannery,' she says.

I push the kitchen table so she can fall forward and be propped, prevented from coming off the chair while I go to get the painkillers. No refinements. No breaking in half or grinding into power. Just the whole tablet and the glass of water. Such difficulty swallowing what she needs. I force her to drink more water after the tablet goes down. Make it work quicker, I tell her. Mother Phrases. Feel the relief in no time. Promise you. I slide the table away and go back on my knees, my shoulders supporting her, my hands softly smoothing the thin back of her. She makes movements with her fingers to indicate that she'll be better in just a minute, doesn't want to impose, and I say 'Shhh, shhh,' as if she has spoken out loud.

We are there forever, my mother and me, my warmth willing its way into her, defeated by the cold of her, my youth a reproach to the chalky frailty that has crept up on her without showing itself until now. Sometimes she moans. The moan is not so much pain as defeat. It stoppers up any future comfort I think to offer. The future is fifteen minutes away, when a narcotic kicks in. No further than that. But it will kick in, I tell her, sure at least of that. Beginning to work now. Worst of it over. Get you into bed. Take your time. That's it. That's right. Don't be trying to straighten yourself up. Just lean into me. That's a good girl. That's it. *Thaat's* it. Nearly there. Two more steps, tha's all. Hold on to me there till I get the cover turned back. Gently does it. No, I'll do that. I'll do that. Shoes off. Now, the tights. Don't be pushing yourself, I can slide them down. Now, promise you won't move? There. Warm blanket against the back. Hot water bottle in it. Shhh. Be all right . . . I sit stroking the thin shoulder as the painkiller takes her, making the mother noises, the old pet names presenting themselves to be played back to their owner. Peata. A cuisle. As the jaggedness of her breathing flattens and softens, I understand, not that I am grown up now, I am *the* grown-up now.

When my father arrives home, I watch him from the landing, unseen, and wonder how I could ever not have known that he knew. There is an expectant dread about the way he stands, interpreting the silence in the house, knowing her to be somewhere within. I check: she is propped with a spare pillow. I go down to him to explain.

He tries to believe it is just an accident. Unrelated to anything more serious. No part of the ongoing illness. A pulled muscle. A trapped nerve. He will talk to the specialist, he insists, having grieved over the ashy figure in their bed. Two days later, they send an ambulance for her. I drive him after it, listening to him talking in half-sentences. It's just you need to check every . . . Wonder if somewhere like the Mayo Clinic . . . ? There'd be the money if needed . . .

He will stay with her while they do tests. I do not fight him for the right to watch them as they tie rubbery tourniquets around her too-slim arm and flick impatiently with their fingers to make a tired vein rise for puncturing. I will telephone the head of his department in college, yes. He has arranged everything to cover this eventuality, it seems. He and my mother had talked about it. I make a list and write my mobile phone number down for him. No, I should not come back that night. He'll stay as late as . . .

I hear him coming in at midnight. I could go down to ask him, but he will write a message on the kitchen surface nearest the kettle in pencil, and I would rather deal with this by remote control. At six in the morning, I read it. She is in Oncology, not Intensive Care. There's no restriction on visiting times, because she is so sick. There are bone breaks and the possibility of infection.

In the hospital, the nurses at the station get prickly at the sight of me, arriving so early, but warm up when I claim relationship with her. She's awake, they say. Very independent, isn't she? I nod, speechlessly. People only remark on your independence when your age or illness presuppose dependence. Mam used to quote Cary Grant saying ruefully that when people tell you how young you look, it's because they remember how old you are. My mother. Very independent. Insists on taking care of herself. That means the eye, I suppose. One of them comes around their bright glass box of a station to bring me to her. First inside the door, the nurse says, and it's lucky she says it, because I would not, otherwise, recognise my mother, sitting up in bed, stary-eyed and dis-tanced.

She forces herself to react to me, but the dying has begun and I am distant, clear but distant through the thick glass wall of it. There is drift and then that staring preoccupation as she sorts the details of the task, residual kindness alone pulling her to talk to me and my father.

We hold her hands except when they come to check the I/V, to syringe it with stronger antibiotic or more painkiller, although she never complains of pain at all. My father talks in corridors of hospice and I keep a handbag on my lap, all the painkillers and the sleeping pills in it, squashed into silence by cotton wool and foam pads tight-stuffed into the containers.

Other patients come back from Theatre and are shouted at to waken them, giving deep groans that flicker her eyes open: was that me who cried out? We tell her, no, no, everything's fine, just snooze for a bit. Evenings and mornings melt into one another in the artificial death-pale neon light. At some point, I come back to the ward, cleaned but without sleep, to find her bandaged as she was after they first took out the eye. Sometimes her thin long fingers – hand estranged through illness – fiddle at the bandaging, but there's no heart in it, no follow-through. It is easy to gather the searching hand in yours and draw it down, gently.

Our names are all she says.

'Edmund,' when he kisses the forehead beside the bandage.

'Oh, Flannery,' with a smile that remembers how happiness felt, when I touch the small foam Q-tip thing dipped in 7UP to her lips.

They stop piling the pillows into a great white pyre behind her, and she slips flatter in the bed, bandaged face upward, hair whitening with every slow speedy empty cluttered day. She is in rehearsal for death and when it happens, it happens unexpectedly and without hospice or help. My father sits, curved into collapse over her hand, the bones sustaining the arch of him sticking out even through the nubby tweed of his jacket. This most gregarious of men cannot even pretend to respond to kindly comments, in wild-eyed incomprehension taking over his face when nurses say soft things about my mother and how she was. How could they know how she was, when what they knew was not her? All they encountered were traces of the self-contained decency of her, struggling for expression through the fog, the distance of dying.

I take him away, drive him to our home where sleep will take him, overwhelming him because now there is nothing to fight sleep for. Whenever I speak, he drags himself to awareness on ropes of courtesy and guilt. Mostly, I leave him be, sagging against the seatbelt like a suddenly old man, hands holding on to his knees. No drape. No pose. If anything, he looks frightened. In the house, he embarks on what might be an apology, an appreciation and I hunt him upstairs, me the grown-up, and begin the phone calls and the formalities. In the midst of the outgoing calls comes one from Amazing Trace. Nicola. Ringing on behalf of Doug. Doug overseas. Doug worried because no responses to e-mails and my mobile phone switched off. I tell her and cut off the spurious intimacy of her sympathy.

Lyn insists on having a bunch of phone calls delegated to

her. When my father wakes up, he is grimly unlike himself in his efficient setting up of services and wording for the paper. I worry that there will be renditions of his every poem about her, and famous friends of his trailing up to the podium on the altar, but the famous friends are all in the congregation and stay there, while an old priest talks about her with knowledge and admiration and humour. There are lives scarce noticed, he says, except in their after-shocks: the effects those lives have on others and the way the learning plays out in later generations of friends and of relatives. That is why even the atheists among us can know that death is never an end, but an enabler. Sometimes a life requires its death, even its early death, to achieve its full totality of impact.

I am not sure I understand all the man says, but I will get the words, written down, later. I will get them, because my mother was not a wife in the way he talked of her. Nor a mother, either. The only near-reference to my father was when the old priest talked of the picture of the girl with the white angel, bright-faced in the sunshine.

The chaotic orderliness of a funeral makes floating wreckage of the bereaved, I learn, being patted and passed from hug to handshake, from generic sorry-for-your-trouble to agonised cries of sympathy. A teacher from school. Meriel, barrelled by early pregnancy. Adrian, sheltering her from wintry gusts of wind-driven rain. TV presenters, smiling right and left but composing their agreeable fame into gravity for comments to my father and dumb handshakes with me. Occasionally, my father tries to introduce, to explain, but mostly it washes over him and me. In sleet, outside the church, Doug appears, grim-faced, holding me by my upper arms while Piers keeps an umbrella over both of us. That is when I weep, because Doug talks of things she did for him I never knew about. I am stone-

faced, otherwise, welcoming the sleety truncation of the fare-
wells, sickened by the shiny black gravestones brimming with
banalities. Mobile phones go off all the time, provoking looks
of reproof, furtive head-tilted conversations by the phone
owners. Cars passing leak Christmas music out of the high
inch-slit of window opened to reduce condensation.

We bury her in a churchyard where there are no angels and
we leave her there on Christmas Eve.

13

Bought and Paid For

———————◆◆◆———————

In the weeks after her death, the letters come in handfuls. Thoughtful letters from old friends. Friends who knew my mother, before she met my father or who knew them as a couple. I sort the letters into the personal and those aspiring to be personal, and he trusts my judgement. When he comes home from college, I feed him and then he goes to work, writing carefully with the good fountain pen she gave him twenty years earlier. He loses many things, my father, but only once ever mislaid that pen.

The phone is busier than normal. Media interest, I have learned, is sparked by many things, but most of all by visibility. There is a relentless neutrality to the interest of journalists and broadcasters. A moral neutrality as impersonal as a tank. It doesn't matter whether you're visible because of triumph or disaster. A radio programme treats those imposters both the same, and so they want my father – as soon as he feels up to it, of course – to come on the show and talk about my mother. My mother means nothing to the wider public, but in my father's words, she will become a figure of pathos. He doesn't even refuse the invitations. Just flaps his hand when I mention them as if even apprising him of them was a waste of our time.

After a couple of months, a columnist who specialises in saying the unsayable on the basis that some nameless person is saying it or will say it, writes a feature ostensibly about grief.

Grief as experienced by the famous, and the pressures it brings to bear on them. Accidentally on purpose, he mentions my father, and towards the end of the piece predicts that if/when my father comes out of the slough of despond and marries again, there will be some who will see that action as a reflection on the first marriage, whereas of course it is an affirmation of that earlier relationship. I am so furious, I make him read the feature and ask my father to consider writing to the letters page of the paper. He looks puzzled as he goes through it, as if he couldn't quite understand the proposition that he might marry again.

'Oh, no, that would never happen,' he says. 'There's no point in responding to that kind of – of flight of fancy. Don't let it worry you.'

It doesn't worry me, I want to holler. Letting this creep get away with this sanctimonious crap worries me. But it drifts away from him and there is no reason I should make him pay attention to something so distasteful.

After any death, there is a little round of deeds and days, and the two of us could be gerbils on a wheel, we do them so diligently, so unquestioningly. As February rolls around, the tone of callers for him is less reverential, their urgency more pronounced. Real life and its routines reasserting themselves.

Doug Rogan drops in now and then, sometimes to do something for my father, sometimes to sit over coffee with me. He seems to have all the time in the world, though the rest of his life is speeding to breakneck point. Amazing Trace has taken over the whole building within which they once had no more than a floor, and are negotiating with the people next door. He employs more than a hundred people and is flying all over the world. In the January 1 predictions of who the important figures in the next year will be, he figures, some-

times on his own, sometimes surrounded by his young management team, laughing, arrogant in their success. They get
CVs in dozens every day, he tells me. Increasingly from
overseas.

He invites me to places, but I do not even consider the
invitations. When I get through this, I say, but I am not sure
what 'this' is. Sometimes he holds me, but gently and without
intent. Mostly, when he is in our house, he is silent or close to
it. Even though, when he arrives, I welcome the break from
the routine of letters to be written, phone calls returned,
contracts signed (for my father) and packing of my mother's
clothes for giving to the Vincent de Paul, I have little to say to
him and am relieved that it doesn't bother him. It is very
comforting to sit silently with a man who wants nothing from
you, not even a vote of thanks. I have no routines of my own
to which I need urgently to return. I am not flatlining, but
peacefully close to it.

I do notice that both he and Lyn are beginning to nag me, in
different ways. Lyn would never say 'Get over it' but she
begins to push the idea of me doing more than research for the
radio station. Maybe do interviews. Or write scripts. I figure
this is an effort to get me out of the house rather than a real
need for different material, although Lyn gets pretty insistent
at the first meeting in her office she cajoles me into attending.

Doug's car (a Lexus, now, we are long past the Land
Rover) is outside the house when I arrive back. I rest a
shoulder against the door while I search for my key, and it
opens quietly. I can imagine the two of them arriving, each
believing the other latched it behind him, and am half-smiling
as I move towards the study where I know I'll find them. The
shout freezes me in the hall.

'. . . that she looks like a horse's ass? A fucking derelict?'

My father's voice answers, but it is so low, I hear no words. The tone is placatory, emollient.

'But you don't *do* anything,' Doug's voice says, in contradiction of whatever point my father has made. 'Nothing. Nada.'

There is a pause, and then my father says something brief, in a slightly more querulous tone.

'Big deal, you got me to take her to the wedding,' Doug says, and as he answers, I hear my father clearly for the first time, because he is opening the study door to come out.

'I see no point in continuing this—' he is saying, but seeing me stops him walking and talking. Doug, whose back is to the hall as he takes a disc out of the computer server, half-turns to see what's caused the sudden silence and sees me, too. The three of us are frozen in position, a rictus of denial forming at my father's mouth. He is hoping I didn't hear what they had been saying. But I did, and they both know it before I scream at them. Bastards, both, I yell. Patronising bastards. The goddam nerve of you, you meddling old fool, I tell my father, smacking his raised hand away from me; comfort, what comfort did you ever offer me, you got him to take me to a wedding; tell me, did you get him to fuck me as well or was that just a freebie with the overall package?

Doug comes up out of the chair and starts saying things, but I cannot, will not, hear him, the static in my head matching the endless torrent of words streaming, slobbering, spitting out of me. He steps past my father and tells me I do not understand, I have taken it up wrongly, and when I raise my hands to hit him holds them until I can hold them rigid no more and let them drop. Get out, I say, quiet now, the static in my head as loud as ever. Get out. Get out. Don't come back. Ever. Go. Get out. Get out.

He gathers his things and goes, leaving my father white-faced and craven, standing outside his study door. I bend to pick up my bag, my papers, blinded by tears and bile, dribble at the corner of my mouth, and warn him off with a Keep away from me, you, as I go to my room and close the door, sinking down behind it, abject in shame at who I have become. At what they believe me to be. At what that belief has empowered them to do.

It is important to me to believe that my mother did not know he invited me to Meriel's wedding as a task, an obligement to a client, my father. My father, the card-carrying sentimentalist. Mr Popularity who can't bear that his daughter mightn't be as popular as he is. Wasn't he the lucky shit to have married someone as beautiful and popular as my mother. She measured up. But a big lump of a daughter who – gimme that key phrase again – looks like a horse's ass? A fucking derelict? Well, you have to take extraordinary steps, don't you, Da? Special measures. Correct the deficit. Make her one of your charities. Kids abandoned or in care or orphaned, you'll make yourself available to those charities. So, here's a good charity subject, right at home. Give her a job and if she can't get herself an escort to a girlfriend's wedding, get her the escort, too. Buy her a man, why don't you?

I can hear him moving around downstairs and then his footsteps up the stairs. Don't even think about it, I whisper, but he does. Comes to my bedroom door and talks about explanations. Over a cup of tea. I sit silent. The door handle moves and I say, not yell, say that if it moves another inch I will kill him. He says he will leave the tea. When I hear him gone, I think about kicking the mug I know to be outside my door, kicking it over the banister, kicking it to smithereens against one of the walls below, but my mother's part of me is saying no melodrama, my own part of me is saying he will never again know, after tonight, anything about me. Not one gap, one vulnerability, one chink in the armour.

Every scene I replay unravels to its implications. The night of the party in Andrea's.

'*Being masterful?*'

'*No. Just practical.*'

Well, tell me, Doug, just how practical was the whole deal? Did you comp me? Or was it a swap? 'You fuck my daughter, make her feel better, I give-a you my business, *comprende*?' No, it would be investment, rather than actual business. Money to burn, my old man has. First generation of Irish poets to become millionaires. I just lodge it for him, lodge the cheques. Someone puts the money in high interest yielding funds. Amazing Trace would be a pretty high yielding investment vehicle. So maybe that was the deal.

My face flames with the humiliation of the illusion destroyed. Who the hell did I think I was? Who was I fooling? At the funeral, when Piers held that umbrella over Doug and me, was he laughing at the artistry displayed in that way Doug held me by my upper arms?

I slide to the floor, my face down on the coverlet, weeping without relief, because from shame there is no relief. Guilt, confessed, expiated, yes. Shame, never. Me, who always wilts at the sound of gurrier laughter in the street, always assumes the kid-sneer is at me. Bruce Green may be a poor thing, Andrea, but your own. But what do I know about poor things, what do I know about reality? Get my father to gift-wrap it, I'll love it. Make sure all my friends know about the purchase, Dad. Wouldn't do for a movie, would it? Plain mousy friend of gorgeous brunette thinks she's got off with the *boss* of brunette's guy. How likely is that? Raimonde, back in the drinking days, you didn't kid yourself that the weekend lay found you special.

I put my face to the wallpaper to cool my cheeks. No make-up to rub off – this is a fucking derelict, remember? Naked, unadorned face. Remember, Dad? You mustn't have paid him enough. He came to you to complain about the goods. Under-groomed, the goods are.

I see it all now, I think, but I am lying. I lie in the effort to claim some prescience about something. No matter how I run the reels, I never see any of it coming. I see none of it linking. I remember this long-legged man, scuffy shoes cocked up, arms folded, asleep in the A & E and I wonder why even now I can't see how I was being set up. I pick and poke at the pictures to find clues to the duplicity, the contempt felt for Daughter Of, and cannot find the evidence. When I am cried into swollen-throated hoarseness, I hear the slow footsteps on the stairs again. This time, the doorknob stays untouched, but I can hear him breathing.

'I'm so sorry, Flannery,' my father says, soft enough not to wake me if I were asleep. 'I'm sorry.'

I sit stone-still with enough bitterness in me to fill an eternity. A long time later, I stand on heavy shaky legs and take my coat and shoes off. I step out of my bedroom and lift the cup of tea from the floor outside. It is silted and scummed, cold for hours. Downstairs, I pour it into the kitchen sink and place it carefully in the dishwasher. I know that exhaustion will make me sleep, but I dread the dreams.

In the morning, I hear him moving about and I whisper to him.

'Last time I've made you toast and strangled eggs, Sun-shine. You used to do a jokey whinge about my mother abandoning you for me, not taking enough care of you. Well, let's see you make with the coping skills you developed, because you know what? Charm and persuasion ain't legal currency any more.'

Judging by how quickly the front door opens, he's not into making toast for himself. I know he will look up at my window, so I stay put.

'Vrrrm, vrrm, off goes the little poet to work,' I say aloud. 'Leaving "my lovely daughter, Flannery" at home. Resident fucking derelict minding the house.'

That reminds me of my mother, never calling me her daughter. Never wanting me to be introduced as my father's daughter, either. Refusing ever to accept that I was plain. Mam, I think, Flannery isn't doing so well. Off the occasional table into the fire, or something like that. From a certifiable sadist to a purchased cynic. That's some progress. When Lyn rings, I am looking at a request from the Franklin Mint in the US to make a limited edition, eight-inch-high alabaster version of the girl and the angel, to be autographed in gold by my father and sold for $500 apiece. I know by the sound of her that she knows nothing of what happened in this house last night. Or I think I know. She has a new job. Same company, but Controller of their national radio station.

'I thought you'd always shy away from management,' I said, glad for her.

'Piers pushed me,' she says. 'They invited a couple of people to discuss the job with them, and he prepped me. I mean, he really prepped me and I figured if I could survive him, I could survive them.'

'He must be thrilled,' I say.

'I have a bouquet in front of me from himself and Doug,' she says.

'Hope there's some freesias in it.'

'Oh, Flannery.'

I ask her the obligatory questions about where she'll be based and what exactly being Controller means.

'I'll have an office and a PA by the end of the week,' she says, giggling a little at the notion of having her own PA.

'I demand to visit you and be given coffee in dinky little white china cups with a gold band.'

When I come home from the meeting, with luck I *won't* hear a boyfriend and my father discussing me as Today's Mucky Problem.

'OK, but after that you'll have to make your own.'

'Sorry?'

'In your own office, next door to mine.'

'Lyn?'

'I made it a condition of accepting the job that I'd be able to offer you a worthwhile post straight away. Doing whatever each programme needed.'

'In the office all the time?'

'In the office as much as you need to be. Obviously, *I'd* love you to be here all the time so I could pick your brains, but you'd probably have to spend time at home to get the privacy to write.'

'That's true,' I say, trying to control the hopeful excitement rising in me.

'Doug's always saying that.'

Wham, bam, thank you, Ma'am. Once you've walked into one wall, you get the hang of it.

'Lyn.'

'Yes, Flannery?'

'Tell you what. Let's not talk about Doug.'

'OK.'

'No, I don't mean now. I mean ever. Let's never talk about him again.'

'But—'

'Because that way, we can stay best friends.'

'Flannery, I don't know what has happened to make you—'

'– Lyn, if you don't—'

'– feel that way, but—'

'– want me to put the phone down on you—'

'– you're wrong. That's all. It's none of—'

'– I wouldn't say another—'

'– my business—'

'– you're bloody right, it's none of your business—'

'– but you are quite simply wrong. OK. I won't say another thing. How soon will you tell me about taking up the new job?'

'Now. I will.'

'You don't know the terms of the contract.'

'I'm not working for a contract. I'm going to work for my best friend.'

'If I never talk abou—'

'Mmm.'

'Flannery, he's Piers's best friend. It's not going to be possible for me never to mention him.'

'Lyn?'

'Yes.'

'I have faith in your powers of concentration.'

She will tell the others, and Piers will talk to Doug and they can do a happy little circle of sneer and snigger for all I care. Except I know whatever way they put it to Lyn, she will not sneer. Again, the moment I tell myself I know that, I am riven with doubts. What do I know? Less and less with every passing day. My certainties are evaporating like fog in blazing sunshine.

I wander into their room, go to my mother's wardrobe, thinned out now, but still with clothes sweet-smelling of her *l'Air du Temps* perfume. Clothes so specific to a particular moment or day that I have not been able to get rid of them, to give them away to charity. On the chest of drawers, silver-filigree-framed, is the old black and white photograph he borrowed to have a print taken for the cover of his book, knowing the negative was long lost.

I'll not let them cheapen your day of summer sunshine, Mam, I think, and fold flat the triangular thing that makes it stand, at a slight tilt. I'll steal you and hide you, vivid with faith in the future, until those books tatter and tear. Then, the picture will be real again, shorn of associations. Just you and the angel. Oh, Mam . . .

14

It Gets Worse

———◆◆◆———

From that point on, I abandon everything to do with my father. I quit buying groceries, getting cheques from him to pay bills, taking messages. I leave him a note telling him how to access the message minder on the phone and another indicating he's on his own from now on. I send on every invitation to Elaine in his office, and she scrupulously e-mails me, at the beginning of each month, a programme of what my father is booked to do. I stick it up on the wall, simply because if he's in Bosnia next week and a radio programme is looking for him, it's not fair to pass them on to Elaine when I could cut short the transaction and save everybody time. But that's as far as I'm prepared to go.

When I'm driving my car, I do notice he seems to be more on programmes than in the past. I'm not sure whether this is because bookings are picking up, now that he's assumed to be out of the woods of mourning for my mother, or because Elaine is so enthusiastically worshipful of him that radio producers find her easier to deal with than I used to be.

I even get my own accountant. She is a partner in O'Hare Barry and at first meeting frightens me to death. I tell her I'm barely numerate and she takes a deep breath before asking me to imagine I make rubber ducks. I agree to be a rubber duck maker and she explains my finances in bathtub terms. It boils down to me keeping receipts for everything and handing them over. She will keep me out of jail.

The process of disengagement from my father is cold, organised and more efficient than I thought I could ever be. The incandescent rage that arose the day I walked in on the conversation between himself and his computer advisor has mutated into a bitter, bruised resignation which allows me, when we meet in the house, to be as polite as a stranger. He has never, since that first night, referred back to it, nor tried to apologise again.

It helps to have an office to go to, although I have never told him that I have taken on the job Lyn wanted me to do. I leave the house at seven most mornings, picking up lattes (skinny, grande) for myself and Lyn. The two of us kick around ideas in her office for about twenty minutes before other people begin to drift in. At which point I take my business-suited self into the room next door and start the day's work.

Business-suited? Purely in the interests of an item for the mid-morning show, I let a wardrobe expert named Billy Dixon decide what new clothes I should purchase for the job. Women going back to work after spending time at home have shag all confidence, I told Lyn, and would be fascinated to hear about one of their number dressing up for business. How the process feels, what it costs. Even though most women in that situation have been at home to have and rear kids, the thing would work, I say, with growing enthusiasm.

Dixon, a quiet sweet-talking Northerner you'd never guess could kill you with the back of his hand because he's a martial arts champion, persuades me into a series of suits that do not make me look thin, but certainly make me look (and, for some strange reason, feel) competent. The item runs for nearly a week, it gets such a good response and is so easy, logistically. Just put Billy Dixon and/or me at the end of a phone and take updates from us. Not all items are so easy to stretch.

'I had no idea radio was such a consumer of ideas,' I say at an early meeting. I am about to add that I further thought presenters came up with their own ideas, but I think better of it. Even though no presenters attend the editorial meetings, you don't want stuff getting back to them. Each of them is broadcasting to a tiny fragment of the general public, but each of them has as much ego as if their audience share was in millions. One of the afternoon girls has to be gently dissuaded from overt identification with Jill Dando, the Beeb girl who was murdered. The girl with the two-hour slot after lunch, known to a very few listeners by voice only, is fearful her magnetic pull would attract mad stalkers right and left. She should be so lucky, one of the producers snarls. I write a note, and another of the producers laughs.

'So we'll be getting something about stalking from Flannery next week,' he says.

'Just remember I need ten competition quotes,' Raimonde reminds me.

One of Lyn's first recruits, Raimonde has developed into a successful radio producer. Partnered with the presenter with the Jill Dando illusions, her shyness works beautifully, so that she serves as background for the presenter's self-directed effusions. Raimonde is also diligent, so once I come up with the quotations, she will search archives until she gets a tape of whatever famous voice I've suggested. In the beginning, we went through what I now think of as 'first cull' quotes. Oh, the humanity. Jairmany calling, Jairmany calling. I knew Jack Kennedy – you are no Jack Kennedy. Now, however, we have moved on to much more obscure voices and quotations.

'We're due to hit child sex abuse again in a couple of weeks,' Sandra says.

Sandra is the youngest of the producers. She has a masters

degree in communication from some prestigious American university, and is a great believer in systems. One of her systems is an eighteen-month cycle of controversies. Up on the wall behind her is a ferris wheel with eighteen flat bits on it, each of them labelled with a particular problem. Alcoholism, says one. Incest, says the next. If you surface, as a victim of Rape (number 6) just after Sandra has devoted three weeks of broadcast time to it, she will pass you on to some other programme. Or save your name and phone number in her palmtop until the ferris wheel turns to that particular problem again.

A few people throw in their tuppenceworth. Raimonde says worriedly that the whole priests and Christian Brothers thing has been done to death. Sandra agrees, but says she hasn't figured out where to go other than religious orders as likely abusers. Damien suggests revisiting it from another angle. He has heard that the level of depression and demoralisation in the religious orders is very high, because all of them now have men accused but not yet put through due process of law.

'They have to be taken out of active ministry,' he says, revealing himself to be considerably more religious than most of the rest of us around the table – 'active ministry' is not a term that readily springs to the other minds there.

'And?'

'You have these guys sitting around the monastery, doing nothing, depressing the life out of the rest of the guys.'

'Tough shit.'

I make another note: Religious orders now the Jews of Ireland?

'Ah, now, hang on—'

'That,' Sandra says tersely, cutting across the emerging

argument, 'that could go in the Unexpected Victims section, but it doesn't belong in the Child Sex Abuse slot.'

We all survey the bit of the ferris wheel that says Unexpected Victims. Last time around, that section dealt with men who get beaten up by their women. It got so much reaction, other programmes throughout the day wanted to horn in on it. You had the anti-newspaper brigade saying women were always beating up men and knifing them and gassing them, but the newspapers only ran stories about women. You had the bunch who believe Government is to blame for everything, claiming it was outrageous, at a time of economic growth, for Ireland to have refuges for women, only. Lack of refuges for beaten-up male spouses was a clear and present need. And you had feminists yelling that most men outweighed and out-muscled most women, so it didn't matter if the occasional woman took a swipe at an occasional man, the ones who got killed were always women and the killers were always men. I doubt if depressed religious will get quite the same response, but you never know.

'We're very close to a pendulum swing on the religious orders,' I say.

Raimonde gets up and writes *Religious Orders* on a chart headed Pendulum Swing. This is a personal coinage of mine. I've this odd ability to spot when something unpopular is going to swing back into popularity, or when a despised group is due for its image rehabilitation. I often think I'd make a fortune if I went into PR. All I'd have to do is work out which condemned despised group was coming up to its next visit to respectability, go sell that group my services, and then take credit for what had in fact happened naturally.

However, right now, it's much more fun to do what I'm doing, not least because of the free books involved. Publishers send them in the hope of 'mentions'. It's my job to read them, recommend that the author be interviewed or brought into a discussion show, ditch them for use as giveaways ('no, that's not today's mystery number, but we'll be sending you on a scratch card ticket and a copy of Joe Buggins's marvellous novel about cornpone hunting in the deep South') or get ideas out of them.

'I'm reading more books per week than I did in my entire time at college,' I mutter.

'But it's not systematic,' Raimonde worries.

'Shurrup, Ray,' Damien says. 'If Flannery's thought processes ever get systematic we're screwed. It's her eclecticism that's her great strength.'

'Her wha'?'

'Eclecticism.'

'None of that filth around here.'

'Magpie.'

'*What?*'

'Flannery's the station magpie. She'll pursue anything shiny and she has the attention span of a – a—'

'Butterfly,' Lyn says.

'We're getting very ornithological around here.'

'More filth.'

'No, that's anal retentive.'

'What *exactly* is anal retentive, anyway?'

'Ask Flannery. She'll look it up and make an item out of it. Look – she's already making a note of it.'

I am, too. The new producer shows signs of wanting to rise above anal retentiveness. Most new producers, straight out of college, have the urge to raise the intellectual tone of their programme. This guy, already burdened with the first name Brad, is bursting with confidence that he can actually do it.

'There's a thing we should look at,' he says. 'Nobody can be found guilty for something that wasn't deemed criminal at the time of the act.'

Wow, I think, but don't say. There's a conversation-stopper. He never notices the cold dampness to the silence that follows his input. Bit of work to be done on you, fella, says Lyn's expression. First skill a radio producer needs is interpreting silence. Raimonde, perhaps because she's so shy, is particularly good at it. She can calibrate two seconds of dead air like a lab technician doing bloods.

'Think about it,' Brad orders, and I write myself a note – *men instruct groups, women entreat groups* – while he goes on to tell us how this Latin tag relates to General Pinochet and, indeed – he includes Sandra in his discursive sweep – also includes religious accused of child molestation.

'No listener is going to care,' Lyn tells him.

'They can be made to care if it's properly scripted,' he says stiffly.

'They can *understand* it, yes, you're quite right there,' I say. (Thinking, you're the kind of drowner rescuers have to knock unconscious in order to bring them home alive.) 'They don't see it, though. See it in the sense of visualising it. Radio listeners' attention is directly related to how much they visualise the topic under discussion.'

'Who established that?' he wants to know.

I flounder and say nothing coherent.

'Flannery did,' Lyn says.

'No, no,' he says. 'Has there been a scientific study?'

'For fuck's sake, Brad,' Damien says, wearying of all this. 'You don't have to do clinical research in order to come up with basic fairly obvious truths.'

Brad, trying to recover leadership in the group, says his

programme is long overdue some serious controversy. (Dig at previous producer.) He's thinking of taking a really hard look at adoption.

'There isn't any, any more,' Sandra says. 'Most babies get kept. Or aborted. No spares.'

'But the issue is whether it's as good a practice as we've always believed. You know and I know adopted kids from our own generation and, let's be honest, some of them, in spite of really good environments, turn out weird. I believe it's time for a gloves-off look at the genetic element.'

'So adoptive parents would be able to get certs three generations back saying this kid comes from sane clean stock, no syphilis?'

'Why not? No, no—' Brad breasts the unworded tide of opposition rising in front of this one. 'If I'm going to adopt Flannery, it's going to cost me more than a million Euros to get her to adulthood. Plus I'm going to invest twenty years of my life and commitment to raising her. So why are the investigations by the Health Board all one way, setting out to see if *I* measure up? I think I'm entitled to know the kid I'm getting does not come from a long line of schizophrenics.'

Lyn warns the group that the Schizophrenia Association listens and reacts to every programme and to be very careful about inadvertently pejorative use of the diagnostic term. The rest of us think about Brad's point. I know I will go away and research it, but I suspect he won't be allowed to do it. It is not a radio idea whose time has come. Ideas are like people. They are subject to an unacknowledged beauty contest. Babies showing Altruism as Young as Eighteen Months is a beauty contest winner in the ideas department. Racism serving a useful morale and survival purpose is an absolute loser.

Suicide as a ruthlessly selfish way of punishing survivors (*pace* Sylvia Plath) is another no-no.

'Beauty contests,' I write down. Some good talker I know on that one. Shit. Doug. I am tempted to cross out the whole idea, but there will be others to articulate what he said. If I need them.

'D'you know a pendulum item we might do?'

Brad's adoption theme is backburnered by general, if silent, consent. He sulks up a storm. A little, seething ant-hill, he is, over in the corner.

'Why the glass ceiling is justified. Lyn has a friend who does a really good rant on this one, and it would get everybody in the world riled up.'

'What about libel?'

'Slander,' Lyn corrects. 'On radio, it's slander.'

'You can't slander a whole gender,' I say. 'Not that they could sue you.'

'Have to be careful of the Equality Agency, though.'

'Good point. Take out the glass ceiling bit and do it straightforwardly as female pains-in-the-arse in the work-place.'

You can see Brad is dying to suggest me and Lyn as the first examples of the species, but he lacks the courage. Lyn tells the group she knows who I'm talking about, managing to give the impression that this person is someone she meets occasionally throughout the year. Maybe on Poppy Day. I look at her with my head held low and she mouths 'Wow' at me. Will he do it? I ask by raised eyebrow. Oh, you know him, comes back the half-critical, whole-worshipping shrug.

I tune in a couple of days later, driving through the city, expecting to hear Piers, and there, instead of Piers, is Doug rolling all over the presenter of the morning programme, rolling over phone callers, too. Allowing them to use his real name is another surprise. I would have thought he'd be more careful of Amazing Trace's image. Because he's saying some very politically incorrect things. Without naming Piers, he's talking about the guy he shares a house with. And the former girlfriend of the guy he shares the house with.

'She comes into the house we share and first thing she says is she can't bel*ieve* we live in these conditions. Like, there's a few things on the floor. Does she pick up any of them? No. She just clears a space for herself to sit down and does it so we all get the message: she's doing us a favour sharing our polluted airspace. She's used to better than this. OK, this woman's an awful oul' bodget, but women, generally, do that.'

The presenter of the programme says they have a million lights on their switchboard because listeners want to fight with Dougal Rogan, and I reach the car park nearest where I'm going. I turn him off without a qualm.

Twenty-five minutes later, when I get out of the shops and drive off, the programme is still running the same item. Rogan's on a roll.

'There's another girl was in our house recently, and my friend warms up some pizza in the microwave,' I hear him saying. 'Like what else is a microwave for? Nuking kittens? And he offers her some and she doesn't say no, straight up, no complication, the way a man would: thanks but no thanks, she makes a f— makes a big issue out of it. "I can't *believe* you're going to eat that." Does this shudder, "Ooh, you're trying to poison me, I just know," as if we'd be arsed poisoning her. When that doesn't get her the attention she wants, she talks right over the conversation going on at the time. She goes: "How can you eat that stuff?" Dead easy. You put your lips together and chew. I'm thinking if you don't shut up about it, you stupid cow, while I'm having my dinner, you'll be wearing the rest of it. So then of course, she does the "Well, I'm *sorry*" lark you've just heard from that caller. I'm sorry but not sorry. I'd be sorry if I offended you, but you're so crass, so tacky, so utterly, utterly naff, you couldn't possibly be offended, therefore I'm not sorry at all, I'm only saying it for effect to show you how sensitive I am, when of course she's not sensitive at all, because that's another thing girls do, they mix up being touchy with being sensitive. Step on their corns, or even hint they might *have* corns, and they get *so* sensitive, but they can step all over your corns, your eating habits, your taste in clothes, what you read or don't read. Women think they can tell their men when to stop eating or drinking or that they're eating the wrong stuff, but if a man as much as *breathes* about a woman eating like a pig, he's the worst in the world, she has an eating disorder and he's probably caused it to escalate into bulimia or cutting bits off her legs with a razor blade. But a guest in my house, a woman guest, just about a fortnight ago, first of all doesn't bother her arse to do anything helpful like put on the kettle, the very first thing you should do as a guest in anybody's house—'

I must be losing touch. I wouldn't have thought a guest in anybody's house would have the temerity to plug in the host's kettle, unasked. Things must be changing very fast. In current affairs terms, I'm up to date, but you don't get much kettle etiquette from the *breaking news* sites of newspapers. Maybe I've been a recluse too long.

The presenter of the programme thinks all his Christmases have come together. Chairpeople from women's organisations are ringing in, outraged, dying to go toe to toe, head to head with Rogan. Don't, I think. There are some guys you won't win against. Gerry Adams is one. Michael O'Leary is another.

Dougal Rogan's a third. Guys who don't need approval. Whose operations do best on the perverse *dis*approval of reasonable people. Whose obnoxiousness is read as fearless (which it is) and visionary (which it may or may not be.)

There is also the irony factor. We've had so much irony floating around, these last few years, half the people listening to this programme (including me) won't be sure Rogan is really a woman-hating stereo-typer. He could be voicing all this stuff as a form of humour.

The presenter, for one, thinks he's a riot. Rogan's now telling the tale of some other woman who watched him, eagle-eyed, while he salted a tomato sandwich for himself, and then asked him, with heavy sarcasm, if he was having tomato on his salt.

'Oh, *there's* a rollicking laugh for you,' he says. 'Not. She doesn't like the amount of salt I take in a sandwich, she should keep it to herself, or they're going to be picking salt and sandwich out of her out in the street.'

Imagining myself in the control room, I *see* the call-in lights on the console coming on, one after another, red, red, red. Red for angry callers accusing him of being violent towards women, stereotyping women, generalising against all women just because someone who has his best interests at heart talks to him about what the Best International Experts on Food have said about salt. He could serve a continuing purpose on that programme, I think, if he had the time to do that stream of consciousness attack on other unattackable groups. Turn the beauty contest inside out. There is a case, in every generation, for an *agent provocateur* whose function is to get people ratty enough to ring radio programmes for a brisk on-air exchange of prejudices. Radio stations love it because the callers provide content for free. Producers and presenters love it because it gives them the brief illusion of being latter-day Woodward and Bernsteins.

I love it because it takes the pressure off me. Most of the time, on our station, I own the stone that gets the soldiers fighting with each other. My script tosses the subject into the arena, and where the presenter is good, they'll get four days straight out of that one stone. One B-team presenter they put on during holiday breaks is so rigid and formal, he reads one of my scripts, a script which would deliver two or three days' worth of response to any of the other presenters, and it's as if he's delivering an ultimatum. There's a teacherish instruction implicit in it, and of course nobody rings in other than the chronic self-exposers who are the mainstay of any phone-in programme. Consequently, next day the guy needs another script. I make more money when he's on, because I'm freelance, but towards the end of his stint, I can feel panic setting in at the thought of running out of ideas.

The same kind of panic, experienced by producers, seems to lead, as day follows night, to them proposing an item on Celebrities' Children. Brad will probably come up with this soon, because he wasn't on staff the last time someone raised it, with the addendum – inevitable – that 'Flannery and her father would be just great'. I smiled as if I had steel teeth and said they were welcome to contact Edmund Stapleton at any time, Elaine in the college was his minder, here was his extension, but they could absolutely forget having me as part of the package.

'I'm a backroom girl,' I said. 'Research. Script. Never on the air. Never in front of a mike. End of story. No discussion.'

Damien was quite persistent at the time.

'Ed Stapleton gives great quote,' he said.

I wrote down on my pad of Possible Items: Clichés people

think aren't clichés, clichés they think they've invented and make them cool: 'Gives great quote.' I tore it off afterwards, though. That's the sort of item – just like any item about typos or infelicities in newspaper usage – that brings every oul' fellow in the country out pontificating. Pontificating very slowly, because that's the dreadful problem posed for phone-in programmes by old men. They have pet theories and if you dislodge them from a ledge within the theory, or try to hurry them along, they have to go right back to the beginning.

I actually developed a series of qualifying questions the phone operator could ask male callers before putting them on the air. Three questions and you'd know to within two years how old they were. Lyn stopped using the questions after a few weeks, though, because she was scared some whistle-blower within the station would tell a newspaper and it would appear as a strike against 'the generation that put the stripes on the Celtic Tiger'. It had been very handy, though. For the weeks it was in operation, the question system radically improved the broadcasting we were doing.

Of course, I'd never say that aloud. A woman would never get away with the half-joking-whole-in-earnest diatribe Dougal Rogan had just done on the programme. Women invented political correctness to protect themselves. From each other. I wonder if there's an item in that for us?

Funny, I think, as I drive towards our house. Barely six months into working with Lyn's people, I am thinking of them as 'us'. They are a lively argumentative bunch of people, and there's nothing like a good argument for taking your mind off your boring self, your griefs and failures.

I close down, in my mind, the thought that one of them must have taken the five hundred quid in clean ironed notes I had in my handbag this week, ready to put in a card with an apologetic note to Meriel, saying 'Christening Present for the twins'. I'm not going to mention this to Lyn until I hear of other thefts. Maybe someone desperate saw the notes – they weren't even in my wallet – when my bag fell open somewhere, and went for it. And will have been got over their problem by my five hundred.

Doug's Lexus is outside my house when I arrive. Sorry. Dougal's. Increasingly, the captions under his pictures in the paper refer to him as Dougal. If his PR company have advised the name change, they are as dumb as trees. It adds no gravitas and – since *The Magic Roundabout* is running again on Channel 4 – invites a cartoonist to make the association. (They've already made the association with *Father Ted.*) Of course, it could be that the PR company is innocent and the new extended moniker is courtesy of Nicola, who, rumour hath it, becometh more powerful in Amazing Trace every day. Dougal apparently believes in her in a big way. Wants to rescue her from her damaged childhood, the sequelae of. Free her to deliver on her huge potential.

Golly gee, I think when I hear this. I wonder if her father had to ask him to take on the rescuer/knight in shining armour role? Probably not. Nicola's not quite as small as Andrea, but nearly. She's also so slim, some asshole always feels called on to describe her as weighing 100 pounds soaking wet. (You can see the women in the group when this is said, wishing she *was* soaking wet, and with a liquid of their choice and temperature.) I have never encountered Dougal face to face since the day I told him to get out. Either my father has finally accommodated himself to the driving entrepreneur's status as a major force in Irish e-business and stopped using him as if he were a freelance computer techie, or the shifting of my father's administrative work to Elaine in the office has taken the pressure off my father's computer so it requires less intensive care and fewer house calls.

However, as I drive up, there is the Lexus, and because I've drifted slowly to a halt thinking bad thoughts about Nicola, I cannot easily rev up and speed off. I could pretend to have forgotten something, but it would fool nobody. Assuming anybody's watching, which they probably aren't. I gather my briefcase and mobile phone, lock the car and let myself into the house. He's working in the study and continues to work in the study for an hour and a half after I arrive. You think I'm going to go offer you a cup of tea, you have another think coming, I say, making one for myself.

When he surfaces out of the study, he doesn't seem to have realised that there's anybody in the house with him, because he's halfway out of the front door when he sees my car parked outside and stops. Dead. After a second or two, he reverses back into the hall and comes down to the kitchen, where I'm reading the *Evening Herald* at the table. I look up silently. No good morning, good evening, kiss my ass. Blank. Yes? You wanted something? Who *are* you, anyway? Do I know you? Remind me? So many workmen, so little time . . .

No good morning, good evening, kiss my ass from him, either. He holds out two components, or at least I assume them to be components of the computer.

'You can tell your father I have taken these with me,' he says.

'You tell him.'

He seems quite surprised by this, but shrugs. Then tosses a single key on the table.

'I will never need *that* again,' he says. Our front-door key must carry typhoid or worse.

I go back to my paper and hear the front door closing, closely followed by the noise of the Lexus pulling away. I stick the key – glancing at it instinctively to see what's wrong with it – into a drawer filled with spare everything, and forget about it. I leave out a note for my father saying Dougal Rogan took away bits of the computer, but my father seems to have abandoned the computer. I never see him work on it again, and since I no longer go near it any more, the thing could have gone extinct, for all I know.

My father goes away for something like six weeks, so you'd think, facing into the autumn term, he'd be rested and rarin' to go. But whenever I see him, he looks worried. Towards the end of October, just in case it's the computer that has him worried, I ask him if he needs replacements for the bits that Dougal from Amazing Trace took out of it. He acknowledges what I have said, but it seems to confirm his worry, rather than ameliorate it. What would my mother want me to do in this situation? Be kind. Make nice.

'You seem worried about something,' I say. 'Is there anything I can do to help?'

It comes out sounding more severe than I intended, but I'm still wrong-footed by the reaction. His eyes fill up with tears and he makes no attempt to conceal from me how fraught he is. No, no, no, he says. Very kind, he says. He has to address this himself, nothing I can help with, very good of me, very good, no, no, no. He does ask me to type up and print out a couple of letters resigning from charities he's been Patron of or on the Board of for a while and then irritates me by photo-copying them on the fax machine, which never produces good clean copies even for filing. It was ever thus, though. Whenever he wanted to show his independence of my mother or me, he would choose something at which he was demonstrably less than competent. I always thought it was a passive-aggressive way of making us pay more attention to him, even if he was letting on he didn't need us.

Because of my track record of missing the significance of the major events in my life, in trying to figure his bothered unhappy look, I add two and two together and get a satisfactory four in the shape of my mother's upcoming anniversary. I indicate I will be helpful about any reminder things he wants to do in December, because that's an older generation thing, but although he thanks me, he never goes back to it, and so Christmas Eve passes with me going to the graveyard on my own. He probably goes at some other time.

Christmas is awful. For the first time it hits me how essential work and routine and all the boring bullshit of non-festive time is. There's a lot to be said for the trivial. I'm listening to our own programmes with clergymen going on and on about the crass commercialisation of Christmas and wishing I had a few people to be more crass and commercial about. The New Year, I decide, is when I take hold of my life. The New Year is when everything is going to straighten out.

The first is reasonably accurate. The second wins the prize for lousiest prediction of all time.

15

Always Start With the Good News

———◆•◆———

Whenever I imagine myself telling anybody else about it, I find myself doing the 'D'you want the good news or the bad news?' routine.

Because the good news is me delivering. First time in my life I sit down on New Year's Eve, all on my own in the house because my father is away at some party. I have, of course, been invited to several parties myself, including a double-celebration 'do' to welcome Meriel's twins as well as the first year they'll face into. I haven't refused any invitation. For the most part, I've portrayed myself as a social butterfly, in demand everywhere, who might just touch down at their particular party briefly during the last evening of the year. I do this while sending myself up just enough for them not to get offended by my wild social life, of which I have none, or my suspicion that they are trying to set me up with someone, which is always the case, even if it's subconscious on the part of the setter-up.

I make drinking chocolate, using half cream, half milk. Now *there's* a last indulgence before rigor sets in. It is a last indulgence after a take-out last meal for the about to be electrocuted. Item for the programme: How, because the ones they execute in the United States are always working class, their last meal of choice tends to be hamburgers and fries. In fact (I think, going to my ever-present programme pad) this

211

would make a competition. If someone famous were to be granted a last meal, what would they/should they eat? I will give the presenter a paragraph suggesting that Victoria 'Posh' Beckham's last meal might be crisps and an apple, since she says she eats crisps all day.

At half ten on New Year's Eve, I've had chips (two biggies), scampi, frozen key lime pie and am sprinkling tiny marshmallows on the top of my drinking chocolate. Across the top of the page of a separate pad bought for the purpose, I print:

THIS COMING YEAR, I WILL:
(1) Take out a year's membership in a gym.

Who do you think you're kidding, I ask myself, when I see this. So I add another one.

(2) Do a serious workout in the gym at least five times a week.
(3) Not eat biscuits, cake, sweets, chips, crisps except during one hour on Sunday.

A lot of thought led up to that one, and there had been some action, too. In September, stricken by some mad back-to-school need to improve myself, I'd gone back on the Atkins Diet, allowing myself time off on Sundays. Of course, any time I went out to dinner on Saturday, I had to break it a bit, and in no time I found myself semi-deliberately arranging Saturday lunches and the occasional breakfast meeting. You might as well be hung for a sheep as a ball of wool, you know? In no time at all, half of Friday got eroded, too, because it was nearly the weekend, and where Friday goes, Thursday aches to follow. It got that only Monday really worked and that by

Wednesday, not only was the diet buggered, but I was eating more mid-week to make up for the misery of Monday than I would have eaten in a normal week.

Atkins' thesis would have aspirants wanting to kick sugar/ cake/biscuits/truffle chocolates completely succeed by kicking them completely, the theory being that your sugar/cake/ biscuits/truffle chocolates taste buds wither and your cravings for the same die off if you keep away from those foods rigidly for several weeks. Not sure I believe it. If that were true, then staying off sex for nearly a year would mean you could take it or leave it in the bonking department and I am the horrible example to prove it ain't so, folks, it just ain't so. In that twilight zone before and after sleep, I am troubled (or pleasured, depending on how positively you look at it) by fantasies of serious committed sex. I cannot seem to disentangle Doug (sorry, Nicola, Dougal, and how's Father Ted doing?) from these exigent semi-experiences, even when I pour hatred all over my imagined Doug like salt on a slug.

Not that I have ever either poured salt on a slug or drowned snails in beer. I will give a wasp or a bluebottle a quick come-uppance, but the torturous and tortuous methods of pest removal appal me. Which is why, this autumn, my mother's wonderful front and back gardens looked like they'd been flittered by a low-flying Super Fortress with a sawn-off shotgun. Scattershot holes everywhere. Chantilly vegetation. The slugs and snails had a feast such as they never had before, and greenfly (the only living entity I ever heard called a wanker by my mother) went orgiastic, leaving their disgusting foam contrivances everywhere. I got a lot of items for the programme out of this: Where to Buy a Gross of Ladybirds (greenfly for the eating of). Whether Beer is all that Humane for Slugs. How We could Eat the Slugs we Find, don't the French?

My father did not seem to notice that the tropical rainforest was breaking out, front and back of his home, so when the lettuces got as tall as four feet, I telephoned a company in the *Yellow Pages* and hired them. They started by spraying everything with a herbicide somewhere between sulphuric acid and Agent Orange. The four-foot lettuces melted like candles into suppurating puddles of putrefaction that smelt like a medieval midden.

Unfortunately, there was a reasonably high wind the day the gardening company did the spraying, so the excess sulphuric acid blew over the wall and putrefied our next-door neighbour's perfectly healthy little round lettuces. He was very civilised about it, but when his apple tree turned nasty the following week, he took it very amiss. Apple trees are very precious to their owners. There's something about the life cycle of the apple tree that gives its owner a sense of being in harmony with life, the universe and the seasons. When our neighbour came to the front door to protest, he was so agitated, you could tell he was dying to say that my mother had been the only decent human being in our house, and I was dying to tell him he was right, so we had this kind of frustrated shared and opposed misery on the doorstep and I promised him it was a once-off. Yeah, he said, like bubonic plague.

This gave me a neat item for the radio station. We threw out a question about travellers picking up bubonic plague and all sorts of people came forward with their stories of the places where it still lurks, ready to hitch a ride with any obliging rat and do another lap of honour around Europe. Not only did we get a week out of it, but it linked neatly to a historian who had published a book about the witch craze and said the plague led to it . . .

I did consider, for a while, learning to garden, but I decided against it. I couldn't live with myself if I managed to kill off my mother's beautiful bluebells, clustered so modestly in shady crevices in the rockery. As well as that, every time I took her gardening tools in my hands, I could see them in her strong hands and it would lump my throat because then I would hear her, humming softly to herself on long summer afternoons as she did that combination of ruthless cutting and gentle supporting good gardeners do.

The gardening company drew up a plan and were hired for the year. They got shirty with me towards the end of the second quarter, because they said they hadn't been paid, when I assumed Elaine would have put a standing order in position, but when I queried it with my father, he said she wasn't doing that for him any more, he had someone different, and he was sorry, to give it to him and he would take care of it. Although he must have taken care of it, because the gardening company got on with the job without any further financial whinges, he failed to take care of either the phone bill or the ESB.

The radio station pays for the ISDN line into my computer, and I use my mobile phone most of the time, so, since I was in contact with everybody in my own circle by phone and e-mail, it may have been out of commission for several weeks before I found out about it. My father behaved very oddly. Said landlines were a thing of the past and he was going to let it lapse. I never heard of a phone line lapsing. I've heard of them being ripped out of the wall by burglars, but *lapsing*? Since my father had already taken the number out of the telephone directory and gone ex-directory, it might have been symptomatic of a desire for greater privacy and reclusiveness, except that most people nowadays reached him on his mobile or in college anyway. Maybe, I decided, he had a point. Renaissance Man upgrades thinking to twenty-first century.

The ESB was, he said, a straightforward cock-up. Genetic traces of my mother prompted me to say that it was an extremely *un*straightforward cock-up, given that the ESB send a series of increasingly urgent reminders and warnings before they cut you off and that each of this sequence of bills must have been ignored over a considerable period of time. I didn't say it, though. Nor did I point out that for the ESB to cut off someone with my father's PR potential was extraordinary. Negative PR potential, I mean. If Edmund Stapleton, widower, were arbitrarily cut off by the ESB, it would make a good victim story with picture. But my father was not minded to blame the ESB, so I cleaned out the freezer, which had defrosted during the time the house had no electrical supply, and asked him if he wanted me to bulk buy anything for him to re-stock it with. He was surprisingly vehement in his rejection of this offer, so I thought frig it, I don't use the bloody thing anyway, so the hell with it. I unplugged it, shoved a box of baking soda into it to stop it mildewing, and forgot we ever had a freezer.

I did have a moment of sadness as I retreated out of the utility room, remembering my mother's habit of storing washed and dried clothes in the freezer until she had time to iron them. It was one way to prevent mildew spots on cotton, but it was unnerving, every now and again, to go to the chest freezer and discover, spread-eagled across the top of it, what looked like half a stiff murder victim, until you worked out the agonised rigid arms belonged to a bundle of shirts frozen hard as iron. Now, my father's shirts get taken to the laundry by the cleaning lady, and he always has a crease across his chest from the way they fold them.

Filling in my New Year resolutions, I briefly consider factoring the freezer into them. I could start using it again, or give it to charity or sell it. I lose interest in it very quickly. You can get absorbed in a chair or fond of a rug, but I've never met anyone who has a relationship with their freezer. So I go back to resolutions I figure will change my life in small but significant ways.

(4) Shift all Edmund Stapleton work elsewhere.

As soon as I have that written, I realise I have already done it. The problem is the ESB and telephone debacle indicate Elaine isn't on that part of the job. I don't know if the replacement is simply an accountant or bookkeeper responsible only for paying bills on time and keeping my father out of debtor's prison, in which case they would hardly be competent for the good-humoured negotiation involved in scheduling him and making sure people anthologising his work paid him the right amount. That shakes me slightly. If Elaine is no longer on the bills-and-payments routine, is she also off the scheduling routine? In which case, who has replaced her? It is quite possible the old landline has been getting calls from hacks and programme researchers who don't know it's dead, in which case my father may have missed a lot of opportunities. I wouldn't even be aware of how much media he has done in the last while. I'd better, I decide, leave a note for him asking for a lengthy meeting where we can get all this squared away.

(5) ?

There is nothing but chocolate grit and half-melted marshmallows in the bottom of the drinking chocolate mug. I spoon out the combination, which is tastier than you might expect, and wonder why it is we feel New Year resolutions must be handwritten. Taking pen in hand makes them more real, more permanent, more memorable than if we simply inputted them. (Programme Idea: How Writing is Still More Precious to do and Receive than Txt msgs or e-mails.)

I should, I decide, make a couple of resolutions to improve my dealings with other people. Lyn spends at least a third of every day rescuing, stroking, minding people. A feature about Dougal Rogan (see, I'm trying, Nicola. I hardly ever call him Doug any more. I mean, *Doug* for a captain of industry . . .) mentioned recently that he had a reputation as a people-rescuer. Prompted or unprompted, I thought when I read that. And do the people being rescued get a choice? Or are they allowed to half fall in love with the rescuer before all is revealed and they learn they are the equivalent of the dummy on which the rescuer might rehearse CPR?

This is not getting me any further with resolution number five, and we're coming up on eleven o'clock. New Year resolutions probably don't apply or work out if they're made any later than midnight on New Year's Eve. They probably fall off, like Cinderella's slipper.

No matter how strong a resolution I make, I'm not going to attract people who need rescue. I say this aloud and immediately question it. Of course I could. If I wanted. Do I want to be a rescuer? Not terribly. I'm prepared to extend a hand over the cliff and haul someone up rather than let them plummet ninety feet to their death on the rocks, but I don't want effing Robinson Crusoe squatting in the spare bedroom, and I sure as hell have no interest in importing Good Friday or whoever that other wanker was. Even if he has refugee status.

I am lonely, I write on the good resolution paper. I cross it out straight away, but I am. If I believed in a religion, this is the time of year, the *precise*, coming up to midnight, last day time of the year, when I would pray to my mother and ask her to help me get happy and productive and contributory. OK, then, get me loved. When we become teenagers, we become contemptuous and dismissive of parental love, but take it away and fail to replace it with anything else, and the prospect sickens. I am unloved and unloving and unlovable, I write. Once written, it invites erasure, but I work the pen over the letters again and again until it is a loud emphasised confession.

I have no idea what resolution will solve that problem, but that's the only resolution worth making, I know, as the fireworks begin and singing seeps out from a party a few doors down.

Just before midnight, I write number five: *I will stop just suiting myself*. Then get parsy-prissy and rewrite it as *I will stop suiting just myself*.

May not look like a life-changer, but it's working as a life-changer for me. I made a list of all the important people in my life, including my father (meddling old fool but well-meaning), Doug (frig off, Nicola, I've lost interest in the whole Dougal-for-gravitas lark), Lyn, the radio station team, Les Girls and my mother. Then I put it up to myself: if each of these people were to say 'It would be really great if Flannery did X,' what would X be?

The end result is I sicken my arse, I'm so positive. Pollyanna was a manic depressive lump of stolid passivity compared to me. I spent all my savings, first of all on a holiday with Lyn and I never said one whingey thing about anything, secondly on a complete new wardrobe, having dropped twenty pounds. I'm going to lose ten more, but in the interim I put the fat clothes in the Cerebral Palsy bin, in order to leave me no chance of going back up to my original weight.

I'm going to move back in with Lyn because, contrary to all

expectations and a whole hell of a lot of the rumours, she *isn't* living with Piers, although the word is they are very much an item. The change of domicile will happen after I have the big meeting with my father. I don't want to abandon him in a house all on his own without giving him some time to adjust. Not that he will need time to adjust. There's been so little contact between us in the last few months we're not even ships that pass in the night. We're lighthouses seeing each other's beam circling, without any direct reference to each other.

But even in advance of the good influence Lyn will bring to bear on me (when I go to live with her) I am already being a Better Person. I am telephoning friends, taking the initiative, I'm going to finish my thesis and if I meet Doug, which, in the course of things in an awful small city like Dublin is quite likely, in fact it's a bloody miracle it hasn't happened up to now, I will be charming to him, because he was only doing what an older authority figure (my father) told him he should do, and he only did it because he thought it would be fun for me, and it was fun for me and anyway, he was probably trying to dislodge me from an unstimulating dependency on my father which life and Lyn have now dislodged me from anyway. He has moved on and I have moved on, and that's in some ways a great pity, because I grew to be as easy with him as a brother (although, in fairness, the night we had together wasn't in any way brotherly, thanksbetoJasus), but feckit, that's life.

Strangely, when I start softening towards my father, and asking him to put aside time for a good meeting about a wide range of things, he looks as anxious and bothered as if I was in some way threatening him. It's so pronounced, this discomfiture, that I back off a bit. There's no rush, after all, to move into Lyn's. I can transfer some of my belongings without making a big deal of it, so that when I finally move out, it isn't a major performance involving a big furniture removal lorry.

I do notice, though, that he is missing little bits of his chin when shaving – something Doug once said was a classic sign of someone ageing fast. But it's more than that, with my father. It's not that he is vain. He has always been able to send himself up when words like handsome come up. (Although the capacity to send oneself up does not necessarily prove one is vanity-free, now that I think of it.) It's that his good looks, his Robertson Davies scholarly theatricality, are part of the product, the branding that is Edmund Stapleton, and failure to look after that asset, while understandable in a less consciously commercial poet, is worrying in him. It makes him look older than he is. No, that's not true. What is ageing him is the look of constant anxiety he now has. My mother used to have that look, I remember, until real illness happened, real disaster struck. But with Mam, it was a kind of low-grade constant watchfulness, whereas my father looks hunted. Urgently. Continually.

I am so saddened by it that I begin to leave more notes out for him, occasionally to cook something and leave it for him to eat, because it appears that he is slowly but surely losing weight. He does, however, appear to have developed a genius for wrecking my reach-out policy towards him. He will eat only the smallest bit of an old favourite dish, then leave a note saying he is most grateful; however, he doesn't have the time for warming up food in the evening (four minutes in the microwave is *such* a chunk out of one's lifespan, I mentally retort). Similarly, when I left a quite funny note for him the night the cops came around, the response the next morning was a scribble at the end of my note – as if even finding a fresh bit of paper was too onerous – that gave me no information whatever and, if the gardai had come around again that night, would have left me, if not obstructing them in the course of whatever duty they were coursing towards, at least not being a good actively helpful citizen.

The gardai came around only that once, though, so I filed their visit in the same slot as the ESB: some form my father must have failed to complete. I did want to be a helpful citizen, if only out of relief when I found that the guards weren't looking for me. Innocent until proven guilty is a great principle, and I hope one day to be able to apply it to myself. Until that day, I'm guilty as charged, from the moment the navy blue shape of a police officer appears within two hundred yards of me. Hell, I'm guilty as *un*charged.

I qualify, in my own mind, as a usual suspect, and feel both relieved and guilty when the officer walks on by. You missed me, I want to yell after him, in the belief that if he finds out later I was there all the time and failed to deliver myself into custody, I'll get life without possibility of parole. Or worse, I'll get community service for a hundred years and have to mop up puke or dig out dandelions. Or be nice to friggers. Or have to stand up in front of school kids and tell them the mistakes of my life that brought me to this awful point. It would be an awful point, too. An audience of purpose-built serial killers specialising in speedy throat-slashing is a doddle compared to an audience of thirteen- and fourteen-year-olds. They are so knowing, contemptuous and cool, they make you want to do away with yourself rather than be subjected to the waves of sniggers disenfranchising you from the body of the hall.

Modern thinking on criminality posits that punishment and terror are not great motivators, but they work a treat for me. Nobody is ever going to have to put me through one of those programmes where hardened criminals show you how they got hardened and why gang rape when doing porridge still has its drawbacks. I don't fiddle my taxes (or my father's taxes), I don't send threatening letters to people (although I've thought about the odd obscure nasty to Nicola), I don't drink and drive (and avoidance of that particular crime led me to a great evening in Doug's), all because I am so terrified of getting on the wrong side of the blue serge arm of the law. The year my mother died, a small background worry in my mind was that the graveyard where my father took the picture of her alongside the angel could possibly claim invasion of privacy of the dead or something even more obscure. Photographic necrophilia. Or that the family who'd put the statue over one of their members might sue us for a share of the royalties generated by the book.

When my father fails to share whatever it was the gardai were visiting about, I quite understand it. He must want to forget about it as quickly as possible, if he feels about them anything along the lines of the way I feel about them. Indeed, his embarrassment must be complicated if they wanted to query him about something as petty, but nevertheless as mortifying to a well-known and very middle-class man, as the ESB cutting off the power. Having the gardai call to your home about an unpaid bill would shrivel my father. Not while they were present. He would be charming to them. Respectful. Self-derogatory. He would seek their guidance on how best to rectify whatever was the egregious cock-up he had committed. (Mixing slightly posh words with very slangy ones is a habit of his to simultaneously distance and embrace non-scholars.) He would mention meeting the Commissioner at some public function, but link the claim with a question seeking their view on the Commissioner. When the meeting was over, he would walk them, not just to the door, but to their car, so the neighbours would see the good terms he was on with them.

I had the entire scenario worked out in every detail. And I couldn't have been more wrong if I'd tried.

16

And Now for the Bad News

———◆◆◆———

Although I've never worked up to getting rid of the car my mother used to drive, and although I still take it around the block in order to make sure its battery doesn't die, I haven't looked after its tax or licence, and the week after the garda visit, I add that issue to the list I must talk to my father about. Of course, because he doesn't drive, there's never a car in the driveway serving as a clue to whether he's in the house or not. Usually, the first sign is music, because he always puts on music when he's at home.

This evening, though, there is no music, despite the fact – as I find out later – that he had been in the house for quite a long time before I arrive. I am in high good humour. Lyn has asked me to have a meeting with herself and Doug about a programme idea he has, and – after the initial jolt, the first wild urge to run and hide – I am proud of the casual willingness I have been able to muster up to deal with that proposal.

She's going to set it up in the next few days. She also quietly let me know, did Lyn the Protector, that Nicola has moved into Doug's house. Or rather, that Doug has moved to a massive old country house and Nicola is sharing it with him. I'm not sure why Lyn makes this distinction, except perhaps as a basis for telling me Piers has bought Doug's old house, but I truthfully tell her I don't care if Doug shares his rural mansion with Nicola, a herd of bison and six Rottweilers.

Although, I add, with Nicola around, would he need the Rottweilers? I don't even get bad-tempered when Lyn says Piers agrees with me, nodding gravely as she offers it. So my view of Nicola as a half-mad crook is now validated because Piers agrees with it? Forgive me if my orgasms at this validation are less than multiple.

Having survived these challenges to equilibrium, I am doubly satisfied with myself because I haven't broken my diet. I am so full of fizzy mineral water, if someone stuck a pin in me, I would spray them, but calories? Not a one. I see a note from my father with my name printed on the envelope, but because there is an envelope, in contrast to the folded-over sheets he usually leaves, my name scribbled on one of the folded sides, it's fair to assume there's a cheque in it for someone, maybe the cleaning lady, that he wants me to process. It's not accurate to assume this, as I later find out, but it's surely fair, based on the information available to me at the time.

Because of that fair assumption, I say 'Feckit, I'll go to the gym,' and do. When I come back home, I have a long shower, already longing for the shower over in Lyn's, which has a pump plus good water pressure. It can beat you into good and productive form even if you are coated and subdued by the mother of all hangovers. I will not cease to miss my mother if I move out of her house, I think, but maybe distance will take the raw edges off the loss.

Lyn gave me a pink coat-like chenille gown at Christmas. One of those safe Christmas presents although, to give her her due, it wasn't a one-size-fits-all, but a Medium, which was flattering. It now fits me comfortably, and I admire myself in the mirror on the bathroom door. Passing the hall table, I tuck the post into one of the big patch pockets, and when I have camomile tea brewed (calming influence preferred over caffeine, this hour of the evening, and no calories) I haul out the letters in a bunch that spews in no particular order over the table.

Which is why I take them in no particular order, stacking them as they resolve themselves into different issues. I am good at this, I think. In many ways I am a slob, but underneath the slob, in my mindset, is a neatnik. I crumple the envelopes and stuff them in the patch pockets, because the garbage container in the kitchen is one of those where you have to step on a pedal for it to open. When I reach my father's note, I slide it out, crush the envelope, and – sharp double-jobber, multi-skiller, me – wash my mug and clutch-cluster the crumpled envelopes out of both gown pockets into the rubbish container on the same journey.

The table, accordingly, is clean and clear and orderly when I address my father's note. No cheque shows when I open the single sheet of his distinctive high fabric paper.

My dear Flannery

it says. No comma. Half-printed, half written. Not his usual style.

Please telephone the Garda Siochana.
I am sorry. But I have no choice.

Please do not blame Dougal.

Your loving father

And then his signature. Not Dad, as he would normally sign a note to me. Edmund Stapleton.

My forehead's wrinkling with puzzlement, my mouth curling up with amusement: think I don't know your surname, Da? But something is settling around me, clammy, inescapable. The *Garda Siochana*? As in the police? Why ever—?

This is a suicide note. Now I know. A suicide note. I am to get the police because he is dead. Has killed himself. Somewhere. Somewhere in the house. But I have been all over the house, casually, carelessly, over the past three hours. I have not been in his study, though. I walk across to it. The door is open, the blind black face of the computer screen as dead as it has been for weeks, no speck-lights on the front of the server.

I have not been in his bedroom, either. Their bedroom. I climb the stairs slowly, trying to prepare myself, knowing at the same time that pain cannot be prepared for, disbelieving it all the time. I'm missing something here, misinterpreting something, adding two and two and getting eleven. The door is closed and I lean my forehead against the dry cracked varnish of it before I open it and go in. The bed is rumpled, but the room looks as tranquilly ordinary as it always does.

Downstairs again, I re-read the letter, stifling the urge to ring Doug and ask for help. *Don't blame Doug?* Does he mean don't continue to blame Doug for taking me to the wedding at my father's request?

Maybe I should ring the cops, I think, before I do anything else. Except that when it comes to doing anything physical, my father is so inept that I might call them out only to find the note signified something completely different and blatantly obvious. That I have greatly embarrassed my father, who, in recent weeks, has looked so brittle, he might not withstand another talk with the gardai. But is this note, this instruction, this situation, related at all to the garda visit earlier? And if so, why has he not left me the name and rank and telephone

228

number of the specific members of the force who might have a clue as to what I'm talking about, if I ring them?

I go into the sitting room, so little used since my mother died it has gradually taken on a shrine-like appearance, the furniture looking old-fashioned and fusty-bright, dust-motes dancing in the disturbed air as I walk through it. I find myself looking behind the couch and laughing awkwardly, the laugh running dry in the hollow silence of the empty, unoccupied, unvisited room with its trophies from my swimming days and the photograph of me in my deb's gown. Like now, I was thinner than usual: in time for my deb's ball. I look at the picture and wonder at how pretty I was, when, at the time, I was quite sure I had to be the worst dog in the ballroom. I can't remember the name of the tuxedo'd boy beside me in the picture. But I do remember his witticism of the night, produced after countless Bacardi and Cokes.

'Fat girls give the best blow jobs.'

I laughed with the rest because I didn't see I had an alternative. I stood there in my Prussian Blue raw silk off-the-shoulder gown and hoped they didn't think he was talking about me, but hoped even more that they were well enough tore not to remember that it was my escort who made that crack, and knew the girls would remember it and wonder about it, just as I would remember it this long afterwards, when I have forgotten his name. It must be ten years. A lifetime.

I have tried all the rooms in the house, even opening closet doors, half-expecting, because it is the story of my life, a jokey figure to come leaping out, arms a-flail, yelling 'Fooldya'. I want to whimper to the goblins in the growing evening shadows: you don't have to do this to me, I know I'm fooled, don't make my heart stand in shock, pins and needles prickle down my arm with fright by letting him leap out at me, large as life and twice as frightening, not that I want him dead, please let him not be dead, I know he's not dead, this is me, I know, misreading the letter and we will laugh afterwards about it, maybe this is what I need to break the freeze in the relationship, just the thing, the very Eye Tee (mother's phrase), work a treat, see you right, O Jesus Sacred Heart preserve us, don't let this have happened, please. Just, please.

The garage I haven't been into in a month and a half. Revving up an unused car about six weeks ago, became one of those onerous routine tasks that suddenly makes your teeth grind. I've been in hock to that goddam battery long enough, I thought, and abandoned the duty. As I step towards the garage, I suddenly think of the painkillers and the sleeping pills stocked up to ease my mother's death and never required, because death overwhelmed my mother, aided by hospital morphine, in an ugly sop-mouthed coercion that left her no time for Victorian gathering around the bed and sweet talk of past times, but swamped her into sleep and slower breathing and glazed eyes opening reddish in response to pain before the next instalment of oblivion and then nothing, gone, full stop, end of her story.

If she told him she was dying, she must have sat with him and told him many things, perhaps including the half-made plans of her and me, the hoarded tablets and capsules, more in each container than the number on the outside, held so carefully in readiness, then thrown with two plasticky concussion noises into a drawer in my bedroom. If he knew I had them, he would know I have them. It is not my style to do the proper thing, to flush them down the toilet, checking afterwards that all have gone through the tubes, the filters, the sanitation systems out to the open sea to slow down passing sharks and stupefy sole to the bone. He would know.

My mother would have known precisely which drawer I'd throw them into, but he would know me enough to figure it out. And it would be his kind of death. Gentle, allowing him to drape himself, his hands hanging from the strong-boned wrists. Jesus, I shake my head like a dog drying itself, this can't be true. I climb the stairs again, and go to the drawer wherein I secreted them, and there they are, the two brown plastic tubes with their childproof lids and their contents packed so tightly, so much more in each than should be that there isn't even a rattle when I lift them. None removed. I put them back carefully.

The lengthening evening is now dark and dusky, the street-lights coming on, yellowy in the initial minutes, turning to a whiter, brighter glare later, sharp against a darkening night sky. I go downstairs and count the number of steps to the door leading to the garage, hoping it may be locked.

He has carried me, easy and sure-footed, on the slip-slidey pebble beach my four-year-old feet shrink from, carried me high on his shoulders, my hands in his shining hair, trying not to grasp but gripping hard when he seems to tilt or slip. No reproach from him, just laughter and the assurance that he'll not let me fall, never let me fall, never will, never would. Then he slides me into a basalt seat, smoothed and scooped, like a saddle in the rock. Goes slant-walking among the shifting scraping pebbles, the white, the navy, the rust-marbled grey round stones to find the flat ones, sheared by centuries of sand, of sea. Stands at the edge of the incoming water, silhouetted against the oblique rays of the evening sun, everything around him silvered, slivered, him bending at the hip, soft fluid set up for the throw, the skimming, sea-striking path of splash and skim, splash and skip, three, four times before it drops below the surface and he swings around for my smile, eyes bulged and bursting, blood spilt, tongue ruptured twice, three times normal, mouth skinned back from the bulging purple out and hanging, drying.

He has found shells for me, at five or six, I could never find. Great perfect scallop shells cleaned to pearl polish inside, rough ribs fanned from a tinier fan at the bottom, on the back. Tiny closed clam shells. Mussels in navy armour, in school uniform, threat-filled, sharp-mouthed. And the great cockle shell, perfect from its tight tulip bud pointed end, evolving, spinning round and out into the great loop filled with smoothness, interior disappearing beyond where the eye can trace its secrets, more secrets, he tells me, in the sea forever trapped in sound inside it, listen, sweetheart, listen to the sea, the ocean, do you hear the waves, puzzling when I hear only my own heartbeat, trying it, head tucked against the wind, turned away from me, tilted, turning back, *creak, creak*, tilted stiff by the long loop of rope dragged against the neck skin, neck tendons, crushing the neck bone, stiff-bending the head to one side, listening, listening, always listening. Listening to an eternity of nothing.

He has held the two-wheeler upright when my wobbles would bring it down, running alongside me: pedal, honey, you can't fall, Daddy won't let you fall, never let you fall, never would. The gentle long fingers tight, strong, the adult balance holding me firm, enough flex in him to sense when I hit that moment of steadiness that unkinks my breathing and powers me with the sense of this is what it is, this is how it works, this is cycling, freewheeling, no more trainer wheels. The hands of him letting go, but near enough still, letting go, turning livid grey, old, now, agonied, now, splinters from the rope driven into the palms and under the nails, the nails, so cared for, broken, hanging down, hanging empty, helpless, lifeless, but no resignation or peace in them, no balance. The fingerprints readable in sharp and shadow on the creaking backswing, speared by rope splinters.

He has hunkered down, bony knees to either side of me, to let me admire the silver chain they have put over his shoulders to tell the world how valued he is, then climbed back to the platform, the eye-level platform from where my mother and I sit, proud of the soft drape of his silk shirt, the slender waist of him, the gathered folds of ironed trousers, the shirt now dragged one-sided from the waistband, the fabric wrinkled, old stains, and as he turns, the voiding absorbed and marked, dark wetness in the front and down a leg, and then the back, still-damp stinking stains coming through and down the skin to sock and shoe.

As long as I live, every picture of my father, every image of him, every memory will carry the horror of his hanging so there will be no more good memories of him, even in sleep. Never, no more . . .

17

Concealing the Truth

It was not in character to do it this way, and that's the impossibility of understanding it, at first. My father was a man for the easy option, so if he were to commit suicide, he would have taken the sleeping pills and lain down, arms by his side, sarcophagus-fashion, his face upturned, age smoothed out of it by gravity, hair waving towards the surrounding and supporting pillow. Or he would have seated himself in the car in the garage, sleeping his way out of life without effort, body-memory habituated to the car seat.

I am so sure of this that when I can pull my gaze away from the horror in front, above, I look to the car half expecting to see a hose threaded from exhaust to window-slit. There is no evidence he tried the carbon monoxide route. Perhaps I prevented that by not keeping the car battery charged. Or perhaps he didn't know where the hose is kept. Or was not sure he could do it. Researching radio items puts you on top of all such details.

The creaking half-movement continues, and the idiot irrelevances of undisciplined curiosity compete with the horrified anguish – is my father's body a pendulum, continuing to echo the great thrashing swings after the drop, when his fingers impotently sought purchase on the rope around his neck (rope splinters testify to it), his feet walked in the air, climbed, clamouring for anything to take the weight off the noose squeezing the life out of him, but slowly, slowly, because there was no hangman's efficiency here, no snapped vertebra short-circuiting consciousness. This was suffocation, strangling, lungs bursting with the last deep breath for courage, bottled, boiling bloody in him, starbursts in the brain, thought-prayers, primeval in their broken-throated plea for mercy to that grim presence black, unsighted and not there, the prayers for rescue melting into prayers desperate for death, the rope-sound loud close to the ears, the convulsions dragging down the hands, but adding to the weight, the infinite deadweight of a slim man still alive and knowing it, full knowledge of the unimaginable agony, that consciousness surviving every other humanness in him, surviving him in eternal punishment.

Nothing could be more horrific than what is in front of me, but I am afraid to go back into the house, afraid of pursuit, afraid this will worsen if I leave it, afraid to turn off the single-bulb light, hanging, hairy with dust and cobwebs, yet afraid to close the door on a lighted horror.

I try out, in advance, the things people will say about him. That he is at peace, now, anyway, except that this coldly purpled hanging thing is not at peace. It is not even inert, but turning, turning. Turning at the end of such an old, thick rope. Who would have thought the old rafter to have so much strength in it?

I am cold. I am standing here so long, there is no feeling in my legs below the knee. I back away until a crate is behind me. Old exam papers or receipts. I sit awkwardly. I must think. I must plan. I must get rid of the note. I must get rid of the envelope it came in. Why? Is it because I do not understand what the note is telling me? I do not understand, true, but do I believe the reference to Doug Rogan means the man hanged him, here, my father, dragged him to a lynch-death in our garage? No, I do not believe that. Who, exactly, do I protect by hiding the note, because I know I will not destroy it. That understanding clicks in like a falling domino: you will not destroy it because it is evidence of some kind, evidence to be used against Rogan, because Rogan's hand may not have fashioned the noose here – it would have been done with greater efficiency had it been his hand – but he is responsible, or my father's reference to him, *in extremis*, would not have happened.

I will pursue and punish, but I do not want the police to pursue and punish at this point, although I do not know why, except perhaps an assertion of my mother's decent discretion. I have wanted to spit whenever, since her death, others have purported to know what she would think or want me to do, but now I know she would not want parading of this act, would want denial, concealment, smoothing over. Better for everybody. I half-sit in the cold garage, at fight with all of that hypocrisy, yet knowing I will do what she would have wanted and that there is a rightness to what she would have wanted, a dignity worth borrowing, a consideration for others and for the memory of a pleasant and pleasing and talented man brought to this, to *this* . . .

There will be pretence only so far, though. Had my father wanted secrecy, secrecy he could have had. You can run away to death, but he had chosen to bring death home with him, create of himself this exhibit for me. I examine this thought and know it to be true. He would never have expected me to telephone the guards first, before exploring the house and garage in search of him. He would never have expected me to do that, even had he ordered or begged me so to do, in the folded note left for me, but even in that, there was no sequence ordained for Daughter Of. Without an ordained sequence, the overwhelming likelihood was that she would be the first to find the body. Your body, father of mine. Although 'body' does not begin to convey reality, catch or communicate the purpled, pallid, putrid reality creaking in front of me. How about we try that great Irish phrase for the dead – 'the remains'. The remains of Roger Casement. That might be true of a man long dead, rattling of scoured bones in a box. But it is too reductive for this bloated hanging thing.

I stand and the standing brings me back, I find, into the circle of stench surrounding it. I move to the door into the house and when I stop to look again, the hanging thing has turned, following me with its eyes. I stagger and hold the doorframe, gazing past it to the wall. In this longer view, the hanged man is mimicked, from another rafter, by the single dusty bulb. One functional. One unfunctional.

When I go into the house, I leave the door open without a reason to, but without a reason not to, and inaction requires no thought when thought is slowed and stunned, when the mind works in a crouch of disbelief, pain lowering. I speak out loud to myself to tie knots in the fray of my ideas.

Would he have written another note?

He might, but to what end? What end, on the other hand, does the note to me fulfil? Did fulfil? I read it again. It means less to me than it did at first reading, because to be sorry for what you did when no imagination could foretell for him what he would look like, end like, suffer – it is empty on the page, that apology, and must have been empty in his heart when he wrote it. A ritual. An expected ritual.

But if he wrote another note, where would he have left it?

He might have posted it. He would never have inputted it into a computer. That I know. But I climb the stairs, turning on lights everywhere as I go against the now total darkness of a moonless night, even in rooms I don't go into. How strange, I think, as I go, how many rooms have tiny green and orange lights on gadgets plugged in ready to serve, pilot lights for power, unwinking one-eyed electronic Boy Scouts, always prepared, cheap at the price, bob-a-job. His room is as it always is, but neatened, perhaps. I go through every obvious place and then try the less obvious, including the backs of the pictures on his walls. I try to pry up the carpet, but it has the feeling of being stuck down for years. I slide my hands in under the mattress, big sweeping scoops, fingers reaching for a touch of paper. Long arms, I have. Maybe as long as his, but with life-glowing hands at the end of them, not grey cemented rigidities.

Long arms, though, I say, voice loud in the empty house. *Could play the double bass if she wanted to*. I am quoting my mother, going to the end of the bed, doing the below-mattress sweep there. I would never have wanted to play the double bass. Bomp a boomp with little slappy hand movements, always bringing up the rear, always the support system for the showy ones. It must have been the only good thing she could think of to say of a teenager whose wrists almost whacked off the floor as she walked, gorilla-style.

No note under the bed.

I try pillows. A poet might secrete something in a pillow case. Even a male poet. No, even a male who is a poet. Was a poet.

Not a poetic death, Father.

Never called him Father in life, why now, in death? Because there is no Dad I will now ever remember, always the Dad figure turning and mutating into the awful permanence of death-blued engorged veins, distended tendons, lengthened by its own weight, bigger than life . . .

I wonder if I carry the smell?

I gag and stand there in the neatness, yearning to open my mother's wardrobe, to bury my face in organza, taffeta, poplin, breathe deeply of her perfume, but to do it would be to pollute a memory, rub raw a lifeline. Now, I am crying. But for my mother. Jesus, Mam? I don't know what question I'm asking her, what help I need, and stumble away out of there, downstairs, sliding half leaning on the banister, lifting the old black phone at the end of the stairs, dialing 999 because who knows the telephone number of the local garda station and telling the voice he is dead, no I know he is dead, no I never touched him, how long ago? I stop answering questions and give the address, monotone. Make the voice read it back to me, put down the phone, heavy in my hand, the plastic warmed by my hand the way inert things can be warmed, the way the hanging man will never be warmed, his body stiffening, probably, into rigor, blood pooling black in hands and feet.

When they arrive, they are good. The woman takes me into the sitting room. The rest of them make phone calls, ribbon off the house, no sirens. An ambulance sits at a tilt, two wheels along one side up on the pavement. Ambulance men and gardai standing together outside, but eventually coming in because it is cold out there.

The woman watches me while she writes, but checks that she has written it accurately. Inserts the kindly phrases as we go. The questioning kindly phrases. Yes, I am all right. No, I don't want tea. Yes, I will talk to her. Yes, I will tell her if I feel I need a break. I came in at this time, I say. Then did this. Then that. Why did I go looking for him? Just, I shrug. But I know it makes no sense. He would be home, usually, I say, and the radio-researcher knowledge warns me: don't fill the holes in your story. Criminals rarely if ever get convicted by the holes in their story. They get convicted by their own waffling attempts to cover the holes.

She nods, neutrally, concernedly. He would usually be home by? I make movements with my mouth, but the ready exceptions crowd my brain. Late tutorials, conferences, meetings. Eating out because it is easier – was easier – than warming something up. He had no regular time of coming home and they will find that out easily enough. I am tempted to go womany on this woman and say, 'Intuition, I just *knew.*'

No payoff there, I think, sighing and surprising myself by the noise of it. This garda knows how and when to make the gestures of sympathy and concern, but there is a clear-eyed observation going on all the time. This is not the police officer to try the intuition line on.

He would usually be home by when? The repetition of the unanswered question is toneless. Oh, around that time, I say. What time would that be? Nine, ten. . . . Tell me again, Flannery, tell me again what time you began searching the house for him? Half nine, was it? Was that not a bit early for you to be getting worried? No?

She nods, even though she is disagreeing, logic is disagreeing, any sane listener would be disagreeing with what I'm presenting. Nod and goes off somewhere else. Before I get over the relief of being let off that hook, I am facing another hook. You looked for your father where? In the bedroom? And did you open wardrobes and cupboards? You did? All of them or just some of them?

I know what you're doing, I think. It's not helping me, though, knowing what you are doing. Every simple single question wriggles as it arrives, implications sprouting, curling around my words, tightening. Yes, I opened all the presses as I passed them. Why did I do it? Who knows? Why do I *think* I did it? I take refuge in the schoolgirl plaint: I don't remember. I just don't know.

There are occasional interruptions, and a slightly older man comes, introduces himself, and sits down, his posture a wondrous mixture of respect and professionalism. Unhurried but urgent. He asks would I like a cup of tea. Time, distraction, yes, this time I would if it's not too much trouble – I stand, make to go to the kitchen, but like a good bouncer, without ever touching me or getting directly in my path, he reverses me back into my chair. They'll find the teabags. No, don't worry if the milk is gone off, they'll take care of it. He goes to the door, talks to someone outside in an undertone and closes it firmly.

I went to the garage at what time? Quarter to ten? Would that be right? I shrug, but shrugs no longer work. The woman officer knows I will not break down, that tears are not going to come to rescue me. A quarter to ten, that was when I went to the garage? Yes. Would you have looked at a clock? Oh, I don't know. I just know. Schoolgirl stuff again and like a heart missing a beat, she is back asking me how I was worried enough at a quarter to ten to go looking for him in the garage when he was sometimes not home until half ten, and then wouldn't have rung me to tell me?

She presents the contradiction to me as if I do not own it, as if she does not own it. Orphan contradiction seeks good home. It is a natural phenomenon, this contradiction, like weather. No explaining it. Except that Flannery Stapleton is the one who behaved in a mindfully mindless way and Flannery Stapleton is the one left alive to explain it. A mad fright like heartburn inside me generates the need to ask, does this mean I am under suspicion, do they think I killed my father? I nearly

voice it. And distract myself by my reaction to nearly voicing it
– dear Jesus, the pointless plaint of every murderer in history.

'I'm sorry,' I say. 'What was it you asked me?'

This time, the older officer takes the facts and presents them
to me. Painstakingly. Leaning forward, he's so eager for me to
see this little fact over here and this little contradictory fact
over there, and this little Flannery Stapleton figure in the
middle, and what do I make of all that, then? What I make of it
is a figure dangling, so near the door to the house, not over in a
corner, not against a wall, not in shadow, but near, right there,
discovering itself to me, not waiting to be discovered, the
colour of it and the mouth of it, knowing who it had been, but
nothing like him.

They both nod. I must have said it all out. But she writes
nothing. Writes nothing. Nods, then moves somewhere else.
Would there have been anything that prompted me to look in
the garage? Slow headshake.

'It was just the only place I hadn't looked.'

That would have been at a quarter to ten, about? Had I at
that point telephoned anybody? Professor Stapleton carried a
mobile phone, we understand? Would you have telephoned
him? Danger, here. Half-remembered evidence from Tribu-
nals: they can find out who called, even if you didn't get
through. Who left messages. No, I say. Keep it simple. Don't
explain. Now a minor theme, insistent, begins in my head:
*What are you hiding? Is all this worth it to conceal a suicide note
that reveals nothing?*

So you didn't ring your father? Before you started to search
for his body?

'I didn't know I was searching for a body.'

Mistake. Don't argue with them. Would my father often
have been in the garage? I shake my head. Hardly ever. He

wasn't a driver, or was he? No. Could he drive? He could, once, but not for years. Didn't drive the car that's in the garage? No, it was really my mother's car. And your mother is dead how long? The car in the garage—

'The car in the garage probably doesn't run, any more. I haven't tried it in weeks. I haven't been in the garage for weeks.'

Civilly implacable, they gaze at me. Gaze, not stare. There is no intimidation in their faces, the intimidation is in the line-up of facts and gaps. I close their faces out by putting my head in my hands, although I do no pretended sobs, simply think. I do not have to answer any more questions, I think. If I was a suspect, they would have to read my rights to me, or is that only in American films? But I cannot be a suspect, so I must have more rights, not less rights than a suspect. I am black-mailing myself into answering more questions than I should. Without asking for a lawyer, because that would imply to a blind drunk dummy that I have something to hide, I must get this stopped. Must stop it. Now, not later. One of them – the man – starts a sentence and I shake my head, then come up out of my hands.

'We can explore why I did particular things some other time. Are there any other factual questions you need to ask me? Because it's getting bright, and I must address who needs to be told and what is said publicly. You understand.'

They do, of course. She flips a page in her notebook and asks me about the body, whether I touched it. She seems surprised, for the first time, when I say I didn't. I cannot bring myself to say that anything looking like what hangs in our garage (does it still hang there or has that white-overalled pathologist arrived to have it cut down?) could not have life in it, should not have that life empowered, even if there were life lurking somewhere within the awfulness. How long would I have been in the garage? I am now testy with the softly conditional questions. I was in the garage maybe forty-five minutes. Doing what? Standing looking at it. Then sitting looking at it. And then? Oh, Jesus, we have another huge time gap coming up between when I left the garage, yes, probably about half ten, maybe a bit later, and five to twelve, when I dialled 999. What was I doing? I try to think of something, then decide maybe the truth will set me free.

'I was searching,' I say dully. As I feel.

'Searching?'

'Yes.'

'Searching for what?'

'A suicide note.'

'Why would you have been searching for a suicide note?'

'Because it— Oh, Jesus, come *on*, why does anybody search for a suicide note? To make sense of something that's like the fucking sky falling, what else? I mean, have you been in the garage? Have you seen what I walked into? My father? My *father*? Everybody knows what my father was like – and then that? Of course I was looking for anything that might tell me what drove him to it.'

'Drove him to it?'

She does not quite jump on it, but there is a giveaway interest. Damp it down. Don't go for a hard spray of water, a directed hoseful that would show her you know she has spotted the sense of intent, the implication that there may be someone to blame, someone pursuing him, but for what? Because of what? Fill the room with fog.

'He was down, depressed, ever since my mother died, but *now*? It isn't an anniversary. I hoped there might be something. But I found nothing. You can search yourselves . . .'

That's right, walk into it. They nod and she formally thanks me for the permission. I am dumbfounded by having given it, by having no way to take it back, but what can they find, and what would it prove?

'You're very tired,' she says with real kindness, and I am suddenly melted down.

'If it was just tiredness,' I choke. 'Now, I'd be afraid even to go to sleep.'

There must be someone I can telephone, he says. Because if I'm going to get any sleep before the media get hold of this, and I'm right, there's no way of avoiding that, given the very public, very much loved figure my father was, I would need someone I trusted to help me, to come over and be here? I nod, and stand, hands still deep in the patch pockets of the chenille robe. She hands me her mobile phone. I look at my watch as I dial. 6.24. It rings for a while, then Lyn's voice comes on, gaspy.

'Sorry 'bout that, I was in the shower. Hello?'

'Lyn. Lyn—'

'Flannery. What's wrong?'

They are listening even though they are talking to each other and pretending not to listen.

'Lyn, my father has committed suicide. I found his – I found – he was hanged in our garage. Last night. Late last night.'

'Ah, Flannery . . .'

As heavy as a petal falling from an overblown rose, the kindness comes and unships me.

'Oh, Lyn, Lyn, it is so awful, oh, Lyn, so awful, my *father*, Jesus, the look of— Lyn, what must he have been thinking? How could it have been so bad? Lyn, it's frightful, was frightful, he must have gone through agonies dying—'

Screaming gulping sodden tears take me over, shake me rat-like, turn me to the wall away from the uniforms and the bright unnecessary lights, nightwashing the place long after dawn.

'Flannery, shhh. Now listen to me. I'll be twenty minutes. No more. Get them to give you a cup of tea and I'll be there.'

She doesn't say goodbye and neither do I, and the officer dithers before taking back her phone and killing the singing open line. I stand, forehead against the embossed flowers in the all-white wallpaper in the hall, imprinting bluebells on my face. She turns me around and brings me towards the sitting room. No, not my mother's shrine. She reads the shudder, moving me instead towards the stairs. We climb it awkwardly, the two of us, me like an old woman. At my room, I sit on the bed and toe-poke my shoes off. Beside my bed is the bag I carried up earlier. Why did I carry it upstairs? Oh, yes, to take away any note I found. If I found one. She goes to sit down and it is in her way. I kick it and it spews contents over the rug. Tampons, tissues, a watch battery, a mobile phone charger, yellow credit card receipts. She goes on her knees and shovels them back into it, tilting it so it half-stands against my bedside unit.

'Thank you.'

When I glance at her, she is shaking her head. No thanks for such a simple favour. No thanks when I have drained and exhausted you. No thanks because you must stay in your role and I must stay in mine.

'You're very good at what you do,' I say, and she nods again. We hear engine noises.

'That must be your friend,' she says.

'This soon?'

'Does she drive a vintage MG?'

I nod, and she goes out onto the landing. This does not give me enough time to slide the letter out of my pocket, but that is the least of my worries. The envelope, crushed, is still in the sani-can in the kitchen, but if they uncrumpled it, what does it reveal? My name? In my father's printing? How would they know? And if they start to question me about it, I will seriously go for a lawyer.

Lyn comes into the room, dropping things right and left to get holding on to me. I cry and make her cry. But then there is a knock at the half-open door and the policewoman is there. A man who says he is a close friend is at the door. Douglas Rogan.

'Dougal,' Lyn says. 'Let him in. Bring him up to us.'

She gives me the kind of look with which you remove irrelevant lovers' quarrels from an equation. This man can help. Never mind that you've had some kind of a tiff with him way back. He comes in and puts his hand to my face, no more than that. Takes it away. Puts it back, dumbed by what has happened.

'Such a bad, bad thing,' he says after a while. 'Poor Flannery.'

He shakes his head as if something has been said that should be taken back. I search his face for clues to why he is not to blame for what my father did to himself, but what I see is a rage at my father for what my father has done to me, and I cannot parse that.

'What can I do?' he asks, and Lyn, with a pat, puts him sitting on the other side of me so we are like three children on a wall. Lyn asks if I have given permission for my father's name to be released.

'Yes, and more,' I say, my voice deepened with weeping. 'I said they could say his body was found in the garage attached to the family home by his only daughter. Which about tells the story, I'd have thought.'

'You're bloody right,' Doug says, and I don't know what to make of that. Lyn tells him we will need more people, because if the eight o'clock news runs it, there'll be a run on the house. He says he will get on to Nicola and get their PR people out to cope with any media. I hear him waylaid outside by the policewoman, but I cannot hear what they say to each other, because they go downstairs together. I tell Lyn I must get clean, and she picks out clothes for me to wear, laying them on the bed in order. Kisses me. Asks me will I get dizzy in the shower or anything like that? Goes off downstairs. I take the letter out of my pocket. Damp, it is, from my sweating hand. Limp, the fabric-rich paper.

There are bookshelves in my room, but if I interleave the note within a book, detectives always shake books and out it would fall. Not on the top of anything. I can't put it underneath a rug. Nor in the frame of a picture, because all of those places are the places I looked when I believed my father might have hidden another letter somewhere in the house. I can hear noises on the landing and, sliding the letter back into my pocket, open the door. A bunch of them look guilty, and one of them says they've just finished with my parents' room, thank you very much. Well, you'll have to wait to do my room until I have a shower, I say, and then say, no I'll shower in their bathroom, go ahead. No, no, straight away. Right now. Get it over with. No, nothing I need to take out of it before you do your search. Nothing at all.

I go into my parents' room and close the door. They have put things back neatly, but the signs of a search are still there. Some of the books on *their* shelves have been put back in a different order. Nobody but the owner of books ever apprehends the rules governing how they will be placed. I reorder them and put my father's letter into a slim volume of Philip

Larkin's work without intended irony. My heart lifts as I shower, and then I reach for shampoo and spot a soap-on-a-rope hanging from the shower head. Hanging from a cleaner rope than my father hanged himself from . . .

I wash and wash and wash again like Lady Macbeth. Not all the perfumes of Arabia. Not all my mother's bird-bottled *l'Air du Temps* will take away the smell that comes with every circling sighting. And that comes sometimes without a sighting.

18

Easy Explanations

━━━━◆◆◆━━━━

I never see the corpse of the hanging man again in reality. It is taken away. It is examined. It is released. It is buried.

I do not want the same old priest to talk about my father as talked about my mother, but a bishop who was on a TV programme with him telephones and wants to preside at the service, so I am grateful and Lyn takes care of the details. Nicola arrives and is fervent, but only for a couple of minutes before Doug embraces her away from me. Is there anything I want media told? I hold my hands down, palm towards him – anything? Whatever? When I look out of a window, I see camera crews and a raincoated girl talking to them, police hovering. Doug goes out and hovers, too, and then brings the girl back into the house. I go to the door of my bedroom and listen to the hissing fury of him.

'You will *not* tell them her father was depressed, is that clear?'

She says something in response, but her voice does not carry as far as his enraged whisper.

'I don't *care* what Nicola told you. You are not to tell them her father was depressed. You know fuck all about her father's state of mind.'

The girl squares up to him. This time I hear snatches of what she says. Reasonable assumption that with Mrs Stapleton dead, and so on, and it's the kindest thing to say, it's what is expected, it lessens, you know, lessens the—

'What?'

The girl is now good and mad and asks Doug very loudly if he wants Professor Stapleton portrayed in tomorrow's papers as mad. Keep her voice down, Doug tells her. He wasn't Professor Stapleton, either. He was only a lecturer. You don't have to be mad to commit suicide, he tells her. Or depressed. Nobody knows why this man did it, so let's not speculate. Give them facts. Yes, his wife died x months ago. No, it's not known that he had another relationship. No, his daughter has no comment. Full stop. Clear?

'It won't answer all their questions.'

'Like I give a—'

'It looks bad, frankly. It looks like he did – looks like he wasn't that caring about his daughter.'

'It looks bad because that's the truth of it.'

The account executive doesn't follow this at all, and says so. If he wanted the truth to be given to media anybody could have done it. He didn't need an experienced PR person to – to . . .

'Put a spin on it. Correct. I need an experienced PR person to hold the bastards at bay so we don't have fucking cameras three inches away from her as she comes out the door to go to the funeral. I need an experienced PR person to prevent bullshit about Flannery just because her father's gone and done this. She's private. She stays private. I don't honestly give a shit what happens to his image, he's dead. Just keep the hyenas on the other side of that garda ribbon and we'll all be happy.'

She walks straight back out of the front door. One of the policemen comes to where Doug is standing. And murmurs to him. I hear Doug talking about having installed my father's computer back when he still did freelancing to support himself. The policeman says Oh, yes, *that's* who you are, and Doug says yeah, visibly bored with who he is. Nicola comes out of the kitchen and Doug excuses himself to the policeman in order to tell Nicola what he has told the PR woman.

'You are ignoring the hurt,' Nicola says, her voice high with emotion.

He stands stock still in front of her, and she puts her arms around his neck.

'You are, you know. You are ignoring the hurt. Pretending it isn't there.'

He stands in the hug, then slowly pulls his hands out of his pockets and holds her at the sides.

'Whose hurt?'

'Flannery's hurt. Who else?'

There is a silence and then she begins to talk again, pulling him towards the kitchen. It can only hurt Flannery worse to have the details of – you know – dealt with in the newspapers and the best way to prevent that, according to the PR company, is to make sure you give the papers loads of stuff. They seem to have stopped before reaching the kitchen, but short of openly peeping, and being caught at it, I cannot know why.

'The more he did it because he was depressed, the less hurt there is for poor Flannery,' she says.

'Nicola, trust me. Leave it the way I've told that PR girl. Just leave it, OK? No more spin, no more soft stuff, no more talk about depression. They have enough, the hacks. They have enough.'

Lyn comes out of the kitchen and asks Nicola to do something which is so obviously beneath Nicola's perceived view of her own role in this tragedy that she audibly bridles, then surrenders. Lyn and Doug have whispered words in the hall, and I wonder, retreating to my room, what Lyn is at, so visibly challenging Nicola and – by inference – Doug. Maybe she's just too busy for it to matter, it's a 'lead, follow or get the hell out of the way' situation, I think.

She has lists for me to inspect and sign off on. I would agree to them all, unread, but she makes me go through them. She has brought me up the newspapers, too. Only the broadsheets have put it on the front pages. Even a Hallmark poet doesn't make it to page one of the tabloids. I put them to one side and ask her to summarise them for me. Amazing outpourings of affection for him, a couple of critics saying that popularity should not make us underestimate the poet's sensibility. One of the tabloids has a two pager on famous people who used his poems at their weddings or the christening of their children. Back-up features about suicide, how women try suicide more than men but when men try it they usually succeed.

Lyn doesn't say, although I find out later when I read through the cuttings, that one of the features maintains my father is a late bloomer when it comes to male suicide. The big bulge is at the start of the twenties and then there's another, largely concealed, bulge in old age. Just as Ireland, in the past, had extraordinarily low numbers of suicides because the need for burial in consecrated ground led relatives and authorities to confect an explanation that took the self-killers out of the stats, so, today, the old do away with themselves with such quiet efficiency that their deaths, too, are often mis-categorised. The feature patronises the past, instancing how often the verdict was 'suicide when the balance of the mind was disturbed'. The implication is that twenty-first-century people are so upfront and honest, they don't need such pathetic euphemisms. Right, I think. 'Depressed' will do.

There must be something, though, I think at every stage in

the obsequies, there must be something, for strangers, for media and for me, to explain the cruelty of it, the suddenness of it, so long after my mother's death, so many months of sustaining life, job, routine. What would have tipped him into this?

They take away the ribbons, the weather changes and I am gathering his clothes to take to the VDP when the doorbell rings. The man outside is my height or smaller, blond. He checks I am who he thinks I am, extending a hand. I take it.

'I'm Brian Deigan,' he says, as if the name will explain much more than names usually do. I look blankly at him.

'Yes?'

'Your father?' he prompts.

'What about my father?' I say, getting edgy.

'May I come in?' he says, looking around him on the doorstep as though he is surrounded by people who will hear highly confidential things if he is forced to stay outside. I begin to step back to allow him to pass me, then stop.

'No,' I say.

'But you know who I am,' he says, amazed.

'I know you say you're Brian Deigan,' I say, and he starts to search in pockets, producing a wallet and out of it a driver's licence with his picture on it.

'OK, now I know you have a driver's licence in the name of Brian Deigan,' I say.

'But you did your father's business managing,' he says, cutting across me.

Vaguely I remember enveloping cheques made out in that name.

'Years back, yes. I handed that over a long time ago to the department in college where my father used to work,' I say. 'You'll need to contact them.'

'You wouldn't hand this over to a university department,' he says, suddenly cocksure and nasty with it.

'I handed everything over,' I say. 'Now, if there's something you want to query, send it to me in writing and I'll hand it over to my father's solicitors. OK?'

It is very definitely not OK with him, but I have run out of courtesy and keep a steely gaze on him while I retreat and close the door. He stands there for ages, shadowed through the frosted glass at the side of the door. It is done to frighten me, I know, but I cannot figure why he would want to. Anyway, it's not going to work.

I get a letter from him by courier later that day:

Dear Flannery Stapleton,
It will help us both and be the best for the memory of your beloved father, if we do not pretend that the past has happened.

I do not wish to have to do with anybody representing your father other than you and this is the best from your position, too.

I will telephone you when you have had a couple of days to consider the best way to approach this.

Thanking you for your attention,
Brian Deigan.

Although it is word-processed, he has left out, I assume, the word 'not' in the first sentence. The letter presupposes knowledge on my part. I sit for a long time trying to figure out if I have that knowledge. No. Any of it? Nada. Where can I get it? I could ring Elaine at the college. She appeared at the funeral and did her formal expression of sympathy. I do not wish to ask someone who was doing a nixer for my father to explain the odd behaviour of one of my father's friends. Or acquaintances. Or former students.

I flip the edge of the letter noisily over my knuckles, as if I were playing the spoons with it. Send it on to his solicitors? They are currently working on contracts and other issues to do with his will, and have been onto me to get permission to talk to his accountants and his bank. I do not, I decide, want to pay solicitors for what is more probably some kind of investigative function; to find out who Brian Deigan is and what the hell gives him the idea he can invite himself into my home. I could go to a private detective agency, I suppose, but the man has done me no harm more lasting than irritation, so siccing an expensive dick for hire on him seems a little excessive.

Process of elimination brings me neatly to the policewoman who questioned me in the immediate aftermath of the death. I open the kitchen drawer where I fired her card, and as I locate it, notice the front-door key Dougal Rogan tossed at me at the end of his last visit. His last ordinary visit, when he took away computer components. Or were they discs? No, not floppy discs of the kind I'm used to, but one of the bits he took with him could have been a hard disc or hard disc drive, I've never seen one of those.

I stand, looking at the closed door leading to the garage, and the never ending circling of the creaking corpse begins, the smell of it and the sound of it. Snap card against teeth, that tick tick tick noise so brittle and immediate, it short-circuits other noises. Telephone her. I turn my back on the garage door and dial.

'Frances Synnott.'

Crisp. Just one notch short of 'Private Synnott reporting for duty, *SUH!*' I look at the card and am surprised, then unsurprised, to see she's more than a private.

'Inspector Synnott?'

'Yes, Flannery.'

Is this woman good, or what? How many weeks since we talked and she can put a name to the voice after a few syllables.

'Inspector Synnott, I had a visit from a man this morning I think I should bring to your notice. I've no idea what he was looking for, but he made me uncomfortable. Sorry. Sorry – this has something to do with my father and my father's death, that's why I thought it might be relevant to you – to the guards, I mean? And he—'

'You're quite right to—'

'– sent me a letter.'

'Sorry?'

'This man couriered me a letter this afternoon.'

'Do you have it there?'

'You want me to read it to you?'

'If you wouldn't mind, yes.'

I read it to her. She says she would send a car to pick it up, if that was all right with me, and – I mentioned cheques?

'I have this vague memory of sending a man with that name cheques. It rang a bell when he said it, but more when I saw the letter. Just, it's not the most usual spelling of that surname, it's usually with two e's. But the address I don't remember at all.'

Two uniformed gardai take the letter away an hour later, and I am so glad to relinquish anything to do with my father, it becomes something else triumphantly delegated. I am going to move to Lyn's as soon as possible, but I don't want to leave the house empty, so I work here except when I go to meetings in the radio station, and I do as much of that as possible.

I also schedule visits, lunches and dinners with all my friends. I meet Raimonde who is still off the booze, but taking anti-anxiety pills, which worries me, because they take the edge off her and I fear will reintroduce her to alcohol. I go to see Andrea and Bruce in their new home, an upgrade to the tune of ¢100K on the first one. Bruce says it was vital to buy on the upswing of the market and that I should sell my house while the going is good, that kind of house with four bedrooms (and a big garage suited for suicides, I think, watching the horror thing with its great dry swollen tongue again) is going at the moment for as much as a million. The mortgage must be long paid off, too. I tolerate him for the benefit of hearing Andrea cut loose about Nicola, who, she says, Doug is over playing and giving share options that will make her a rich woman when they get bought over, which, mark Andrea's words, will be within sixteen months.

There's a great comfort in listening to other people's hatreds, even if you don't share them and even if you should share them. I twirl a glass in my hand and feed Andrea all the questions that will fuel the flow of bile and venom. What was it again that she had said about Nicola's very difficult background? It wasn't she who had said it, she snaps, it was Doug and Doug, for all his brainpower, can be an awful gullible nerd. Nicola filled him up with this big dysfunctional family thing like Sinead O'Connor, her mother getting hauled off to the mental hospital and Nicola witnessing electric shock treatment when she was seven and then her brother on his deb night coming off that pedestrian bridge in Fairview killing not just himself but an unfortunate taxi driver underneath as well, the selfish sodden shot. Shot? Sot, she says and giggles. We all try saying it, because if we make ourselves laugh, it will distance us from the terrifying thought that Andrea has called a suicide something nasty, and I might have to take offence on behalf of my dead father.

'How could a seven-year-old witness electric shock treatment?' I ask. 'I wouldn't have thought it was exactly family therapy. I mean it's not one of those tough love things where everybody gets to come and tell you how much of a pain in the tits you really are to them. Electric shock is under general anaesthetic and so on?'

'Don't think they do it any more,' Bruce says.

'Worked, though,' Andrea says. 'Of course she couldn't have seen it,' she goes on. 'There's no way. A child?'

'So why's she claiming to have seen it?'

Bruce hands around a plate of savoury biscuits shaped like tiny goldfish. I shake my head at them. In the aftermath of the suicide, I am almost permanently nauseated. The minute I stop being nauseated and eat something with any kind of enjoyment, something on the plate reminds me of some texture or shape from the hanging man in the garage, and I am cold-sweatily trying to control the urge to throw up. If my friends didn't know better, they would assume I was pregnant. As it is, I am losing weight. Not an amazing amount, but enough to make clothes loose on me. I wish I cared enough to enjoy it.

'Glamorise herself,' he offers. 'Make her important.'

'I don't think she's making it up, actually,' Andrea says. 'I think she has told it so often, she believes it, now. She makes it incredibly believable when she tells it – I remember she told it to me shortly after I hired her, it was the first thing that made me worried I had made a mistake.'

'You wouldn't have hired someone with a background of mental illness?'

'No, I wouldn't have hired someone who claimed – in such im-impelling detail – to have been present when electro-shock treatment was administered to her mother. I've read enough about false memory syndrome to be worried when anybody claims to have been around when someone else did something awful.'

'So she's nuts, Nicola,' Bruce summarises.

'I don't think she's nuts,' Andrea and I say together, and laugh at each other, pointing. You go first. No, you.

'She remembers things that didn't happen, and you think she's sane?' Bruce is looking at the two of us as if he thinks *we*'re nuts.

'Some dame in the US did this thing where she told a cousin he'd been present when his older brother fell to his death or drowned or something, and that nobody had told him because he was only three at the time and they knew he'd forget. Sure enough, within weeks, he was able to tell them memories he had that up to then he believed to be just dreams or random images, but that fitted what was known of the tragedy perfectly. When she then told him she'd made it up and that he was somewhere else entirely when the brother died, he literally wouldn't believe her, because he had such faith in his "retrieved" memory.'

'Doesn't explain Nicola,' Bruce mumbles.

Andrea and I start to play out the possibilities. You grow up in the Ireland of the seventies in a small country town. Your mother suffers from serious depression. Was there much of a stigma about mental illness in Ireland in the seventies? Bloody right there was. Still is. Upwardly mobile family does its best to conceal what's happening when mother disappears for a while and comes back softened, confused but not quite so terminally sad. Bright middle daughter listens at doors. Reads books. Mixes it all together in a mélange with personal applications. Finds that when she 'confides' claimed experiences on the edge of her mother's illness, the lingering stigma around that illness prevents too rigorous interrogation and elevates the daughter to hero status. Everything she then achieves becomes a double triumph, a triumph against adversity, a win against secret hardship. Or semi-secret hardship.

'Well, she's doing well for herself now, anyway,' Bruce says.

'True,' Andrea says, much happier, always, dealing with pathology than success.

'Have you seen the house they're living in?'

I shake my head.

'Makes this look like a shack,' Andrea says.

'Lean-to shed?' I ask.

'Out-house,' Bruce says.

'Doug explains away anything she does wrong in the company by telling people she's just not good at dealing with delaying tactics,' Andrea says. 'Which means executives who question her judgement in any way, who want to do things by some agreed protocols and at some sensible pace, find themselves at management meetings being made out to be dragging their heels over nothing, stopping the onward march of Nicola, getting in the way of the triumphant flotation. Or whatever it is that's going to make them all richer than they are right now.'

I ask what Piers, the dynamic second-in-command, makes of this. Not a lot, is the answer.

'He uses the "c" word about her,' Andrea says out of the side of her mouth.

It takes me a minute to work out what the 'c' word is.

'Does he, then? Unwise, to do it where Doug can hear him, I'd have thought.'

'Wise is not what Piers majors on,' Andrea says. Bruce is watching her closely. Can it be he realises how very bright this little squashed down woman is? I wonder.

'Arrogance is what Piers majors on. Piers thinks he is the brightest guy since Einstein, the sexiest old charmer since Clinton, better-looking than Pierce Brosnan. It wouldn't cost him a thought if Doug fired him tomorrow. He'd be sure he'd pick up something just as good somewhere else. Lyn encourages him, of course.'

'In which?'

They both look perplexed. I haven't the energy to explain, but Andrea works it out.

'In everything. Lyn thinks the sun shines out of his arse. She doesn't even pretend not to. He is going to hurt her so badly.'

I drive to my parents' house (I can no longer bear to call it my home) thinking about this. Lyn, for a couple of years, was regarded with fear and loathing by most of her girlfriends and all her female acquaintances. Anybody that good-looking had to be about to do great damage to anybody already in a relationship, because she would take the man just to show she could. Mothers of her girlfriends commented favourably on Lyn's gentle way and nice manners, but they feared her, too, feared that wand-like flower look, that great fall of shining black hair, that constantly concealed intelligence. Cross-generational threat among women reduces the older woman to a caricature. But she is not always wrong. Except in Lyn's case.

Now, the boot's on the other foot. Lyn's girlfriends are circling wagons to protect her from the only man they think worthy of her. Lyn, meanwhile, is circling – no, not that creaking circular movement and the dark-stained trousers at eye level, no, think of something else, anything else, Lyn, what was it Lyn is doing, Lyn is circling the wagons around me, keeping me busy, pushing me to push the lawyers to get the probate or the will or whatever needs to be processed so that I can put the house behind me, put my father's royalties into the care of KPMG or Deloittes and get to what she thinks I should be doing. I have a meeting, first thing the following morning, with her and Dougal Rogan, I remember. A meeting initially set up before my father died. I will attend the meeting and I will begin to explore, to delicately interrogate, the sentence in my father's letter adjuring me not to blame Doug.

The meeting is in the radio station, and Lyn meets us in the control room of one of the studios.

'Remember the first-person script you did about your debs?' she asks, as Rogan arrives in our eyeline in the studio itself with a woman in her mid-thirties and a man who is a little older.

'Not necessarily about my debs,' I say untruthfully. 'It sets out to crystallise all the hidden awfulness in many people's debs. Not people like you, Lyn. Plain people.'

My eyes adjust, unbidden, and I find myself watching, not the settling-into-place going on in the studio as Doug and the man make the woman comfortable at the microphone, but my own reflection in the glass. I am not plain, I think. I have been plain, but misery must suit me. I look grave and a little weary, but attractive. This surprises the hell out of me. Nearly as much as when I saw myself as being pretty in the deb picture. Take a quick picture of that glass reflection, boys, this attractiveness won't strike again for another ten years, if it follows the pattern up to now.

'I showed it to Doug.'

'You showed what to Doug?'

'Your script about the debs' ball.'

The only appropriate answer to that is 'Why the fuck?' so I don't give it.

'You know the way Doug is always trying to rescue people?'

Not recently, Lyn, I think he may have killed my father. Not personally. Indirectly, maybe, in some way I haven't yet figured out. He certainly was not in the business of rescuing my father. Before his death. Or after his death. But I nod, because that will keep her running. She gestures towards the studio, where the woman is now seated with a script in front of her. The man is seated beside her, filling a glass of water for her. There is an anxious solicitude about him, as if she were fragile, although she is a plump, well-dressed, well-pleased looking woman.

'Why doesn't he shut up and let her go through the script?' I mutter, and Lyn says I'll see why in a minute. Doug Rogan appears behind us and I extend a hand over my shoulder for a cursory shake. Lyn works the faders on the desk and a red light comes on in front of the woman, who jumps.

'Dorothy,' Lyn says in a soothing tone. 'Dorothy, I'm going to count you down from five. OK?'

The woman nods, but in a vague way, rather than directly at Lyn in the control room. Lyn goes 'Five, four, three . . .' and then cuts off her own sound. The woman waits the two final beats and then starts to read. Chills go up and down my spine, because she takes it and owns it. It comes out of her, not as if she was reading, but as if it was happening in front of her, as if all the wounds the script mentions were being experienced by her as a plain, overdressed deb, even though you would only have to look at her to know that she herself was pretty, even as an adolescent.

When she comes to where the page has to be turned, there is an instant of complete, abandoned panic. The man strokes her arm gently and takes away the finished page. She settles to the next one and reads. It is all discovery, and yet the pacing, the small hesitations are masterful.

'Lyn, you better be recording this,' I say and Lyn's head

bobs to confirm, her eyes not coming off the gauges for a second.

At the end, I am in tears. In the easy tears of remembering adolescent misery touched with laughter and with the post-factum knowledge that what seem at the time to be hurts terminal to one's hopes and dreams are not terminal at all, are just stages on the way. Stages on the way to grimmer things, I think, banging the arch of my wrist against the tears.

The woman in the studio, though, is not looking to the people behind the glass for applause or confirmation. She is simply looking frightened. Frightened in the way you see in faces in news bulletins. Mothers running, babies cocooned at their chests, screaming terror as shells hit the earth behind them. The man gets her turned to him, and leans behind him to pick up the discarded pages from the floor. He orders them, sets them into her hands, and Lyn leans forward.

'Dorothy, I'll count you down from five,' she says, but this time touches no buttons. 'Five, four, three . . .'

After two more beats, the woman starts to read the script again. Except that there is no 'again' about it. She reads it *exactly* as before. Not close to the first time. Exactly. The slight hesitations are the same, the sense of discovery the same, the point at which her eyes gloss with tears the same. To the second. To the inflection. To the half-indrawn breath. Lyn fades the sound from the studio and the three of us sit. My arms have goose bumps down them, although the space is warm. I spin the chair to see Doug Rogan. He is sitting on a table behind the two of us. The table has been jammed against the control room wall to hold audio tapes and commercial cartridges.

'Dorothy is Dorothy Brandon,' he says. 'Good actress, but brilliant voice-over artist.'

'Female equivalent of Bill Golding,' Lyn confirms.

'Read anything at sight, get it right first time. Lyn?'

Lyn spins the chair and pushes the fader. Dorothy has finished the script and is looking frightened again. Lyn tells her she will count her down. The script in hand, she waits those two extra beats and then starts. The performance is eerily, creepily identical to the first two. Lyn douses the sound from the studio and turns back to us.

'Married to Len Bolton, great friend of my father's,' Doug says. Len Bolton must be the man in the studio. 'Great friend of mine in recent years. Just good guy, OK?'

Nothing to be lost in agreeing with that, I think, so I do.

'Eight months ago, Dorothy got a form of viral encephalitis. It destroyed her short-term memory. There's more technical terms for it, but that's the bottom line. She can remember something for maybe sixty seconds. No matter how many times you tell her what has happened to her, she does not know it. She can never learn it. Never learn anything, ever again. She remembers people and skills up to the illness, nothing afterwards. In hospital, the moment she woke up in the morning, every single morning for nearly three months, she was terrified, because she had no idea where she was or why she was there. She would listen to what the nurses said, and calm down, and two minutes later would be screaming with terror all over again. When Len would arrive, she would cry like a child, clinging to him, wondering what she had done to be put in this place without explanation. Every day like a videotape of the previous day. Every single day. Watch.'

The woman at the microphone is reaching the end of the script. Lyn thanks her through the talkback and she looks towards the monitor the voice comes out of. When it doesn't say anything else, she begins to search that area of the room for the person she evidently believes to be hidden there, but as she searches with her eyes, a bottomless terror comes into them. Although we cannot hear him, we see her husband saying something, and she turns to him, clutching him as if she has not seen him for days, weeping in relief and grief as he strokes her hair and looks empty-eyed at the three of us in the control room. He calms her down, mops her face, gives her a gold compact and a lipstick. She looks at them, bewildered. He opens the compact and she smiles at her own reflection, automatically, then, unscrewing the matching gold cap from the lipstick and applying it expertly.

He holds open her handbag for compact and lipstick to be dropped into it, hangs it by its strap on her arm, and offers her his tweedy arm. Giggling and confident, she allows him to take her to the door, talking to him as they go. The big padded studio door swings slowly closed.

'I knew of Dorothy, but sort of as a legend,' Lyn says. 'Remember, I'm not in radio that long? It was really Doug who made me learn her.'

'Why? What was this for?'

Len has taken his wife home, they tell me, each taking bits of the story, falling over themselves but giving me a sense of what is involved. He has given up his job to take care of her all the time. Some of her friends help him, too. There are things you can do to take the pressure off. If you get her to listen to music, put earphones on her, she might stay there until she needs to go to the toilet. Music seems to take her over. But she is never going to improve, never do anything.

'It was really curiosity,' Doug says, looking hunted and embarrassed. 'I just got curious to see could she still read scripts and then when I heard her doing some, I thought it was a waste that she wasn't. She could earn bits of money, not that she'll know. Get Len and herself out of the house. I don't know.'

I bet you don't know, Mr Logic, Mr Women-Hater, I think. For once in your life, you want to rescue the unrescuable. You've come up with a solution that you know bloody well is not a solution, because this woman's husband, sooner or later, will have a heart attack and she will spend the rest of a possibly long life in a mad circle of daily, hourly grief and terror and explanations and grief and terror. Sickening images of the hanging man superimpose themselves on our reflections in the glass as I wonder if she would kill herself if she understood the sentence of worse than death that has been passed on her by a virus. I wipe my face with my hand a couple of times.

'We could do a late-night thing,' Lyn says. 'Never give Dorothy a name. Just a script, first person, every week. About something that is so painful, so real that she can experience it and deliver it the way she did that script. Then just take calls, put them on the air. If the scripts are good enough, it would work.'

'I would have to do the script telling of what has happened to Dorothy herself,' I say, knowing I have thereby agreed to all the foregoing.

Lyn says she wants to catch Dorothy and her husband before they leave the building. She abandons us and runs.

'Lyn runs like a girl,' Dougal Rogan says, with annoyance, as if nobody should. Even if they *are* a girl.

'Not helped by the high heels,' I say, determined to be his pal.

He looks at me, querying.

'How you doing?'

None of your business, you murdering judgemental bastard.

'Oh, fine, fine.'

'Yeah, right.'

Much you care.

'Am I another project for rescue, like Dorothy?'

Oops, that one escaped before the cuff got clipped around its ankle and the ball and chain attached.

'You know you're not.'

'You know something, Doug? I don't know anything any more. Once upon a time, I knew great stuff. You know the kind of stuff. Doctors fixed you when you got sick. Your parents were always – what's the great cliché – "always there for you". Until they became grandparents and did baby-minding for you. At this point, if this' – I opened my hand to show my tiny mobile phone – 'turned into a bag of maggots, I wouldn't be that surprised. It'd be congruent with the rest.'

He nods but says nothing. I remember, I remember, the silence with you a long time ago and how easy it was to sit in its warmth.

'Doug. Remember the day I came home and you were working on my father's computer. You took stuff away out of it and threw the key at me.'

'Not at you. I left it on the table.'

'Whatever.'

Watch that impatient tone, Flannery. Got to keep this guy onside until you get information out of him. I stretch. Message sent: It's just me, I'm so tense.

'You took components with you that day.'

'Components?'

'Bits from inside the computer.'

He does a marginal movement with his head as if to say taking bits out of computers is something he does all the time, how can I even suggest he might remember one particular incident so long ago? Not that long ago, friend. And big entrepreneurs don't actually spend that much time in other people's homes removing the innards of their computers and taking them away with them.

'Have you been having problems with it?'

I force myself to do an all encompassing smile. Appreciative of how caring he is, trying to work out what computer problems I might have, and indicative of my awareness that Mr Rescue Squad will speed to my home and boot me back into full operation at the drop of a hint. Upgrade me. Fill me full of free downloads.

'It's never been used since then,' I say and he looks interested but baffled: Your problem, Flannery, is, exactly?

'I was just wondering what were the bits you took away and why.'

He leans back and looks at the ceiling as if this would help him work out the answer. Shakes his head. Golly, gee, I jes cain't 'member, Miss Flannery. Doesn't say anything. Neither do I.

'I could come over and get it operational again.'

I smile at him and shake my head. *Not* the issue, Dougal, me oul' flower. *Not* the issue, and you know it. Zebedee said it was time to deal with the issue, Dougal.

He roots in the pockets of the brown leather jacket for his keys.

'I must have a look at my notes.'

I know what I am supposed to take out of that. He will look at his notes, his notes will remind him of whatever he took out of my father's computer, he'll get back to me to pass on the information and I will stop worrying my little head. None of it said. Nothing subject to discovery. Nothing to defend later in court. Why am I thinking of court? He is at the door of the control room now, all biz, turning out the lights. Action Man. Thinks all this busy business will get me off my arse and walking out on to the corridor with him. I sit still.

'You coming or are you planning to squat there?'

'Doug, what were the bits you took away and why?'

'Do you think I stole something?'

Hey, Inspector Synnott, I've learned something from your interrogation style. I'm doing something right, if I've got him to the same point you got me to: *Are you accusing me of killing my father/Are you accusing me of stealing computer parts?*

'What were the bits you took away and why?'

Silhouetted against the light from the corridor, he stands there, leaning against the doorframe. Tossing his keys in the air and catching them backhanded.

'Because if you do think I stole something, the thing to do is go to the guards.'

'Doug, you took something out of the computer for some purpose. What was it and why? And why won't you tell me? What have you to be afraid of?'

The key-tossing stops. He is very still, I presume looking at me, but no light is on his face, so I can't tell.

'Not a thing, Flannery. Thankfully. I have nothing to be afraid of. Now, you can charge me with theft or you can assume what I took was between your father and me, part of a confidential business arrangement between a businessman and – and an investor, and leave it alone. If you want my advice, you'll leave it alone. But that's up to you. I've an appointment. Seeya.'

A few steps down the rubber padded floor of the corridor, I hear the sounds of him meeting Lyn coming back. Brief encounter. Then Lyn, long hair swinging free, is standing in the door of the control room.

'The hell are you doing in the dark, Flannery?'

'Thinking. There a law against that, here?'

She laughs.

'No, but as Controller of Programmes, I could bring in a regulation. No thinking permitted unless you have a computer in front of you to catch the thoughts as they crystallise. No point in non-commercial thinking, right?'

19

Beads in a Necklace

————◆————

'Tragedy, in my experience, carries in its wake a shitload of little clearing-up jobs.'

I say this in the house on my own, checking for echoes. No echoes. Hollow sound, but no echoes. (No creaks, either. Only in my mind is there the heavy creaking of an old, weighted rope.)

'Tragedy, in my experience,' I say, trying out the sentence a different way to distract myself. 'And I have, you will agree, a *lot* of experience, teaches you shag all and improves you not a teeny tiny bit.'

The wall-clock in the kitchen has a red minute hand. The clock's ticking seems to originate with that hand, so it twitches from second to second, going 'Tsk, tsk.' All the way round the face of the clock, all day, every day, like a disapproving spinster aunt. When the battery runs low, it slows the pace of the disapproving noise, so it becomes 'Tsk . . . tsk . . . tsk.' Other than when it's slowed by a low battery, it keeps in perfect time with the clock in the sitting room some company gave my father at the end of a talk he delivered at a dinner for them. A faux carriage clock, all determinedly tarnish-free visibly moving parts, this one has a high-minded tone. 'Tink, tink, tink,' it says. God's in his heaven, all's well with the sitting room. To which the kitchen clock responds in gloomy contradiction.

This is my life, at the moment. Bits, every day, so empty I end up listening to clocks talking to each other. Then there are flurries of activity. Or is it activity? Maybe a better way to look at it is to think of the flurries as beads on a necklace. Bead #1 of today coming up. (I can see the solicitor's navy blue car pulling up outside, so this one is a safe prediction to make.)

He comes up the path, all briefcases and documents under his arm. You'd think I was a tribunal. I open the door before he gets to the doorbell and it is commendable how he hangs on to all his materials in view of how surprised he is. I hardly know him, this fortyish local lawyer my mother dealt with about mortgages and contracts. But because we've seen each other down through the years, we behave as if we know each other well. I have china cups out. Tea or coffee? Tea. I bring it to the kitchen table, making no excuse for not seeing him in the sitting room as my mother used to. I shove the biscuit plate to him. Individually wrapped biscuits. Sign of someone living on their own. Families have biscuit tins full of unmatched, unwrapped treats.

This man does some lecturing on night courses and it shows. He wants me to understand the background to my father's will. Probate and other issues. I half-listen to him. I wouldn't listen to him at all, except that almost everything I do listen to I can turn into a script later, and make money out of. He is well into it before I establish that this meeting, which I thought was a wrapper-up, a final sign-off, is 'still in the nature of' (his phrase) a preliminary.

I sign papers for him, to allow him to undertake various tasks he says he cannot undertake without my signature, and watch him take his documentation back down the path to the navy blue car.

My notes from Bead #1 meeting say:

Mortgage almost paid.
2nd mortgage? Why? How much?
Advance paid on UK royalties.
Car paid for – hold off on selling.

I wash the china, the teapot, dry them and line them up for the Sherry FitzGerald woman. Confession: I have made like Daughter Of. Telephoned Sherry FitzGerald, because I know nothing about property companies or real estate or whatever the hell they're called, but I read something somewhere that the head guy at Sherry FitzGerald is a Son Of someone famous. So I ring and ask to talk to him, mentioning my father's name. Sure enough, he comes on and tells me he'll send someone out this very afternoon to look at the house and give me a steer. I'm now waiting for the steer-bringer.

She turns out to be a tall pale twenty-five-year-old with russet hair around a porcelain pale face. Memorable. Also weighed down with paraphernalia. Hers include mobile phone, PDA, clipboard, handbag, briefcase and Mont Blanc ballpoint.

'I could walk you around the house, but I imagine you'd much rather go around it yourself without having to be nice to me about all the crap you find,' I say and she laughs and nods.

'Off you go, then,' I say, and she does. She is heavy-footed, so I can, by the sounds, track her progress. Spare bedroom. Parents' bedroom. Other spare bedroom. My bedroom. Downstairs now. Out into the garage. Hollow sounds from garage. I go make tea. She's having tea even if she would prefer coffee. Sound of garage door closing. Sitting room. Dining room. Father's study. Kitchen. (Where she left most of her goods and chattels before she set off.) She walks around the kitchen, making notes. Goes into the utility room, makes more notes. Comes back, sits down.

'I have to tell you, straight up, that you can add to the value of the house if you're prepared to have publicity about – about—'

My father strangling himself in the garage? I hold up my hand.

'I don't think the famous owner advantage really applies in this case,' I say, and am quite proud of myself, the way it comes out.

'May I clarify a couple of issues?' she asks. I nod.

'As I understand it, you want to sell the house, but you're not in a hurry to sell it.'

'My father's will has turned out to be as complicated as you'd expect a poet's will to be.' I smile. 'As a result, I expect it'll be a couple of months before it's free and clear for me to sell.'

'*Aw*right,' she says, on a long exhalation.

'Don't tell me,' I plead, laughing. 'I must change the garage into a conservatory, add skylights in the spare bedroom, paint the whole place white and kill off the bats in the attic.'

'You're not allowed to kill off the bats in the attic.'

'I don't actually *have* bats in the attic.'

'I know, but if you had, you have to keep them. Environmental law.'

'Do people inform on you to the EPA if you don't tell them that stuff about their bats?'

No, bats are not that often involved in her business, because she mostly does this (gesture) kind of area, and it's not really the typical bat haunt. On the other hand, painting the house white wouldn't be a bad idea. Painting a house white allows potential buyers to imagine what it would be like their way. Sort of neutralises the influence of the present owners. She will send out a surveyor and somebody else, but the house looks to her very solid, well built. Big enough gardens to play with extensions. Not that most people would need to extend a four-bedroom house, but the footprint is getting bigger all the time. I nod as if I know what the footprint is and she goes.

My notes from Bead meeting #2 say:

Clear and paint garage interior.
Up and over doors? (Gap bottom right. Rot.)
Mini maids. Ask for blitz.
Leave awards, pix with President, etc.
Cut flowers, baking on day buyers visit.
Talk gardeners.

Inspector Synnott comes to lunch. No, she comes at lunch-time. She will have a sandwich, she says. In fact, she'd bring it with her. No, I say politely, I can do sandwiches. I can do a couple of other dishes, too, but I decide to be literal-minded. Tea and samwidges. Samwidges triangulated and with the crusts cut off, nestling in carefully checked lettuce leaves. She, too, has a mobile phone and a PDA, but that's it. An unmarked car draws up, she gets out of the passenger seat and it drives away.

'You're not going to bring down the tone of the neighbour-hood, I see, leaving a squad car outside,' I say, smiling as if this were social. She's in civvies, but her suit is so formal, she might as well be in uniform.

'Garda car was here, I gather, a couple of weeks before your father's death,' she says, turning off her phone and shoving it noticeably to one side: *definitely* social.

I keep my movements fluid. Difficult, when your blood has just gone solid. *Not social.*

'You were aware of that?' She scans my agreeing face. 'You aware of why?'

'No. My father dealt with them.'

'OK,' she says, as if this item has been completed, whereas its little legs are waving, naked, from the sea like Icarus's. 'Brian Deigan.'

She takes a sandwich, puts it on her plate, ignores it and starts to tell me about Brian Deigan.

'His mother's name was Deigan, and hers is the only name on the birth cert. He was one of three kids. Different fathers. She was on welfare. Spent some time in England, came home very sick. Kids taken into care. Brian, at eight, difficult to foster, bit old for it. Charity called The Traveller—'

I react without thinking and it stops her.

'My father was a patron of it. It was named after that poem about the guy who knocks on the door and nobody answers.'

'They began to send visitors to the institution where he was kept. Take him out for the day, for half days, matches, the circus, go to the pictures. Bit like the American Big Brother approach. Your father did a lot of the visitation. When Brian left school early, your father paid for him to be taught the drums. Supported him to a certain extent while he tried to get into the music business. Continued to send him occasional cheques, to underline his commitment. Saw Brian as a talented drummer.'

'My father could spot the most deeply disguised talent in anybody outside his own family,' I say, lightly. Well, I try for lightly, but what comes out is heavy and sour, informed by years of him enthusiastically reading crap written by some orphaned seven-year-old (when I was seven) or deprived nine-year-old (when I was nine). He was always about to get to anything I wrote, but ultimately my mother was the one who sat down with it, and she proof-read like a bastard. Every writer's worst nightmare and best teacher, my mother. When you handed her your two or three pages, she would take it, one-handed, and the other hand would reach out for a pen. To sub-edit it. To leave criticisms ('*Cliché!!!!*') in the margins.

'The cheques would have been reasonably regular and sizeable until recently and Brian believes they were part of a – a – almost a contract, an agreement. Between your father and him.'

'Does he have a disability?'

She looks startled. I laugh.

'No, I don't mean he's imagining this therefore his lift doesn't go all the way to the top,' I say. 'I mean is there anything that would make it difficult for him to earn his living?'

'No. Although he feels there are a lot of strikes against him, psychologically. His upbringing wasn't what you'd call ideal.'

'So he should become a pensioner of my father?'

She raises her eyebrows at me, inviting me to explain why this man thinks my dead father owes him a living.

'You said sizeable cheques. Like what? What constitutes sizeable?'

'Eleven thousand. Eight thousand. Twelve thousand.'

'In what period of time?'

'Those three were in the last year.'

'*What?*'

'You didn't process them,' she says hastily, lest I think I'm being accused of something. 'He had a series of temps doing work for him. I gather.'

Thirty-one thousand to this total stranger who arrived on my doorstep and demanded to be let into my house?

'My father's judgement was always a bit soft when it came to the underdog, but if this is normal generosity to an underdog, tell me where I can get on an underdog course, because that's the career for me,' I say.

She says this doesn't add up, and I agree with her. That she's going to get it looked into. When I repeat 'get it looked into?' she smiles and says I may not be aware of it, but there's a gift tax in Ireland. If my father had given the thirty-one thousand to *me*, his daughter, there would be a substantial tax liability, but gifting it to a near-stranger meant there was even more tax due. It would be worth exploring if that tax liability had been met, and see where that took things. Would I be prepared to authorise . . . ? Catch that creepy guy not paying tax on what my father gave him? Sure, I'd be prepared to authorise. Would I excuse her a moment? She goes out to the car, which has returned in the interim, and comes back with a plastic folder of pages. Cleverly done, I think as I sign dotted lines. Draw attention to the fact that you made no presumption that I would agree to this investigation. She comments, lightly, on how easy I am about tax matters and my father.

'I'm easy for a good reason. My father's university salary would have been taxed at source, PAYE, no fiddling possible. Anything else he earned would have been artistic, so no tax on it.'

I have no worries, I think, as I watch her get into the passenger seat of her car and drive off, sorting the pages I had just signed. It never ceases, my ability to read the signs upside down and inside out.

My notes from Bead meeting #3 go:

Insp. S to check all charities Ed. S Patron of, Board memb of.
Go through accounts – talk to Ronan, DeLoitte's. Bank Mgr?
Raise with?

The bank manager is the fourth bead on my necklace that day. Him agreeing to come to the house to see me is surprising, but my call has obviously happened at a time when he wanted to be in touch with me anyway. He tells me he'd like to bring one of his assistant managers with him. I wash the cups and saucers and plates but don't put out another set. I've stayed on my diet all day in spite of the sandwich-consumption, so I don't have the energy for digging out more china.

When the two of them arrive, I'm struck by how uncomfortable they are, compared to the earlier visitors.

The manager does a formal introduction to the session, referring to the fact that my father and I had joint cheque-signing rights and this continued, despite me not being so involved in recent months. He seems to feel this allows us to speak freely. His need for permission seems strange, but I let it pass. He puts documents in front of me and waits for me to read them. I laugh.

'I'm really sorry,' I say. 'I have a feeling I'm doing an exam and I'm going to get an F grade. I have no idea how to read this kind of thing. Why don't you tell me the most important things?'

The assistant, who wears a low-slung T-shirt filled with burgeoning breasts, which is kind of encouraging in an aspirant bank manager, now does *her* introductory bit. All of this is preliminary, I am clear on this. Oh, so clear. Other factors may come into play, I do appreciate that? Factors are always coming off the sub's bench and into play, I agree. Indeed, there may be other accounts, in fact overseas accounts, of relevance in due course. I concede this, too. (*My father? Overseas accounts? My father was challenged by the complexities of his credit union membership, for Chrissake.*)

I'm now looking at the two of them wondering which of

them is going to get to the point and how big and bad the point is going to be, if they have to work up to it at such portentous length. The manager advances one document towards me and rings a figure on it.

'This is the current state of what we'll call the main account,' he says.

Not as much as I would have expected, but OK. I look up at him. My expression must not be right, because he frowns, directing me to look back down at the document. I do. He clicks out the nib part of his Parker and uses it to point at the little minus sign in front of the figure. I look up at him disbelievingly.

'Overdrawn? The main account is a hundred and fifty thousand in the red? You must be kidding.'

He silently puts other documents in front of me. Special savings accounts and a couple of others. Smaller. But all either empty or worse than empty. He wants to make it very clear to me, he says. Let there be no doubt. I should inform you. His hands move among the folders of materials to show me letter after letter going to my father over the past year, the tone of the letters moving from mild concern to semi-legal ultimatum. One of them, I notice, refers to his delivery to them of the deeds of the house in which we are sitting, and draws his attention to the fact that he failed to disclose to them the second mortgage on the property, undertaken through another financial institution.

The two of them sit, clenched, as if they expect me to head butt them or at least attack them verbally.

'What the hell was he *at*, my father?' I ask the air.

They relax a little. Justify themselves some more. I shove the papers towards them. Yeah, yeah, yeah, OK, I see yiz did your job. All *right*, already. Do we have records of payments made?

He nods and takes me down through them. Big cheques to B. Deigan. I point to them and say I know about them. Other cheques at least as big to two other names. I don't know the names, although there's the illusion of a far-distant bell ringing a few forests away when I look at one of them. Then, for a period stopping maybe three months ago, constant withdrawals from ATMs and payments by debit card with cash withdrawals as well. Every day, including Saturdays and Sundays. Then that pattern ceases completely. The manager has left the Parker on the table. I use it to trace the ATM withdrawals, so many and so similar, they are a shout on the page, and put it like a silvery bottom line under the final one.

'What happened here?'

They exchange glances.

'The bank stopped payment. We had notified him, of course, and sought—'

Oh, shut *up*, why don't you? I gesture. So on this date, six weeks? Seven? Seven weeks before my father died, everything stopped. No money from anywhere. I flinch before I can prevent myself. O, my beloved Father, you stole from me. It was you took the 500 clean flat banknotes out of my bag. The clean flat notes. I blamed some nameless villain in the radio station, considered blaming our cleaning lady.

The two of them are looking at me, expectantly. None of your business, I think with a sudden onset of lordliness. You are financial servitors and I'll not sell my thieving, hanging dead, purpled stinking . . . I get suddenly so overwhelmed that I put my head down on the table. After a minute she rubs my back, which is unwelcome and irrelevant, but she means well. Don't we all? Didn't you all, Dad? Or did you?

I get my head back up and say aloud: 'Correct me if I'm wrong. On this date, nearly two months before my father died, he had no money. No available money. Literally, he would have had to borrow money from a friend. You people wouldn't have let him have a cent.'

The two of them start to talk together, but even out into sharing general agreement. The credit union, I remember, wearily. The poor oul' credit union, jammed into a tiny old workman's cottage on a by-road, manned by the kind of people who run the meals-on-wheels. The manager worries at me until I get to the understanding that this is not *my* problem at all, this is *his* problem. He doesn't quite get to the stage of asking me am I going to get into selling my body on Leeson Street to make up the deficit on his books, but he leaves me in no doubt that he would have moved faster and more punitively if the debtor had not been my father.

Remember your beauty contest, Dougal? I think. In banking terms, it works both ways. You can be at the loser end of the beauty contest, a slaty-eyed fear figure like CJH, and the bank will let you run up an overdraft as tall as Liberty Hall because you're the Prime Minister and give them a right bollocking if they look crooked at you. Or you can be at the winner end of the beauty contest, a gentle, forgetful, famous poet like my father, always on radio and TV, loved by all. Go up against him, foreclose on him and the publicity will do the bank harm, not the poet. Instead, you get coy and persuasive. Heere, Poet. Pishwishwish, Pretty Poet.

'I've already been in discussion today with my legal advisors and with the police,' I say, reaching – fairly successfully – for my mother's most authoritative tone.

Their eyes widen. Police?

'Something very strange was going on, and I have authorised the police to get to the bottom of it.'

Stretching it a bit, that one, but not an outright porkie.

'As soon as I have Probate, I shall present a plan to clear this debt.'

Shall, did both of you hear it? Shall. It's far from shall I was reared but when you're giving the impression you've outrun the Pamplona bulls even as one of them sticks a horn up the leg of your shorts, a shall comes in handy. I instruct them to leave copies of the paperwork because Inspector Synnott will need to see it. (Bloody right, she'll need to see it. Whether I'll let her see it is another story.) Thank them very much for going to the trouble and inconvenience of coming all the way over here, they're very good, much appreciated, thank you, be in touch, absolutely. Door closing. I stand behind the wooden bit, leaning against it, for quite a while before I go into the kitchen to wash the still-full cups of tea.

Notes from Bead meeting #4:

No painting. (Garage).
Cancel gardening company.
Check lawyer: my own earnings safe?
Check credit union.

The following day, I am efficiency on steroids. I ring the gardening company and say I have to terminate the contract. No, nothing to do with the herbicide going on my neighbour's apple tree, I appreciate that was an accident, it's just circumstances have changed and I'll be sending them a letter today, they should bill me any outstanding amounts. There is a half-hearted noise about cancellation fees and I smile through gritted teeth down the phone at him. Don'teventhinkaboutit.

I give the lawyer a truncated version of the figures.

'I propose to fax you the most instructive of the pages the bank manager left with me,' I say, and do it. I sound more like my mother every minute. Hey, Mam? Now, I'm not *the* grown-up. I'm the only grown-up left standing, and it's scary.

Around seven that evening, I go down to the credit union and they tell me, very properly, what they can't tell me or give me, but I am given to understand, in a way that wouldn't stand up in a smartie box, never mind a courtroom, that my father withdrew the few thousand he'd been saving in the last few weeks before he died.

Bingo, I think, getting back into my car. Except that I don't think I'm winning anything. I think what I'm doing is confirming a major loss. Financial. And worse.

Outside the door, when I arrive home, is the Lexus. Whatever way he has it parked, as I get out of my own car, it draws my eye to the bloody big hole at the bottom of the garage door. Cannot get that fixed, I think, no matter what it cuts off the value of the house. But a hole in a garage door, in the currently complicated scheme of things, is not going to have life-changing implications for me, personally. Wrong again, but I'm beginning to realise I wouldn't recognise an implication if it came with a passport, visa and coupon for a free steam clean.

Rogan waits until I get the front door open – does he think to get into the house he's gonna have to fight me for the lone key, out here on the driveway? Then he follows me. Carrying flowers. *Flowers?* I stop in the open doorway and wait for him to reach me.

'You here about the missing computer bits?'

'Among other things, yeah.'

This leaves him holding the flowers. Frig him.

'Dougal. Very recently, I remember, the computer bits you removed from my father's property were important, or seemed important. Other events have made them considerably less important, so why don't you and I call it quits on the components?'

He hands me the flowers and I retreat like a fool into the hall. His hand is at my waist, guiding me into the kitchen. One bit of me wants to hit him with the flowers. Another bit hopes he notices how slim that waist has got. Not that it's any of his business. And not that it could ever compete with the teeny weeshy, handspan waist of Nicola the Midget. In the kitchen, I put the flowers down on the table, and like a moron put the kettle on. He reaches into a press overhead and produces a vase I haven't seen in years.

'How the hell did you know that was up there?'

'I put it up there for your mother one day when I was here – longer reach.'

I recycle the uneaten wrapped biscuits from the lawyer, policewoman, bankers, etc., and when I serve us, find he has arranged the flowers very creditably in the vase and got rid of the wrapper and ribbons.

'Woman of property, are you?' he asks, and the question is so wildly inapposite, I gape at him. He looks slightly defensive and points to the good china.

'Oh. Oh, no, that's not for you,' I say. Queen of Tact, me. He smacks himself on the back of the hand for effrontery in thinking I might have given him the good stuff deliberately. 'I had lawyers and police officers and bankers and you name it here yesterday.'

'Ah,' he says.

'And the "ah" means what, exactly?'

'You're tidying up your father's estate.'

'If that's what they call the Kalahari, these days.'

'Kalahari?'

'Desert.'

'Desert?'

'Hey, you know something, Dougal, if I wanted to ask myself questions, I could do it without your physical presence. No offence, the roses are nice, but if Ms Waldron has stolen your brain since the last time we talked, could you get a transplant?'

'Warden.'

'Like I care.'

'Pretty obvious you don't.'

'Oh, for Jasus sake, I really haven't the time for this cutprice argumentative shite.'

'Your father's estate is – is . . . ?'

'Insolvent, I suppose someone like you would say. However, that's not something that really concerns you.'

'No, it does. I owe your father money.'

'For stealing bits out of his computer?'

'Flannery, shut up, would you?'

I can't think of anything to say to this, partly because I am suddenly deadly tired.

'Just listen to me, OK? I trace things on computer. That's my—'

He blithers around, looking for a word other than 'speciality' or 'genius'. My hand twiddles an acknowledgement. *I can't think of the word, either, but I'm with you. Keep going.*

'Your father is an investor.'

This seems a bit out of sequence, but I nod.

'I'm installing software, cleaning up things on the computer, and I find evidence he's been doing things he shouldn't have been doing.'

Like insider trading? My father?

'Any kind of deviation from the standards laid down by the Stock Exchange endangers Amazing Trace,' he said, opening his hands to me in a 'see?' gesture.

He says no more, and I cannot ask him any more questions, because if he told me until I was drawing the old age pension about Stock Exchange standards, I wouldn't know what he was talking about, and I do not, really, want to know details I might pointlessly reveal to Inspector Synnott.

'I liquidated his shareholding,' he says. 'Now, here's the problem. You can't check any of this because the early part of it was before we were properly set up, and so I could extricate him without it causing him problems. You have to trust me that I'm giving you the proper value, not gipping you.'

He hands over a funny-looking cheque. It is made out for one million, three hundred and forty-five Euro. I want to cry. I want to laugh. I want to hug him. I want to check over have I told Lyn any of my father's financial disaster, and would she have told him and could this be another of his high-minded pain-in-the-tits rescue operations.

'Thanks, but no thanks,' I say. 'I don't know what's behind this particular lifeboat, but you know something? I'd rather drown.'

He stands up, plants his hands on the table and waits until I look up at him. Then he smiles a mad triumphant smile at me.

'Thought you'd say that,' he says. 'Flannery, you want to do the same as your cowardly and very cruel father, that's up to you. Drowning, hanging. If you want to live up to his standards or, rather, *die* up to his standards, you will drown in such a way as to do maximum hurt to those who love you, and a good few do. But my debt to him and to you is fulfilled. That's not a cheque, Flannery. It's a bank draft. That means the money has already exited my account and nothing you can do will put the money back into my account. You can tear it up, set fire to it or roll it up tight and stick it up your arse for all I care, but I've paid to you what I owed to your father and I sincerely hope you use it to get you out of the shit he's left you in.'

Smack-smack of the right hand on the table, and he's gone. Gone with such speed and such a swing of the front door that the bank draft floats up in the air as if it's going to follow him. It settles down beside his cup. Still full, the cup. Something of a special cuisine, I'm developing here. Looks good, stays undrunk. On the other hand, if someone's going to force you to take a million and a half you desperately need, it looks better if it settles down beside good china as opposed to Polish workmen's aluminium mugs.

Cruel and cowardly. The words gyrate in my head. About my father. I leave the bank draft where it is, face down on the table, and walk to the door into the garage. Open it. Step down into the shadows. Over at the door, a puddle of sunshine coming in through the hole where the wood has rotted away. Rot. Decay. Damp. Such sweet sickening smells. I stand where I stood that night. Did he do it in that way, in that place, from that rafter, to hurt me in the worst way? To position himself so I could not but see him? The suicide note was not written to a biddable stranger. It was written to his daughter. The daughter he called – briefly, after an American lecture tour – feisty Flannery. He would have known I would never call the police before I searched for him, before I found him. I slowly, with the familiar cramping dread, lift my face, my gaze to the rafter the old rope was wound around.

Out of the darkness overhead something comes at me, at my face, neck, dribbling down the front of me, wet, warm and dead, bloodied, mucoused, boneless.

I am still screaming when Doug Rogan comes at a run in through the hall door, grabs me, searches me, puts two big hands flat on either side of my face, over my ears, so the screams roar around my skull. I can see his face, his head shaking, no, no, no, mouth pursing, shh, shh, my name in his mouth and slowly, the screams lose power, lose strength, lose volume and I stagger. He lets go of my face and gets his arms around me. I cry, shuddering, for a long time, and he gets me into the kitchen, holding me still, talking almost behind my head. It was a cat, I hear him saying, again and again. Cat. Got in through the hole in the garage door. Only a cat. A cat looking for somewhere to have its kittens. A cat up in the roof. One of the newborns, that's all it was, what fell, one of the newborns. Dead. Kittens often die, the first time a cat becomes a mother. That was all it was. A dead kitten. Newborn.

He gets me sitting down and pulls the jumper off me, so I can't see the blood any more. Leaves me and comes back with a dressing-gown out of my room. Gets it on me as if I was half-crippled. Wets a tea towel and wipes the dried stuff off my face and neck. Then throws the tea towel in the sani-can. You could be expensive, I think, then remember. You can't complain that a man has thrown out a serviceable tea towel if he has given you enough money to buy thousands of tea towels.

'What made you come back?'

At this, he laughs so much he has to sit down.

'Jesus, woman, the screams could be heard in Manchester. Instant replay, Amityville Horror. I'm surprised you didn't trigger Dublin City's Emergency Plan.'

'But you hadn't driven off?'

'No. I'd forgotten to give you a note for your accountant about gift tax, and I was searching for it in the car when the screams started. Whoo. Fortunately, the front door hadn't latched.'

Happened before, with you, I think.

'Poor frigging cat,' he adds. 'Creeps into this unused garage, old car sitting covered in dust, nice bit of tarp thrown over the rafters underneath the roof, nice and warm and dark and quiet, starts giving birth for the first time – "what *is* this godawful pain?" – minding its own business, lets the first poor misshapen outcome fall and motherajasus, the siren from below.'

'Fuck the cat,' I say.

'Some tomcat did, that's why we're all gathered here this afternoon,' he says, producing the letter for my accountant.

'Doug?'

'Make up your mind. Am I Doug or Dougal?'

'I only call you Dougal to send up Nicola.'

'I frigging well prefer Doug, with or without Nicola.'

'Oh. Anyway, should we go back out and check on the cat?'

'No. She'll go daft altogether if her space is any more invaded. I'll put a little water and food in the gap in the door. That'll hold her until tomorrow, and we can have a look at her and the kittens then.'

He finds a can of tuna fish and decants it onto a saucer, puts water into a porridge bowl and carries both out of the front door. When he comes back, he washes his hands. He has a thing about clean hands. I've never seen him with dirty hands.

'The hell were you out in the garage for anyway?' he wants to know, as he gets ready to finally leave.

I finish the tea he has made. Think about standing up. Think against it. Look at him levelly.

'What you said about the way my father did it. I wanted to – almost see it again, I suppose. You think he wanted me to see it.'

'He didn't make much of an effort to prevent you seeing it.'

'Well, the note was—'

'What note?'

The silence is absolute.

'Do the guards know there was a note?'

'No. Nobody knows but me. And now you, by accident. You going to rush off and tell them?'

'Why didn't you show it to them?'

'Mind your own business.'

He looks at me silently. Trying to figure out what would have been in the note, probably.

'Flannery. Show it to the guards. If there's something bad in it, better they know about it than you start messing around in dangerous areas. Show it to them.'

I say nothing and don't look at him. *Do not blame Doug . . .*

20

Negative Equity

———◆◆◆———

I ask the accountant to meet me at the bank, where I present him with the note about gift tax and hand the bank manager the bank draft. They both know the name Dougal Rogan and are aware of the buzz of flotation or takeover by one of the biggies. Impressed, they pass the bank draft from one to another with reverence. This man must have been very fond of your father? I bring my shoulders up around my ears. Sure, wasn't everybody? Do you know this Dougal very well? Depends on your definition of knowing someone very well. First time I met him, I broke my arse while he watched, most recently was on the receiving end of recently dead near-kittens on the site where my father did himself in. I guess you could say I know him pretty well. Do you trust him? What's to trust? I'm not giving *him* a million three, he's giving *me* a million three.

The bank manager gets severe. The fact is that because there is so much negative equity in the home, and because so much of what you could only call asset-stripping went on before he died, and even if you get 800,000 for the house, which at the moment you might, the million three will still leave you somewhat in debt. I talk about royalties coming in, he talks about my father having taken a two-year advance on the British royalties, I open my mouth, then close it again. This poor bank manager had me in debt to a million and a half yesterday. Today, somebody the bank manager has never met has surfaced to improve the situation to nearly even steven. He's trying to figure out how much of my father's pre-terminal spending spree was due to flawed genetics and how soon the heritage will show up in me.

I sign a lot of papers and get out of there. When I get home, Inspector Synnott is waiting for me. May she come in? Of course she may. As I put my key in the lock, the Lexus pulls up behind her car.

'This a neighbour?' she asks.

'No. Guy who used to do computer stuff for my father.'

In a Lexus? Right. Dougal gets out of the car, clutching an oblong plastic box, a sack labelled Organic Kitty Litter, and three cans of Kit e Kat. He follows us into the kitchen.

'Inspector Synnott, this is Dougal Rogan.'

'Of Amazing Trace?'

Dougal, who is very suited and posh behind the cat litter, nods. I try to work out who to explain to the other in which order and decide the hell with this.

'I'll make tea,' I announce. 'Doug, you'll go out to the garage and Inspector Synnott will go with you and you'll explain what happened yesterday and then we'll have tea.'

Surprisingly, both go along with this. I can hear the voices murmuring to each other, and the odd clatter as he opens cans and lays out dishes. When they come back, Synnott has unbent more than I've ever seen her.

'Two tiny little kittens,' she says. 'Two! Eyes closed and so fragile.'

'Don't want to know,' I say and offer Dougal tea. He refuses. I hand him his old key.

'If you're in charge of the cat department for the next couple of weeks,' I say.

He tucks it into the pocket of his waistcoat (*waistcoat!*) and leaves, closing the front door very carefully. Synnott doesn't open her folder of papers, just holds her cup and looks at me over it.

'Did Mr Rogan tell you why he was here yesterday?' I ask.

'Before the cat, you mean? No. He didn't.'

'He was here to pay off what he sees as a moral debt to my father. My father invested in Amazing Trace at the beginning, and then did something that wouldn't have been good for the business, so Dougal cut him out of it, but came through with the amount of money my father's investment would have earned if it had still been there, if you know what I mean.'

She looks at me as if I have just confessed to an ongoing erotic relationship with a jellyfish.

'Nonsense,' she says.

Shut up, I tell myself. Talking too much, you are, you walked into that one, because you don't quite believe Doug's explanation, either. But you didn't need to tell her about it.

'Let's put that to one side, just for the moment,' she says. 'I need to talk to you.'

She starts with a reference to the name of the police force. Garda Siochana.

Guardians of the Peace. Not just in the business of rounding up the suspects and getting the convictions, this police force is in the business of guarding the peace. Preventing crime. I try to convey that I'm with her so far, but have no idea where she's headed with this general exposition.

'I have absolutely no doubt your father wrote a note before he committed suicide and that you have it in your possession,' she says. 'I'm raising it with you because it is my job to prevent crime, and you are endangering yourself by holding on to that note. You are involving yourself over-confidently with a dangerous, monied international sub-culture.'

I'm looking at her pop-eyed. Dougal Rogan? Part of a dangerous, monied and international sub-culture? If she knows all this, why was she making nice out in the garage with him, looking at the two kittens? I drink my lukewarm tea with a sense of sitting on cracking ice. And the worst of it is, I never knew there was ice in the vicinity at all.

'Because there has been so much publicity about it, people like yourself believe it's all been exposed, all been dealt with,' she says. 'You are wrong. It is highly organised, characterised by high levels both of collusion and of denial.'

She lets that sink in and pours herself a fresh cup of tea. 'Well?' she demands.

'I know you're not going to believe this, but I have genuinely no clue as to what you're talking about,' I say. 'I would—'

'I'm talking about paedophilia,' she snaps. 'The sexual exploitation of babies and children by adults and the international propagation of the practice on the Internet.'

I'm sitting, mouth open, trying to get a handle on this.

'You mean Amazing Trace is some kind of—?'

She leans forward, batting Amazing Trace out of the way.

'Flannery, let's cut the pretending, will we? Your father, Edmund Stapleton, was a paedophile.'

This is worse than the dead thing coming off the rafters onto me, this is a crawling many legged thing, part of the pewter grey horror swinging and creaking and I cry out against it and know it to be true. My despair terrifies her, and she clutches my hands, hard, across the table while I do some kind of begging against this, some prayerful attempt to roll back the tide until it swamps me, shivering, and I just cry.

'I have cried more these weeks than since I was a child,' I

eventually say, apologetically, withdrawing my hands, conscious that in some way she may feel tainted by touching me since I am so closely related to him. She waits until I have blown my nose and put away the hankie, then gathers my hands again. I let her, feeling destroyed back to childhood, bombed into infantilism.

'Are you sure?' I ask, and correct it. 'How sure are you?'

There was a complaint, she says, naming the year after I was born, but it never became a charge. Nobody really believed it of a man like my father. Plus, the child was a damaged, untrustworthy kid who came from a bad home. Looking for attention, went the rationale. Making up things. Very hurtful to this nice lecturer who does so much for boys from broken homes.

'But he *did*,' I say. 'He was so committed to them.'

'C'mon, Flannery,' she says, all blunt banging of back door closed so I am offered no escape. 'Your employer has shown me scripts you've done on this topic. You know the truth. You know the score.'

'My employer? Lyn, you mean? Oh, please, don't tell me Lyn knows?'

'About your father? I suspect she does. She passed on two transcripts of calls to one of the programmes there which pretty clearly identified your father as the accused perpetrator in a couple of incidents. The calls were recorded but not broadcast. She was keeping strictly within the intent of the law by letting us hear them. She said she trusted they came to nothing and that she would bring them to your attention only if they *did* come to something.'

'In that case,' I say, attacking, spitting fury, 'Lyn knew before I knew. If it's true. *If* it's true.'

She opens her file and takes a folder out of it. The top of the folder has been poking out the top of the file from the beginning. Moss-green, the folder, with a string through a hole at the top to hold the contents, the string finishing, both sides, in a T-shaped metal retainer. Printing on the front, including the government harp. It is taller than A4, this folder. Foolscap, I remember, it's called. Long time since I saw foolscap.

'I'll go see how the cats are doing,' she says and moves away into the hall.

Opened, the folder contains typed pages. Perhaps six together. Fuzzy lettering and wrinkle dirt on the pages. Carbon copies, rather than originals. I am engaged with it before I mean to, sucked into the bare narrative. So formal, that narrative. No adjectives or colour of any kind. Nothing simply happened. No impressions. Just on the fifth day of the sixth month of 1979 (approx.) Professor Stapleton did something. Or the Matron did something. I read it to the last page. It ended with a formal note that this was a statement given in the presence of a named garda, that the subject of it had read it and to the best of his recollection it was true.

When I was a toddler, this was being typed by some garda. Probably a ban garda. Wasn't that what they called the women, then?

'Coming along, coming along,' Synnott says, brushing her skirt as she comes back in. 'They'll be fine, your kittens.'

She sits down again and takes back the moss-green folder without comment. Behind it is a print out of a spreadsheet.

'What do you know of a company called Fresh Starts?' she asks.

'Nothing. Why?'

'Because if we analyse the movements of your father's money, we find, in one period of little more than six weeks, a lot of odd transfers.'

She puts the documents in front of me.

'See here? Withdrawals from ATMs, virtually on a daily basis, the maximum possible sum every time. Cash advances on two credit cards. Cheques written to cash. It adds up to almost £200,000 and seems to end up in this account, which otherwise was fairly inactive. Then a cheque goes to Fresh Starts. Which seems to have been set up around the same time.'

I shake my head.

'Don't worry about it,' she says, accepting my ignorance.

'Why do you believe me when I say some things if you think I'm lying about a suicide letter?'

'Some people are bad liars because they lie rarely,' the inspector says. 'You lie rarely.'

'It probably comes of being an only child,' I say. 'Your parents know you too well for you to deceive them easily, and you don't have competitive siblings to need the lying weapon against.'

When she's gone, I ring Lyn.

'Need to see you, Lyn.'

'When?'

'ASAP.'

'ASAP as in take you to A & E or ASAP as in after work?'

It is half three. There is a half-knock at the front door, then the key turns. Rogan gives me a curt wave and disappears into the garage.

'ASAP after work would be fine.'

'Why don't we meet on the beach, our spot?'

'OK.'

Our spot was a corner of dunes identifiable because it was opposite the high-prowed wreck of a wooden ship out in the bay where we once or twice met as teenagers in crisis, inflating it beyond its real role in our lives by calling it 'our spot' and promising to meet there more frequently than we ever did.

I go upstairs until I hear his car going away, then I come down, in jeans and a wax jacket, and drive to the beach. As I pull away from the house, I wonder what price it will earn. Never thought I would be even half-interested in all these reports by some man named Bacon about how long the boom in house prices will last, but then I never thought, either, that I would know, understand or care about concepts like 'Negative Equity'.

'Sums up the value of my life, right now,' I say as the car picks up speed. 'Negative equity. Still, you can't fall off the floor. It can't get any worse than this.'

The minute I have it said, a chill comes over me. I believed that about my mother's eye, my mother's death, the swinging, creaking horror in the garage and, every time, life has managed to get worse. It can do it again.

I lock the car and turn the collar of the wax jacket up. At least an hour before Lyn will arrive. Time to walk and work out the next step. Except that, walking into the wind, my eyes half-closed, vision ghost-sliced, up and down, by my own eyelashes, I begin to put life, flesh, hopes and dreams around the typed chronology in the statement Synnott showed me.

If the unimaginable were true, if my father was what she said, then of course he would have supported charities filled with little boys tossed out of damaged families, little boys who had no rules to be sure of, no guidelines to trust, no authority figures to rely on. Little boys left in a maelstrom of shifting norms, desperate for affection, their neediness aching out of them in every move, every syllable. How they would have loved him, this tall, ascetic, angular man with the soft dark blond hair, a little long, always, curling over his shirt collar.

Loved his gentleness, his way of talking to you as if you were the most important, most talented, most insightful person he ever met, the way he would fasten on something you said and make you repeat it, it was so clever he wanted to hear it again.

How the individual, singled out, would have felt specially validated, rewarded for an individuality nobody else had wanted or valued. How the little boy would have looked forward to the man's arrival, listening out for the distinctive noise of his car's engine, because to a boy, each car has a voice as unique as that of a human. There would have been the electricity of the meeting of eyes across cold corridors, shining institutional floors beneath them as they walked, the boy's back warmed by the casual comradely pat delivered by the man as they met, shoulder hankering for the crushing hug, wishing it would never end.

And then the extra quiet reassurances as they walked the woods around the institution. Shh – touch of palm at back of neck – shh. Listen. The hand left there, as if forgotten, warm, comforting. D'you hear it? The bird? D'you know which it is? The man dropping to his hunkers, arm around the boy's waist, the man looking upward, but the boy watching *him*, the big eyes of him, all the better to spot you with, my dear, the smiling mouth, the hand dropping in a caress so inconsequential, the least squirm would have transformed it into a schoolmaster's mild reproof for not knowing the birdcall, or approval for knowing.

Every visit would be threaded through with secrets that became secrets because of the little boy's need to own something, anything, but above all, to own a connection with this beautiful adult, to be special to this special man, more than the generic of the boys receiving his other kindnesses, more worthy. Each small perfect gift given by the man would have provoked a need in the boy to reciprocate, to give in return, but what to give, from poverty, from overseen poverty, from state-owned, state-regulated saved pittances? The exquisite sensitivity of the boy selected for that sensibility, for those fragile, infinitely responsive needy nerve ends would have sensed without ever a word passing, sensed what pleased this lovely man, what was a gift to him. And then there would be the covert, wondrous sense of a small point of power, a capacity to bring this man to near helplessness, a near helplessness that could be repeated and that led to more time, more secret time with him, more of the touches and excitements that isolated the child from others, because the boy knew enough not to tell. Unwarned, unarmed, he would be silent.

And when the helplessness turned into something sickening for a child to see, the hands of the adult would turn bony and strong, the aquiline profile predatory, the gifts would become payment. The little, growing boy would be suddenly old, knowing more than he understood himself to know, his flowering short and sour, every forced servicing a confirmation of what no child wants to be. But at least, the boy would believe, as he moved into new classrooms, new sporting leagues, at least there is this special thing.

There would be no words around the mutual dependence, because it was a thing that happened in hushed silence where moans broke through and were stifled instinctively. It would always be there, the boy would believe, reaching hungrily, because such is the imperative of adolescence, for everything that will ensure its death.

He would relish, sour-faced, the boy, the prophetic prognoses of its death, the calls of My, how you've grown, aren't you a big boy now, shooting up all the time, got put out of the

sopranos, happens to us all, nice lookin' lad, no girl will be safe
from you.

The absences, at first, would be understandable. This overseas conference or that. The gifts less frequent. Then one day,
he would realise the last gift had been precisely that; the last.
The greetings would become the raised, tilted hand – how's it
going? Nice to seeya. In time, the man would be of equal
height to the boy, always courteous, warm, gentle, dredging up
the name from among so many others, denying, by the very
act of dredging, that it had been unique, what they had shared.
Or special. Not to the man. And the boy would know he was
one of many, qualifying not because of the essence of him, but
because the man perceived him to have no essence, not
because of the fullness of him, but because the man perceived
him to be an empty vessel, rattling with need. There was
nothing more to it than presence and age and type, the young
man would know, cringing at the memory, shrivelled by fear,
because what would be different, now? Any future caress,
every future caress, would come tainted by the gentle duplicity
of the way he had been trained and thrown away.

The instinct would be to conceal, pretend, deny. What's to
be done? Each young man would believe himself, as he once
believed himself uniquely privileged, uniquely cherished, now
would believe himself uniquely used. Until the television
programmes started. About orphanages visited by smiling,
smiling, damnéd clerics, where little girls and little boys were
offered up for private counselling, poor troubled minors, the
party dresses spread over the black trousered thighs,
the terrifying sounds and smells, the beatings later when
the children told and were branded liars. Even then, the rage
would be more toxic, because Edmund Stapleton was no Fr
Brendan Smyth, no filthy ugly mad old man, gloating in the

black maria in his sixties, flaunting an erection occasioned by some little girl, some passerby on a street corner.

Edmund Stapleton would not easily be accused. He was a beauty contest winner, was Edmund Stapleton, a man of whom it was not possible to believe what some young man might accuse him of, and then the young man would have, comparatively speaking, the wrong track record, would he not, no pun intended, but why does he always wear long sleeves and the police in England have records of charges and he's been seen in the Phoenix Park, you know where in the Phoenix Park, late at night, could you possibly put his word up against a man of such probity, a married man with a family, I mean for his family's sake, you couldn't run that sort of story, it wouldn't fly, or if you ran it, it would be coloured, in the tabloids, by sympathy for the man smeared and the broadsheets would have lengthy editorial meetings, their ethics in a twist further twisted by the fact that Stapleton is such a nice guy, no side to him, and gives great quote . . .

Parents are there to protect their children, but these children had no parents, or worse than no parents, parents in squats living between syringed instalments of oblivion, their children half remembered as illustrations of how wonderful the parents were once, a long time ago, when they were clean. Or nearly clean. And when you're clean is when it works best and then the children are just mumbled endearments and if they're in care, it's only for a while, because parents are best for their kids, right, right?

Parents are there to protect their children, but maybe I was protecting my father without knowing it. By just existing, I was testament that he couldn't be one of those perverts. You could understand priests being that way. It explained itself with a double excuse, like a lying teenager. Either they knew they were that way and went into the priesthood because it was the best place to get at kids, celibacy covering everything, or the celibacy in the priesthood drove them to it. But a man with a wife about whom he wrote love poetry, a man with a little girl he constantly talked about, 'My wonderful daughter, Flannery,' of that man, it could not be imagined. The accusation would sheer off the Teflon coated steel of him, rebounding.

But the young men and sometimes the young wives to whom they had told the choking secrets of their non-childhood, would be led by many things. By the critical mass of reaction to the church stories, as one order after another had its men and its women accused. By the strange turnabout that, once unbelievable under any circumstances, the victims were now unassailable under any circumstances, because to challenge a detail, the smallest detail, was to deny their victimhood, to further victimise them and no reasonable man or woman wanted to do that.

The young men would begin to conflate the exposes, believing themselves to have as much chance of fame, of television stardom as the middle-aged women featuring in the docu dramas. But the women would be rounded by age, sag-faced and unthreatening, cleansed by their own mother-hood, bunched together with other women, whereas the men would be loners, thinned and thinning on top and thinned in the lips, unshriven by fatherhood because it is the mothers who carry, clean and swaddle, some worse than innocent because 'stable relationship' with another man serves in suburbia to feed the self-congratulatory illusory tolerance of the middle-aged and middle-class, but is a devalued currency against the gold standard minted by the poet quoted at their wedding. The ones without that currency would begin to find their damaged present investigated and used to question their veracity about the past. That kind of person, doing those kinds of things, would always have been . . . The argument would never go the other way, that a round-eyed open optimist could be warped into a sly sliminess.

I have walked much, much further than intended, driving, head hunched, against the wind. Now, when I stand, it almost revolves me, faces me back where I have come from, my face burning, sparking with the sudden relief of shelter, every pore alive, scoured, reddened. I haul my hands out of the depths of my pockets as I half-walk, half-run, pushed by the wind, palming my cheeks to find them icy to the touch, yet wonderfully warm inside the tautened skin.

Out of nowhere comes a stray remembered fact from a script written months ago. The married paedophiles blame their wives for getting too involved in social work, or too involved in the kids. No time for the husband any more, so what could he do? I suppose I was lucky, I think, that he didn't say 'Don't blame yourself' in the note.

Lyn appears around a car, hoods her face into the wind with her arm, drawing it back and down so the thick scarf of black hair is held low at her neck, and waits for me until I am within a hundred feet of her, then comes to meet me, letting the black hair go.

'Whassup?' I ask, the two of us turning out of the wind.

'This 'n that.'

'Nuthin' much?'

'*Bor*ing.'

'Same here.'

'Happens.'

'Days like this.'

Neither of us can think of another offering, and we laugh, knowing we used to be better at it. Back when the two of us would sit in a bus and go for maybe four minutes, never missing the beat of it, knowing middle-aged couples were glancing at each other, trying to remember what we were saying to share with each other later as examples of the impoverished vocabulary of the young.

'What'll you give me?'

Another of our games, designed to cheat payment for something out of the other before revealing what the purchased item was. We got so good at this, last year in school, we had to agree to a financial ceiling for fear we'd bankrupt each other.

'Fifty quid.'

Lyn laughs out loud.

'You're supposed to start with pennies,' she says.

'Haven't time to piss around at the lower levels any more. Cut to the chase. Get to the point. I have this boss in radio who shits all over introductions. So I go straight to the big money.'

'I'll take fifty quid.'

'What do I get?'

'Chips.'

'*What?*'

We're nearly at the dunes. She pulls up the tote and reveals it to be one of those squared off, brick-shaped insulated food carriers. Helping each other, one-handed, we get up the snowy side of a dune and coast on our heels down into the nest in the middle, where she slides a greaseproof wrapper and miniature salt packages out. We eat out of the same bag, hunched at each other to keep the salt from blowing away.

'Need something to drink,' I mutter between mouthfuls.

Out of the side pocket of the food carrier, she produces two bottles of Diet Coke jammed into round insulating sleeves. They are sweaty with condensation, as cold as the chips are hot.

'Ririculous lengsto gofor chips,' I say through a mouthful of them, nudging the food carrier with my toe.

'Chips deserve it,' she says. 'Chips rule.'

'These chips rule,' I agree, eating more.

Her hand goes into the carrier and produces another bag.

'These are not McDonald's chips,' I say.

'Fries,' she corrects.

'These are not even Beshoff's chips.'

'Better'n Beshoffs.'

'Who made them?'

She looks into the carrier. Furtively.

'My mother.'

'You rang your mother from work and asked her to make two bags of chips?'

'I asked her to par-fry them and finish them when I arrived at her house.'

'In the middle of the afternoon. What was your mother's reaction to this?'

'She wanted to know who she was making chips for.'

'Why?'

'Because if it was Piers she could disapprove.'

'She thinks Piers eats too many chips?'

'No, she thinks I am putty in Piers's hands.'

'She's right.'

'That's true.'

'What she say when you told her they were for me?'

'Wanted to know if you liked salt and vinegar because she'd put in a little bottle of vinegar.'

This chokes me up ridiculously. She hands me a napkin. It is linen and has embroidered daisies on the corners.

'Couldn't be bothered bringing me a decent paper serviette, though, could you?'

'Nope.'

'Why are you putty in Piers's hands?'

'Oh, you know us bimbos.'

'Yeah, and that apart.'

'I'm mad about him.'

'As in lustful?'

'I love him.'

'Oh, shit.'

'But it doesn't *matter*,' she reassures me. 'It doesn't do me any harm.'

'He flaunts the "take 'em or leave 'em" uncommitted crap.'

'He works very hard, though.'

I scrunch up my eyes, ostentatiously trying to make this make sense, and she laughs.

'Plus he's very talented.'

'Your point being?'

'He's talented, good-looking, witty. He can be very kind, too.'

'So you don't play hard to get, you just let him know you love him?'

She nods. Probably everybody close to her knows she's daft about this bugger because she feels no need to pretend. I've spent roughly twelve years pretending I am sought after, lusted after, yearned for. I've bored the arse off myself, attracted nothing worth a toss, convinced nobody, yet if I went all nakedly honest, I wouldn't win the way Lyn wins. I say a version of this aloud.

'I'm not winning,' she says, wide-eyed that I can't see the simplicity of it. 'It doesn't matter that other guys fancy me if I don't fancy them. Piers is the most interesting person I know, more interesting even than my father. Why would I pretend he's not the most interesting?'

'Too available is dangerous. Masochistic. Makes you exploitable.'

She smiles at me with what is either great wisdom or a new brand of good-looking dumb and I don't know which.

'I know an equivalent,' she says.

'Oh?'

'Dougal.'

'Lost you.'

'Dougal's never pretended not to be in love with you, he always comes back after you've thrown him away, and he never loses by it.'

This is so off every point that I don't know which angle to tackle it from.

'So he's out there in the mansion, hiding in the east wing from the predatory advances of Nicola Waldren?'

'Something close to that. Warden, anyway.'

'Lyn.'

'Yeah?'

'Don't tidy up and don't do any more girltalk, OK?'

'OK.'

'My father.'

'Yes.'

'D'you think he did it?'

In spite of what I have said, she tidies everything into the bag and pokes it behind her knees.

'Do you?'

She says nothing and my heartbeat in my head is a muffled drumbeat, the lifeless timekeeping of the military with the stepping hesitation behind the riderless horse. I don't hide the tears that scorch my eyes. She puts her arm over my shoulder and we sit there, sheltered by the surrounding dunes, listening to the whistling wind in the low-flying white sand.

'Don't tell any of this to Piers, all right?'

'Oh, *Flannery*.'

'You told Synnott.'

'I told the guards what I had to tell them. No more, no less, and I didn't tell Piers about it, either.'

'Why not?'

'I was friends with you first.'

'That's ridiculous, you know that?'

'Yes, but whatever works.'

'I think he was paying them off.'

'Your father? Paying someone he – he had— The victims?'

The plural is like a stab.

'Who else?'

Why would one single victim be less awful? I wonder. Because it would be an aberration? A visitation of a devil, fought off, thereafter? An evil brought under control, regretted.

'Who else could he be paying off?'

'Blackmailer?'

'How would they know?'

The two of us ponder this.

'D'you know the worst thing, Lyn?'

'Your mother.'

'She must have known.'

'No.'

'There was a complaint, although it never went to court. When I was just a toddler.'

'It doesn't mean she knew. It doesn't mean she believed it. You wouldn't believe it about someone you totally loved. You could never believe it.'

But you could never quite *not* believe it, either.

I wonder if this was the cause of the watchfulness of my

mother, down through the years, the wariness, especially when things were going well, that unexpected relief she would show when disaster struck: God has hit us with this, He wouldn't let the other happen at the same time . . .

Conscious of the deepening darkness and cold around us, I get to my feet and haul Lyn upright, too.

'What I don't get,' I say, in a softer voice in the quiet of my car, 'is why my father felt he had to die. Why did he not just continue to pay them?'

She looks wonderingly at me, unable to come up with the reasons.

'Thanks for the chips. One other thing. You know about this dozy bint of a cat that decided to go into the maternity business in my garage and scared the living bejesus out of me? Inspector Synnott says there are two kittens doing well. One white, one black. D'you want one of them?'

She nods.

'Which one?'

'Black one.'

'OK, now I just have to find some other humanitarian willing to take the white one.'

'Why don't you keep her?'

'She'd have kittens of her own and I'd have to drown them.'

'You didn't drown these ones.'

'No, but that was because the way they announced themselves kind of put me off freestyle drowning, that week.'

'She could be a man kitten.'

'And go around knocking up other kittens?'

'When they stop being kittens.'

The infelicity of this strikes us both simultaneously.

'Lyn.'

'Mmm.'

'You're blushing. Lyn, I'm the only other person here. If you start editing everything you say after you've said it because of a small possibility it might mean something about my father, we're going to have to write to each other.'

'We do anyway.'

'I mean, even when we're together.'

'OK, if it was a man kitten, would you keep it?'

'No, I shagging well wouldn't.'

'Why not?'

'I never had pets.'

'Why did you never have pets?'

'Disease.'

'Which disease?'

'All diseases. Pets carry diseases. My mother said turtles, particularly.'

'You wouldn't want a turtle. They hibernate half the year.'

'And then come out and give you their disease.'

'If you take good care of dogs, they don't give you diseases.'

No, they just knock you over and kill you the way that stupid dumb eager happy black Labrador knocked over my mother.

'They do so. *Toxicara Canis*.'

'What the hell is that?'

'It's this really awful parasite kids can get. My mother had a book by a woman whose little boy got it. It made AIDs look like a paid holiday.'

'You read about it?'

'When I was about twelve. My mother gave it to me because I wanted a dog.'

'Flannery, no offence, but your whole family was kind of the family from hell. I mean, your mother was *nice*, but giving you a book about a lethal parasite to prove to you you shouldn't have a pet . . . You could have had a budgie.'

'Budgies give you psittacosis. Hey, you know something? There's a great radio series in all this. Diseases You can Catch from Your Pet.'

'You'll probably find the only pet you can't catch something from is a snake, but it can get big enough to eat you.'

'Everything else does, why not snakes?' I asked rhetorically, making a note of the item.

'You should keep the white kitten, Flannery.'

'Don't "should" me, Lyn.'

'But have you *seen* them?'

'Lyn. I have more on my mind than effing felines. Cat person, I ain't. I would rather spend the rest of my life frying goats' willies for my breakfast than have anything to do with effing cats. Plus, I have rather more sizeable problems right now. Problems that will not be softened, much as your trivial sentimental soul thinks they will be softened, by having the softer side of Flannery Stapeleton stimulated by a roof-dwelling goddam cat.'

I sometimes think there must be a case for treating someone who can get it so wrong so consistently.

21

A Ball of Twine Unravels

———◆◆◆———

Of course, I did not tell Lyn that Dougal Rogan, best friend of the man she loves, took investment money from my father, didn't bookkeep records properly, caught my father at some kind of insider trading, stole my father's hard disc drive and used it to cause or contribute to causing my father's death. Or that Inspector Synnott has cast doubt on everything Dougal has come up with in the nature of an explanation for me, and put it all in the context of an international paedophile ring.

Conflicted doesn't begin to describe the way I feel when I come home from the office supplies store a few days later and see the Lexus outside my front door. I've managed to miss him on several of his recent visits, or maybe he's skipping days, now that the kittens are doing as well as they're reported to be doing.

I go very quietly upstairs, on the basis that he will leave, without talking to me, if I'm not rattling crockery around in the kitchen. Just after I have closed my bedroom door (which I wouldn't do if he weren't in the house) I hear him coming out in the hall from the garage, but not closing the garage door. Bloody eejit, I think, is going to let those vermin into the house. I can hear him moving around and then I realise it's on the stairs. I'm up off the bed, about to fling my door open in a towering rage, when he calls from outside.

'Flannery, open the door, would you?'

I fling it open and he is there, his two hands clutched, open-fingered, to his chest, fragile paws, two black, two white, between his big fingers, two sparky-eyed kittens, the black one doing a yawn that closes its eyes and shows off a mouthful of the tiniest teeth in the world.

'Sit down on the bed.'

I reverse. He puts the kittens on my lap and what can I do but stroke them? They are so small, I stroke them just with my forefinger, feeling the bones of them inside the silky fur. Before I hear the black one purring, I can feel it vibrating the fabric of my skirt.

I raise my head to argue, but Rogan frowns down at the two little shapes on my lap. The white one raises its little face and I see blood seeping into the fur around the right eye.

'What happened to it?'

'The mother cat seems to hate it.'

'Does that often happen?'

He looks at me as if I'm a Martian.

'You know, cats and dogs,' I say.

He doesn't bother to answer, just looks around him and asks if I have 'a hatbox or something?'

A hatbox? He must watch Audrey Hepburn re-runs.

'This'll do,' he says, opening my dirty laundry wicker basket and turfing my used underwear on the floor. This should be so embarrassing, I think. This should be so invasive. There are so many things I should be doing, right now, of more importance than this. But, half-dragging the laundry basket one-handed, he gets me standing up, clutching the tiny kittens (helped, I have to admit, by their natural instinct to get those tiny feathery claws out and cling onto my dress for dear life) and down the stairs in front of him. I have no idea where we are going, but the little white kitten's eye looks so pathetic I feel I should do anything to help it, and so find myself sitting in the passenger seat in the car with the driver door open. Through the hole in the garage door, I hear vile throaty screams, a few equally vile curse words, and then he comes out with the laundry basket in tow, its noises indicating that it is full of mad mother cat. He jams it between the back of the driver's seat and the front of the back seat so the lid cannot open, but even when the engine gets going, the cat can be heard screeching.

'*Fucking* feline,' Dougal says, sucking the back of his hand.

'You'll get catscratch fever,' I say before I can stop myself.

'What do you know about catscratch fever?'

'Nothing. But it would make a great radio item.'

When he puts his hand back on the steering wheel, a line of tiny red beads of blood appear.

'Would it be too much trouble to inform your passenger as to the purpose of our journey?'

He brushes the dark blond hair off his face and glances sideways at me.

'Want to watch the pomposity, Flannery.'

'Dougal, the marvellous thing is that I have only myself to please.'

'That makes two of us. We're going to my friend Federico the Vet.'

'Freder—'

'*Fede*rico.'

'He Spanish?'

'No, Afrikaans.'

'*Is* he? Oh, shut up why don't you.'

I've been automatically stroking both of the little kittens, who are in a kind of Yin/Yang sign in my lap, and both of them are purring up a storm, in marked contrast to their mother, who is getting as close as a cat can to berserk between the two seats.

'I'll buy you a new laundry basket.'

'You've bought me everything you're ever going to buy me.'

'He-ere we are.'

He takes the basket and goes ahead of me. The vet sounds pure south Dublin to me, but doesn't say that much. Takes the white kitten from me and *tsk-tsks* to it before handing it to his assistant. Dougal is standing, embracing the laundry basket. The cat seems to be trying to climb the inside of it. The vet opens a door into an inside room and Dougal and friend go in there. A moment later, Dougal appears with an obviously lighter laundry basket. We sit, side by side, on a bench seat and I look in the laundry basket.

'How about leaving this here?' I say and Dougal shrugs.

'D'you take Punter here?' I ask, wondering how to get around to doing an Inspector Synnott on his story about the hard disc drive.

He looks momentarily chuffed at me remembering his Golden Labrador's name, which it's taken me the whole journey to recall.

'When I ran over him, I did.'

'You ran over your own dog?'

'Well, his leg.'

'Where?' I meant on the leg. As in, did you just squash his paw a little or take the assault higher?

'Outside the new house.'

'All that extra space made you reckless?'

He nods miserably. Sometimes this man is not adequately protected by humour.

'Did you hurt him?'

How to win friends and get people softened up for questioning.

'I broke his leg.'

'Oh, God. Did he have to be exterminated?'

'Put down or put to sleep is the way normal people describe it, Flannery. No.'

'Does he hate you, now?'

'Why would he hate me?'

'I'd hate you if you broke my leg.'

'I'm sure you would. Dogs haven't got quite your appetite for blame. Punter thinks I am wonderful.'

'Him and Nicola.'

'No, I had to exterminate Nicola.'

'What, broke her legs, too? I always thought they were a bit on the short side.'

All this time, I am holding the little black kitten, who has decided we're boring and gone to sleep in the most perfect little coil I have ever seen. I can't take my eyes off him.

'Nicola and I have separated,' Dougal says with sudden gravity, as if levity about her bendy little brackets of legs would be disloyal to the precious thing they once had.

'That didn't last long,' I say, dizzy with dislocation and confusion of purpose. 'You do the speeded-up version of serial monogamy, don't you?'

'I believe I have been as useful to Nicola at this point in her life as I can be.'

'Dougal? When it comes to pomposity, you have me beat, hands down. "Useful to Nicola" my arse. You bonked her until you were blue in the face and then got bored with the deranged bullshit that comes with her bonking.'

'That would be another way to put it, certainly.'

I don't feel, given the bizarre-ass multiple trauma I am going through, that I should laugh, but I can't help it. He seems to feel that in deference to Nicola the Nutcake, he shouldn't laugh, either, but he does. The vet, emerging with the white kitten, doesn't seem to think either of us should be laughing, and we sit there, abashed, while he tells us he wants to keep the mother cat in for observation, but the kitten can go home. This kitten has no home, I want to tell him. Squatter's rights in a garage is as far as it goes. I get distracted, though, when Federico the Vet says he thinks the mother cat has blinded the white kitten in one eye although he can't be sure. I burst into tears, which surprises the hell out of me, Federico the Vet and Dougal.

'I have drops for you to put in the eye,' Federico says, in a 'there, there' tone. 'And antibiotics to sprinkle on its food.'

I mop up my tears using the white kitten, before I realise it's not a hanky. Not only does it not mind, it purrs.

'Dougal will take care of that stuff,' I say. 'These are not my cats.'

Federico looks warily from one of us to the other. Dougal does that blinking thing guys do to convey that although, right now, I may not be on top of this kitten business, he'll have me up to speed in no time, and the ownership matter will be sorted, also.

In no time, we are back in the car, the two kittens are back doing yin/yang in my lap, and Dougal is telling me that on the kitten front, for the next two days I am on my own, because he has to fly to Munich first thing in the morning. The penulti-mate meeting with the big prospective purchaser who is so gung-ho it looks like there won't be banks big enough to store the loot from the takeover of Amazing Trace. Forty-eight hours of work, after which due diligence investigations will start, and a sale announced within weeks. I wish him luck, but don't specify what kind of luck. Because I am as yet unclear as to how great an enemy he was to my embattled, probably guilty, but none the less frightened father.

I am coping – and coping pretty well, though I say it myself – with the eye drops for the white kitten the next day when the phone goes. I hang the kitten on my shoulder and pick up the phone.

'Miss Stapleton?'

I am uneasy before I know who it is.

'Brian Deigan here.'

'I told you to write to me if you wanted something from me—'

'Don't put down the phone on me, Miss Stapleton, you need to know what I'm phoning to tell you. I have given my story to the *Sunday Times* and I just thought, in fairness, you should know what is going to appear before it does.'

I can say nothing.

'I could come out to see you this afternoon, if you want to meet me.'

'When?'

'Three o'clock?'

I disconnect, pull the phone onto the kitchen table, kittens on my lap, and find the card with the number I need. Dial. Is Inspector Synnott there? She is. I get put through to her. I tell her. Long silence.

'D'you believe he has told the *Sunday Times*?'

'I don't know.'

She arrives before he does, sets up a tape recorder and some kind of remote listening device and then finds the time to be delighted with the kittens' progress.

'Keep them with you,' she says. 'Keep them with you when he's here.'

'Why?'

'Just.'

This makes about as much sense as the rest of my life at the moment, so I put the kittens in the dented-down button-held middle of an old cushion and wait. He has a docility to him, Deigan has, and I wonder if it predated what my father did to him or resulted from it. If my father did anything to him. I have a flask of tea and one of coffee, and as he serves himself, I find myself trying out various formulae.

I am extremely sorry for any damage my father may have done to you is too conditional.

I apologise for what my father did to you too accepting that he abused this man.

I'm sorry is presumptuous. I've never done anything to him and I don't speak for my father.

Lack of an apology does not seem to bother him, though. He sits opposite me, his hands on his lap rather than on the table, which makes him look as if he's doing an oral exam with me as examiner. He starts with his own background and how he ended up in St Alice's. I lift the cushion with the two kittens asleep on it, put it beside me and stroke them. It may not do much for them, but it calms me a lot. As I listen, I'm picking up anecdote and allusion from something I have already encountered. I widen my eyes when appropriate, nod, let my brows knot as I concentrate on details he posits as hinting at what is to come in his story. I have already read it somewhere else. Where? Oh, yes, the transcripts Lyn gave Inspector Synnott.

This man has been eager to tell his story for a long time. I ask occasional questions, and even the simplest gets him to talk on, and on, and on. The concept of what he maintains my father did to this man when he was a vulnerable little boy is heartbreaking. Told by the man he has become, it is not heartbreaking at all. Is this just beauty contest thinking, I wonder, watching him. No. The problem – and it is a problem for him, rather than for me – is that he has for so long not been listened to, for so long rehearsed the outrage in his mind that, untutored, the ghastly details are put side-by-side with irrelevant irritations. It's as if Marie Antoinette, interviewed post-guillotine, said, 'And not only did he cut off my head, but that executioner, wait till I *tell* you, he stepped on the lace of my collar, which my great grandmother the Duchess of Austria had imported with her on Shrove Tuesday a week before the bells of St Michel cracked because of the summer heat that year.'

I keep waiting for him to come to some sort of conclusion, but it goes on and on and on like a big ball of twine. The *Sunday Times* people must have had to work overtime to get a tellable story out of him.

'What are you thinking?' he demands to know, so suddenly that I start and tell the truth.

'I was thinking the *Sunday Times* people were probably very helpful to you in getting a shape on your story.'

He goes off on another tangent of complaint, this time against media people who only want to nail religious orders, but people don't have to be in religious orders to do the sort of thing my father did. Inspector Synnott appears in the doorway behind him.

'Mr Deigan.'

He leaps a mile and when he's capable of speech again, tells her she could have been responsible for him being very ill, he has very high blood pressure and the doctors have told him. This man, I think, isn't one ball of twine. He's several balls of twine. But none of them are any more than twine, tightly rolled, ready to unwind. I stroke the kittens wondering if it's their presence has me so caught up in twine balls. Isn't that what kittens are always playing with, in pictures?

Synnott is so crisp, you could cut butter with her diction. If he has talked to the *Sunday Times* (and the implication hangs in the air that he probably hasn't, yet) he must give her the name of the person to whom he talked, instanter, because the gardai are in the process of a major investigation into paedophile rings and it must not be jeopardised in order that one individual can profit from the past. He rises off the seat in a thoroughgoing fury at the idea that profit is in question at all. She cuts through the unwinding ball of twine and says it's great profit isn't the motive, especially given the amount of money he received from the late Mr Stapleton and the problems he has already encountered with gift tax. Since he is not motivated by profit, he will want to ensure that all paedophiles are brought to justice and she will be able to stop the *Sunday Times* going to print on this issue this weekend without having to take out an injunction, which, he should have no doubt, she will be able to obtain like that (snap of fingers which startles the kittens, who, between them, open three eyes.)

But what he needs to be very careful about, in all of his talks with media, she tells him, is this issue of profit. He is a novice at dealing with the fourth estate. (The fourth estate, I think. Not often called that, any more.) There's a lot of cheque-book journalism around, but there is a thin line between cheque-book journalism and blackmail, and an innocent man like him could awfully easily find himself on the wrong side of it. He keeps trying to puff himself up into a fight, but she golden-syrups him into sodden defeat.

He gathers his belongings and allows her to escort him to the door. Me and the kittens have become minor figures in the drama. Props, maybe. Brian Deigan and the Inspector are the ones to be reckoned with. The front door closes behind him and she goes first to the room where the other end of the recording device was secreted, coming back into the kitchen rolling the flex around her extended fingers.

'Nice one, Flannery.'

I am pathetically grateful for this.

'Thank you, Inspector Synnott.'

'Frances.'

'Frances.'

'OK, now we have *him* sorted, another matter. Remember I told you your father, in an amazingly hamfisted way, gathered together a lot of money and then issued a cheque to a company you'd never heard of? Well, the company has two share-holders. D. Rogan and N. Warden.'

I sit, stunned by this confirmation. Dumbed down, I am.

'This company isn't very active in its trading. In fact, the only major transaction I can find is your father's cheque going into its account, and about four days later, a matching cheque exiting the account. Made out to Nicola Warden.'

'How long ago was this?'

She gives me a date. About four weeks after Dougal took away the disc drive. They told me you were a genius, Dougal. Punch in your name on the Internet and all the profiles add up to that: big, *big* brain. Big money-maker. Morals? Minuscule. Mercy? Well, who the hell has mercy towards child-abusers? Specially if the merciless can make money out of the deal. Funny, I would have thought you were due to make enough money to last you several lifetimes without forcing my father to buy your silence with his pathetic clawed together couple of thousands, but what do I know? Daughter Of is all I ever was, and now I'm Daughter Of Famous Paedophile.

I smile at the policewoman. Or try to. The smile melts off the trembling sides of my mouth.

'You know, I wiped away my tears the other day with the poor white kitten,' I say. 'Mixed her up with a hanky. Might have to do it again. Better get rid of her before I wash her in the washing machine.'

'You have a customer for the black one? Why don't we do a deal?'

I look at her with difficulty. It's difficult to concentrate on mundane things when you're chest deep in the slough of despond.

'You keep the white kitten and give me the suicide note.'

Laughter hijacks me and I laugh like a fool.

'That's crazy. I don't want the white kitten.'

'You do, you know. Look at it.'

I look at the white kitten. The white kitten looks at me. One-eyed. Blissfully unaware of its other eye being closed, completely forgetful that its mad mother tried to take the eye out of it a few days after it was born. This dumb half-blind kitten thinks it has the whole world sewn up.

'But if I keep the kitten, I have to give you the note?'

She nods, suddenly very serious.

'I get it from the book I've hidden it in. She reads it. Her eyes narrow and I know why. *Do not blame Doug.*

'No point in not showing it to me, now,' she says, and I nod.

'We both know what it means – now,' I say.

Which might have been true if I had checked what she believed it to mean.

The following day is when the two kittens are to be separated. Federico rings in the morning to say their mother is still erratic, which I take to mean she is chewing and clawing the shit out of the inside of his cage the way she did in my laundry

327

basket. Unless he has a kitty straitjacket. He says his recommendation is that he should hold her for another week, after which I will be in a better position to make a decision about her. I ask how much it costs for the clawed cage per night. He tells me. I tell him I will send him a cheque for that multiplied thirty times. Board and lodging for the crazy catmother for a whole month, I say. At any time during that month, if you find someone desperate enough for company that they'll take a cat that takes the eyes out of her own babies, they're welcome to her. If you don't, put her to sleep and send me the bill.

Federico takes the dimmest of dim views of this. When only Inspector Frances Synnott and the odd patch of peculiar good luck prevent the entire nation taking a dim view of you and your parentage, a vet being reproachful because you don't take ownership of every violent half-mad cat that wants to drop dead bodies on you from the rafters of your garage is the least of your worries.

I also, that morning, get a letter of sympathy on the death of my father from Luke. This redefines that joyous radio programme concept, a blast from the past. God be with the days, I think, when standing on an occasional table seemed a problem. Right now, I'd pay to stand in peace on an occasional table. I send him a brief handwritten reply and squash down the memories of his mad rantings on my father's Internet address. I am working, two kittens on my lap, when Lyn rings.

'You're picking up the kitten this evening, aren't you?' I ask.

'Would it be dreadful to ask you to drop it over to me?'

No, not dreadful, but quite surprising, since Lyn almost never asks anybody to do anything for her convenience.

'He's small enough not to need a cage. If you just put him in the car, he'll be fine. I mean, with you driving. See you around eight?'

I end up OK-ing into a dead phone. That night, I fling on the nearest clean item (my dirty clothes are still piled in the floor because I haven't got around to buying another laundry basket), make sure the white kitten has access to water and the litter box, grab the black kitten and drive off. The black kitten tries out the passenger seat. Then decides to compare it with the back seat. In the rear-view mirror, I see it climbing with great difficulty up the back of the back seat. Fair dues to you, kitten, I think, as it hoofs it over the top and lies on the back windowsill.

It's still there when I find parking with some difficulty outside Lyn's place and lean in to collect it. Still there, and not that pushed about moving. But I tell it who's boss, and it surrenders, then pretends there was never a disagreement. I have it, gently nestled in the big patch pocket of my overcoat, when Lyn opens the door, presents me with a glass of champagne and leads a round of applause for me. As it dies down, I hear Andrea's bark: 'Ah, would you *look* at that little kitten?'

One small black face is poking up over my pocket, unbearably cute. I scoop it out and hand it over to Lyn, who gives it a saucer of milk and warns everybody against frightening it.

'Never mind frightening the kitten,' I say. 'What about me? What the hell is going on?'

Piers takes centre stage, to nobody's surprise. Flings out the long arms.

'We are the Friends of Flannery,' he says. Pushing it, I think, seeing Brad from the radio station in the background. On the other hand, if, as seems likely, he's attached to Raimonde, maybe he's a friend at one remove.

'We Friends tend to get together in plenary session only when the hormones rise and a wedding happens—'

Meriel takes a little bow.

' – when the temperature falls and we have New Year or Christmas knees-ups, or when someone belonging to us snuffs it.'

Andrea wants to know what about christenings. This causes a giggling stir and speculatively congratulatory pats on the back to her and Bruce.

'But because we are fresh thinkers and innovators,' Piers goes on, highmindedly, 'we had the insight to realise there are other reasons for a get-together. One of the best being when one of us is under pressure. Because when someone is under pressure, they can feel isolated. While their friends are all saying "better leave her alone, she needs time to herself". So, Flannery, we decided to cut through all that oul' shite and get together, simply to say you're important to us, nothing anyone else does or did is gonna change that, and hump the begrudgers.'

Adrian suggests Piers should hump the begrudgers on his own, given his reputation. Piers says he would, but he has to 'be here for' Flannery. And to pass on Dougal's regrets that he couldn't get a flight out of Munich until tomorrow morning.

The black kitten, having finished the kitten milk, stretches and yawns luxuriously. That gets a laugh.

'Now, about Nicola's absence from tonight's important meeting,' Piers goes on. 'What can I tellya?'

The suggestions as to what has prevented Nicola being present, what she might be up to, what the people present would *like* her to be up to, are many. The kitten walks confidently to the edge of the table and Lyn shepherds it back to safety.

'One last thing,' Piers says, pointing at the kitten. 'We have to name this feline.'

'Black Velvet,' someone says.

'Oh, come *on*,' Piers says. 'It's not running the goddam Grand National.'

'Velvet, then.'

'This kitten is a fella.'

'You couldn't possibly know.'

'Couldn't take the chance on a fella being called Velvet. Imagine its teenage years.' He does a Dublin gurrier. 'Velva? Didja score last ni', Velva, didja?'

'Sable.'

'Girls,' Piers observes, 'are shite when it comes to naming cats.'

'Afro.'

'And fellas of a certain age are not much better. C'mon, folks, look at this animal.'

We all look at the kitten, who is standing looking sideways, not happy where it is, but not actively considering alternatives.

'What picture does this kitten remind you of?'

We look back at the kitten and it looks like no picture I've ever seen. Piers taps a cigarette out of a packet in his jacket pocket, sticks it on his lower lip and turns up the collar of his jacket.

'James Dean,' someone says.

'*Boulevard of Broken Dreams*,' someone else says.

'The wet street and the raincoat,' a third offers.

'Dean,' Piers says and makes as if to pour his champagne over the kitten. Lyn fends him off. But then he puts down the glass and drops on his hunkers, gathering the kitten to the edge of the table.

'Here, look,' he says to Dean, pulling its own tiny tail around. 'A tail! Whooo! Eat ya, it would. Gone' – he disappears the tail and the kitten is mystified – '*back!* Tickle your nose.' He does so, with the tiny tail. 'Chase it. Go on. Kill it.'

He has the little cat bewitched, racing around in a mad miniature circle, threatening its own tail with imminent destruction. You are very funny, I think. Pity about your choice in business partners.

One by one and two by two, my friends come to me for quiet off-line votes of sympathy. Nobody mentions child abuse accusations, or makes what I could see as coded references. Either they don't know, or they're doing an awfully good job of pretending they don't know and that the reason for the party was to give me a lift after the horror of the way my father died. As I talk to Raimonde and Brad, out of the corner of my eye I see Piers and Lyn taking the kitten away. No doubt it will have the feline equivalent of a four-poster or a waterbed. When they come back, I tell Lyn I must go because my own kitten is on his or her own.

'Your own kitten?' Piers repeats. 'I thought you wouldn't be seen dead with a kitten?'

'C'm'ere to me, you,' I say, and the two of them follow me out onto the porch. 'Piers, thank you for the speech. Just one bit of it – Dougal sending his apologies? When you see him, tell him no need to apologise. And tell him I know all about Fresh Starts.'

He tries to ask me questions, as does Lyn, but I ignore him, kiss her and drive home. The minute I open the kitchen door, I know something is wrong. For a second, I think my floor is ant-infested. No. Not ants. These little dots do not move. Coffee. Ground coffee. Everywhere. Knocked-over packet on the floor. The white kitten comes out from behind a tea towel looking as if it has black dandruff, its fur is so completely speckled with coffee.

'You did this, you half-blind halfwit,' I say, and it comes over and winds itself between my legs: yeah, aren't I *so* smart? I wait until it's good and finished (you don't want to interrupt an experience like that) before I get a sweeping brush to clean up the place. When everything is perfect again, the kitten, which must have been trying to lick half a pound of coffee grinds off itself, throws up in the middle of the floor.

She (God alone knows why, but I'm convinced she's female) comes over to me, having accomplished this, and purrs like a little motorbike. I clean the puke, then find a fine comb and get most of the coffee grounds out of her snowy fur. I leave the grounds in a pile on the floor while I get a dustpan, and when I come back, the kitten is paws in the air, rolling on her back in the grounds I've just cleaned off her.

'Cats are supposed to be clean,' I tell her. She walks into the table leg on her blind side and takes it personally. I know what I'll call her. Scruffy. Looks like an effing derelict, I think, with misplaced sadness.

22

Scruffy

———◆·◆·◆———

I am tweaking a knotted string along the hall for Scruffy to pounce on and kill when the phone rings. Lyn.

'You OK?'

'No, Lyn, I'm not OK. I now know I can sell my house any time I want to, and if the force is with me, the buyers don't notice the hole in the garage door, and rumours of suicides from the rafters don't screw up the sale price, I might walk away with 20K. Which would just about, these days, give me a deposit on a birdcage. I don't know whether to move in with you and pay you the 20K or stay put and fix the garage door.'

'If you stay there, I'll need to move in with you,' is the response.

'To prevent me getting terminal depression?'

'Well. You know.'

I do know, Lyn. I jam-pack every day with minutiae to distract myself from what feels like the destruction of my whole life; if my father was doing what I now know he was doing, then he was pretending fatherhood, kindness, altruism. If my mother knew about it, then was she somehow colluding?

Popular belief is that they're all sophisticated evildoers who go to endless lengths to achieve what they want to achieve, never fighting against it, never admitting they were in the wrong. But maybe my mother saw it as like being born 5'2".

You might prefer to be a six-footer, but what can you do? Nobody feels contrition about irrevocable inborn traits.

'I'm re-reading his poetry,' I say. Lyn's silences have a way of hooking me into confession.

'I am, too,' she says.

'Looking for clues?'

'I suppose so. No, more looking for reasons to forgive him.'

'For child molesting? Not in our gift, that forgiveness, Lyn my friend. Wrong generation. Clean, uninvolved hands can't make it better.'

'No. I'd like to forgive him for what he has done to you, but I'm not finding any reasons. Anyway, that's not why I rang.'

'You wanted to brighten my day with news, gossip and scandal.'

'Some.'

'Oh?'

'Dougal is being sued by Nicola. It's in the papers.'

'I didn't think breach of promise was much of a flier these days.'

'Not breach of promise. Constructive dismissal, bullying and sexual harassment.'

'*What?*'

'Well, it's hedged around with "it is believed" and they have no response whatever from Dougal, but that's the gist of it.'

'Constructive dismissal?'

'Well, you knew he fired her?'

'No. He doesn't need to visit Scruffy any more, so I would have no occasion to talk to him. Especially not about his ex-girlfriend.'

'Piers needs to talk to you.'

I do the anti-vampire sign in the air, and Scruffy tries to kill it. She's about three feet away from it, but lets on she was within *that* of it. Then she walks into my leg and sulks at it for creeping up on her. Scruffy reminds me a lot of me.

'I'll get him to ring you,' Lyn says, and cuts herself off.

I sit there, trying to figure the significance of what she's told me. Scruffy decides I'm going to be boring (not totally dumb, this cat) and goes to sleep. On me. I feel pleasantly trapped. When the phone rings, I can just about get to it without fecking the white kitten on the floor. Katria Tyler, the voice says. The tone says 'All kneel and kiss the ground.' I try to figure out why. I'll know the work of Tyler Productions, she tells me. I make a noncommittal noise, because I don't. As she talks on, I deduce who Tyler Productions are. The TV people who do documentaries.

'Our programme about Edmund Stapleton is nearing completion,' she says. 'We felt it was only fair to offer you, as his next of kin, an opportunity to put your side of the story.'

She's off on a flurry of logistical details. They could bring a camera crew to my home Tuesday next after lunch, or if I like to go to the studio, they could take me on Wednesday or Thursday. I make wordless noises that keep her going while my mind rattles like an abacus, beads adding up the sums of her phrases. 'Only fair to you'? 'Your side of the story'? This ain't no documentary about my father's poetry. This is about child abuse. This is Brian Deigan and maybe the guy who gave the statement in the moss-green folder. Trying to sound as if I don't suspect it's about anything but his poetry, I ask casually who else is appearing in the programme, and she makes like I've proposed phone sex to her. Oh, *no*, she couldn't possibly reveal details like that.

'Sorry?' I say, reaching for the kind of confused manner a poorly informed Daughter Of might credibly use. 'I don't follow why you wouldn't be happy for me to know about other guests on the show?'

It's not a *show*, she says, enraged. It's a documentary. Oh, I say, I thought Tyler Productions did kind of docudramas? (As in, don't patronise me, you. Put little actors playing little parts in little dramatic reconstructions in your programme and it ain't no documentary, and it sure as hell *is* a show.) This woman suffers from poor anger-management, and in no time at all is talking about 'victims' and 'lives devastated'. I get even more stupid. Her desire to crush me with terror about what the programme will say about my evil father competes with her need to keep me in ignorance of the details of the programme.

'Katy, I'm a bit—'

'Katria.'

'Oh, I beg your pardon. Katria? I must have misheard you when you came on first. What a pretty name. Oh, you're going to be so offended with me that I've never learned it off the credits at the end of your programmes. Is it a foreign name?'

Because she can't decide whether I'm dumb as a tree or smart as a snake, she tries to cut through all of this and I deliberately misinterpret her impatience as modesty and get into a great long wandering parcel of drivel about the importance of giving children unusual names because it makes them live up to them. (Item for radio programme, I think in a mad side-bar.) When I have her good and confused, I say that really I don't make this kind of decision and my father's lawyer's name is X, his address is Y and she should address any queries to him, he's really very efficient and he runs me (giggle, giggle) like a train. Anyway, it was great to talk to you, Katia, and hope this is useful. Must fly. Bye.

I ring Piers's direct line.

'Amazing Trace,' a male voice says. As if hedging its bets. As if it was really Guinness's Brewery dressed up for the day impersonating Amazing Trace.

'Piers, need your help. You use a PR company, don't you?'

'Flannery? Yes.'

'C'n I talk to them?'

'I've been trying to talk to them myself,' he says, through gritted if not grinding teeth. 'They seem to be all meeting with Nicola.'

'In your office?'

'No, *not* in our offices. In her new apartment. Nicola is out sick. Officially. Meanwhile, our Managing Director, Mr Rogan, is out doing his civic duty, chatting up detectives about something to do with your father's death. No offence, Flannery, but I'm just a little bit busy. I have no problem being omnipotent and omniscient, but it takes concentration, you know?'

'Piers, I'll get out of your hair. Talk to you.'

I leave a message on my solicitor's phone saying he may be contacted by a TV production house and maybe he'd talk to me before he agrees anything with them? Scruffy is still sleeping on my lap.

I lock my hands behind my head and look at the kitchen ceiling. Amazing, the crap you see on ceilings. Spider webs in corners. Thinking about ceilings reminds me that the one place I haven't simplified and tidied in preparation for moving out of the house (or taking in Lyn as a lodger) is the attic. Not a bad time to have a look up there, I think. Nobody's going to need anything from me later this evening. I lift Scruffy gently onto the rug and go searching for torches. I have exhausted most possibilities when, visiting the downstairs loo for other appropriate purposes, I open a press and get lucky. Sure enough, my mother at some point had purchased one of those portable lamps that will sit and that has a big shiny face on it. It takes one of those brute batteries the size of a square jamjar.

One of those is nearby, still in its box. I fit it into the lamp and it lights up, somewhat to my surprise. My mother's competence still showing up; a place for everything, everything in its place, and fuses replaced regularly.

Upstairs, I find the A-shaped ladder and open it beneath the trapdoor into the attic. At this point, Scruffy wakes up and decides I'm interesting again. Not only am I interesting, but I have this toy with steps for jumping between. I climb the ladder, hindered by a white kitten, get the trapdoor open – and the phone rings. I'm standing on the top of the ladder, a trapdoor on my head, and for a moment, I consider running to the phone.

'The hell with you,' I tell the caller and shift the trapdoor to the left, horsing the lamp into the space and following it. I am fitter than I used to be, but jeans and running shoes might be the preferred wardrobe for this kind of operation, I think. I am in a knit dress and medium heels. Feckit, I think, what harm? Nobody's going to see me and I'll only be up here a few minutes. Another to add to the catalogue of judgement and prediction errors. This one, as it turns out, is a doozie, even by my standards.

The attic is new to me. Never been in it before. Although there is one skylight, it is in the lee of a chimney and probably never lets in that much light. Now, as the light fails anyway, the attic is a place of dusty darkness, ribbed by joists, with secretive cartons and boxes in corners. I make my way to what I judge to be the oldest of the collections, get the light set up above the majority of the cartons, and start to go through what turn out to be souvenirs of my babyhood. Mysterious inside so many thicknesses of polythene that the most determined moth would give up and turn in its wings at the sight are pink hand-knitted baby blankets. Lace christening robes.

White crochet caps and bootees with pink satin lace threaded through the stitches. My mother's mother made them, I know. I've seen myself in pictures, wearing them.

In another pile are accounts from twenty years ago. Bank statements showing a modest mortgage and even more modest savings. That was before the royalties began – and before those royalties were made tax free.

I suppose every attic in Ireland is filled with bank statements nobody ever needs, but decent law-abiding people keep just in case someone at some point needs to check up on. Yellowing, tied together, month by month or year by year with thick rubber bands, all perished now, so that the moment you decide to go through one bundle, the rubber band parts without even a snap.

A third grouping of boxes contains everything to do with Christmas. This one gives me the sensation of meeting an old friend unexpectedly. Meeting Christmas out of season is particularly pleasurable for me because the last two Christmases have effectively been postponements. I still have two of my mother's puddings, sitting in Pyrex bowls with greaseproof paper tightly tied with waxed string over the top.

Here, in the attic, is the huge broad oblong box my father used to hand to me when I was three or four. He would do it with ostentatious carelessness, knowing I would panic at the prospect of holding this big person's box, then find it as light as if it had nothing in it, so I could carry it confidently, even though I could barely see beyond its furthest edge. Beside it, the smaller, but much heavier box containing the ornaments my mother had made. She had come upon them in a magazine, the year they were married. Round shapes with bright pictures, for you to cut out and paste onto cardboard, then paste another matched set on the other side of the cardboard before threading twine through the top and hanging it on the tree, where it would turn, showing first a set of Victorian carollers, then a set of camels guided by a star. I hold them, shuffle them, imagine my mother making them because the newly-weds couldn't afford expensive spun glass ornaments.

When I have them stowed again, there is just one more assortment of boxes unexamined, over to my right. I am in a crouch, moving from joist to joist, when the phone rings, startling me into a misstep. Down goes my foot between the joists, splintering the floor, going through, going down, even as I struggle to get my weight onto the other foot, something tearing into my leg, other leg slipping, more weight, more splintering, knifing into my thigh, pain robbing me of sense.

When my mind begins to work again, the phone has stopped ringing and I have stopped falling. My right leg is trapped, at thigh level, in the splintered floor of the attic, or the splintered ceiling of the room below, depending on your viewpoint. I must look as if I'm trying to ride a joist, on the other side of which my left leg is bent into a kneeling position. I try to think past the pain. Something is dribbling down the leg that's gone through the ceiling of the room below. Blood, I think. I'm not imagining the sensation of being cut by something. A nail in the wood? Tetanus. I'll die of tetanus before Scruffy ever gets old enough to give me a cat disease.

I brace myself on the joists and pull upwards. The pain puts spinning lights into my head and the dribbling becomes a running stream. I stop bracing myself and sink back. This has the single advantage of stopping the bleeding, although I have no idea why.

My mobile phone starts to ring. It goes for five, then switches off. The caller is now getting my voice inviting them to leave a message.

The floor starts to make a noise and for a second I am terrified that I have undone its support systems and will plunge twelve feet to the floor of the room below. I hold very still, to prevent this. The noise continues. It is a smaller noise than a floor about to collapse would be expected to make. It's also coming from the trap door. While I watch, Scruffy's head appears over the edge and she scrabbles frantically, creating a little cloud of dust. Somehow, she gets enough purchase on the edge to shift her weight and the next thing is in the attic along with me, swanning along towards me between two joists, her tiny weight no danger to the thin floor.

'Yo, Scruff,' I say as she gets close.

She jumps onto the joist I'm straddling. I lower my face and she gives my nose a lick. That settled, she wanders off into the darkness behind the Christmas decoration boxes. I wonder about tying some kind of a note to her and putting her out of the skylight. *Am trapped in own attic. Please help.* Except that I can't reach the skylight, can't reach anything with which to write a note or on which to write a note, haven't got anything to tie a note to the cat with, haven't got the cat handy and would probably be done for cruelty to animals if I shagged a half-blind kitten out on a roof, forty feet above the ground.

The fax phone rings. This is someone who knows I'm here and isn't going to let go. Lyn, maybe. Lyn, hopefully. Because I am going to need rescue by an external third party. I berate myself for lack of survival skills and look around me for something with which to enlarge the break I have made in the floor, to let me draw my leg back up. The only thing within reach is the box of hand-made Christmas decorations. I look to see if there are splintered bits I can pull away, but any pointy bits must be angling down into the room below. In fact, the ceiling of the room beneath must look like one of those tabloid boasts where graphically torn shards of a newspaper page circle a punched-through claim.

There is still pain up at the thigh, but lower down seems to have gone numb. I make the effort to move my distant foot, and the shoe falls off it, clattering on the floor below. *Sorry, my right leg just stepped into another room. My foot is in another office right now.*

Two of the phones are simultaneously ringing, now. More the merrier. The more unanswered calls, the sooner people will mention to each other that for no good reason I have ceased to communicate. Lyn will be the hub of the spokes. She has a key to the house, too. However, realistically, nobody is going to get anxious for at least twenty-four hours. Worst scenario? Forty-eight hours? Worse?

Radio item: How to Survive on a Joist for a Long Weekend. No food. No water. I know from my research that you can live without food for weeks. Classic quiz question: Name the man who undertook the longest hunger strike in history. Answer: Terence McSwiney, Lord Mayor of Cork. Duration of hunger strike? Seventy days. Or thereabouts.

Nobody's going to leave me joisting with death for seventy days, so hunger isn't the problem. Thirst, though. Thirst will be a problem. What's the survival time without water? Five days, maybe. Lyn? Get anxious quick, OK? Don't get so focused on Piers in the next day or so that you forget your old leg-in-ceiling friend, Flannery. Radio Item: Don't knock the glass ceiling. Glass doesn't give you tetanus. Nice clean cuts you get from glass.

I can't feel blood flowing any more, so maybe we're winning on that front. (Who's this 'we', Tonto?) Let's test how much play we have, here. Maybe we could go to sleep. (Ring, ring, from downstairs. Landline.) I bend as far forward as I can.

Effortfully, it is possible to get my arms folded on the joist in front of me and my forehead touching them. Restful it isn't, but in time, I may get sufficiently weary to be able to sleep in that position.

I try going the other way, like someone doing Pilates or yoga. By the time I'm bent back maybe eighteen inches off plumb, my head's spinning and some bit of the ceiling is poking into my thigh with such force I come back up straight very quickly. Sideways I try, but no options. What time is it? Half eight. Time to do some serious thinking about something other than ceilings, entrapment in.

By now, Inspector Synnott will have presented Dougal Rogan with the accounts of Fresh Starts, Ltd., and gently but firmly dislodged him from the position that my father was some kind of investor. My father (I say aloud in the attic) was a paedophile. Therefore, whatever Rogan found on the computer was related to paedophilia, and the reason he took it away with him was to preserve evidence in order to get money out of my father, because my father was no investor and I don't know why I bought that crappy scenario for even a moment. OK, so Rogan blackmails my father. (Join the queue, why don't you? You and Deigan and probably others this Tyler woman has lined up for her programme.) Gets two hundred thousand or more out of him in bits and pieces. Mixes them all into one nice cheque for bracket-legs Nicola to cash.

There's something slightly off in this scenario, too, though. Or maybe I don't want to find Dougal Rogan guilty of blackmail and ultimately guilty of inducing my father's death. My father's death, hanging from one of these rafters, these joists. As a child, I would go to sleep in imaginary flight, seeing my bedroom from above, seeing our garden, the roof of our house, the neighbourhood. Now, I see the grey hanging thing from above, eyes, tongue still visible . . .

It couldn't be – or could it – that I am astride the rafter round which the old rope was wound? No, that was in the garage, and although I can't be sure precisely which room I am above, I am definitely not above the garage, because that's a single storey building with a roof.

Pull thoughts away, substitute a live, if hated, face. Rogan the Rescuer. Rescued Nicola, then shagged her out on her ear a few months later. Rescued my father, then made money out of him. No, rescue is not a word that could be applied to my father. You took away the evidence. To face him with? I have it at home, Professor, and you'll never know where, so paying up is the only way to ensure I don't give it to the cops. But why would Doug Rogan want a few hundred thousand when he stands to make millions if he floats or sells off Amazing Trace? The really bad part is the recurring thought that he gave the money to her. Part of the pissoff? But did he tell her where it came from?

It all makes near-sense, which is worse than no sense. But Inspector Synnott's questioning will allow the bits to fall into place. I just wish they wouldn't fall into place. Bad enough that they have fallen into place about my father. I can still sadly love the remembered remnants of my father, although never free of the encircling trails of shame. There is no loving a man so monied as Rogan, still clawing for more, no understanding the callous compounding of the discovered outrage by capitalising on it.

You have one sorry life, I think to myself. If you ever get rescued out of this attic, you better get your aching arse out of Ireland and get to know some normal people. If there are any, anywhere. Funny thing. My adolescence was filled with annoyance because of the awful middle-class ordinary normality of my life and its surroundings. God, how I wanted to be real. Real as in working class with people who said fuck all the time, instead of my mother frowning if you said feck. Real as in getting throwing-up drunk or injecting substances that carried a blood-stopping jolt of pleasure, rather than a glass of good wine with dinner. Real as in unplanned sex with strangers, nothing remembered but the pleasure, knocking hell out of dated commitment and fidelity concepts. I yearned for eccentricity, exceptional status.

Pretty exceptional, it'll be, to die in an attic, not waving but starving. Festering Flannery. Leave me here long enough, maybe the leg will come free. Locked Door Mystery: One Leg Found in Poet's Home. (Paedophile Poet's lair?) Pretty exceptional to have a suicide father suicided by the only man you've ever fancied. Be honest, now. You lived with Luke. You lived the half-life of the newly cherished. The incarceration of the gladly needed. But you didn't love him.

And, yes, there have been crushes. Those three-day or three-week periods of raised emotional response, when the mention of the man's name spasms the heart and breathing, when a word from him heats the face and trembles the hands. They come and go, those crushes, laughable in retrospect, short-lived at the time. Never did any one of them take on the easy unthinking comfort you took in Rogan's company before you knew your father had him bought and paid for. There was such pleasure there, such a sense of being able to breathe easier with him, not have to pretend. And all the while, he thought you looked like a horse's ass.

I'm sitting astride a joist in an attic lit by a big torch, hungry and thirsty, trying to get over someone nobody in their right minds would ever have fallen for. Life-crisis.

Unwitnessed. I try to move my leg, but there is no sensation at all, now, below where I can see. I run my hands over my hip and what I can reach of my thigh, then do a comparative sweep of the other leg. My right thigh is swollen, a bit like one of those corks that has a fattened bit, mushroom-style, above the bit stuck in the mouth of the bottle. Ditto my arse on that side. They may be responding to trauma, or the floor/ceiling may be acting as a tourniquet, cutting off the circulation to and from the leg.

Implications of using a building as a tourniquet would be serious. Without a flow of blood, the leg will start to die. All its little cells keeling over and snuffing it. Gangrene. Amputation. Peg-leg. Prosthesis. Listen, how bad would that be? Paul McCartney fell in love with a woman with a prosthetic leg. I try desperately to move my leg, but no go.

The time now is 9.15. Little known natural law: Time moves at half-pace when you're trapped in an attic. How long have I been here, now? Couple of hours. (Silly tune, silly tune, silly tune. Mobile phone again.) And not a child in the house washed. Shag all achieved. Look at all I could have done by now, if I had used what my mother always called my Inner Resources. I could've come up with a hundred radio items. I know I came up with two, but can't now remember what the hell they were. Must make notes. How?

(Ring, Ring, Ring. House phone again.) I try my pockets. No pen. No paper. Precisely what is in reach? The joist I'm on. Plus two others, one on either side, plus the valley between them. I could make notes in the dust. I try it. They are going to need to be very big and simplistic, I think. Not to mention the fact that I will never, as long as I live, go into any attic after I get the hell out of this one, so how am I going to read them, later? (Ring, ring, ring. Slightly more discreet noise of the fax phone. Someone is methodically checking. That's about the third time the sequence has been gone through.)

Something stirs at the other end of the attic and puts the heart crossways in me. Scruffy. Stretching luxuriously. Ooh, what a lovely snooze. Yesss . . . She advances towards me along a joist, stands about three feet away and squawks at me. As in: OK, had enough of you doing the joist thing, let's go downstairs and you get to feed me. Sound good to you? Thought it would. She jumps a joist or two and walks away from me in a valley until she reaches the trapdoor. Glances back. Squawks again.

'Sorry, Scruff. Would if I could, but I can't.'

She comes back with this 'humans are *so* stupid' attitude, and explains to me what the issues are. I nod and fill in the gaps. She heads for the trapdoor again. I don't follow. She comes back and gets close enough to be stroked. This she accepts, but looks fiercely at me and does loud meows to make it clear to me that stroking has its place, but hunger comes first.

'You are so right, Scruffy. Not a thing I can do about it, though. For either of us.'

Mobile phone rings. Stops. Landline rings. Stops. Fax phone rings. Stops. The kitten decides that company is better than nothing, and curls up on the joist in front of me, presenting me with her elegant arse just to make it inescapable that she's pissed off at me. I stroke her. The warmth is comforting. She goes slitty-eyed with pleasure and after a while, falls asleep. Wonder if this relates to that bit of research they did years ago with the orphaned baby monkeys, where they starved the poor little friggers and then gave them a choice of two makey-up 'mothers', one made of wire with a bottle of milk attached, the other made of soft cloth with no

348

bottle. The babies all chose the soft mother. Warmth and softness even at the cost of starvation. But then, that's probably part of the passivity of the abused child, buying present warmth and softness even at the cost of betrayal. No, that would not be true. It would not be experienced as warmth and softness.

Those children can never have faith in anyone. Do I have faith in anyone? I have faith I will be rescued. My parents can't have done so badly by me in that. Mobile phone rings. My mouth is as dry as if it were one of the dust-coated joists surrounding me, velveted, all sharp angles softened by the grey, the dirt matt grey. I try leaning down in order to get some sleep, but I cannot get into position without waking up Scruffy and I am loth to do that, lest she stalks off and leaves me up here alone. Even a sleeping one-eyed hungry cat is a bulwark against the nightstalking terrors, its silk-furred little sides rising and falling as it breathes.

The fax phone rings. The pattern is getting more random as respect for normal sleep time kicks in with the callers. Soon, that reassurance of outside interest will die away. I can hear the house settling around me. The central heating is going off around about now, and the warmth in the pipes will cool with clicks and squeaks, the floors over them contracting.

Downstairs, there will be noises I cannot hear at this distance. Clocks ticking. Thermostats clunking from one phase to another. A house breathes and lives. My father had a poem about the memories a house stores, but – rehearsing the lines in my head – I reject the thought. The house in Ekaterinberg had stains on a flowery wallpaper in a basement, those stains laden with clues carrying no guilt at the time, no traceable links to the bleeding boy, the teenage girls weighed down with the heaviness of the grand duchess titles, the missing waif turning up speechless in a hospital, saved from a river. The carpets may have picked up fibres from the starched laces, the few velvets the family clutched around them as they retreated from the poking guns, the drink-smelling peasants briefly elevated to the worst power, the power to enjoy suffering caused. The dust might even contain cells shed, hairs lost. That I know. That I believe.

It was only the eleven-year-old me who could be chilled and thrilled by the possibility of the house at Ekaterinberg retaining more, retaining the essence of the nameless fears and un-crushable hopes. My father's poem was anthropomorphic. Or does that apply only to the projection onto animals of human characteristics? He was amused, at the time, by a critic who wrote that he was the Disney of modern poets. Or was he amused? I hear again the radio programme, my mother shushing me and Lyn to hear him talk, so easily tolerant, so liberal in his humour, of the great critical battles, the cruelty visited by Dickey on other poets, how time is the ultimate critic, relegating the venom of past-tense humans to the books of quotations or to true oblivion, preserving what is worth preserving with an inhuman perfection of taste. My mother nodding in fierce affirmation of the implication he was, of course, too modest, too self-effacing to articulate: that his work might now be subject to the envious cruelty of lesser poets, but would be lifted out of the sinking mass of twentieth-century Irish poetry by Time with a capital T.

I am loth to believe her wrong, my mother, because so much of his work was about her, because if the scumbling hand rubs out his work, it rubs her out, too, the girl dancing with the angel. Except, as that old priest said in the church that day, her coffin shining darkly at the altar rails, she is remembered in me, those big, beautiful hands, the thick strong hair that never had time to grey, the laugh that was like a trophy won, the pride in every syllable of my name, my name that will never sound the same, never sound so worthy, so loved, so softly believed in, without her to say it. I must not lose sight of you, Mam. I must not lose sense and smell of you. I must work past the easy words he used to remember the reality of you.

Scruffy shifts in sleep, long slim front legs a-stretch, translucent tiny claws reaching out, then furled. The torch burns brightly, casting long, ecclesiastical shadows. I am unafraid of the house. Rightly, I suppose. The twisting, creaking horror that has replaced – because that is the truth of it, it has replaced my father in my mind – is internalised. I carry it with me. It is not imprinted in the house. My house.

I will live here, I decide. I will tear the garage apart, insulate it, paint it white, paint it white again, gloss paint going over undercoat, ceiling hanging where the rafters span like bones. Bright lights hunting out the shadows. No wallpaper anywhere. No flowers to count. I will install great glass doors in the front of it.

I look at my watch. No wonder the phone calls have stopped. It is one in the morning. The morning of the next day. What is that idiot poster Raimonde stuck on the wall of her office in the radio station? *Tomorrow is the first day of the rest of my life*. Banal, but, like all good banalities, useful. Today is the first day of the rest of my life. No longer Daughter Of. Flannery Stapleton. Feckit, it's a great name, all the same. Flannery Stapleton, What? Activist for Victims of Child-abuse? Great PR move, that would be. I could announce it, tearfully, on the Tyler programme. They will probably leave four minutes at the end for an apology from me, and in those four minutes . . .

I shift, to move the growing pain, since there is nothing I can do to get rid of it. Just shift it to another set of muscles and bones and swollen tissues. There will be no such four minutes. I will not take on his guilt and I will not do a distanced and conditional apology. Daughter Of might do that, but not me. The solicitor will set up a fund from my father's royalties. An expiation fund. Outside my control, my influence, untouched by my name. His money, his sin, his reparation. I'm not like Goering's son, my life and identity sucked out of me by the dead villain.

My hand checks the swollen area. It is now hard, hot, the skin unlike any skin I have ever touched. White cells, collecting in the location, fighting infection. A war zone, above and below the ceiling, I am. Why have I not an overwhelming desire to pee? Because I have had nothing to drink. But more than that, because I have bled. Maybe shock keeps your liquids somewhere other than your bladder. There must be a radio item in this, somewhere, but it eludes me. The thirst is bad, bad. I must not talk out loud any more. Conserve energy. Maybe saying things aloud makes my mouth drier.

Sleep must have happened, because Scruffy's whiskers are against my face and a clawed paw is scraping my neck. I scratch behind her ears and she vibrates with purring. It is half three. Darkest hour before the dawn. When is dawn, these months? Will I know when it happens, or will the torch keep everything at the same unreal localised brightness? Scruffy gets bored with purring and wanders the attic, jumping up on cartons, moving where I cannot see her.

She comes back and meows loudly at me.

'Scruff, go downstairs,' I say, breaking my own vow of silence.

My voice sounds as if I have a sore throat.

'Go downstairs,' I say in response to her exigent meow.

'There'll be water in the kitchen sink, because the washer on the cold tap is worn. You'll get enough liquid to keep you going. Go on. Go downstairs.'

She meows at me furiously, and I hope she will stay with me, in spite of telling her not to. Even if all she can do is give out to me. Better than nothing, a kitten's complaints. Better than a poke in the eye with a sharp stick. Better than a kick in the arse. Anything is better than silence. The great fear is silence. But was it always? Radio item: that we in the twenty-first century are more afraid of silence than any earlier generation. Because we have trained and technologied our way out of it. Every walker, every cyclist with an ear-piece plugged to Britney or Beethoven or continuous news programmes. Every house filled with the bright noise of televisions never turned off. Silence is the great weapon against sanity, the worst element of solitary confinement, so the footsteps of even the most hated jailer are welcomed.

The careful crouching cat is preparing to go down into the house. Cats are so cautions, never leaping from a height, always crawling forepawed as far down as they can before giving in to gravity, as she does now. Far below, she meows up at me. Instructions. Dogs do pleadings. Cats do instructions. Sorry, Scruffy. Can't obey. Can't help. Faint noises come from below, then nothing. Four o'clock. No signs of dawn.

Don't just stand there, do something. Don't just swell there, do something. I remember a script I wrote about a man named Carbine Williams. Williams? An American. Nineteenth century. An ungovernable. Undisciplined and gormless in his fights against army discipline, incarcerated in a tin cage without light. A tin cage so small he could neither lie nor stand. Left out in tropics, so that during the day, he roasted like a dinner, and at night he froze. The cage opened, now and then, to check his humility levels. You cowed yet, sojer? The dismissing oath forced out between blistered, breaking, crusted lips. The cage door closed hard, clanging. Your problem, sojer. Stay there some more. No skin off our nose.

The imprisoned man working inside his mind on the gun he would make. Fitting the pictured parts into each other. Pulling them apart in silence, brain-cell silence, to solve the flaws. The end result, when they caved in to him out of fear of killing him, a gun, the carbine, that worked as he had worked it in his enforced dreamtime. If Flannery Stapleton were worth a toss, she'd be coming up with something like that. Not a gun. But something, not this mad repetitive conveyor belt of trivia, like that old TV programme where you got to take home with you whatever you remembered. There was a kettle, a liquidiser, an ice-cream maker . . .

The shadows are weakening. There's the answer to your question. You will see the dawn. Seeping up through the trapdoor. Spilling softly through the dirty skylight. Forgotten the skylight, hadn't you?

Wonder if it's possible someone in the area might notice the skylight lit during the daytime. It could be the point of rescue. Yeah, right. Like someone is going to stand back from this big old house in order to notice that a half-hidden skylight in the lee of a chimney is lighted from inside, do the deductive reasoning – *why would a light be burning in an attic during the daytime?* – overcome their own sceptical logic – *because some plank was up there and forgot to turn off the light* – and make the imaginative leap to the conclusion that someone is imprisoned up there. Need waxed moustaches for that kind of deduction, methinks.

The kitten has never come back, and since I cannot hear any of its movements downstairs, I am tempted to call out for it. I don't. If Scruffy has found some water for himself/herself, that's a mercy. Dragging the poor cat up here on the illusion, carried in my voice (assuming I could get my voice to be heard that far away) that I have food for her would be so cruel. Not to say impossible. Doubtful if at this point she could muster the strength for that last leap through the trapdoor. What is it – four times their own length cats can leap? That marvellous gathering of strength in haunch and thigh, so fluidly done, the watcher has the delusion that faithful imitation would result in the same graceful distance on the part of the human.

My mother was funny about physical delusions, when she took me to see the Royal Ballet in the Gaiety for my eighth birthday. *Giselle*. Afterwards, I came upon her imitating for my father the way all the matinee-going girl children had danced up and down the aisles on their way for ice cream during the interval, convinced they were now *en pointe* and ethereal, rather than mired, for all outsiders to see, in the squat flat shoed stubbiness of the pre-teen. It wasn't unkind, her mimicry of us, but it felt like a blow. She knew it, too, when she saw the reddened face on me, and made no attempt to make it right, because once you have been summed up for the laughter of others in a word, a phrase, a gesture, the offence is permanent.

The grossly swollen area around my hip and thigh has no feeling in it now. It is hard and hot to the touch, but inside there is no pain. Where there is pain now is in my head. Predictable, after these many morning hours with no coffee. Caffeine withdrawal. It will hammer and hound for hours, this one, but its very normality, its recognition by my body as having precedents, is somehow less worrisome than the anaesthetised feeling elsewhere.

The phones begin. Someone is doing the same thing as

yesterday. Ringing my mobile, then the landline, then the fax. Batteries, I think, looking at the torch, which is looking paler in the relative daylight, whether from loss of battery power or increase of ambient light, I cannot tell. The mobile phone will run out soon. True enough, by ten o'clock, the caller doing the magic triad is reduced to the landline and the fax phone. By eleven, I am sure of it. The torch battery is beginning to run down. It's mid-morning. By dusk, it will be dying. I will face the night in darkness.

I am crying out loud now, but trying to stop because even tears are taking liquid out of me, and I am so dehydrated, my hands look withered and small. It's getting more difficult to lean my head on the rafter. I try to work out why this is. Is it because the swelling is going higher up my torso, making it difficult to bend over? Or – it could be some other reason, but I can't think in straight lines. Each thought is like a hook-and-eye fastener, joining onto any other thought that's handy.

No sleep, now, but long patches of nothing but pain and then I look at my watch and two hours have passed. The torch is flickering, so it probably won't even make it to dusk. The phones ring every couple of hours. I keep imagining I hear familiar car noises outside and sometimes give a start when I imagine I hear the front-door key. When I really do hear a familiar car and the front-door key, I don't believe either noise. Then I hear a faint cry and another, and foot-steps in the hall. Scruffy, I think. Scruffy begging for food and drink. There are clattering noises in the kitchen and then his voice.

'Flannery? Flannery, where are you?'

I try to call back, but what voice I have goes no further than half the distance to the trapdoor. I hear him going through rooms. Checking the garage door. Coming up the stairs at a run.

'Flannery?'

I bang the heels of my hands in the hollow between rafters and know, from the wordless sound he makes, that he has heard me and worked out where I am. Then the trapdoor is shadowed from below and he comes, in silhouette, over its edge. Like a man long used to walking in attics, he crouch-runs along two rafters to me, drops to his knees astraddle, close to me, puts his shoulder to mine so my head is supported.

'Ah, Flannery,' he says in soft protest at the circumstances.

'Thirsty,' I say.

He puts his hand to my forehead. His hand feels cold against the burning heat of my skin.

'Where d'you keep painkillers?' he asks me.

I tell him and he pats me, promises he'll be back in no time, reverses along the rafters and is gone. I hear him on the phone. Then in the kitchen.

'Feeling like a human again, Fluffy?' I hear him asking the kitten.

I know he has the name wrong but I can't think of the right name. Then I hear him in my room at my chest of drawers. When I see the shadow in the trapdoor, the relief is so huge, even though I have known he will come back, that I cry, noisily and childishly.

'One drink,' he says and holds a plastic cup to my mouth. Iced 7UP. I have never experienced anything so wonderful. He takes away the cup, puts it behind him.

'Now, I've stuck pins in these painkiller capsules to make them work quicker,' he says, and puts them in my mouth as if my hands won't work. I swallow. Gives me another sip of

7UP. And another. He puts the drink beyond my reach, tells me he'll be back in a minute. I cry out not to be left in the flickering, gathering dark, but he says he will be back before five minutes have passed, just keep an eye on my watch. I can hear him go down the ladder, then run onto the landing, downstairs and open the front door. Then he is running back upstairs, coming back up the ladder, getting to the 7UP, feeding me gulps of it. He goes behind me and sits, legs out on either side of me, clamped up against me like the back of a chair. Something to lean on. I am crying all the time now, in relief, no noise, no sobs, just hot salted tears running black through the dirt on my face, and he hooks his arms like haversack straps under my arms and up over my shoulders, so I am secure, held.

The sirens sound competitive and many, screaming up from the distance, filling the house, spinning bright blue lights leaking up through trapdoor, down through skylight. He leaves me, goes to the trapdoor, shouts 'Up here'. Must have propped the front door open, because they come up the stairs like an army of entitlement, and like a rescued child I abandon myself to gratitude and grief. One of them comes through the trapdoor with some difficulty, because he is so garbed in stiff plasticky stuff and walks around me, stepping from rafter to rafter. He goes back down and we hear him shouting for individuals and tools and two men to go here, one there. A paramedic climbs into the attic and another after her. They cut away some of my clothes and ask me questions. I hear one of them talking to him.

'D'd'you give her something?'

'Painkillers.'

'What?'

'These.'

'Shit. How many?'

'Two.'

'Jasus. You don't mind me saying so, very unwise to give someone in shock painkillers. Quite apart from them being pure morphine. I won't ask where you got them.'

'I'm sorry,' he says. 'I have poor judgement. Just, she was in a bad way.'

'I know, I know,' she says more gently.

The two of them go down to let the big fireman back up to us. He tells us what is going to happen. I am without care or fear. Dougal Rogan gets back into position with his arms bracing me like the straps of a haversack and the fireman looks like he's going to argue and then doesn't. A grinding, driving noise begins. Drill. They are drilling.

They break away bits they have weakened and although I can feel nothing directly, there is a sudden, startlingly sudden shift in pressure, deeply, threateningly uncomfortable, sickening, frightening. Someone below is shouting, then two or three of them are on the rafters with us, the paramedic now in charge, forcing her arms between my leg and the containing splinters, shouting, counting and then some different pressure takes over and the counting slows. Some of them swear.

The drilling happens again, followed, more speedily now, by breaking noises and then they are blowing up something in the attic like a bed you might float on a swimming pool and I am being laid back, two legs together, covered in blood, one of them, swollen to twice or three times its size, dozens of hands on me, fast, expert and unafraid, all the time, his face down into my hair, whispering, murmuring nothing that has words to it, or maybe the pills in me, powdered, are powdering the words.

359

Then they are shouting to each other and sliding the stretcher, me on it, helpless like once I remember on the carrier of my father's bike, no choice but to rely on him. No choice now but to rely on them.

23

Contributions From the Floor

━━━━◆◆◆━━━━

If you're going to Accident and Emergency, your vehicle of choice is an ambulance. Arrive in someone else's car and stumble across the pavement to A & E, they subject you to triage and assume, even if you do a pretty continuous scream, that you're All Right, Really. Arrive on a stretcher in a state ambulance, and teams of professionals come together to take you seriously. It's as if you're their property, whereas if you come in under your own steam, you're just visiting.

I have been examined, X-rayed, had a drip inserted, been extensively stitched, painted yellow (they say this is disinfectant, but, because I'm on a morphine high, I tell them I know the real reason is to prevent over-tired surgeons stitching the wrong leg) and bandaged. They are determined, all of them, to impress me with what has happened to me. Not as an illustration of me as a great sufferer. More as a way of showing their incredible professionalism. I apparently encountered, on my way down through the floor, some protruding 'metal sharp' which sliced me from below the knee to the crotch, encountering and slicing open an artery along the way. In trying to pull myself out of the hole, I jammed myself worse than before my escape efforts, and this jamming closed off the ruptured artery. Until they cut me loose. Which was why that paramedic was yelling and getting tourniquets in position.

'According to your partner, you had already lost a lot of blood,' one of them tells me.

Who the frig is my partner? I look around.

'He said to tell you he'd be back by eight,' a nurse says.

It is seven. In the morning. I have no idea which morning. I am in this bed that has rails on it. Making me feel like a felon. Potential felon. Potential *paediatric* felon: there are definite playpen implications to the metal bars.

'How could he know how much blood she'd lost?' someone else asks.

'There was a shoe filled with congealed blood in the room below,' the first person says quietly. This squashes the sceptic, but makes me want to argue. I take a size five, for Chrissake, and we're talking shoe, not boot. How much blood can a size five hold?

'Can I go home?'

This provokes a laugh. I look rattily from one to another.

'Your husband said that was the first thing you'd say,' the nurse says, smiling affectionately.

'Well, can I?'

I am poking at my arse and thigh as I ask. There is a distant tenderness, but the hard swelling has receded a bit. The feeling has come back into my leg, but compared to when I was stuck in the floor, it's a doddle.

'And here he is – *early*,' the nurse says meaningfully.

The meaning being: appreciate this wonderful husband of yours more than you do, because you never asked for him at all in the last few hours. That, nursie, is because my husband he isn't, my partner he isn't, my father's blackmailer he probably is, my rescuer he undoubtedly is, and this complexity reduces my capacity for appreciation.

I look at Dougal, who has poked his head around the curtains that separate me from the drunk on the left (who fell down three flights of stairs and is bothering the hell out of his observers because he is continuing, literally, to feel no pain) and the suspected myocardial infarction on the right (who is stoic in the face of a wife who cuts to the catastrophic chase and is silent only when planning his funeral). Dougal looks at me. The team around my bed look from one of us to the other.

'OK, I'll say it,' I say, eventually.

His hand appears from behind the curtain in an 'after you' gesture.

'We can't go on meeting like this.'

The other hand appears and the two meet in applause. The medical team find this unsatisfactory.

'A & E has played a major part in our relationship from the start,' Dougal explains, as he comes over and kisses me on the forehead. It is a clever kiss. The kind that lends itself to a multiplicity of interpretations, invades nobody, commits nobody to nuthin'. 'Have the wheelchair,' he says, and pulls a folded set of wheels and plastic seating around the curtain, propping it against the leg of the trolley.

This announcement decides the team to let me go home, but the way they plan the operation, you'd think I'd banged my head through the floor, not my leg, and couldn't be trusted to understand or remember any instructions. These are the things he is to bring home, they say, presenting each container by name and function. Here's how often he is to cleanse the lesions. My *arse*, I think. If I have lesions, I'll cleanse them myself. My lesions are personal. You should be telling me about lesion-cleansing, not a fecking stranger. However, rather than slow things up, I just eavesdrop on lesion instruction until they get me into the wheelchair (tight fit, one side of me is still much larger than normal life) and hang my bag of lesion goodies on the handle behind me.

In the car, silence obtains. Once, he asks me if I'm all right, and I say I am. Other than that, he concentrates on driving and I consider my options. He gets the car as close as possible to the house, puts the wheelchair beside the open door on my side, locks the brake and holds it for me to shift myself from car seat to wheelchair. When he comes to the front door, he reverses the wheelchair and tips it backward. Bump. Bump. Up the two steps. I am about to give instructions when I find him wheeling me into the sitting room, where the mattress of a single bed has been placed on the floor and dressed with sheets, pillows and a duvet. He stands me up, takes the coat off me and lowers me onto the bed.

'What d'you want to eat?' he asks, folding up the wheelchair. Because it involves a lot of well-directed kicks, this seems to be enjoyable.

'I'd prefer, frankly, if we could—' I begin, and he goes slitty-eyed. Instantaneous don't-fuck-with-me, I'm-an-Alpha-male. I can't be arsed to fight with him, so tell him tea and toast. He lashes folded newspapers down on the bed beside me.

'You might have a read of the business pages,' he says, departing for the kitchen.

In my own time, I think. Business pages? Last part of the paper I ever go to. Scruffy lands, four-pawed, on me from nowhere, picking the injured thigh as runway. I control the yell rising in me and tell her she is the coolest kitten in the world. Look at her, all silky and unbothered by a day's starvation and dehydration. She curls up on the sorest part of my leg and goes to sleep. Purring.

Clattering from the kitchen reminds me I'd better have a read of the business pages before Rogan comes back to ask exam questions. Across the top of the first one, the headline goes:

BULLY, HARASSMENT SUIT
HITS HIGH-FLYING CYBER-FIRM

Since I know no cyber firms, I ignore this. There seems to be shag all of interest on the page, so I shift to the other paper.

AMAZING TRACE BOSS
ACCUSED OF SEXUAL HARASSMENT

it says. I go back to the first one. The cyber-firm is Amazing Trace.

> Dougal Rogan, charismatic founder of Amazing Trace, the high-flying software development company, has been accused by one of his top management of sexual harassment and bullying. It is understood that a case of constructive dismissal has been lodged with the Employment Appeals Tribunal by Nicola Warden, who has resigned as Head of Human Resources at the company. Mr Rogan could not be reached last night for comment.

The bullying sexual harasser is standing at the door, holding a tray. I shift the papers to make room for it on my lap.

'No,' he says. 'Not putting it down where you were damaged. Move over a bit.'

I horse myself and Scruffy over and he puts the tray down beside me. I take up the mug of tea and scorch the mouth off myself.

'Jesus, you cost-cutting on effing milk?'

He goes off silently and comes back with the carton. And another paper. I flap a hand to establish that I don't need it, I'm across this sexual harassment issue.

'Those were yesterday's papers,' he says. 'These are to-day's.'

Yesterday? Shit, I thought Saturday was today. Today is Sunday. All of the Sunday papers put the sexual harassment story on their front pages, but one has a big exclusive. See inside, it says. I put down the mug and, lifting the broadsheet as high as I can, so as not to tickle Scruffy with the corners of a page or get butter on it, find the inside page, fold it open, fold it back, and get organised. The exclusive turns out to be a transcript of the diatribe Dougal did ages ago for Lyn's radio station about women and how awful they are. He sits down at the end of the mattress. Even if I didn't have Guinness Book of Records lesions, I couldn't do that. Fold down so neatly and flexibly. I throw the paper at my feet, since I have no space either side of me, and begin to sip tea.

The silence goes on forever. Whatever way I phrase the question will imply my acceptance of the accusation, or some satisfaction in him getting his come-uppance, and neither is the truth, mainly because my concerns are elsewhere and my confusion, at this stage, too deep for simple satisfying single issue condemnations. I am so grateful for rescue, and so guilty over lack of expression of my gratitude, that a slobbering thankfulness could slosh past the deeper need for him to answer for what he did to my father.

'You have no judgement,' I say. 'That's what you told the nurse this morning.'

He looks a question.

'Did you mean it? Or did you mean it just about painkillers?'

He thinks about this for longer than it merits.

'I meant it generally. Last year, I knew everything. This year, I know fuck all. That's about the size of it.'

'Insight into one's progress is always good.'

'I wouldn't, at this stage, trust myself to have *that* much insight,' he said, getting his forefinger and thumb about a millimetre away from each other.

'Insight isn't the issue,' I say. 'The issue is evil. Power. Coercion. Lack of mercy. Lack of humanity. Intellectual and entrepreneurial arrogance at the expense of any kind of human decency. Blackmail. Profiteering. Extortion. Fucking around with people's hearts and minds and jobs and lives.'

The eyes don't go slitty, but he looks at me long and unyieldingly. He may be confessing new humility, but Alpha Male will be a long time a-shrivelling.

'Flannery, do not ever assume that being victimised entitles you to behave like a complete asshole,' he says calmly. 'You've had a tough time. Acknowledged. Now, can we deal with facts for a change?'

'A change from what?' would sound like a teenager having a tantrum, so I just look at him in silence.

'First of all, the conversation you eavesdropped on – overheard, whatever – between me and your father. I stand over everything I said in that conversation. I told him it suited him to surround himself with emotional and financial dependents, but he wasn't doing it to me and he shouldn't do it to you.'

My expression makes him revisit what he has just said.

'Your father had insisted on giving me five thousand pounds early on when I was fool enough to tell him some of my plans, my big dreams. Once I set up Amazing Trace, I gave it back to him, doubled, as a loan repaid. Didn't want him as an investor. Just didn't, all right?'

'Why not?'

He examines his own fingers one by one. All present and correct.

'Your father would have wanted to make Amazing Trace

part of his act. Poet on Board of High Tech company. Everything about the way he thought wasn't . . . Look. If you look at the people I choose to have around me, they tend to be direct, no-shit, tell it like it is people. Piers. You.'

'Nicola?'

He lets a big deflated sigh out of him.

'Flannery, c'n I let you in on a secret? You don't have to come up with the smartarse contradictions. They're all up there in my own head, circling to land. Doesn't matter that I don't know what I'm at, I knew I didn't want to owe your father anything, be dependent on him for anything, and I also knew, and on this one I was bloody right, that it was wrong for you to be hidden behind him, Daughter Of. You'd make jokes about being Daughter Of. It wasn't a joke. It was a fucking tragedy. It wasn't even an accidental fucking tragedy. I think it was deliberate. I think he knew you were him and your mother multiplied. Two and two making five. And he didn't want you to be more successful than him. It suited him *so* well to be 'protecting' you, to have you where you didn't have to take care of yourself, didn't have to dress up, look like anything but a slob. Didn't matter to him that you had no sense of achievement, nothing that you could point to: "This is mine, I won it, I developed it, I created it." Everything second hand, every pleasure referred, every pride belonging to someone else. Jesus Christ, they used to write plays about oul' spinsters kept at home in rural Ireland as servitors by their domineering oul' parents. He'd just invented a newer, softer version of that for his daughter.'

I close my eyes to get away from the angry accuracy of it, and there, behind my eyes, is the sluggish turning slimed similitude of him, turning on the rope, tongue lolling.

'The thing about your father is that nobody knows, nobody

knew, including him, where self-interest ended in him and altruism began. That day I shouted at him, I think he honestly was taken aback when I mentioned being asked to take you to that wedding. It was like he didn't deliberately do it to make you more dependent on him, indirectly, to stop you having to move your arse and either ask someone to escort you or go on your own and maybe meet someone there. It was all about control, but how much of it was conscious, I don't know.'

'But you went along.'

'Same as you did. You're bucking right, I went along. For the ride, if you want to be really crude about it. Not many fellas get the father of the girl they fancy to hand her over on a serving plate. I thought all my Christmases had arrived together.'

I keep looking at the duvet cover. It has been put around the duvet inside out, which gives me a small frisson of suppressed superiority.

'The problem was you arriving, hearing bits of the conversation and deciding you're the Ugly Duckling and your father is pimping for you with – with the Evil Gigolo. Jasus. I decide not to fight with it, that there's going to be no changing you, pity, but at least we'll stay in contact and that's fine.'

He stands up the same way he sat down – without needing to balance himself against anything. Stretches much the way Scruffy does. This reminds me to stroke the sleeping ball of fur, which repays me by vibrating with purrs.

'You don't have the time for this,' I say quietly, knowing that anything I say will be tacit acceptance of what he has said. 'You need to be addressing this sexual harassment thing.'

'No, actually, I don't,' he says. 'Nothing in my life is as important as the sustained misunderstanding I have had with you over the past few years.'

A car pulls up outside. The door is banged, but someone is running up our path without pausing to lock it. Doug picks up the tray and is halfway to the front door with it before the doorbell rings. There is some conversation, but I have the impression that he has put his head out into the porch to talk in a low voice rather than let the newcomer into the hall to talk at full volume. Another car pulls up outside, the handbrake pulled on with such vigour, the driver must be muscled like a gorilla.

The town hall meeting on my front doorstep seems to be attracting a crowd. Scruffy sits up, licks her ass and saunters out to see who's there. This cat expresses my feelings more often than she knows. I stretch the leg she was sitting on, pleasurably grateful to find that I can stretch it.

Dougal comes back in and closes the door. Hundreds of people seem to be gathered in my kitchen, but that's beside the point. He sits down on the bit of the bed where the tray was. Being that low to the ground folds his legs up around him like a cricket'.

'I didn't discover what your father was up to in time to do anything useful,' he says. 'He made with the humility a lot, your father, but behind it, he was ridiculously confident of his abilities. He thought all you had to do on a computer was delete the document and delete it again out of the recycle bin, check that there were no back-ups, and it was as if you'd never created the document. Or had the correspondence. Or visited the web site. When I said I could give him an upgrade of his virus program, he probably did all that, did the deletions, and allowed me to walk into – well, to find stuff he wouldn't have wanted me to find.'

He watches, in his mind, the screens coming up, one by one in response to his prompts, revealing an addiction to paediatric porn, contacts with other practitioners and sustained correspondence with victims moving from wounded dependency to aggressive entitlement. I remember meeting him, that day. Him clutching the hard drive, tossing the key on the table: *not coming back here, not for any money*.

'It was the time Gary Glitter got done, remember?'

I see the black and white newspaper pictures, the ridiculous shock of shoddy dyed hair, the pantomime-aunt remnants of what had been an ironic, over-the-top Elvis prance, the furtive crouch of an old pervert caught out by an anonymous techie kid fixing a laptop. My head droops. O, Jesus, that my father would have come to this, this association with the living definition of talentless tawdry tackiness. Dougal pulls my hands into his as if we were friends, allies.

'I probably should've gone to see your father, but I admit it, I didn't have the moral courage. I just rang him and said I had the stuff and I was going to hang onto it in a safe place. Let him think safe-deposit box. Someone his generation would. I said I wasn't shopping him because I figured he was in such shit, someone of his victims was going to, sooner or later, and one way or the other he wouldn't have the time or cover to do any more of it in the short term. I suppose I knew there wouldn't be a long term. And he knew, too.'

He brought the bits of the computer home to the new big house. The new big house in which Nicola had recently joined him. He did not tell her where he had been. Just boxed the components and shelved them in a room he planned as a library, telling her they were important and not to touch them.

'I'm sorry, Flannery,' he says, now, letting go my hands. 'That was so stupid.'

My father's suicide Dougal assumed to have resulted from an agglomeration of guilt and emerging threat. He knew nothing about Nicola investigating the box of components. Knew nothing about her getting one of the juniors in Amazing Trace to fit the hard drive into her PC as a secret nixer, knew nothing about her meetings with my father or the money going into and out of a ghost subsidiary. Until Inspector Synnott called on him and showed him the cheque stubs, he saw no connection between my father's destruction and Dougal Rogan.

'And I never showed you his note.'

'No, you didn't, Flannery. Not bad enough that he'd kill himself in the best way to destroy you, you who'd never done anything to him, he manipulated you right up to the end, right fucking *past* the end. "Do not blame Doug." Yeah, right. Meaning: "*Do* blame Doug, but whatever you do, don't blame me, your father. I'm pretty damn perfect. Few minor flaws like destroying the lives of damaged kids, but gloss over that. Don't blame the bitch who took the last of my money, because you don't really know or love her. But because you love this bastard Rogan, I'll fix him and you for good." Yeah, Flannery, I didn't know you loved me and I suspect you didn't either, but your father had special antennae for who could be exploited, built up and then destroyed, and his final poetic offering . . .'

There's a knock on the door. He dithers. I catch his hand. Try to indicate, yes, let whoever it is in, we've gone as far as we need to, I believe you.

'C'mon in,' he says.

Piers erupts into the room, followed by a total stranger. Female. She is tall, Barbie-shaped and has short spikey hair, bleached platinum white.

'Flannery, we've been so worried,' she says in Lyn's voice.

'Don't step on Fluffy,' Dougal tells Piers.

'Who the fuck is Fluffy?' Piers wants to know.

'Scruffy,' I say. 'My cat.'

'Attention-seeking,' Piers says, sitting in the only chair in the room. The doorbell rings and blonde-with-Lyn's-voice goes to answer it.

'What?'

'The hair. Pretend you don't notice it.'

Even if I wanted to, I can't, when Lyn returns with Andrea and Bruce and Raimonde.

'Chairs in the kitchen,' Piers says and they obediently go off to get themselves something to sit on, with the exception of Lyn, who sits in front of Piers and leans against his legs, and Raimonde, who sits at the end of my bed and tweaks my feet through the duvet. The tweak communicates sympathy, solidarity and a soupçon of rage against the random but persistent injustices of life. Gotcha, Raimonde. Andrea lets someone else in. The someone turns out to be Meriel, who stands in the doorway closing her eyes dramatically to convey how totally she shares my pain until Andrea bunts her with a tray with flasks and mugs on it. Meriel climbs down off Histrionic Hill and hands biscuits around. She sits on the floor.

'OK, folks, votes of sympathy taken, we're now in formal session,' Piers says. 'You will all have read in the papers that we're being sued by that dozy deranged bint Doug Rogan was dumb enough to bring into Amazing Trace in the face of all available good advice.'

He gestures at Andrea to leave us in no doubt as to the source of the good advice. Andrea doesn't wave it away. Nor does Dougal, who still sits on the edge of the mattress, looking swamped by self-realisation.

'You may wonder why it's me who is telling you all this,' Piers goes on. 'I wonder myself. I have spent the last week wondering. No, the last three weeks. This day three weeks ago,

I'd've said we were rocking. We were the high tech company to buck the trend. Yeah, sure, the dot-com disaster had happened. Yeah, sure, the Motorolas and the Dells were laying off employees right left and centre. But we had a product that wasn't dependent on unrealistic expectations of Internet use. That was central to many enterprises. We had an offer for substantial minority shareholding from the world leader in forensic software development. Doug was just back from Germany, due diligence about to start. Plus, he's shown some sense at last, and a few weeks earlier booted Nicola the hell out of his private life, so we figure we gettin' places.'

He stops and drinks some of his cooling coffee. Lyn puts her blonded head back to look up at him and helpfully prompts 'And then?' He gives her a dig with his knee and tells her to stop trying to take over his meeting. *Our* meeting, Dougal murmurs, too softly to be heard by anyone other than me.

'Nicola is being an even more major pain-in-the-arse at work than usual, but she's kind of peripheral to our priorities right then, so we don't pay that much attention to her. The accountants are in, doing the due diligence, when the CEO loses it.'

Dougal explains Inspector Synnott and gives them a shortened version of Nicola's accessing of my father's secrets and blackmail of him. I wonder how long all of them have known about my father, because they seem more shocked, now, by Nicola's intervention than by his original crime. He stresses that he went along with Inspector Synnott's instructions.

'In other words, he didn't go find Nicola right then and beat her into puree,' Piers says. '*NO*. He leaves her out there, comfortable with her ill-gotten gains, pissed that he has gone back to the love of his life—'

'If that's me, he hadn't,' I say, indignantly.

'He's over there every *afternoon*,' Piers says, in Nicola's voice. '*Every* afternoon. I mean, what do *you* think he's doing? Feeding her fucking kitten?'

'That's what he *was* doing,' Dougal says, beginning to tire of the passive eejit role assigned him. Lyn leans forward and pats his knee: We know, Doug. We believe you, too. Thousands wouldn't, but we do.

'Effing Scruffy,' Dougal mutters.

'Poor little yoke is blind in one eye,' Lyn tells the room and gets a collective sympathy croon in response.

'So because this evil witch with the sausage dog legs doesn't know she's heading for Mountjoy on blackmail charges, what does she do?' asks Piers. 'She decides to screw the screwer.'

No, Piers, I think. Zebedee was the screw. Not Dougal.

'She talks to the PR company which is being paid a frigging fortune by Amazing Trace, and gets them into the same sympathy and sex frenzy into which she worked yer man here, gets names and phone numbers of a select number of hacks and shares her tragedy with those hacks. Including – ta *ra!*, by way of objective evidence of her boss's anti-female bias – the transcript of an item he *ackshully* broadcast *on de wireless* ages ago.'

Dougal raises his head and points out that most of what he said in the celebrated radio programme was drawn from outbursts of Piers's over a period. Piers responds crushingly that nothing counts in court except what was recorded and broadcast and by Jesus, nothing had ever been broadcast by Piers about fat girls giving the best blow jobs.

'That didn't get broadcast by Doug, either,' Lyn fair-mindedly inputs. 'I edited that out.'

'Even before this appears in today's papers,' Piers goes on, waving the folded-over pages showing the transcript, 'our rectitudinous friends in Munich were on to me. Well, they were on looking for our CEO, really, but this last week, our CEO went walkabout. So head-the-ball here had to fill in for him. Bottom line, our prospective investor ain't no prospective investor no more. Bottom line, half our staff are circulating their CVs in the marketplace. Bottom line, the value of our shares is one-tenth the value they had last week.'

'If that,' Doug says helpfully.

'That's a lot of bottom lines,' Meriel says. It's like she wants Piers to know someone appreciates the drama of his presentation.

'Where's the light at the end of the tunnel?' Raimonde asks.

'Raimonde, there is no light. Norra chink,' Piers says, grimly serious now. 'In the words of the poet (you should pardon the expression, Flannery) we're fucked. Royally, collectively, corporately, individually, severally and decidedly fucked.'

The phone rings, and I am somewhat fazed when Doug goes off to answer it. Particularly by the way everybody else in the room seems to figure it normal that he, rather than anybody else, should substitute for me when I patently can't get to answer it. There is a flurry of compensatory activity. More coffee is made, more biscuits found. Someone turns on the lunchtime news programme in the kitchen, and we can hear reference being made to Amazing Trace in the middle of a question about the ongoing collapse of Internet based companies. When we gather together again, Doug brings a chair. I mouth *who?* at him. *Synnott*, he mouths back.

'Going back to the difficulties Piers outlined—' Doug begins.

'I didn't outline difficulties. I said we were fucked,' Piers snarls.

'We're not,' Doug says. He says it with such calm assurance, people around the room begin to nod and smile at each other. I giggle and they look at me to see if it was a moan of pain or malaise.

'This is like one of those old musicals,' I say, 'where someone says, "Why don't we put on a show – right *here!*" And they do and everybody can dance like Fred Astaire and Ginger Rogers and sing like Cliff Richard and get rich.'

The minute I have it said, I lose faith in it. Yet another example, I think, of me making predictions anybody with half a brain cell could see were going to be proved wrong. Of course, if you second-guess yourself constantly, sometimes it's the second guess that'll be proven wrong.

24

Flannery Stapleton and Friends

———◆◆◆———

'We have two problems,' Dougal begins.

'The *Titanic* had only one,' Piers points out glumly. 'Little hole below the waterline.'

'The first problem relates to Flannery's father,' Dougal goes on. 'The second is Amazing Trace.'

'Great to have that sorted,' Piers says.

'Piers, shut up if you've got nothing better than smartarsery to offer, OK?'

'Two weeks ago,' his boss says, mostly addressing him, 'you and I were regarded as the frigging crème de la crème of young managerial brain power in this country, Lyn was the ultimate radio high-flyer, Andrea was a power in the land of HR – look around you. We've got almost every discipline, every talent you could want if you were trying to rescue a truly shit situation. Now, you can spend the next few hours admiring the size of the problem or see if we can use this powerhouse to pull together a solution.'

Piers does a shrug that manages to indicate unwilling willingness, suppressed sensible doubt and heroic commitment to a doomed ideal, all in one. If I could reach him, I'd hit him. Everybody else seems pretty tuned into the concept of being part of a powerhouse of talent. But then, they would, wouldn't they? Bruce takes A4 paper out of his briefcase and writes FLANNERY'S FATHER and AMAZING TRACE on one, then sticks it on the wall, using the corner of a framed picture to retain it in position.

'Flannery. Outline the key practical elements in relation to your father's problem.'

'First one, I suppose, is Nicola. The money she got out of him.'

'D'you want it back?' This is from Andrea.

'D'you want her punished?' Meriel asks.

'Both, of course,' Bruce answers and is cordially invited by his wife to stop putting words into Flannery's mouth.

'I'd love to see her punished,' I say. 'But if you take her through the courts, everything gets published about my father. I don't even know if I can charge her or if it has to be the State. The money . . . well, I don't want her to gain from it. But Nicola is really a more immediate problem for Amazing Trace.'

'Your garda woman has talked to her, right?' This is Meriel, getting excited, as if this was one of those management games based on a murder mystery. 'So she knows they have her – knows they have the evidence of where the money came from and it ending up with her. There isn't any way she can suggest Doug got some of it?'

He shakes his head.

'So whether it's your Inspector or the Criminal Assets Bureau, sooner or later they're going to get her for extortion or something.'

'And every detail of Professor Stapleton's actions will be all over the media,' Lyn says.

'Not necessarily,' Meriel says. 'She could plea bargain.'

'Meriel, that's the United States. We don't do that stuff here.'

'If people confess, it prevents the details of the case coming out. We do *that* here. I was reading the other day a judge saying she was going to shorten this guy's sentence because he hadn't wasted the State's time. And that was for *rape*.'

'She won't go to prison at all if she pulls the I-am-a-poor-sick-victim bit,' I say, and immediately get knotted up over what the group will think of me for talking contemptuously of victims. Listen, I want to say, I know most victims are really victims and we must never question what they say, but on the other hand . . . Interesting, I think. I don't have the 'other hand' option any more. Because of whose daughter I am, I must always take the side of the victim in any situation. The alternative would be *Daughter of Child Abuser in Hate Campaign Against Victims*.

'D'you need her to go to prison?'

Dougal asks the question very quietly.

'I don't,' I say. 'But does society?'

'She has a point,' Andrea says. 'If she's convicted, she has a record, it helps prevent it happening again.'

'Does it?'

' 'Course it does,' Bruce says. 'Soon as she goes for a job, her records will show—'

'Show what?'

'Imprisonment. Sentence. Conviction. Whatever.'

'She's going to put all that on her CV?'

'No, but when the employer calls the people who gave her references—'

'When Doug decided to give Nicola a job,' Andrea reminds us, 'did he even bother to check with her then employer?'

Dougal mimes shooting himself in the head.

'Your point being?' Piers is getting as impatient as Bruce.

'Just playing out all the options.'

'Well, what's the other option?'

380

'The medical model.'

Andrea's on a roll at this point. Mistress of Human Resources.

'Meaning?'

'Meaning,' I offer from the mattress, 'that she checks herself into a mental hospital suffering from – oh, I don't know—'

'Manic depression,' someone offers.

'Cognitive dissonance,' another voice pipes up.

'Mental exhaustion,' says a third.

'Prescription drug addiction,' someone else says.

'– gets whatever treatment is needed and all the bad things she did get attributed to mental illness. Or disorder. I don't know the difference.'

She isn't mentally ill, Piers says. He knows mental illness, and this isn't it. She shouldn't be allowed to hide behind mental illness when she doesn't have it. She shouldn't be allowed to – to—

'Bring mental illness into disrepute?' suggests Doug, and Piers is jolted into laughter. But he's still rabidly high-minded.

'*Qui bono?*' Lyn asks. '*Qui malo?*'

She sounds like an exotic bird. I know she's quoting her father, who would always calm us down, as outraged teenagers, when we would recount to him some malicious act perpetrated against us by an erstwhile friend. Half the time, once he got to work on our problems, they turned out to be random circumstances, rather than clever conspiracies. Which was always a disappointment.

'Does it do anybody any harm if the medical route is taken?' Lyn clarifies.

Of course it does, Piers roars. It renders unclear the line between criminality and madness. Bruce tells him both of those terms are dated and that the line is completely unclear anyway. The fact that this point comes from Bruce seems to upset Piers much more than the point itself.

'It's an option open only to one class in society,' Raimonde says quietly. 'You're poor, you go to jail. You're well off, you go to hospital.'

'Like fucking Ernest Saunders,' Piers says, encouraged. 'Only man in medical history to recover from Alzheimer's. Or General Pinochet.'

'Would Nicola have quite that significance?' Lyn asks, mildly.

Precedents don't have to be set by the famous, I think. Nor patterns by the notorious. The Holocaust was not a function of a handful of Nazis but of a fostering context.

'Isn't this what the Church used to do with paedophiles?' asks Raimonde. 'Take them out of wherever they'd been caught doing it and move them somewhere else. Solve the problem *here* by creating a problem over there?'

'But what problem are we creating "over there"? Do we want to make this woman unemployable when she comes out of either hospital or clink?'

Yes, Dougal, I think but don't say. Don't you reason me down the rehabilitation rather than revenge route. Been there, don't believe that. Revenge has its place. An eye for an eye has a symmetry to it. On cue, Scruffy pads in. She takes a more or less straight line to me, using people as a path. Settles down as if she plans to contribute to the meeting. Everybody but me says aloud that of course they don't want to make Nicola unemployable.

'Well, whether we admit it or not, the stigma of being in a mental hospital is not that much worse than having a suspended sentence on your record,' Doug points out. 'Especially if planks like me don't check the records anyway.'

Doug as Mrs Gummidge, I think: *Wot's the good of anyfink?*
Why, nuffink . . .

'I think we should be looking at our objective,' Bruce says,
and I nearly laugh, because for a while he's had *OBJECTIVE*
printed out, very large, on his next sheet. Doug and Piers do
almost identical movements, like tigers assessing how much
effort it would take to tear the throat out of someone.

'Wouldn't it be great if Nicola confessed everything, withdrew her accusations against Doug, and was able to get the
care she needs?' Lyn said, in a garden-party voice.

'*What* fucking care?' Piers demands. 'That's the whole
issue.'

'No, Piers, that isn't the whole issue,' Dougal says. 'The
whole issue is us. Flannery. You. Me. Amazing Trace. Employees who don't know if they'll have a job tomorrow. Not
whether or not Nicola is being let off some hook by being
allowed to claim that she's half-mad.'

'Which she is,' Bruce says, fearlessly going where no man in
his right mind would go. 'Nobody sane would blackmail
someone in such an ill-planned way.'

'And the Nobel Prize for Psychiatry goes to Bruce Green,
with his discovery of the new truth that if you don't plan your
crime properly, it's because you're as daft as a bag of wire
hangers,' Piers says.

'Like *you're* a psychiatrist?' Bruce snarls back.

'None of us are psychiatrists. All we can do is nudge things
the right way or the wrong way,' Lyn says, standing up and
brushing non-existent creases out of her skirt.

'Where the hell are you going?' Piers demands.

'Oh, you know,' Lyn says vaguely.

'No, I don't know,' Piers responds.

'I'd probably be able to talk to Nicola,' Lyn says, and we all immediately recognise that the likelihood is that Lyn has stayed in touch with Nicola, maybe through e-mail, right throughout this disaster, just as she stays in touch with all ex-boyfriends, employees, schoolpals and school enemies. She goes out into the hall with that swing she always uses on exit. It used to unfurl the flag of black hair.

'It doesn't work so well, now you're bald,' Piers calls after her and a few people in the room stifle guilty laughs. Having thought much the same thing themselves.

'Even if Nicola paid back everything she blackmailed out of my father, even if she got a doctor to say she was sick at the time, it doesn't prevent someone like the Tylers doing programmes on my father and it doesn't solve Amazing Trace's sexual harassment reputation.'

'Which, by now, stretches to Munich and back,' Piers confirms.

Raimonde has to be brought up to speed about the Tylers. Meriel's Adrian puts up his hand like a schoolkid waiting to be called upon. Dougal smiles at him, acknowledging their joint exclusion from the inner circle of Les Girls. Les Boys, I think, haven't been doing too badly in the talking department, but if Adrian wants to make with the tentative diffidence, let him.

'I hate to sound like an accountant,' he says, and Bruce mutters his way through an accountant joke which none of us quite hear, 'but that's where we should begin to address this TV programme possibility. With the numbers. The programme is a product for sale. A half-finished product for sale. Part of a monumentally successful product line, over the past couple of years: exposés of loved authority figures as child abusers. Right?'

All of us except Meriel nod in response. I wonder if he has a habit of asking her to agree with him.

'Right,' he confirms, not noticing the standout. 'But the market for that product is slowly but surely shrinking. Why is it shrinking? Because religious orders are not taking it any more. Look crooked at them, and they get litigious. Plus, the very fact that there have been three or four of these programmes means we're close to saturation point. Which, in turn, necessarily implies a certain diminution in the enthusiasm with which prospective purchasers will look at this latest offering.'

No wonder you sat over there, silently, for so long, Adrian, I think. The way you talk requires a long rev.

'This, in turn, means that Flannery is in a neutral to positive situation, rather than a neutral to negative one.'

'Why do I not feel much better?' I ask rhetorically.

'Because you're still in shit,' Piers says. 'What Adrian is doing is working out whether it's birdshit or whaleshit.'

'Ah,' I say in a satisfied way.

'It matters,' Adrian tells us, working hard on being patient with people who so patently need his help but are insufficiently grateful for the manner of its presentation. Piers and I send signals of pious attention.

'In this situation, you have at most five potential purchasers,' Adrian goes on, gathering speed. 'RTE, BBC, UTV, TV3 or Lyn's lot.'

'Now, the one thing no TV station wants to do is get itself caught in the crosshairs of competing litigants.'

Shit, I think. Another of life's great truths I never knew about.

'A pre-emptive strike, therefore, to negatively prepare the marketplace would be indicated.'

'If I understood the hell what you're talking about,' Dougal says pleasantly, 'I'm sure I'd go along with that.'

'Flannery's father paid off some of his victims, right?'

'Right,' I say. 'Well, not paid them *off*, exactly. They didn't go *off*.'

'How many?'

'I only know of two, for sure.'

'But the bank statements your garda pal has would establish it pretty clearly?'

'Probably.'

'Then you might take legal advice on informing each of these TV stations that they are likely to be offered a television programme in the foreseeable future which names Professor Edmund Stapleton as a child molester. That, while this charge was never made against the Professor in life, it is understood that he financially supported key individuals likely to be telling their story in the programme offered. And that his estate has put the bank documentation relevant to these payments in the hands of the gardai. Full stop. Don't name the guys who were paid, because they may be quite different guys from the ones who appear in the programme. Don't name the guys you know or suspect may be in the programme. Don't breathe a word about blackmail. Just give them a big unpalatable fact to chew on that will influence the way they view the programme when it lands on their desks. My betting is that it will lead most of them to either pass on the programme or to send it back to the makers for amendments, and it won't, one way or the other, find a place in the autumn schedules. The longer the time intervening after your father's death, the less saleable is the programme, because it becomes a case of Professor Who? Which poet was he, now?'

If I were the praying kind, I should now, it seems, pray for the reduction of my father to the ranks of us unmemorable nonentities. Better make sure nobody makes a movie like *Four*

Weddings and a Funeral and revives the dead popularity of one of his poems. I make appreciative noises at Adrian, while pointing out that the Tylers may be a handy hate duo, but will not be on their own among broadcasters and journalists eager to expose my father, once the word gets around, as it will.

'For everything else, you need a two-line statement,' Meriel says. 'Third party. Saying Professor Stapleton's daughter confirmed she turned over all of his papers to the gardai as soon as these allegations came to light and will make no further comment.'

'That's kind of cruel,' Raimonde ventures.

'Cruel?'

'Well, it says she doesn't care—'

'On the contrary,' Meriel snaps, but goodhumouredly, 'it puts a cork in the whole thing. If you, Ray, go on a radio programme and say "this means his daughter doesn't care", you've slandered her and you and the programme are in trouble. It sends a strong signal that Flannery doesn't own her father or answer for him or plan to spend the rest of her life being Daughter Of. She's her own man. Woman, I mean.'

Lyn told me some time back that Meriel was doing a night course in PR. It must be a good one.

'Some of us need food. Some of us need a cigarette, although you'll die of it,' Andrea says to Bruce. 'We all need to stretch legs—'

Right on cue, Scruffy rises and does that long reversing-from-the-front-paws stretch, ignoring the laugh she gets for it.

'—I propose we break for half an hour, call for food, clean up and continue at nine.'

The rest of them drift off and Doug unwinds himself from the wall he's been leaning on and comes over, extending his two hands. I grab them. It hurts, getting upright, but not as much as I expected. I make my way to the downstairs loo, watched by him but unassisted by him. When I come back out, he's watching from the room we were in.

'I could climb the stairs.'

'Go ahead. I'll come behind you to catch you.'

'Crush you, if I fell on you.'

'Naa. Dent me a bit, maybe.'

On the landing, I have to halt for quite a while to let the misery die down. Then I get quite enthusiastic. I will have a shower. He will set up the kitchen for the rest of the meeting. I will come back downstairs. He says going downstairs may be more difficult than going up, but if that's what I want, he will send Raimonde to break down the bathroom door if I don't come out within reasonable time.

Twenty minutes later, I'm sitting in Victoria's Secret red satin pyjamas and matching gown at the kitchen table, my leg raised on a chair. The Victoria's Secret motif surprises the hell out of everybody, so I make like I always sleep in sexy flimsies rather than the rugby pullovers and saggy knickers which are the normal truth. I bought the red outfit about a hundred years ago to encourage myself to lose weight and then forgot about it. It turned up a few weeks back, flattened and defeated at the bottom of a drawer. I look (I tell myself) inappropriately bouncy and refreshed, whereas, at least until they get food into them, most of the others are looking a bit frayed at the edges.

'If we eat up all our cabbage, will we get to sort out Amazing Trace?' Piers asks. Plaintively. The phone rings and Dougal picks it off the kitchen wall. What ensues is one of those infuriating calls where the caller makes all the running.

'Lyn'll be back in about half an hour, maybe less,' he says, and the way he looks, nobody has the temerity to ask if she

found Nicola, talked to Nicola or anything to do with Nicola.
It's one of the problems about being as modest as Lyn. She
would never boast of success on the phone, but that doesn't
mean we're not awaiting an account of total failure.

'Flannery has to be sorted first,' Dougal says.

'I think I am sorted,' I say. 'I like the idea of the letter to the
TV stations. Love the statement. I just—'

'Get on with your life?'

'Fish or cut bait?'

'Shit or get off the pot?'

'Start producing scripts by the dozen for me?'

Raimonde, from whom this last offering emanates, is down
on her hands and knees in the corner, pouring out kitten milk
for Scruffy, who is purring in one continuous vibration.

'For maybe another month, but after that I'll stop.'

'Oh?'

'And?'

'Longer term, I'm going back to college. I'm going to be a
vet,' I say.

'Shit,' Piers says. 'The single most difficult course to get
into.'

I suddenly realise Doug's eyes are filled with soft gentleness
and that he's looking at Scruff's little white self, poised over
the saucer. Frig that sentimentality.

'Specialising in horses,' I say.

'Great, we'll all go to the races all the time and you can put
down the ones that fall,' Meriel says. We can hear Lyn letting
herself in. Piers ostentatiously fails to make room for her
beside him. She sits down opposite him, smiling at him as
if she knew he preferred to be able to see her. Lyn must be *so*
irritating if you're trying to turn her nasty. Meriel fills her in on
me becoming a vet and specialising in horses.

'Wow,' Lyn says.

My very own wow, I think. Life's a bitch, but then you get a wow. And, because of the marvellous disproportionality of things, it can lift the heart after grimly serious traumas.

'You must do research into crib biters,' she tells me. 'I had a mare who was a bad crib biter.'

'What the frig is a crib biter?'

'Oh, it's dreadful,' she says, with another toss of the non-existent hair. 'They just chew the wood of their stable.'

'Do they have a twelve-step programme?' Piers wants to know. 'Because I'm going to become a crib cruncher if we don't cut to the chase. As in Nicola.'

Oh, yes, Lyn says maddeningly, as if it had slipped her mind. Of course. Well, she did meet up with Nicola. And they talked. And Nicola is really not in good shape.

'Nicola was never much in the shape department,' I say.

'She brings "short" to a new low,' agrees Piers and I feel a great sisterly affection for him. Doug stretches out a piece of pizza so the cheese strings become as thin as spider's webs and concentrates on them.

However, Lyn goes on, Nicola, underneath it all, is very clever. She got a solicitor and they drew up a letter and a statement. Plus, her GP has got her a bed in the private psychiatric ward of Tallaght Hospital immediately, where she'll be under observation. The letter was faxed to Inspector Synnott there and then, Lyn explains, and Inspector Synnott asked to see the statement and didn't find any fault with it, so really, there it is.

The statement says she withdraws accusations of sexual harassment against Dougal Rogan, that there was never any truth in them, that the breakup of an important relationship caused her to behave irrationally at work and outside work, that she had given the gardai information on some inappropriate actions she had taken as an officer of Amazing Trace and awaited whatever action they would take. In the meantime, she was entering psychiatric care and would be unavailable for further comment.

' "Inappropriate actions undertaken as an officer of Amazing Trace" presumably covers blackmailing Flannery's oul' fella and storing the money briefly in one of our subsidiaries?' Piers asks, looking up.

That about covers it, we decide, and Piers goes ballistic all over again. This evil two-faced shortlegged cow dalmation ('You mean dachshund,' I correct, 'she's squat, rather than spotty') is going to be allowed to crap euphemisms instead of owning up to being a murderous shit, despite helping to clean Flannery's father out financially so he committed suicide. I make gently contradictory gestures. Down on a paper plate goes Doug's pizza.

' "Do not blame Doug"?' he reminds me. 'Your father knew bloody well you'd find out at some stage where he'd been paying money to, and that I owned it. He was making it clear I wasn't behind the extortion, but he was also making clear that this final extortion made suicide his only option. Don't dismiss Piers's "murderous". This woman did not care, and I suspect, although none of us has asked Lyn, *does* not care, that someone died a ghastly death as a result of her deciding to make money out of him.'

'She was your girlfriend, for Chrissake,' I say.

'Yeah, and the guilt by association is no fun, Flannery,' he says.

'That little spat out of the way,' Piers says, 'we now have something to show.'

He lifts the page and waves it. As soon as it goes back down on the table, I reach for it, but encounter Lyn's smiling reassurance. *I have copies*, she mouths.

'To show who?' Andrea asks.

'The Meedja,' Piers says.

'You going to use the PR company she used?'

'And we paid for? In my arse we are. Remind me to fire them first thing tomorrow.'

I make a note. Hell, until I'm fully occupied learning about crib biters, I have the time. Meriel says that, thanks to her night course, she can handle a press conference.

'Who said it would be a press conference?' Piers wants to know.

'It *has* to be a press conference,' Meriel says, managing to sound both crisp and dramatic. 'Only a press conference will make your worthwhile employees stay. Only a press conference will stop the banks foreclosing.'

Doug says he can help prevent this because he has sold his house and so has some money he can plough back into the company.

'Bruce and I would be prepared to make a small investment,' Andrea says.

'No, but thank you, Andrea,' is Dougal's response. 'If you're our new Head of HR, then you should probably get a carried interest.'

Andrea's expression is a mixture of astonishment and smugness that would make you want to hit her with the litter box. I want to know what a carried interest is. Adrian says it's when you get a shareholding as a present, without having to pay for the shares.

'Meriel, a press conference it is,' Piers says. 'The ultimate press conference. Oh, man, are we going to have fun?'

Doug suggests we concentrate. That way, we could have the

whole thing planned in an hour and get some sleep. He doesn't say where he's going to get the sleep. It is just collectively assumed he doesn't plan to leave the house. My house. Which is why I am quite surprised when, after they've all taken off into the night, he escorts me back upstairs and shakes hands with me on the landing.

'Jesus, the first time I've ever worn Victoria's Secret satin, and all it gets me is a handshake,' I say, and then wilt down in guilt because tomorrow may be the first day of the rest of my life, but it could be the end of his career, even livelihood.

'Flannery, I have a radio item for you,' he says, stroking my shoulders, enjoying the satin nearly as much as I do. 'The myths of trauma. Myth One: that it deepens and matures people. In fact, it leaves people just as shallow and immature as ever they were. They're just shallow and immature at a different level. Myth Two: that it taints life forever. That's the one you buy into. You feel it's your duty to be tainted, that God will strike you dead if you ever have a trivial moment ever again. You'll always have your nightmares, but you don't have to attend matinees of them. Myth Three: that survival is about counselling and "working through the issues". Survival is about denial and hard work and laughter.'

He pats me in a general way, turning me in the direction of the bedroom and goes down the stairs.

'So great sex and mutual commitment aren't worth a shite, then?' I say and he turns.

'Might be worth a try,' he says.

25

Specialising in Horses

———————◆◆◆———————

Exactly a half an hour before the press arrive, Meriel tells us next day, there will be a staff briefing. Half an hour ensures the ones who immediately run to the gents' loo or the ladies' with their mobile phones, ready to do dual purpose leaking, will have no great lead time on the journos who arrive at the main press conference. But having the press briefing after the staff briefing will make all staff understand the corporate priorities.

I've got myself positioned where, if my leg gets sore, I can discreetly stick a foot up on the chair in front of me. Doug goes up on the platform and seats himself beside the podium. Piers leaps the steps to the platform three at a time. Lyn follows him.

The staff meeting is short and to the point. It is also so effective that what the press meet, as they make their way up the stairs, is like the Red Army on speed: there's an awful lot of them, a hell of a comradeship, and every last one of them is high as a kite and planning (according to overheard promises) to get considerably higher as soon as they quit the office this evening.

This, of course, simply deepens media cynicism. Yeah, OK, you may fool the poor staff, but, us relentless probers who never get spun by spin doctors, we're waitin' for ya. In the long grass. A colour writer from the *Indo* sits beside me and does a sideways handshake to introduce herself and ask who I am. I mutter my name and say, truthfully, that I work with the radio station. I don't tell her that I am down here among the hacks in order to get a feel for their reactions as those reactions happen, so's to be able to report to the performers how they performed.

The colour writer asks me if I've ever met Nicola Warden. Yeah, I say. She gets very interested in me, does the colour writer. What's Nicola Warden like? A dachshund, I say truthfully. Low to the ground. With really short bendy legs. Although I have heard, from dog lovers, that dachshunds have nice natures. But I shouldn't say bitchy things like that, I giggle girlishly, as – up on the platform – Doug stands up and thanks everybody for attending this briefing, which is to announce a major strengthening of the Amazing Trace management team. At the far end of the table, he says, and all heads swivel, is Andrea Grogan. He names the company where she has headed up HR, and welcomes her as incoming Amazing Trace Human Resources Director. Andrea lifts her head, nods curtly, and goes back to making notes. Sitting beside Andrea is the former Controller of Programmes at Radio Live, he goes on, who is taking on the new post of Overseas Marketing. Lyn, all shiny white hair spikes, glows at the journalists. Every woman there hates her. Every man there decides she'd be worth a try.

Dougal waits for the heads to swivel back in his direction before telling them that substantial new funding has been injected into the company. By private investors, he goes on. I suppose you could call the five hundred thousand scraped together by pals last night substantial. At least from their point of view.

Because he knows the press will be aware of some controversial recent allegations against him personally, he says, he should deal with them before going into any more details about corporate plans. He stops and looks at the audience. Silently making no point. You have shag all judgement in women, I think, and you're as dumb as a rock to have set out to rescue that cannibal, but you didn't deserve this public confessional.

He states, without emotion, that the allegations have been withdrawn, but that perhaps the best way—

Prers touches the keyboard and up behind all of them comes Nicola's statement. Doug stays silent to let them read it and then says Meriel will distribute copies immediately. Now, he says, he will hand over to the new Managing Director of Amazing Trace, Piers Watson, formerly General Manager.

'Nice of you to contain your applause,' Piers says, alluding to the silence in which all of this has been achieved. He gets an unwilling laugh. 'I'm so new to this job, I figure speeches are a bit beyond me, yet, so why don't I just try answering your questions?'

'Could we backtrack a bit?' one journalist asks. 'A week ago, you people were boasting, off the record, about the fact that you were about to sell out to a major German interest. Would you care to enlighten us on what changed so totally in that short time?'

'Be a pleasure,' Piers assures her. 'Where would you like me to start?'

'With the reaction of your potential investor to the scandal within your company.'

Please, Piers, I think. Don't lose the run of yourself. Remember what Meriel said. Never repeat the words of an accusation. Don't tell them there was no scandal. If you do, tomorrow's papers will headline *New MD Denies Scandal in Amazing Trace*.

'That was a bit complicated, all right,' Piers says, looking very young and bashful. He can do this at will. 'Baron von Richthofen telephoned on – what day was it?'

Andrea shrugs. Before my time. Lyn looks bothered: I really should remember, but I can't. One of the journalists says *Who?* Dougal, trying to stay grave, gives the German's real name and spells it out.

'When he telephoned, our Managing Director was out of the office, attending to the complications caused by the controversy already referred to,' Piers says, now giving the impression of an earnest management student parroting words a PR agency has crafted for him. The German rang three times, and eventually, balked of the MD, talked to him, Piers.

'What did he say?'

'Well, the discussion covered a wide range of issues.'

'What did he say?'

'He expressed a number of concerns.'

'Such as?'

Piers admits that they would have been the kind of concerns you'd expect a man in the German's position to have. Given what had recently happened, you know?

'What exactly did he say?' a business editor asks.

Piers looks at the others along the table and hesitates. You can almost see the sharks turning over, teeth baring, going for the soft underbelly.

'He said that there—'

His voice has gone soft and someone shouts that they can't hear. He gathers himself, holding the podium tightly with both hands.

'He said that there could be no investment of the scale envisaged if Amazing Trace was to continue as currently managed,' he says. Because he is obviously trying to lay it all out for them, they buzz, but give him space.

'I pointed out to him that we knew the allegations against Mr Rogan to be untrue, and provably untrue,' Piers continues, after a deep breath. 'While I could not tell him how soon we would be in a position to publicly establish this, I could assure him that we would in due course be doing – well, be doing what we're doing today, what we've shown you today?'

This unexpectedly questioning tone is because he's gesturing towards Nicola's letter, which is still on show behind him. He then leans across Dougal and turns off the laptop, so the screen goes dark.

'And his response?'

'While he was glad to hear that, he – he' – Piers grimaces. Dougal continues to watch him calmly, supportively – 'he was not reassured.'

'He said they were pulling out?'

Piers looks at the questioner in astonishment.

'Oh, no. There was never any doubt expressed during the conversation about the worth of the product we have developed – sorry, that Dougal Rogan developed. In fact, Herr' – Piers ducks his head down to take a prompt from Dougal, then names the German correctly – 'he said they were more convinced than ever of the viability of the product, even going so far as to comment on the fact that it was not going to be affected by any of the electronics turndown we've been seeing in the last few weeks.'

'But?' someone prompts.

'But they would not take the due diligence process any further and would withdraw the indicative offer if Dougal Rogan did not immediately step down as Managing Director.'

AhAA, is the general feeling. Everybody watches Dougal Rogan. Including Piers. Dougal nods solemnly at Piers. There is an uproar as conclusions are leaped to. So this is the major investment spoken of earlier. Dougal gets done in and the king is dead, long live the inflowing money.

'He said there were moral principles involved, and that a multinational like the one he represented could not afford to make and continue to make the offer unless this condition was met,' Piers says, looking like he's back on message.

'And your response?'

'Well, obviously, any response I made . . .' he dithers. 'I wasn't the Managing Director at the time, and he was aware there would have to be extensive consultations, there were legal implications in what he was demanding, you know? But of course, the sum being offered was unprecedentedly large—'

'What did you say to him?'

Just as the journalist gets convinced that he has run the new MD to earth, a smile of world-encompassing delight slowly takes over Piers's face.

'I told him to roll up his offer very tight and shove it up his arse,' he says, distinctly.

There's a sort of double-take as the journalists, particularly those from the classier papers, wonder for a split second if they have misheard.

'In those words, I told him,' Piers goes on. 'His English is very good, so I only had to say it once. I told him that we didn't need moral lessons from him or any other multinational and that we had been having serious doubts, well in advance of his call, about the wisdom of being taken over at a time when so many multinationals are running like scared sheep, shedding talented people and closing plants everywhere except where they could get cheap, if not slave labour. I also told him that Amazing Trace's management and people were fast-moving, flexible and focused, unlike his management and people, who, in our experience, were slow-moving, over-paid, over-cosseted, cover-their-ass cretins, and I hoped he had a happy recession. I may have said a couple more less formal things, but that's the gist.'

In a way, I think, as I watch the thing take off, in a way, Piers, I'm sorry Amazing Trace is continuing. Because you could make an awful good living as an entertainer. But maybe you don't want to be Son Of, and a few years as a Managing Director will put that possibility a long, long way away from you. Lyn is not watching him at all. She's making eye contact with individuals she knows in the audience. Isn't he something? her expression says. I MEAN, WOW. Isn't it strange? I think. To Lyn and Piers, separately or together, they are the story. Whereas to me, right now, they're another story. Another story worth telling, but not yet.

The hacks now want to know why – given that he'd claimed to have told the German to roll up his offer tightly and shove it up his arse – Amazing Trace had gone and done what the German had wanted anyway? If they didn't need to lose the charismatic leadership of Dougal Rogan, why had they?

'You saying I've got a charisma deficit?' Piers demands, squaring up to them. 'I can out-charisma Rogan any time. Watch me. Read my lips: No charisma shortage. Plus, we've appointed a new PR company to sell my charisma to you.'

Effortlessly, casually, he brings Meriel to the front and introduces her to them. Some of them make noncommittal noises, but go back to asking what Dougal Rogan is going to be doing from now on. Piers leans down to him and does a stage whisper.

'Frig it, what *are* you going to be doing?'

Doug laughs and whispers back. Piers straightens up.

'He's going to be doing what he was always good at, which is software development,' he says, and goes back down for another prompt.

'He's going to stop doing what he self-evidently has no talent for, which is managing a corporation,' he goes on and dips his head one final time.

'And he says he's going to devote some time to getting a life.'

Doug shakes his head fiercely and pulls at Piers's arm.

'Excuse me,' Piers apologises and listens. It looks as if Doug wants something corrected, but Piers shakes his head at him and Doug gives in.

Piers does the fastest, strongest summary you have ever heard. Quotable quotes all the way. Strong don't-give-a-shit attitude. High good humour. Confidence. And, above all, the cleverest positioning of Amazing Trace as the one computer company with the wit not just to see the future, but to pioneer it for the rest of the Irish electronics industry.

26

Time to Heal

———◆———

Confession is not only good for the soul, but turns out to be good for laughs and business, too. The next day's papers portray Dougal Rogan as a kind of brainy pillock. It's as if he were Hugh Grant confessing to the blow job without there having been a blow job.

Some of them – to prove they haven't been taken in by a PR ploy – write about a PR ploy, but they don't seem terribly clear on what the ploy was to achieve or distract from. They mention 'putting a brave face on the collapse of a multi-million pound takeover bid' from the Germans, but, since they also have to report one multinational computer company after another either pulling out of Ireland or reporting losses, they also pick up Piers's hint that a multinational takeover bid in this particular year is the equivalent of a frequent sinker ticket on the *Lusitania*.

The Sunday papers run pictures of Piers, on his own, or with Lyn. One columnist opines that even if Dougal Rogan is innocent of sexual harassment, which the columnist is sure he is, his continued public personification of the company would always have served as a reminder of the allegations, whereas now the company is to be fronted by an equally personable executive who carries no baggage.

The fact that Rogan's been able, in the middle of a crisis, to promote someone so self-evidently on top of his game as

Piers and recruit high-flyers like Andrea and Lyn is also seen as showing his skill. He has, one paper suggests, arranged to step aside for a period, but has left his options open for the future.

What works best, however, is chauvinism. Just as Finance Minister McCreevy's national popularity shoots up any time he's seen as saying YahBooSucks to the big boys in the EU, so Piers telling the Red Baron to roll the offer up tightly is seen as our smart lads telling them big Huns where they can get off. The fact that Germany continues to be Amazing Trace's biggest market escapes attention. In order to use Red Baron and von Richtofen in their headlines, the papers go to endless lengths to say Piers wasn't actually being racist when he didn't use Mr Bendt's real name: he used, instead, a term widely used in a generic way and a name associated with all that is positive in the German character.

The story is picked up as one of those inch-deep funnies in papers as widely distributed as the *International Herald Tribune* and *France Soir*, many of them carrying pictures of Piers looking handsome, and captioned (in the *Herald Tribune*) 'Irish freebooting businessman . . .'

'It's had the most fantastic effect,' Lyn tells me on her mobile from Gatwick, on her way to yet another round of marketing meetings, Piers with her. 'They're all dying to meet the guy who told off Niklaus Bendt. It's like meeting Robin Hood. And then Piers is so witty when they actually meet him, they end up just *loving* him.'

'But does this result in sales?' I demand.

Short answer? Yes. Long answer? They're exceeding by a mile the sales Bendt AC had envisaged in the first year after the acquisition, and that was with the massed power of Bendt's sales force behind the product.

'How you getting along with Piers?' I ask. I can hear him in the background, giving out that she should be getting him a sandwich from Upper Crust instead of running the effing sewing circle from a mobile phone Amazing Trace effing pays for.

'Very well,' she says.

'Tell him to shut up complaining about costs.'

'Flannery says you're to shut up about me using the mobile,' she tells him.

'Tell Flannery I'll go over there and microwave her cat,' I can hear him respond. 'She thinks she's dealing with the old Piers. Not the freebooting Piers. I'll stick my freeboot in the arse of her cat before I microwave it.'

'I heard all that,' I tell Lyn. 'I imagine most of Gatwick did, too.'

'They love him,' she confirms.

'Has he got over your hair?'

'Getting there.'

'Doesn't like it though?'

'I'm sure there's some accuracy in that.'

'You using it to indicate how absolutely independent you are of his every wish . . . ?'

'Oh, Flannery, would I?'

'Lyn.'

'Mmm?'

'I think you're a great bit of stuff, but I also notice you do tend to end up in the jobs you want, on the money you want, doing the travel you want, with the people you want. I suspect you have discovered that sainthood is so rare, these days, it's a real good approach to take, because nobody expects it.'

'Flannery, your brain. Wow.'

Piers, in the background, says the noticeboard says it's nine minutes' walk to their gate and that means nineteen minutes for birds wearing five-inch heels, so they're going to miss their flight. He further tells her to tell me to draw up a dress code that prevents people like Lyn wearing skirts up to their over-sized arses—

'Ooh, how can you say that?' she asks, as if wounded at having her thirty-inch ass so described. My waist measurement matches Lyn's hip measurement.

– and blouses open to their navels—

'You don't call them blouses any more,' Lyn says to him. 'You only use "blouse" in phrases like "big girl's blouse". I'm wearing a silk shirt.'

– as if they had good-sized jugs to show off, which they don't.

'Oh, I'll just have to go,' Lyn says in an exasperated way and Piers shouts a rude farewell to me.

Because Lyn is away for a few days, her black cat is in my care. He is feeling very sorry for himself, having just been 'done' and won't play hide-and-seek with Scruffy. The great thing is, Scruffy is so thick she thinks him sulking is part of the game. So she goes off behind the nearest wall and works herself up into a pretend tiger about to make shit out of a passing antelope. She does this with her blind eye on the outside, so any passing antelope that wasn't brain dead would see her ten miles off. James Dean (not the best name for the newest member of the castrati) sees her, but gets sort of mesmerised, trying to work out what the hell this mad white cat is up to, failing to hide behind walls and feinting at nothing. Because he gets mesmerised, when Scruffy suddenly pounces on him, it surprises the shit out of him, he rolls over, Scruffy pummels his sore bits and he sulks for hours. At me. I think he rates Scruffy as such low-grade opposition that when she startles and overcomes him, he goes into denial and convinces himself I really did it.

Scruffy's been something of a distraction today, between half-killing her brother and searching high on the walls for mice. She seems convinced that there is some secret passage in our walls filled with mice. High-flying mice. Mice at knee level. When I mention this to the guys who are rebuilding the garage, the lead guy says they found evidence of mice when they were clearing stuff into the skip. Mmm? I go. Well, he says, they didn't kill them, so maybe they migrated. Into the house. Good deal, that. Get your garage done and you get a free bonus of a houseful of mice at knee level.

On the other hand, the lead builder has given me a number of great ideas for radio items, one of which is going to run and run. He's an environmentalist. When I say this to Raimonde, who is Acting Controller until they either seduce Lyn back at twice the money or officially replace her, she says 'Yes?' almost tersely. Raimonde? Almost terse? Shit, we're all growing up so fast.

'Raimonde,' I say merrily, 'builders are the anti-Christ, environmentally. More crap goes into landfills from builders than from any other single group in the country. If we did away with builders, we wouldn't have any waste management problems. Well, not many, anyway. Builders just go in, knock down things and shove the bits into skips and trucks and lorries and feck them wherever is handy. This bloke recycles everything. D'you know who he's like? He's like the funny sculptor in *The Iron Giant*.'

The cold hand grips my heart, the way it does two or three times every day. *The Iron Giant*, Ted Hughes' animated film. The one the Americans are still thinking of emulating, based

on one of my father's poems. They're not making progress,
and I dread the possibility of their ever making progress,
because then I'll have to flag them that this film (meant to
appeal to children, with their parents amused by hidden witty
references within the dialogue) is based on work by a possible
child molester. Who am I kidding with the 'possible'? But
then, Ted Hughes was a serial womaniser an awful lot of
whose women seem to have killed themselves. In the moral
lexicon, though, serial indirect killing comes a long way behind
getting kids to—

'Will he talk?' Raimonde wants to know.

'Who?'

'Your Iron Giant builder,' she says, doing a real terse now.
She has limited tolerance for me forgetting what subject we're
on.

'Good question.'

Scruffy is making a funny noise. Just as I'm about to go
investigate, she hoves to. The funny noise is occasioned by her
having a real live mouse in her mouth, its tail curling in a way
that says 'still alive'.

'Oh, sacred heart, O Jesus, O Mother of Divine God,' I
squeal, proving that, under stress, we skip a generation and
become our mothers. 'Ring you back, Raimonde.'

Scruffy puts down the mouse. Round of applause, please,
her expression says. I'm going to throw up. The mouse gets up
and runs towards me. I get both my legs up on the kitchen
table, which at least shows how mobile I've become in spite of
the attic scars. Scruffy goes under my chair and catches the
mouse again. She stands back and makes the odd loud noise
again. Her back legs fold down. Don't even *think* about the
kitchen table, James Dean and I roar at her. I leap over her and
run to the front door. Because she can never resist a chase, she

thunders after me, mouse and all, and is down the front steps before she can stop herself. I've the door closed on her in a heartbeat, which I presume that poor mouse is not going to have many of, but what do I want, a houseful of knee-high mice or a good one-eyed mouser cat?

I put this question to James Dean, who has shifted onto the kitchen surface beside the phone, which lifts him a foot off the Formica by ringing right beside his ear. I answer it.

'Well, Raimonde, you've scared the shit out of an already troubled James Dean,' I tell it.

This gets complete silence.

'Raimonde?'

'No. Doug. James Dean?'

'Lyn's cat. I'm minding it while she and Piers fly around Europe selling your wares. Anyway, to what do I owe the call?'

It's a full month since I've seen him or heard from him. At the end of the press conference, he said he thought we should wait until I healed before we discussed anything. I got ratty at him deciding he could schedule my life, and said I didn't know what we needed to discuss, anyway, and he said well, maybe spending the time it took to heal away from each other would clarify things for both of us. I did a casual shrug and got myself involved in so many conversations with so many different people, anybody could tell he had zero importance to me. The sort of guy you wouldn't waste red satin Victoria's Secret nightwear on. Which was just as well, because two days later, I washed the nightwear and it not only shrank small enough for the trousers to serve as pedal-pushers for Lyn, but turned everything else I wear pink. I'm now standing, phone to ear, at the kitchen sink when Scruffy leaps onto the windowsill outside, mouse still in mouth, yelling.

'What the frig is that?' Dougal wants to know.

'Scruffy's caught a mouse. I fecked her out the front door, and now she's on the kitchen windowsill, screaming at me.'

'Why'd'you feck her out the front door?'

'Because there wasn't an open window handy, and I've never tried breaking a window with a thrown cat.'

'Why'd'you feck her out at all?'

Scruffy is now doing some serious screaming, over which I can hardly hear him.

'She's only looking for approval,' he adds.

'Oh, Jesus, Scruffy, you're mighty,' I assure her, through the glass. 'The best mouser in the world. I'm proud of you. Live for ever. Yess.'

'That'll be enough,' Doug says. Scruffy says different. I enthuse some more.

'Why do I have to do this cheerleading?' I demand, when she quietens down. 'I thought hunt and kill was satisfaction in itself?'

'She thinks you're her mother.'

'*What?* Jesus, she's bats as well as blind and thick.'

'She wants to please you.'

'Waving dead mice at me is going to please me?'

'Bringing you her trophy.'

'Well, she can shove her trophy.'

'If you haven't been over-feeding her, she'll probably eat it.'

I look. She has the mouse laid out on the windowsill. Din-dins. I retreat to the full length of the phone cord and turn my back on the window.

'How's your leg?'

'Fine. Thank you.'

This could awful quick become the end of a beautiful phone call, I think, but he should not think he can cut off all contact and expect a slivering on his return. I can't be rude, since he did rescue me from the rafters, but I am definitely not going to be what my mother used to describe as Too Available.

'I'm ringing to ask you for a date.'

I roar laughing.

'You can't do that,' I say. 'Nobody asks for dates. Nobody real. In this country. These days. If they ever did.'

'I want to take you sightseeing next Wednesday morning.'

If he's inviting me out for Wednesday morning, he wants to have something like a formal meeting. Well, maybe it's time to relinquish a relationship that has never quite gelled, I think. Everything is moving on, I'm finishing the last of my scripts for Raimonde, the garage is nearly fixed. New life ahead.

'Wednesday morning, pick you up at ten?'

'Drop me back when?'

'Oh, let's not tie ourselves down.'

'No, I'm not into bondage.'

'You're pretty good at locking yourself in fixed positions, Flannery,' he says so heavily I don't know if he means attic or wider issues.

'What kind of sightseeing?'

'Why would it matter?'

'Because if you're taking me to the Sistine Chapel, I need long sleeves, whereas if you're taking me to look at the Port Tunnel, I need waterproofs.'

'Wear whatever you feel good in on the day.'

I hear another call wanting to come through, so I tell him I have to go to the other line, see him Wednesday unless I run into a problem, in which case I'll leave a message on his machine. I switch to the other line.

'So will he talk?'

'Who?'

Raimonde lets such a long-suffering sigh out of her, it makes me remember.

'Oh, my builder. Well, he talks to me.'

'Would he be able to talk with a microphone on?'

'I'd say so. D'you want me to ask him?'

Raimonde says this would be helpful and gives me a list of the other items she'd love to have from me before I quit at the end of the month. I write them down and we discuss Lyn's hair. Raimonde likes it and is afraid Piers will persuade her to go back to black.

'If Lyn doesn't want to go back to black, she won't go, no matter how much he dances up and down,' I say. 'On the other hand, going from black to white might make it all fall out.'

Raimonde tells me hair is dead and colouring the bits outside your scalp cannot affect the bits inside your scalp. And, now that she thinks of it, would I do her an item on dyeing your hair and whether or not it gives you cancer. I add that to the list and ring off before going to check on Scruffy. No cat on windowsill. No mouse, either. I cautiously open the front door and Scruffy comes in. I don't quite frisk her for concealed mice, but I want to.

The phone goes again. Scruffy goes off looking for James Dean to frighten the shit out of. (I think she's doing it literally. He's spending an awful lot of time in the litter box. Or maybe it counts as sanctuary. You can make like the Hunchback of Notre Dame, in cat terms, in a litter box, knowing no other cat will violate you while you're there.) The call is from my bank

manager, verbose with relief, to tell me the money, restored by
Nicola to the Amazing Trace subsidiary and restored by the
Amazing Trace subsidiary to my father's estate, has finally
come through into my account, now amazingly healthy. I tell
him how much I want taken off the mortgage and he talks
some more. James Dean is lurking behind the kitchen door.
Lurking? Lurking with intent, it turns out. As I watch, Scruffy
comes busily barrelling in from checking up on the builders.
She's on the short-sighted march to report to me when James
Dean comes out from behind the door, claws at full stretch,
the Evel Knievel of cats, hits her amidships, rolls her over and
boxes her in her bad eye before standing back to see what kind
of a fight she's going to put up.

'You're *siblings*,' I tell them, shrilly. 'You're supposed to get
on.'

Scruffy gets to her feet quite calmly, but I figure Dean's
attack may have been a shock to her when she throws up on
the floor. Mouse. In three instalments. Head. Body. Tail. That
done, she rubs affectionately up against James Dean and the
two of them stalk off together.

When Doug Rogan collects me on Wednesday, I am
casually dressed. Meaning I am dressed in casuals. My bedroom floor is full of clothing worm casts where I have tried and
discarded whole outfits.

'Where we going?' I ask as he blasts onto the dual carriage-
way at RTÉ.

'Arklow.'

Other than pottery, Arklow has no associations with me.

'You're not bringing me to a pottery factory?'

He looks at me sideways.

'Do I look that stupid?'

'Well, what else is in Arklow?'

'Oh, lots of things. An Open Prison, for example.'

'Great. I get to look at killers picking oakum.'

'What the frig is oakum?'

'I don't know. Didn't Oscar Wilde have to do it for hard labour?'

'He wasn't a killer.'

'No, but oakum-picking was the corrective activity, was it not?'

He hands me his mobile phone.

'I know you'll need to look it up for a radio script,' he says.

It's one of those ones you turn sideways and get onto the Internet. I give it back.

'I'm interested in oakum, but not that interested. Plus, I have no more scripts to do, so all the trivia in the world is going to have to float past me, unharvested, for the next couple of years.'

'Starting with oakum.'

As he says it, he pulls out suddenly from behind a truck and accelerates so fast I'm pasted to my seat. I close my eyes. When I open them again, he's staring at me.

'Look at the road,' I yell.

'Why don't *you* look at the road?' he asks. 'Why had you your eyes closed?'

'That's what I do when drivers do dangerous things.'

'Oh. If you can't see it, you can disappear it?'

He does another manoevre that's so iffy I instinctively close my eyes again, and when I open them, he's in stitches.

'Dangerous driving is nothing to laugh about.'

'I'm an incredibly safe driver.'

'Says who?'

'Says my record. I'm twenty-eight and I've never had a serious accident.'

'You're not a millionaire, either.'

'Sorry?'

'You told me you were going to be a millionaire by twenty-five and retired by thirty.'

'May have to extend the retirement age,' he says, tranquilly.

'Because of the problems at Amazing Trace?' I can feel myself softening towards him.

'Not at all,' he says, so arrogantly I hope none of the softening showed.

He drives for a while in silence, then mentions he's finally out of the big house he had bought. And shared, I think, with the jellyfish dachshund. You can't mix species, a mental censor tells me. Yeah, I can, I think. There's no limits to my creative venom.

'I'll be tying down somewhere to stay for the short term – probably later today,' he says, looking at his watch. 'But long term, I'm looking at property around The Curragh.'

I try to imagine The Curragh. Any time I have driven through it, it has seamed featureless and so flat they put signs on the motorway warning against wind shear. How many roads carry windsock signs? I wonder.

'Expensive, I'd imagine,' I say.

He talks about property prices flattening out. Halfway through what sounds like expert guff, he laughs.

'Flannery, c'n I make a personal observation?'

I can feel the red gathering in my chest area, ready to break for the border and come up my neck and into my face. What have I failed to wear? Which label is sticking up where and making me look ridiculous today? I look at him.

'One of the reasons I love you is your absolute transparency. You used to pretend to be interested in stuff you weren't really interested in, mainly in the hope someone like me would work

up to something you could get a radio script out of. Now that
you don't need ideas for scripts any more, God help any poor
hoor who isn't telling you you've won the Lottery.'

I apologise for my bad manners.

'It's not bad manners, it's lack of pretence,' he says. 'Whatever you're thinking at any moment is written all over your
face.'

Please, God, if there is a God, let that not be true, I think.
Because, right now, I'm rattling around in a little cage with
the phrase. 'One of the reasons I love you'. Parsing is such
sweet sorrow. It could mean the same as a girly hairdresser
compliment: '*Love* you in pink, dear.' Only an ingrown
adolescent would be subject, at my age, to surges of the
bloodstream, leaps of the heart. I should have more self-
respect.

'Here we are,' he says, slowing the car to take an exit off the
big road.

'Arklow', the sign says.

'Where do we go now?' I ask.

'Prison.'

'Real prison?'

'As in real oakum? Yeah.'

'I only know Mountjoy.'

'Frequent visitor, are you?'

I sit very still, flummoxed by that. I don't do anything good,
and visiting prisons is one of the quintessentially good things
to do. As a child, I remember reading about Elizabeth Fry in a
girl's annual and thinking better of her, of the Quakers and of
Fry's chocolate as a result. (Not that I ever thought badly
about Fry's chocolate, even before I knew it was pacifist.)

'What this real prison called?'

'Shelton Abbey.'

'Do I keep my eye out for signs, or do you know where you're going?'

'Oh, I know where I'm going,' he says, with deep satisfaction. 'I've been here before. Many times.'

'I really admire you,' I say reluctantly.

'Oh?'

'It's something I always thought I should do, but never did.'

'What is?'

'Prison visiting.'

'You giving me credit for visiting prisoners? Don't. I haven't been. This' – he gestures – 'is Shelton Abbey. Former seat of the Earl and Countess of Wicklow.'

He does a little lecture about the Earl of Wicklow's connections with the Gate Theatre, and speculates that the Wicklows must have died out, as a dynasty, since the Department of Justice now owns Shelton Abbey, using it for low-risk prisoners. Meaning prisoners convicted of white-collar crimes, I propose. Not necessarily, he tells me. When prisoners reach the latter end of their sentences, it can be part of their rehabilitation to put them somewhere from which they could, theoretically, abscond, knowing they won't because it would be pointless, since they'd be free so soon anyway. But it's not Shelton Abbey itself he wants me to see, he says, parking the car.

I get out. The air is singing, full of late-summer midges, circling around ferns growing at the roadside. On the other side of the road from Shelton Abbey is a small, old church. Protestant. Dougal walks alongside me until we reach the gate, then ushers me into the deserted grounds of the church. He leads me through the grounds to the graveyard, which is filled, to capacity, with gravestones varying from old (as in eighty or more years old, by the inscriptions) to very old, where the inscriptions are crusted, eroded, unreadable with age. Lichened, hand-hewn stone, softened by time and weather. Granite, mostly. There are few of the harshly sharp black shining marble advertisements filled with gold lettering and photographs of the deceased you see in modern graveyards, none of the impassioned shallow avowals that the dead will be like lodgers in the minds and hearts of the living, no puce-pink toys attached to children's graves, no data-filled gravestones like CVs with little roofs on them. These dead are anonymous, minimal in their claims. They lived. They died. Bees hum between the stones and the long grasses shift, whispering, as a wind passes on its way to bully the trees at the back of the church grounds.

Dougal sits down on a wooden bench with wrought-iron frame, but I wander, loving the warmth of the mid-day sun on my shoulders. I am trying to remember the title of a play my mother loved. A play about a tiny Protestant community running out of people to attend the local church. The last something. *The Last Eleven*, I recall, standing in the stillness of a place filled with memories with none to remember them. This must be what it's like after *The Last Eleven*. Deserted, but not lonely. Unvisited – or rarely visited – but not sad.

I hear him ambling up behind me. He takes me by the top of my arms.

'You missed it,' he whispers, and gently turns me.

On its own, towering over the rest, glorified by the sunshine into a triumphant white, there it is. My mother's angel. Great feathered wings furled in graciously postponed strength. Robes rope-gathered into folds untouched by any breeze. One hand raised above its head, its lovely tranquil face inclined, as if listening out for the laughing girl who once stood, warm in colour, bright in hope, in its embrace. Listening for an eternity.

I weep, but there is no pain in the weeping, just a great wistfulness, a wonder if the expectations of the girl sheltered in the Italian marble embrace came to be, or were crushed. How much of the great happiness the laughing face owned and expected eventually came to pass.

His hands are light on my arms, and I hold to them. Then he leads me, silently, back to the bench, and we sit, his arm around me, watching the statue. The wind fusses clouds along in front of it, so rolling shadows alternate with patches where the sun warms, suffuses the figure. I imagine the skirt of my mother's light summer shirtwaist blowing against the marble and the imagined feathering sound of it brings slow tears.

By the time I look at him, pretences – and any need for them – are cried out of me.

'If I never loved you before, I'd love you for finding this,' I say.

He smiles at me and thumbs away the tears from under my eyes. I go back to looking at the statue, and he comes closer, sitting slightly behind me, gathering my wind-blown hair in his hand so he can get his face close to mine.

' ". . . with bright hair flapping free," ' he quotes. ' "The woman who I loved so, and who loyally loved me." '

I don't know the poem, but he has no need to repeat the line.

'I told your mother I loved you,' he says softly. 'Haven't got much right, but I got that right.'

I turn, startled, disbelieving. He nods.

'What did she say?'

'She said I'd have to cut off my pony tail, that you hated it. So I did that, too.'

I am laughing and crying simultaneously, but trying to be quiet. It seems disrespectful to make noise in such a bee-loud quietness. I stand up and walk away from him, to stand close to the angel, look up at its infinitely sweet peaceful face, touch the sun-warmed folds of its robe with a palm. I must come back here, I think, briefly in despair at the loss of my mother and her protecting angel.

Dougal is standing on the pathway between headstones, hands in pockets. He stays put, one hand coming out to take mine as I come level with him.

'We'll come back here,' he promises as we walk.

'We will,' I nod.

The gates swing closed and he shepherds me so I don't step in the path of oncoming cars. When we get to the car, I impede his opening of my door by hanging on to his arm.

'Did you really cut off your pony tail for me?'

'Who the hell else?'

He opens the door and I sit in. He runs around the front of the car, waits for traffic to pass, then slides in at the driver's side.

'You do appreciate,' he says, getting the car moving, 'that changing your name is the single most effective way to stop being Daughter Of. Flannery Rogan sounds good to me. "This is Flannery Rogan. The vet. Specialises in horses." '

He looks at me sideways.

'Fecking *horses*, Flannery?'

'That why you're moving to The Curragh?'

'Well, if you're going to insist on horses.'

'The horses are a negotiating position,' I say.

'It's really cats, right?'

'I could probably be talked down to cats,' I agree. 'Quote me that poem again.'

' "Oh the opal and the sapphire of the wondering western sea,
And the woman riding high above, with bright hair flapping free.
The woman who I loved so and who loyally loved me." '

I sit, sodden in eye-swollen happiness, and he gathers my hands, one-handed, while he drives, the car gathering speed as we merge onto the motorway on the way back to the city.

TERRI PRONE

Racing the Moon

Darcy and Sophia are twins, non-identical but equal, until their fourth birthday silences one and makes a leader of the other. From then on Darcy is conscious of the disadvantages of being a twin, as well as the benefits: it is easy to let Sophia speak – she is the small, pretty, polite one. But Darcy, bigger, lumpier, is locked in silence, defined by her relationship to her twin, taking refuge in rebellion.

As the twins grow up in an Ireland that has changed utterly in one generation, they move from a cautious Dublin convent background to international careers, work on different continents, and grow closer through business triumph and family tragedy. Admiring and hating each other to the same degree, their differences always remain more obvious than their similarities. Until they both fall for the same man.

FLAME
Hodder & Stoughton

TERRI PRONE

Running Before Daybreak

Cassie Brown has it all: married to a man who is famous, funny and rich, she is also a successful cartoonist and adores the baby she never planned to have.

Then she loses not only the happiness from her life, but her belief in happiness itself. Her car is found at the water's edge . . .

So why does her best friend believe she is still alive – and why is one man determined to find her, if it takes him the rest of his life?

'This warm, original novel is a real tear-jerker'
WOMAN'S OWN on *Racing the Moon*

'Light but never trivial, it casts an acerbic eye on the excesses of the media age . . . and contains nuggets of hilarity which would do Bridget Jones proud'
THE IRISH TIMES on *Swinging on a Star*

FLAME
Hodder & Stoughton

Other books available by Terri Prone

Racing the Moon	0 340 72853 1	£5.99 ☐
Running Before Daybreak	0 340 73325 X	£5.99 ☐
Swinging on a Star	0 340 73824 3	£5.99 ☐

All Hodder & Stoughton books are available at your local bookshop or newsagent, or can be ordered direct from the publisher. Just tick the titles you want and fill in the form below. Prices and availability subject to change without notice.

Hodder & Stoughton Books, Cash Sales Department, Bookpoint, 39 Milton Park, Abingdon, OXON, OX14 4TD, UK. E-mail address: orders@bookpoint.co.uk. If you have a credit card you may order by telephone – (01235) 400414.

Please enclose a cheque or postal order made payable to Bookpoint Ltd to the value of the cover price and allow the following for postage and packing:
UK & BFPO: £1.00 for the first book, 50p for the second book and 30p for each additional book ordered up to a maximum charge of £3.00.
OVERSEAS & EIRE: £2.00 for the first book, £1.00 for the second book and 50p for each additional book.

Name ....

Address ....

....

....

If you would prefer to pay by credit card, please complete:
Please debit my Visa / Access / Diner's Club / American Express (delete as applicable) card no:

Signature ....

Expiry Date ....

If you would NOT like to receive further information on our products please tick the box. ☐